Deliverance in
SHANGHAI

Deliverance in SHANGHAI

by **JEROME AGEL** and **EUGENE BOE**

DEMBNER BOOKS • NEW YORK

Dembner Books

Published by Red Dembner Enterprises Corp., 1841 Broadway, New York, N.Y. 10023

Distributed by W.W. Norton & Company, 500 Fifth Avenue, New York, N.Y. 10110

Library of Congress Cataloging in Publication Data
Agel, Jerome.
    Deliverance in Shanghai.

    1. World War, 1939–1945—Fiction. 2. Shanghai
(China)—History—Fiction. 3. Jews—China—Shanghai—
History—Fiction. I. Boe, Eugene. II. Title.
PS3551.G43D4   1983   813'.54   83-7349
ISBN 0-934878-32-3

FOREWORD

The winds of war also blew twenty thousand frantic European Jews to the Far East—to the wickedest city on earth, to Shanghai, "the Paris of the Orient." The refugees had no choice. Nobody else wanted them.

In less than a century, subtropical Shanghai had bloomed from mudflats into a teeming, exotic, surpassingly rich cosmopolis. As an aftermath of the Opium Wars, businessmen from America, France, and Britain had carved out for their personal use the choicest precincts. They made their own laws, built empires on the backs of drug-besotted coolies, and worshipped money, success, and the gratification of sensual appetites. For the four million Chinese, the realities were poverty, hunger, and the ravaging, raping Japanese armed forces. By 1939, the Japanese had occupied all of Shanghai except for the sacrosanct French Concession and the International Settlement.

The Jewish refugees—for whom life had begun with such shining prospects—had escaped the lethal fanaticism of the Third Reich. For a time, it seemed that in that wondrous port on the East China Sea they had found the beginnings of a safe, new life. . . .

Though fictional, DELIVERANCE IN SHANGHAI is based in part on exclusive interviews with survivors and on the translation of many personal documents, including those of Americans stationed in Shanghai during and immediately after the Second World War.

Jerome Agel
Eugene Boe
April 23, 1983

July 25
1943

SHANGHAI

Rebecca Langer-Wolf had never seen anyone so repulsive.

The Chief Examiner's face was the brown of spat snuff and riddled with warts. His ears, shaped like bedpans, stuck out at right angles and sprouted clumps of black fuzz. His brow had a simian slope. His black hair rose spokily like the quills of a wary porcupine. He was nearly noseless and chinless.

The Chief Examiner was also a dwarf.

Rebecca anguished for the muscular woman cowering before the scrutiny of eyes coal-black under a thicket of eyebrow. The woman was middle-aged, creamy-skinned, and plump. Her platinum-blond hair was braided in a figure eight across the crown of her head. Her bosom was pitching and she was shuffling a frayed string bag from hand to hand.

"Stupid woman," the Chief Examiner bellowed, two prized gold incisors flashing in a snarl, "who are you? You stink like whore."

"Hilda Weiss, sir. I am Hilda Weiss."

"Not name, idiot. Who?"

"I am masseuse, sir."

"Masseuse? Again right. Whore!"

From her bag the supplicant fished a letterhead. "See, sir. Hotel says Hilda come back."

"Even coolie can steal paper and forge. Cathay Hotel people high-class. All English-speaking. Your English smells."

"I do not speak there, sir. Only 'Good afternoon, madam.' 'Thank you, sir.' I only rub."

"Lie! You are fat sow that makes dirty love to dirty men."

The masseuse who had kneaded hippopotamuses broke into convulsive sobs.

"Whores who speak bad English get no pass."

It was Rebecca's turn. She had been waiting eight hours.

3

Chief Examiner Minobe never saw anybody before noon. But the queue always formed in Wayside Road at dawn. This race was to the early. Who knew when it would be his whim to call it a day? So two hundred or more refugees wilted under a merciless sun for the chance to be heard. A boil upon their boils.

Throughout the morning, Rebecca had drifted in and out of the reminiscences of a babbling, slightly stooped corsetmaker from Leipzig, "the city of Wagner, Bach, and books, Mrs. Wolf." As if she had to be told. He was just ahead of her in the queue and so eager for an audience.

" . . . as I was saying, Mrs. Wolf, my avocation became my vocation. 'Your roses, Mr. Hofmeister! Your delphiniums!' Even the Nazi Blockwart used to say, 'Your garden is a little bit of heaven, Mr. Hofmeister.' A few days after I got off the boat, some wealthy Ashkenazics from the Avenue du Roi Albert beseeched me to be their head gardener. Very upstanding people by the name of Lipschitz. Been here since the Bolshies took over Petrograd. Fur, real estate, and vodka. Believe me, they've made fortunes. *Fortunes.* But with all their influence they could not save me from the Proclamation. 'What am I to do?' Mrs. Lipschitz pleaded with the Japanese. 'Abraham Hofmeister is the finest gardener in all of Shanghai . . .' "

Delusions of glory. Their unassailable keepsakes.

"Sign nothing," Mr. Hofmeister warned the people around him. (A petition was being passed along the queue.) "Never sign anything in this place."

The blazing sun looked to Rebecca like a luscious grapefruit, maddeningly beyond reach. Poetic imagery springing from psychological extremity—thirst turning the sun into a thirst-slaking grapefruit. She took off her conical straw hat and put it in front of her face. For a moment she could hide from grim reality . . . the attacks of pesky gnats, insidious in their invisibility . . . the whorls of dust turning the air vaporous as fog . . . the human panzer of peddlers and beggars and the deformed and blind . . . the narrow stalls selling dried grasshoppers, ginseng, and lotus roots . . . the gritty fan-shaped leaves of the tired ginkoes . . . the festering garbage . . . the pathetic Korean girl hawking the baby at her blue-veined breast. ("Healthy son. Strong worker. Sell, cheap, cheap.")

Submission. The word had come to haunt her in its macabre application. They were here because of their *submission.* Authorities—by what authority?—had proclaimed they must uproot and deny themselves, and they uprooted and denied themselves. *Again.* Who could ever explain the links in the chain of absurdity that had snatched a well-born woman from the lap of northern European bourgeois comfort and dumped her into a gummy roadway in this sweltering malodorous slum?

"You see? You like?"

An urchin of eight or nine in ragged Kuomintang breeches poked a palm-leaf fan into Mr. Hofmeister's ribs. The boy unfurled a hand-painted rendering of dreamlike vistas of misty lakes and weeping willows. Hangchow. Beautiful, mister? You like? With a flick of the wrist the poetic scene was transposed into a pair of long-tressed concubines meshing in rapturous cunnilingus. You like, mister? You want? Mr. Hofmeister gave the boy a furious shove.

The queue inched along. Gradually, the pass-seekers disappeared into the cavern at the top of the shallow stone stairs of the Wayside Police Station. Rebecca again stepped out of the queue to see if she recognized anyone. There was still not one familiar face. She saw no one from that other Shanghai, the white man's Shanghai. She saw no one she could recall from the *Hannover.* The *Hannover.* Four and a half years ago—an eternity. Where was David Buchbinder? He had promised her, albeit grudgingly. Such an appealing young man, and such a stubborn and perverse one at times.

In the hazy sky of early afternoon the sun had become lemony. (Another image out of a parched throat.) It was the same lemony sheen that would filter through the pearl-gray skies of a winter afternoon in Lübeck. Gothic, gabled Lübeck. With its great towers and cathedrals and cobblestones and ruddy bricks and watery parks. "O, Lübeck, how your spires rise along the flag-decked riverbank / in ancient pomp before my eyes . . . " the poet had rhapsodized. Lübeck, home sweet home to us all . . . the Herschels, the Langers, Samuel, Kitty. And Meyer, oh Meyer.

"Atten-SHUN!"

A ramrod-straight, stern-looking goose-stepper was brandishing a bamboo baton under her nose.

"Back in line, madam. No bunching up. No pairs. Single line. Heads up. Eyes forward. Backs straight. No passes for slouchers."

He was wearing olive Lederhosen, knee-length white woolen stockings, cleated desert boots, a white short-sleeved shirt, a yodeler's green hat with a tired yellow feather in the crown, and a red band around each bare arm. The glare that he cast in passing sent atavistic shivers along Rebecca's spine.

"It's only Wassermann," Abraham Hofmeister explained through cupped hands. "Wassermann the Junker. He likes to play drillmaster. 'Shape up, Jews. Do what I order, Jews, or it's. . . !' " He pantomimed the slitting of a throat. "Empty wagons rattle the loudest. Wassermann hasn't worked a day since he was released from Dachau. He has a bunk in the Alcock heim."

Bitterly ironic, like so many tales that had come out of the concentration camps. The jailed imitating their jailers, brutalized prisoners turning with a vengeance on fellow prisoners. Out-kapoing Nazi kapos. "I can't believe it," Rebecca had said to her husband. But neither could she doubt Meyer's grisly documentation of betrayals at Buchenwald, of victims becoming the executioners.

A hooded rickshaw clopped by, carrying a singsong girl and her amah. High in the sky, two Japanese Zeroes charged toward the interior. Rebecca was bemused by this incongruous coexistence of pleasure and pain . . . a Chinese maiden, delicate as porcelain, on her way to exercise exquisite arts of coquettishness in a salon along the Bund, the august shoreline drive, while fighter planes sped like meteors to obliterate whom? what? in the Sino-Japanese carnage.

"Emergency paper! Emergency paper!"

Too bad this brash young vendor's ingenuity couldn't match his stamina. To expend so much energy marching back and forth on a day like this with sheets of toilet paper. He couldn't possibly think *these* people would use his wares for their intended purpose *here*. Had the euphemism "discardable towels" occurred to him? It had to Rebecca, and she used two of the grainy, yellowish sheets to swab her face, neck, and arms. It was like planing her skin with sandpaper. The coarseness seemed a metaphor for the coarseness of her whole existence. She was depressed and weary at the very hour it would behoove her to be keen and persuasive. She should be anticipating the confrontation. But how to prepare for someone so enigmatic and explosive? If he said, "Show me evidence, proof," what could she show? *Then* what would become of her?

"There they are."

Abraham Hofmeister directed Rebecca's attention to a flurry near the police station. A man was handing a coin to two small women. One of the women turned the crank of a portable Gramophone. Strains of *Tales from the Vienna Woods* stirred the stunned air.

"The Springer twins from Dortmund. They're out here every day," her informant intoned. "For a penny you can hear one of their scratchy records. *Indian Love Call, March of the Chocolate Soldiers, Flight of the Bumble Bee,* a Caruso aria from *Il Trovatore.*"

"Better than no music at all," Rebecca sighed, "I guess."

Music. How they all loved their music! Music, too, may have contributed to their undoing. While Rome burned, they had kept their eyes averted and their ears filled with Beethoven and Brahms. The country of the Music Mad. Hitler was nourished by Wagner. Himmler cried over Mozart. And Nietzsche had said that without music the world would be a mistake.

The pungent odor of cooking overwhelmed the other smells. Bent like a wicket under his impossible burden was a withered husk of coolie—a perambulating restaurant. From the ends of a bamboo pole thrust across his rutted shoulders dangled pails of cabbage, fish, pork, noodles, and tea. From a rope looped three times around his concave waist hung a brazier, a pan, a chopping board, a cleaver, utensils, and a stool.

"A cup of tea, Mrs. Wolf?"

Hot tea on a torrid afternoon? Not all that insane an idea. Somewhere, Rebecca had read that wise Burmese in their jungles drank steaming cups of tea all day long to *cool off*. The tea was smoky—Lapsang Soochong would never be to her taste—but it was revivifying. She felt braver, almost hopeful.

A typical summer afternoon in Old Cathay. Queues. Dust. Dirt. Maggots. Molten streets. Foul-smelling trees. Baby sales. Talk of castles on the Rhine. Vendors vending themselves. Dung in the air and underfoot. Singsong girls. The Great Enrico crooning "Ah! Cai ben mio."

The stone steps of the police station were hot as burners under her feet. From out of the inky interior came a barrage of muffled imprecations. An older couple a few steps ahead of her looked at each other, bowed their heads, and retreated hand in hand. To have come this far and then lose heart!

Inside the Wayside Police Station, Hades. A windowless inferno. Heat trapped, ignited, distilled as in a pressure cooker. To stifle the stench of urine, Rebecca pressed against her nostrils the "emergency paper," now wadded into two drenched balls. Before her eyes adjusted to the darkness, she heard doors banging open and shut and boots clodhopping on an upper floor. She climbed more stairs, steep, narrow, stone. She reached for a handrail, but there was none. The braying became decipherable. "Out! Out! Not your baby, hag. You think me fool? Out! Never back!"

The second floor was wanly illumined by one weak-watted bulb. Dirt-caked Japanese soldiers—so many of them bowlegged; was bowleggedness a prerequisite for military service?—bustled in circles and at angles and cross-purposes. They chattered and strutted, their swords scraping the stone floor like pennynails on slate. An old woman whose hair was covered with a red lace snood—the mother manquée—brushed past Rebecca with a wailing toddler in tow.

The Office of the Chief Examiner of the Bureau of Stateless Persons at the end of the hall was square and bleak. On the wall behind the Chief Examiner was a collage of portraits and photographs covered with cellophane, the Emperor—the God-King—as boy and man, reposing against a backdrop of pock. The tiny Crown Prince. The young Hirohito on his tour of Europe—the first Japanese royal personage to leave the floating kingdom in more than twenty-five hundred years. The meditative ichthyologist at a fish tank. The triumphant Emperor—February 1942—riding his beloved White Snow across a bridge near the palace in Tokyo. The serene Son of Heaven on the Chrysanthemum Throne.

Propped up with pillows, the Chief Examiner sat at a chipped wooden table, his feet dangling in mid-air. He was not so much interrogating as castigating. The putrid air crackled with insults, obscenities, threats, innuendoes, dismissals. And now this sickening assault on the masseuse Hilda Weiss.

"Please, Mrs. Wolf," the pallid Mr. Hofmeister said, stepping aside. "You go. Ladies first."

"No, thank you. We all go in turn here."

"Please. I insist."

She *saw* his insistence. He had cold feet. Feet that must get cold day after day. Of course. That explained his omniscience, his familiarity with procedures. That explained his peculiar embarrassment when she had said quite innocently, "I admire your perseverance. I wonder if I would have the courage to come out here again and again if Minobe kept turning me down."

Rebecca took a deep breath and looked straight into the Chief Examiner's knobby brown face. He was regarding her benignly, the more reason to be on her guard.

"You are good-looking woman. You surely have man. Why you need pass?"

"It is not as you think, Mr. Minobe. I have responsibilities."

The caterpillar eyebrow lifted and fell like a Yo-Yo. "Yes? So?"

"I am a widow. I have myself and a young daughter to support. I have no wish to become a dependent."

"Uha-uha-uha-uha-uha." He shut his eyes and drummed his thumbs on the table. "You look like intelligent woman. Tell me, why do Nazis hate you people so much?"

A consummate toad. Putting a question like that to her. A question of no relevance whatsoever to her being here, quaking behind the brass rail. How could she have anticipated this? It was as if he had been waiting for someone who would not answer him with a banality like "It is totally irrational" or "We would like to know that ourselves." She kept her eyes locked on his and prayed for inspiration to strike.

"Mr. Minobe"—after how many more deep breaths?— "their hatred is not confined to Jewish people. The Nazis have a bottomless reservoir of hatred, and it flows in ever-widening circles. They see themselves as the master race. On the most superficial level, they hate all peoples who don't conform to their idea of what a master race should *look* like—people with fair skin and blue eyes and blond hair and tall, straight bodies." She paused to let that much sink in. "For the moment, you are partners because it serves their purpose. But, believe me, the Nazis are haters of all people except themselves. They are jealous. They have a deep-seated inferiority complex. They distrust civilization. Their gods are death and destruction. They hate you and they hate us because we have cultures that go back thousands of years. Their hatred would be a compliment, if it were not so lethal."

The heavy-lidded eyes, obsidian crescents, went blank, inscrutable. Some genie must have escaped from a bottle and was dancing on her tongue. But she could not let it go.

"Shintoism and Judaism have many similarities," she went on. "I know. I have studied comparative religion. In both your religion and ours, ancestors are revered, and strict codes of ethics are observed. The Japanese people and the Jewish people have long enjoyed a harmonious relationship. Surely you recall the prompt and sympathetic response of Jews from all over the world when Japan had that awful earthquake twenty years ago."

"Yes-yes-yes-yes-yes. Much help from American Jew Most Honorable Schiff. Also helped sink Russians in Yellow Sea. Hee-hee. Port Arthur, poof. Schiff only white man given Order of Rising Sun by Emperor Meiji. Good-good man."

The Chief Examiner grinned, his lips stretching wide. His gold pegs shone from a mouthful of gray teeth. He swung his little legs. But if she kept blathering, she would risk having the wheel come full circle and putting to him, "Tell me, why do the Chinese hate *you* people so much?" As if she didn't know.

She held her tongue, and he said, "You have fair hair, blue eyes. They kick you out."

"Many Jewish people have fair hair and blue eyes, and Hitler's hair is very dark. That, I should think, gives the lie to the Nazi theory of racial superiority, sir."

Minobe rubbed his stomach and shifted his weight on the prop of pillows. She stood at stiff attention. She must not flinch or cringe.

"You want pass to fix typewriters outside?"

"Yes, sir. That was my business on Boulevard St. Honoré."

"Repair typewriters? No more English, no more Americans, hee-hee-heehee . . . " His right fist mimed a key locking prison gates. "*We* fix machines, lady."

He knew she was lying. But it was too late for her to renege or reconstruct. "We were still getting some business from White Russians and a few Chinese," she said.

"The yellow poppyheads? Poppyheads typewrite? Hahahahaha."

"Come, come, Mr. Minobe," she said, ignoring his slur. "You know as well as I that Shanghai has thousands of stenographers who are Chinese. Many of them work for Japanese companies on the Bund."

"You know what you know and you know what I know. I will tell you something you don't know. You are lucky woman." His smile teetered between mockery and menace. "You get pass. Be sure you fix typewriters, Mrs. Wolf. Shalom."

"Shalom," she echoed uneasily.

"See, I talk Jewish. Do you know what you people call me? 'King of the Jews.' Chief Examiner Minobe is King of the Jews."

King of the Jews? Abraham, Moses, Saul, David, Solomon—and now Minobe.

David Buchbinder was not his friend Ignatz Stern. He did not have Natzie's glibness nor his powers of persuasion. "Tell the warthog you worked with me in Frenchtown," Natzie told David, "and that I still need you for deliveries." It was a stratagem that David had no intention of trying. He was done with pig fat. If he told the Chief Examiner that he was looking for work in his chosen profession—a futile goal—he would at least have a measure of self-esteem.

For him, the queue was a waste of time, a punishment, an empty gesture. "You owe it to yourself," friends said. No, he owed this effort to Uncle Moritz. And the promise to Mrs. Wolf should be kept. "Let's neither of us procrastinate another day," she had said. "Let's ignore the weather, David. And do dress in your best."

His "best" (and only) was a three-piece tweed suit. Putting it on was a mistake. Sweat coursing in rivulets down his long frame pasted his underclothing to his skin. The collar of his shirt was a pond. Hot streams poured from his arm pits. He would have a rash for days. Three-piece suits were fine for summers in southeast Germany but not in the tropics.

"Pencils sharpened. Put a point on your pencil."

The pencil-sharpening man was burnt scarlet by the sun, and he had a severe limp. He was wearing short pants and an undershirt, not unlike the refugees in tatters and Red Cross flour sacks whom David had seen begging along the Embankment even before Pearl Harbor. It was sad, demeaning that a man who might once have been a doctor of philosophy or a skilled barrelmaker had been cut down to pandering with a toy pencil sharpener. But it was not so sad or demeaning as it was for all those who were lying down and demanding the penny without offering anything.

"Pencil sharpened. Only a penny, please, only a penny."

Neither the person in front of David nor behind him interested him, and he let talk dribble away. In front of him was a smelly, foul-mouthed barber from Warsaw. ("I asked the blockhead with the farshtinkener ladle who put Minobe's balls in the kreplach.") David pretended little understanding of Yiddish, which was denigrated as piggish jargon by some German Jews and celebrated reluctantly by others as a wise and humble language, the idiom of frightened and hopeful humanity. Behind him, Mrs. Bessie Rosensomething with her clattering store teeth wanted to acquaint David with each of the seventeen relatives she had left behind in Germany. "Cousin Rolf—that branch of the family was in ironmongering in Danzig—he planned on studying agricultural sciences but a girl from Lower Saxony got her nails into him and that put the kibosh on that. The trouble with Rolf . . . "

David closed his eyes. With an imaginary pencil, freshly sharpened by the crippled peddler, he set to scribbling on an imaginary pad. ("Bored?" Papa had said. "Reach into your mind and you will never be bored.") He would take his mind off this ignominy by nurturing his journalistic embryo. ("Write about what you know," instructors of journalism-creative composition had always exhorted.) He would compose an essay about the here and now, a kind of threnody for displaced lives in an alien place:

"This 'designated area' is a ghetto. We are living in a ghetto. We cannot set foot outside it without permission. The ghetto is within a native section of Shanghai called Hongkew. It is a scab on a scabrous sore.

"Conjure up a gnarled hand. Call its major veins Chusan, Wayside, Tongshan, Ward, Kwenming, East Yuhang. From the veins run mazes of capillaries. These are the lanes, alleys really, most of them culs-de-sac. Each lane has as many as forty flimsy houses, Bleak Houses, some so cheek-by-jowl they could share a common window. The houses are an excrescence. They crept out of an earth scorched by Chinese soldiers foiling the Japanese invaders. They are made of dirt and dust and shards and shingles and splinters and ashes and stray bricks—but mostly they are made of spit and hope.

"In these shacks in these few squalid blocks dwell at least fifteen thousand 'stateless persons'—Central European Jewish refugees 'lucky' enough to escape their homelands. We are contained by fiat. We are confined as if by electrified barbed wire. We could not feel more threatened if attack dogs were about to spring for our throats or if rifles were sighting on us from guard towers. The atmosphere is depressing. Depression is deeply rooted in mass dormitories called heims. The less fortunate of us exist there like orphans in an almshouse . . . "

David's painting of word pictures was indeed an immersing, distracting exercise. (Hadn't Kafka said that even he forgot his miseries when he was writing?) Vaguely, he was aware of a woman keeling over and being carried off by two men whose hands formed a seat. He was only dimly conscious of drifting with the tide, of climbing stairs, of an obscene riddle put to him by the barber from Warsaw, of stepping inside the Wayside

Police Station, of someone shrieking past him, "I got mine! I got mine!" How had Mrs. Wolf done?

In the dock, David was tremulous with the interview that he had been dreading. There was a long silence while the Chief Examiner subjected him to an insinuating head-to-crotch scrutiny. "What for, pretty-boy?"

"I worked for the *Tribune*, sir. I would like . . . "

"Shut down. All newspapers shut down."

This again. The loud mouth and the pygmy mind. Brown shirts. Brown dwarfs. "Newspapers serve . . . "

"Newspaper people make up stories. All liars."

"There are many good newspapers that try . . . "

"Only Japanese. We give them truth, they print truth." Minobe surveyed him again and snorted. "You don't look like newspaperman."

David kept silent. He would not be trapped by self-defense, curiosity, or impertinence.

"Newspapermen don't wear vests and neckties. They aren't pretty-boys like you. Want job? I know job for you."

The Chief Examiner hooted, wagging a stump of forefinger. David still refused to play the prompter.

"Hee-hee. Newspaperman asks no question? I say I have job for newspaperman, and he don't ask what job? I tell him. Pretty-boy should be ladies' man. No pass needed. Hundreds of ladies right here starving for diddle. Married ladies. Unmarried ladies. Make them pay. You'll be rich, pretty-boy." Minobe jerked his thumb in dismissal. "No pass. Not today. Not ever."

1938

LÜBECK, GERMANY

Rebecca Langer-Wolf was sure that the news would be bad. She detected it in the sound of her husband's retreat up the staircase—the pauses, the stealthiness of foot as he adjusted himself to face her. Presently, in the slump of his shoulders and in that sheepish, lopsided grin, she also saw his defeat, *their* defeat.

She could have gone downstairs with him. She could have stood beside him, and together they could have confronted Mr. Jäger. On principle she would not. Better, too, that she not be witness to the latest of Meyer's humiliations. With a trace of vindictiveness, she was almost pleasured by the idea of his rejection. Maybe, at last . . .

"He doesn't want to renew," she greeted Meyer.

"He doesn't want to renew."

"How did he put it?"

"How did he put it?"

"Yes. They have all become such experts in euphemisms."

"Yes. He said we had been exemplary tenants and that he could have wished for nobody worthier," Meyer sighed. "But the times, alas, are so unfortunate. He, in common with others, must look for whatever security he can find. It was out of the question that he could offer us another one-year lease. He must look for people who would sign for ten years. And he would have to require deposit money in the amount of one year's rental . . . "

"We're on the street," Rebecca said.

Evicted! Evicted from this salt box. Evicted from three small rooms that would have fit into the parlor of the old house on Kurfeinstrasse. Evicted by the greengrocer Jäger, their landlord. In the old days, Jäger would have been nothing more than a vendor, someone whose greatest professed pleasure would be in serving *them*.

"We'll find another place."

17

"I daresay," Rebecca said drily.

Meyer, was there no end to it, Meyer? No end to your patience and rationalizations? To your obstinacy? To your blindness? How much more, dear God, was tolerable? The closing doors . . . the chilling smiles . . . the rising voices . . . the constrictions and the expropriations . . . the defamations and the disenfranchisements . . . Meyer's dismissal from Radio Lübeck . . . that odious, balloon-nosed weasel downstairs, Jäger. What was the deed, the ultimate degradation, that would convince Meyer? She must keep trying, repeating her monotonous litany.

"It is time, Meyer. It is time to leave."

Roles long ago struck in performances revived again and again. Like two protagonists in a didactic drama, they articulated their conflicting views. Each claimed the superiority of logic. One threw his weight on history. ("Our roots are here. Germany is *our* home, too. Are we to be driven out by a few hoodlums and by a few firecrackers going pop-pop-pop? Patience, Rebecca.") The other argued for gimlet-eyed pragmatism. ("We've seen this before, you say. I say this is something different. How about the thousands who have left? Are all of them wrong and you're right?")

Everything would be all right, Meyer always insisted. Meyer, you are a fool. A sweet, gullible fool.

Her well-rehearsed speech went unsaid. He was too shamed now, too vulnerable. "With or without you," she could not say to him in the wake of Jäger's notice, "I am going to leave. I know that I made a marriage vow. I vowed to myself that I would never oppose you in anything important. In crucial matters I held that it is the husband who makes the decision. But not when it is also a matter of life and death. Not when it is a matter of a life other than our own. Our child must not be sacrificed to my vows or to your stubbornness."

Tomorrow. She would tell him tomorrow. She could predict his response. "Rebecca, Rebecca, you are distraught. You don't mean that. You would never leave without me."

Oh, yes, I would, Meyer. I *will*.

The genders were reversing themselves. Women, the primordial angels of the hearth, the nestbuilders, confined to Kinder, Küche, and Kirche, were proving the sex quicker to sense danger, to resign itself to flight. Men like Meyer belonged to a fraternity of faith. They had fought in the Great War for the Kaiser. They clung to their Iron Crosses and their memories of the old order.

Yes, she could turn her back on the pleasant, comfortable city that had been her home all her life. Lübeck had never been a city to inspire sentimental ballads, like Heidelberg or Vienna. The Hanseatic crown jewel was too provincial, too conventional, too mercantile to indulge in nostalgia. Minds in a brisk northern clime tended toward the mundane and the expedient. Had not the city's celebrated son captured the smugness and the self-satisfaction of the burghers almost too incisively in his *Buddenbrooks*? She could leave knowing it was a matter for grim conjecture whether she would ever see Lübeck again.

The Lübeck she was born into was receding into the ominous, lengthening shadows. Long behind her were the vistas of childhood and young womanhood . . . the memory-haunted, three-tiered Gothic home of stone and timber with the leaning gables—built, Grandfather Herschel claimed, the same year that "the Admiral of the Great Ocean Sea set sail for Cathay and discovered a new world." Generations had dwelt under that roof. Certain images would be unexpungeable . . . the Biedermeier parlor, the high corner cabinet glistening with silver and gold wine cups, the Gobelin which covered one entire wall . . . the carpeted halls, the tapestried sofas . . . the heavy green taffeta drapes framing the windows . . . the white satin coverlets and the intricately woven laces on the bureau and tables and backs of chairs . . . the pink tile oven that reached almost to the ceiling . . . the sepia portraits of stern-looking ancestors staring down reprovingly from the galleries . . . the herring-shaped brass knocker on the thick oaken front door. The house on Kurfeinstrasse. The house of ghosts, the ghosts of Herschels and Langers. The day she had left that house she knew all other partings were bearable, probably inevitable.

Meyer bowed to the will of Jäger the greengrocer-landlord. The Wolfs would go in good form. They would not create unpleasantness. Meyer found two rooms in the home of a blind woman, a Mrs. Markheim, who lived in a gray-shingled house on the edge of town.

"So what!" Rebecca told herself. "It is only for a moment."

Kitty Rosenthal Kohn visited, and in maniacal laughter they fell into each other's arms.

"A castle," Kitty whooped. "Mad Ludwig would be jealous."

"And you're in Hannah's room?"

"Yes, remember it?"

Rebecca indeed remembered the "Tom Thumb suite" on the third floor where Hannah, the Rosenthals' laundress, had slept. She and Kitty used to sneak up there to prowl through Hannah's forbidden picture magazines. "For a Schottische," Kitty's father had sold the house on Lindenstrasse to a manufacturer of rifle slings, who needed it for his mistress. Kitty and her husband, paying an exorbitant rent, were permitted to stay on and live in Hannah's old room.

"She's no Marlene Dietrich," Kitty said of the kept woman. "Fat, dark, porcine. Eats like a pregnant elephant. But Herr Roentgen starts unbuttoning himself before he's even through the front door."

Darling Kitty, even sharper of tongue in adversity. Kitty with her delicious gossip that she swore was nothing less than the gospel truth. ("Hitler is at least one-eighth Jewish, Becky, and he defecates on actresses . . . Klaus and Erika Mann, the twins, still sleep together—in their twenties!") Irrepressible Kitty. Rebecca and Kitty were of an age (thirty-seven) and always had been closest friends. In recent times they had seen each other too seldom. It was regrettable—wasteful—that the mutual dislike of their husbands for each other ("A windbag and a blowhard," Meyer said of Harry) had been allowed to stand in the way of their constancy.

"Harry and Meyer should have been friends," Kitty said. "They think so much alike. Harry tries to convince me that as long as they need baskets for bicycles, they won't bother him or his factory."

"If only for a second I could believe our husbands were right."

"We're the last, Becky. The *Titanic* is sinking and our husbands are saying there's no need to jump into the lifeboats."

Kitty recited the roster of the departed, of those who had breathed their last of the noxious air of Nazi Germany. Kitty's brothers "absolutely loved" Melbourne and couldn't wait to take out Australian citizenship papers. Ursula had fled to Canada, to Winnipeg. Rhoda was in the United States, with cousins in Chicago. Helen had joined her parents in Capetown. Hermann was in the Belgian Congo. Only Kitty's parents were sending back miserable reports. They were in the kibbutz Elena Haym and didn't have one good word for Palestine. (Kitty had written them sternly, telling them they were lucky to be anywhere and especially lucky to have made it to Palestine under the wire. John Bull was playing it safe there; with all that oil under the desert, the British had Arab feelings to think about and had closed the doors to further Jewish immigration.)

"What's left?" Rebecca asked.

"Brazil. Brazil is all I hear."

"Brazil?"

"The Wittensteins got their visas last week."

Rebecca went to a second-hand bookshop run by a young man "retired" by the State from his profession as language teacher, and bought a Portuguese primer. She kept the book hidden from Meyer. To their sharp-eyed little Esther, who wanted to know what Mommy was reading so slowly she almost never turned a page, Rebecca explained, "I'm trying to learn a lot of new foreign words. Let's not tell Daddy until Mommy's learned them perfectly."

Four weeks into her secret preparations, Rebecca heard that Brazil had slammed shut that "open door" and thrown away the key. The blow was one more in a series of events aimed either to induce hysterics or harden resolve. The Anschluss earlier in the year, the annexation of Hitler's own Jew-ridden, Jew-hating Austria . . . the Sudetenland, reclaimed with the promissory note of "peace in our time" . . . the Evian Conference of Great Powers convened by President Roosevelt to "resolve the Jewish refugee problem," a hollow pageant of rhetoric signifying nothing. (Calling their bluff, Propaganda Minister Goebbels told the "Jew-loving" countries, "You can have as many of our Jews as you want.") For the multitudes of latter-day Josephs and Marys there was simply no room in the inn.

Rebecca made plans to visit her brother and coached herself to announce her trip in the fewest possible words.

"I must see Samuel," she said to Meyer. "I am worried about him. I'll stay only a couple of days. You keep Esther with you in the office."

To her daughter she said, "Mommy will be back from Uncle Samuel's just in time to celebrate your birthday. I know you are going to be an angel while I am gone. So I shall be bringing home a surprise suitable for an angel."

Rebecca sold a single-strand pearl necklace—her sixteenth-birthday remembrance from her parents—to purchase her ticket on the Berliner Express. She boarded the train with conflicting feelings of exhilaration and apprehension—and of guilt for having told Meyer a half-truth.

Rebecca soon put aside the *Duineser Elegien* as too heavy for a railway journey. Her mind was in too much of a tumult to read anything. Just getting to the station and boarding the train had been taxing. She had not been on a train in aeons. And to be traveling in such luxury. She had a compartment to herself at least until Schwerin—and she was beyond earshot of the beery camaraderie of Nazi officials also aboard. She must open her pores and absorb everything. She must try to see and feel like a prisoner reentering civilian life. When again would she be so private, so free to savor impressions and revel in comfort?

The November landscape passed as in a slide-show of somber camera shutterings. Flat potato fields. Stalks of wheat shivering in their coatings of frost. Black and white Holsteins standing motionless, snouts frozen in stubble. Wild geese, a perfectly choreographed corps, arrowed southward.

Rebecca closed her eyes. Presently, her whole life was coming back to her in some encapsulation of memory . . .

Grandfather Herschel. Naughty Grandfather Herschel. Like Scaramouche, he had the gift of laughter and knew the world was mad. In his seventies he still stood tall and as erect as a Doric column and had the gait of a boulevardier. Trailing bay rum and swinging his Malacca cane, Grandfather Herschel, a retired cattle dealer, set off whistling on his mysterious morning forays, his thicket of pure white hair waving in the breeze like drifting snow. No one questioned where he was going and no one had a clue. ("The business of a man of commerce is never concluded.") Until the time he was missing. In due course a note arrived from the widow Brinckerhoff. "Mr. Herschel joined me for a cup of coffee," she wrote, "and I could see he was distressed. It was most close and I suggested a cool bath. Directly, I heard a cry of pain. Mr. Herschel had slipped whilst emerging from the bathtub . . . " A week passed before Grandfather Herschel could be borne back (by horse-drawn cart) from the home of his flame-haired hostess.

The mystery of human attraction . . . Grandfather Herschel and the Black Crow at the Feast. Grandmother Herschel, silent, immense, unfathomable. An obese Buddha mute under her fortress of berthas and bodices and blouses and slips and petticoats, maintaining her eternal post in the black leather chair behind the bay window. Between her and the street fell a gauze curtain. Mirrors on either side of the window—"her spies," Grandfather Herschel called them—gave her a stereoscopic view of the passing parade. She could see everything without moving a muscle. She never told what she saw.

17 Kurfeinstrasse. Grandfather and Grandmother Herschel had the street floor, seven rooms with maids' quarters. The Langers lived on the second floor. Mama, Papa, Samuel, herself. In the front flat of the third floor were the Sternvogels—Aunt Emma and the war-splintered ex-Hussaren Cavalry officer she had married in her thirty-ninth year. (Strange, strange Aunt Emma, more spinster than spouse, with the large red-purple horseshoe of birthmark on her right cheek she so pathetically tried to hide with a hair-style that blinded her in her right eye.) In the rear flat, Herr Heinz Alfred Fachenheim, a bachelor who worked as a floor walker in a general merchandise store and whose "family" consisted of a pair of black watersnakes named Adam and Eve which he had clandestinely spirited into the house.

"Anyone looking from the outside," Rebecca was to say to

her husband, "would have assumed this was the home of just another conventional, well-off family."

Her parents had met on holiday in Bad Brambach. Frieda Herschel was nineteen and Paul Langer was twenty-five. A few kilometers to the south and east of Sagan, Bad Brambach had a certain celebrity for being near the place where the Curies had taken samples of pitchblende that led to their discovery of radium. The Herschels and the Langers were stopping at the same inn. The Langers were from Kolberg, once a salt-trading center, on the Pomeranian Bay. Paul's father owned a store that specialized in feminine apparel. Reluctantly, Paul carried his father's wares to subleases throughout that part of northern Germany.

The wedding portrait in the oval silver frame had bewitched Rebecca as child and woman. Mama's face under the high-peaked hood of her Alençon lace gown, so lovely, so serene, so solemn, and Papa gazing into the distance with a slight look of bemusement. She wondered about them, too. The attraction between two such handsome but elusive people must have been galvanizing. But after the waning of sexual ardor, what was the paste that held them together? Habit? False respectability? Quiet affection? They shared no community of interests besides their children. Papa was too guileless for opportunism, to be drawn to Mama with some notion of quitting his father's business and moving into 17 Kurfeinstrasse and his father-in-law's cattle business, though that is exactly what came to pass. Papa's heart was no more in the cattle business than it had been in fine lingerie. He wore the air of someone denied, unfulfilled, vaguely unhappy. But what did he yearn for? He was neither artistic nor musical nor bookish nor inclined toward the sciences. It would not have occurred to either Rebecca or Samuel to ask him, or their mother, anything that might require an answer from the heart.

Mama. How did I love thee? You were gentle but undemonstrative, inquiring but detached, smiling but unmerry, silently injured but never rebuking. Kind, quiet, insular. Mechanically trilling at the Bechstein her Chopin polonaises and Rachmaninov preludes. (Was it because of Mama's joyless virtuosity that neither she nor Samuel could abide to touch the piano again after their three years of obligatory lessons?) Was there anything of moment in Mama's life beyond duty and sufferance?

"My claim to immortality," Rebecca would jest, "is that I was born on the day that Queen Victoria died."

It was as auspicious an omen as any for a girlhood poignant in memories . . . home and school . . . ice-skating on the Trave . . . riding Prince Otto at the Praeger stables . . . waltz classes at Frau Heuningen-Haupts . . . hot chocolates and madeleines at Niederecker's . . . overnights with Kitty and Susanne and Trudie . . . Julys with Samuel in Kolberg at Grandfather and Grandmother Langers' . . . her horrified fascination watching balky Herefords and Holsteins being auctioned to farmers who would fatten them up for the abattoir—a grim intimation, had she but known, of the time when men, too, would be rounded up and shipped off to pens for slaughter.

Papa and Samuel, her confederates. Papa, indifferent to commerce, ready to concede the progressive view that unconventional daughters were as deserving of education as sons. Samuel, innocent of jealousy and envy, proclaiming her accomplishments: "Becky's teacher said she can conjugate as well as a monk . . . Herr Dietrich told me Becky has strong cognitive power. What does cognitive mean, Papa?" Not even her mother suggested that Rebecca should place the maidenly virtues of modesty, self-effacement, duty, and submission above learning and self-improvement. Or that securing a husband should become her raison d'être. She could not follow her brother to the exclusively male Katharineum (the *Gymnasium*). But at the convent of the Sisters of the Order of Saint Cecilia she spent three happy, stimulating years studying European history, English, mathematics, the social sciences, and composition. Sister Marina marveled at Rebecca's strong logical turn of mind and at various times compared her to Miriam, Deborah, Esther, Abigail, and the Four Matriarchs. "It's a wise Sister," Papa observed wryly, "who knows her Old Testament."

The years at the convent school coalesced with the years of the Great War. It was also a time of sadness at 17 Kurfeinstrasse. Grandfather Herschel died of cardiac arrest, and within a year Grandmother Herschel followed him to the grave. Fortunately, Papa was not conscripted. He was too valuable as a civilian. The Herschel cattleyards were helping to feed the valiant armies of the Kaiser. Because of a chronic asthmatic condition, Samuel was not called up; he spent the war years studying art history at the University of Hamburg. (He happened to be visiting in Kiel when the German navy there revolted against the Kaiser a week before the Armistice.)

Lübeck was far from the fronts. No enemy soldier, in fact, set a foot in Germany. But nearly every day there were reminders of the war. Pine boxes arrived at the railroad terminal, and the hospitals became crowded with the maimed. Nor was Lübeck spared the war's deadly epilogue of the Great Influenza. Thousands, in this city of fewer than a hundred thousand, died. Paul Langer came home feverish one noon, and by the next morning his body had gone up in flames. Shocked, grieving, Rebecca mourned the passing of this good, sensitive parent. He had given her strength and confidence without apparently being strong or confident enough himself to find satisfaction in life. Grief gradually softened to regret, but without Papa what was to become of them? She reached out to support her mother and discovered that Mama did not need that support. "What's meant to be, happens," Frieda Langer said. "We shall find a way of going on."

Rebecca and Samuel shared their father's distaste for dealing in animal flesh. They did not even want to control the business at second hand through the stewardship of managers. It was a propitious kind of business to put on the block—Germany was nothing if not a country of carnivores—and a change of ownership was soon maneuvered. The payment was converted by Rebecca into Dutch guilders and deposited in an inflation-secure bank in Rotterdam.

Samuel was straining.

"Lübeck is so suffocating," he had been saying since his first days at the university.

"Go to Berlin, then," Mama said, "if that is your wish."

"We shall manage," Rebecca assented, wondering how she could endure without him in that mausoleum of phantoms.

"Becky, Becky," Samuel said, tears spilling out of his eyes, "I'll make it up to you. I'll find a way for us to be together again."

It was an awkward time to be coming of age. The terms of the peace were more humiliating than the losses in battle. The army accused the politicians of stabbing Germany in the back. The problems of inflation and unemployment and poverty were gargantuan. The Republic was in convulsion. There were strikes, assassinations, putsches. Recalling the advice of Sister Marina, Rebecca tried to read the classical philosophers. But what relevance was there in Plato's *Republic?* Or in the unities of Aristotle? What did it matter if Kant had answered Hume? Philosophy! Was there a philosopher, as Shakespeare had asked, who could metaphysize his way out of the pain of a toothache?

Young women from good families did not seek paid employment, however hard the times, but Rebecca longed to be doing something. She fought shy of the well-meaning, "make-busy" type of volunteer work that her friends were doing. Kitty Rosenthal, three afternoons a week, was at Holy Ghost Hospital pushing wheelchair patients from one spot to the next as the sun moved across the rolling greensward. Lena Josefson escorted distinguished visitors about the city, explaining, "Bach walked more than two hundred miles to hear Dietrich Buxtehude play his own fugues on the organ here at St. Catherine's . . . " Lisl Schwabe read to the blind. Renata Gottlieb taught a prekindergarten class in her home.

Drifting, foundering, peeved with herself for her inertia, Rebecca sat one night at the feet of Bertha Pappenheim and was mesmerized. A rich Frankfurt spinster animated by steel springs, Bertha Pappenheim had pledged her life's energies to reconciling German, Jewish, and feminine identities. She had founded a league of Jewish women known as Jüdischer Frauenbund. The principal aims of the J.F.B., as it came to be called, were to fight white slavery, to seek equality for women in Jewish community affairs, and to train disadvantaged women for respectable employment. (Only in some Jewish quarters was the J.F.B. considered radical.)

"Sisters," Bertha Pappenheim addressed the inchoate Lübeck chapter of the J.F.B., "we must face reality. Many of us will never marry. Today in Germany, due mostly to the attrition of war, there are two and a half million more women than men. Many of us will never become biological mothers. But motherliness is the primary feeling of a woman. That feeling can be delightfully experienced even by one who has remained untouched . . . "

Bertha Pappenheim had lectured throughout Central Europe and in Moscow and New York and had personally conducted municipal officials to brothels in Constantinople and Alexandria. She had translated Mary Wollstonecraft's *A Vindication of the Rights of Woman*. And with Shelley's wife she agreed that women should be men's companions, not their adornments or willing servants. Intellectual companionship was the best foundation for a fulfilling relationship in marriage. To become self-supporting, women must be given vocational training. Humble girls should learn the "domestic sciences" so they could find work and shelter in a good home. Girls from "good" families who would not marry must train for paid employment. "Our married sisters who are sinking into economic hardship must learn to do for themselves what servants always have done for us—even home repairs. Jewish husbands, for some reason, are not as handy as gentile husbands."

Men, in the creed of Bertha Pappenheim, were the mortal enemies. Men denied higher education to intelligent women and told them that their function was to have babies and manage households. Men scorned the efforts of dedicated volunteer social workers and imposed laws that exploited women. Men—and men alone!—induced girls into prostitution and kept them there. In the world-to-come, if it was to be a just world, women would be the law-givers and men would have the babies.

"We must conduct ourselves in a way that reflects favorably on Jewish people," the tiny, elderly woman cautioned her audience. "The weaknesses of a few are generalized to reflect on all Jews. We would do well to heed the warning of our own newspapers and not drape ourselves in glittering jewelry or speak in loud voices when we are in public . . . " She paused dramatically, her blue eyes blazing with the zeal of a visionary.

How many of them had read that venomous manifesto, *Mein Kampf?* The viciousness of a hatemonger, that militant messiah from Austria. Lies upon lies. The most dreadful threats and slanders concerning the Jewish people, insanity beyond refutation. The Jews were accused of shamelessly profiteering in white slavery. The vilest of treacheries, and one that must be dealt with. German Jews were not trafficking in whores. Of the half million German and Austrian girls involved in that wretched business, very few were Jewish. The Jewish girls who were in prostitution were refugees from the East. They were fleeing from the pogroms and poverty of Poland and the Pale. The motherly Jewish women of Germany must stretch out their arms to shelter these unfortunates from further degradation. . . .

Rebecca could not respond to Bertha Pappenheim's hatred of men. That had had to come out of some personal and painful experience that she had transferred, projected into generalization. Nonetheless, the woman* was spellbinding, inspiring, a Vesuvius in eruption.

In a burst of idealism, Rebecca enrolled in a school for typewriting. Typewriting was a skill that she could pass along to the immigrant girls. She studied Yiddish so that she could reach the girls and teach them to speak, read, and write German. With sister volunteers, she scoured and furnished the house that the J.F.B. had leased. The top floor became a dormitory with a dozen cots. On the lower floors were classrooms, a library, a calisthenics room, a music room, a sewing room, a recreational parlor, a kitchen, and a dining room.

The girls who passed through the "doors to the Mothers" on Landestrasse arrived there via the houses of ill repute on the Reeperbahn in Hamburg. Some of them had been sold into white slavery by parents starving in shtetls and ghettoes. Others were victims of a bogus marriage: Two men traveled the ghettoes together, one posing as the rabbi who would solem-

*Bertha Pappenheim was revealed in 1953 to have been the pseudonymous "Anna O.," whose hysteria—brought on by her father's lingering death—was treated successfully by Josef Breuer's "talking cure." Her case history, written up later by Breuer and Sigmund Freud, was the precursor of the revolutionary discipline of psychoanalysis.

nize the wedding rite after the other had professed his sacred and deathless love for some gullible maiden, who would then be ravished and abandoned.

What diversity was contained in the name of Jewry! These pathetic young women had only their Jewishness to identify them. They had no sense of place, no sense of family, no sense of worth. They were the children of fugitives who had been fleeing their persecutors for a millennium. With their gratitude and their abject docility, they were an embarrassment to their Lübeck protectors. "You are so grand and pretty, Miss Langer," they said with their eyes. "Why are you bothering with us?"

Rebecca's days were full now, and she had something of substance to write to Samuel. But his letters from Berlin left her feeling that she was far removed from the pulse of life.

"The murder of Walther Rathenau has shocked the city to its foundation," Samuel wrote. "One editorial called it the greatest tragedy of its kind since the assassination of Abraham Lincoln. Rathenau was a great statesman—he was trying to keep Germany from being carved up. His enemies blamed his 'Jewish' policy—insisting on paying the reparations—for turning the currency to mush. (Not true, though it takes a wheelbarrowful of marks to purchase a loaf of bread!) They're now blaming us for everything—unemployment, poverty, hunger, even inflation. And for all the isms. Marxism. Communism. Socialism. Pacifism. Internationalism. Adventurism. We Jews are supposed to belong to a world-wide conspiracy of financiers and industrialists bent on keeping Germany on her knees. In our omnipotence we control the press, literature, theater, films, department stores, stock exchanges, Parliament. We are accused of starting the war and then of losing it. We are called slackers and cowards, and they claim we were only clerks in the war. Clerks! Eighty-thousand German Jews at the front, thirty-five thousand decorated, two thousand commissioned, twelve thousand *killed*. Worst of all, Aryans fall in love with us and we intermarry and pollute the national bloodstream . . . "

Rebecca was relieved that at least she was not in the thick of that particular ferment. The Jewish community in Lübeck numbered less than a thousand. It was cultivated, and until present times inconspicuously well-off. The country's renascent anti-Semitism rarely rose above a whisper here, and there was much regret in the newspapers that the brilliant writer Rosa Luxemburg had been murdered for her revolutionary ideas. But hard times *had* arrived, and the capital in the Dutch bank was eroding. She told Mama that they must sell some of their silver and their Meissen china and let rooms to strangers if they were to go on managing in the big house. Mama sighed—the world was beyond her understanding—and lapsed into reciting the symptoms of her declining health.

Still, Rebecca's early and mid-twenties passed agreeably enough. Sharp economies indeed had to be practiced, but everyone else was practicing them, too. The work with the wayward girls was involving and fulfilling. And there was the occasional sojourn to Berlin to be with Samuel and become infected with his excitement.

"Everything is in explosion," her brother marveled. "This must be the most vibrant capital in the world. The new architecture. The painting and sculpture. The literature. Politics. Medicine and the sciences. Theater. The cinema. Photography. Composing, conducting. Not since the Renaissance . . . " Heady Berlin sparkled with names like Max Reinhardt and Georg Grosz and Elisabeth Bergner and Max Liebermann and Arnold Schönberg and Kurt Weill and Lion Feuchtwanger and Stefan Zweig and Franz Werfel and Martin Buber and Bruno Walter and Otto Klemperer and Artur Schnabel. "A breed unto themselves, these Berlin Jews, Becky. So cosmopolitan, cultured, self-assured, witty, cynical."

Fleetingly, Rebecca thought that she should be thinking of marriage. She was as well aware as Bertha Pappenheim of the statistical odds against it. Whether she would marry was not an obsession. She was not without suitors. Amusing Otto Haas—amusing the first evening, but a lifetime of hearing and rehearing the same japes, epigrams, and anecdotes? Theodor Schnell, "the most promising trial lawyer in Lübeck." Lionel Hellmann, the bespoke haberdasher, whose style far exceeded his substance. Each in his own season . . .

"You are a classic," swooned Nathan Jacoby, a forty-year-old architect who was by far the most persistent of Rebecca's suitors. He was ridiculous, embarrassing, tiresome. He de-

clared her a Botticelli, the Venus de Milo, the Duchess of Alba
. . . her hair was as golden as the harvesting flax . . . skin like
alabaster . . . impish, impish, those spit curls . . . that high
wide brow, *such* nobility . . . the neck of Leda . . . her eyes,
dazzling azure pools . . . did she know her chin was shaped
like an inverted heart? . . .

As tactfully as she could, Rebecca broke off with the rhap-
sodic architect. To her astonishment, and further embarrassment, he did a volte-face. "Who do you think you are, Miss
High and Haughty? Cleopatra? the Gioconda? Whom do you
think you are saving yourself for? The Prince of Wales? Let me
tell you this, young lady, you are well on the way to becoming
an old maid . . . "

Otherwise, things were looking up. The inflation was
abating. The famine was ending. Farmers, who had been holding back, were bringing their produce to the cities again. Civic
disturbances were quieting down. And Samuel had been
kissed by inspiration.

When he first got to Berlin, Samuel boarded with second
cousins in the Bayrisches Viertel of Schönberg. The city did not
exactly open its arms to an aspiring young art historian from a
northern duchy. To subsist, he walked Afghan hunting hounds
for a bedridden widow and served as a guard in the Herz Gallery on weekends and held flashpans for portrait photogra-
phers. He guided tourists through the wonders of the Tiergar-
ten's African Village, and he worried out pieces of criticism for
minor art quarterlies.

Rebecca had her J.F.B., Samuel now had his invention. The
paperweights on the market were a particular offense to his
sensibilities; they were so banal, so sentimental—glass globules entombing coy cupids or duelling knights or shy maidens
or swirling snowflakes or artificial flowers and fruits and butterflies. Why not try, Samuel had ruminated, to uplift the soul
of the bourgeoisie with representations of illustrious paintings?
A painting could be reproduced in miniature and laid on a
felt base inside a globe of eight-power magnifying glass.
A. Reinhardt, the venerable manufacturer of office supplies,
agreed to distribute the products of Samuel's Paperweight
Classics. Soon, the glass emporia of Clichy and Baccarat and St.

Louis were being kept busy with the new account. Demanded the paperweights that proclaimed their appreciation for esthetics. They wanted their own *Don Manuel Osorio de Zuñige*, by Goya, *The Gleaners*, by Jean-François Millet, *Morning*, by Ferdinand Weldmüller, and later, demand rising, *The Sleeping Gypsy*, by Rousseau, *Spring*, by Böcklin, and *Seated Female Clown*, by Toulouse-Lautrec.

Samuel prospered and, in general, times *were* improving. But anti-Semitism burgeoned. The Jews must never be forgiven for Germany's miseries. Brown-shirted youths and unemployed war veterans crowded the streets and poisoned the air with ugly epithets. Students in parochial schools and universities were beaten up. Race and religion were redefined. Newspapers published shorter and shorter lists of resorts where non-Aryans were welcome. Portraits of a man with a mustache began staring menacingly from posters.

"This is just another manifestation of an ancient tradition," Rabbi Leo Baeck, the spiritual leader of Berlin's quarter-million Jews, reminded his congregation in a Friday evening service in the magnificent synagogue on Oranienburgerstrasse. "Its roots go back to the Protestant reformation. When Martin Luther failed to lure our forefathers to his movement, he turned on them with a vengeance. He said synagogues should be set on fire. Jewish men should be stripped of their prayer books and all their other property and made to work in the fields like beasts with yokes around their necks. Generations upon generations of good Germans have heard denunciations of Jews from the pulpit. Only a hundred years ago, zealots were demanding that the Jews be driven from the country or be exterminated. But as you can see, we are still here . . . " (Beyond Germany, the seeds of anti-Semitism had sprouted in antiquity. In the first century, Romans massacred hundreds of thousands of Jews.)

"A business has to grow," Samuel boomed in the first long-distance telephone call that he placed from Berlin. "If you stand still, Becky, you go backwards. I want to expand to the north. I'll need someone there. I know you can do it."

Samuel, dear Samuel, making good on his vow that he would find a way of uniting them again. Rebecca Langer, Division Manager, Paperweight Classics, North Germany. Promising herself to donate two evenings and Sunday each week to her J.F.B. work, Rebecca rented office space in a tilting medieval building on the Trave which had been a granary in its Hanseatic heyday. The listing floor gave her a slight vertigo; others complained of mal de mer. Out of the classified advertising pages of the *Hamburger Blätter* she hired a sales manager to make calls and create markets.

Rebecca would be the first to admit that she was little more than a competent expediter of orders. But she was *seen* as the mistress of a successful enterprise. "Just another salty herring in the Baltic," she demurred modestly. She might have been seen by some as unconventional—a young woman in an unwomanly position—but Lübeckers worshipped success in business and looked at her admiringly.

With success came acquisitions. It had been easy to make a virtue of asceticism when she had nothing to spend. Now she discovered that she had perfectly defensible needs. She needed the Opel to get about, and she became absurdly attached to it, naming it Maxie. She must "keep up." With Kitty Rosenthal she attended the BBB Evenings (Bach, Beethoven, Brahms) and the new dramas put on by the Masque and Wig Society. On a dare she flew in a dirigible to Stockholm and back. The exhilarating long weekends with Samuel in his spacious white flat in privileged Dahlem were also necessary for business. The sable coat was not an extravagance but a sensible insulation against the fierce winter. (How could she possibly have known that the sable would be her most negotiable asset a decade later in a subtropical city thousands of miles away?)

Life was—what? It was a perplexity of things. The days were short of hours. There was not enough time for everything . . . the business, Mama, her continuing social work. Evenings beckoned with a host of pleasures. But she was becoming insomniac. At three o'clock in the morning she wept into her pillow, "Is this all it's ever going to be?"

She went by herself to the subscription series of the visiting Hamburg Opera. A woman alone there was not conspicuous. A man alone was. He sat in front of her, between a middle-aged couple (the Steinways, tanners) and a family of six (the Reiters, flour millers). He must be passing through. Lübeck men were not given to light gray suits with black windowpane patterns and paisley silk handkerchiefs flowering from breast pockets.

During the interval of a lackluster performance of *Die lustigen Weiber von Windsor,* the stranger stayed in his seat and never lifted his eyes from the program. When he rose at the end of the opera, Rebecca got her first good look at him. He was rather more interesting-looking than handsome. His head had an elegant shape. His brown eyes were large, and soft as a spaniel's, and his hair was dark as bitter chocolate and parted in the middle, floating in waves above a high brow. Well-barbered sideburns fell to his ear lobes. A mustache thin as the stroke of a fountain pen traced the outline of his upper—and more prominent—lip. He looked to be in his early to middle thirties.

He was no visitor. He was there every second Monday evening. Through *Der Rosenkavalier, Salome,* and *Das Mädchen des goldenen Westens* she stared at the back of his head, tracked his retreating figure after the performance, and thought about him. *Das Land des Lächelns* concluded the series. At the interval he broke precedent and went to the foyer. Rebecca went there as well and stood in the corner opposite him. She lit a cigarette and felt his eyes upon her. He came toward her and her heart fluttered.

"We're neighbors, so to speak," he said shyly, with a pleasant smile. "May I introduce myself?" In the next breath he was inviting her to have supper with him and she was accepting.

"Yes, I am new in Lübeck," Meyer Wolf said, as they sipped an apéritif in the Café Geiger.

"Strangers are quite rare here," Rebecca said, "and so we're always interested in them."

"I don't know how interesting I am. I can do it all in one breath. I'm here because the Republic has made me Director of Operations for Radio Lübeck. We shall begin broadcasting soon. I am from Ulm. My grandfather Philipp Reis was *the* Reis—he invented the telephone sixteen years before the

American Bell. My father is a retired railways traffic manager. My mother, God watch over her, died of poliomyelitis last September after being encased in an iron lung for three years. In the war, I served the Kaiser as a machine gunner. I was at Brest-Litovsk when the Russians were forced to sign over those five-thousand factories and industrial plants. I was so confident that we would be the victors. I had hoped to go to the university after the war, but there was no money, and I had to look for work. It was a very difficult time, Miss Langer. My opportunity came when interest in radio became keen. I studied and passed the civil-service examination and was sent to Bayreuth, then to Augsburg, and now here. What else? I am thirty-three years old. I have such plans—oh, but I must be boring . . . "

"Not in the least."

"I have such plans for the station. I want the programing to be both eclectic in classical music and dynamic in discussion and lecture and literary appreciation . . . "

"To Radio Lübeck," Rebecca said, raising her glass of Moselle.

"To Lübeck." He smiled mischievously. "I should like to have been here when Thomas Mann lectured his former townsmen on their 'crass materialism' and accused them of 'accruing riches on the broken backs of the working classes.' "

"Everyone who heard him thought of course, 'But he isn't talking about me.' "

"Still, he thought well enough of one local citizen to marry her, yes?"

"And a Jewish girl at that."

"Proving he's a man of taste and culture."

"Like you, Mr. Wolf," Rebecca said boldly.

"Except for this difference. I happen to be Jewish myself."

Later, there was an accident at table. A young waiter spilled a demitasse of black coffee onto Meyer's suit jacket and shirt front. "Don't fuss," he calmed the quaking youth. "The stains will come out. A blessing in disguise, actually. I shouldn't be drinking coffee at this hour anyway."

Such gentleness with a clumsy serving boy. German men did not suffer ineptness in service easily; most of them would have had the waiter's head.

Rebecca became tremulous with a giddy perception. Here was a man who could matter to her. What charming manners and modesty he had, and his conversation was precise, well modulated, candid, informed. He did not patronize her nor did he condescend to the familiar inanities of a man on his first meeting with a woman.

"May I be so personal and trite," he said softly, his fingertips glancing hers, "as to tell you what you must be weary to death of hearing. You are a beautiful woman, Miss Langer."

"Say anything you like," Rebecca laughed, "as long as you don't compare me to Botticelli or the Venus de Milo or the Duchess of Alba or say I have a Gioconda smile . . . "

The courtship lasted six weeks.

The second time they were together she knew it was more than the wine, the candlelight, and the tender compliments in the Café Geiger. To see Meyer Wolf, to be with him, gladdened her heart. He aroused romantic, even erotic fantasies. He was no dashing hero come to sweep her off her feet. But she could not think of him—and she thought of little else—without the stirrings of desire. Here was a sweet and decent and solid man, sensible, endearingly modish, quietly ambitious. Here was the man with whom she could walk side by side.

"This has been the happiest time of my life," Meyer declared. They had been to the cinema (George Arliss and Joan Bennett in *Disraeli*) on a lilac-scented evening in June and were drinking chocolate in the café of the Hotel Stadt Hamburg. "You must know how I feel about you, Rebecca. If I am not wrong, you have some of the same feelings for me. I don't think you or I are the kind of people to be enslaved by convention. If something good is to happen sooner or later, why not let it be sooner?"

After their marriage and brief seaside honeymoon at Travemünde, Meyer moved into the house on Kurfeinstrasse. If a woman marries to make two women happy—herself and her mother—Frieda Langer could not have been happier. She adored her son-in-law to distraction. He gave rapt attention to her increasingly complex medical recitals, he indulged her craving for forbidden caramels, and, as glaucoma drew a thickening veil over her eyes, he read to her the vacuous penny novels that she found amusing. "I always wanted a brother," Samuel said when he met Meyer, and that said it all.

"Teach me how to please you," Rebecca whispered in their bridal bed. With her index finger she traced H-A-P-P-Y on his back. "I so want to make you happy."

"You have. You do. Just by being here."

Meyer was the considerate lover who transported her to joys she had never imagined. She would never ask him how he had gained his experience and finesse. What had happened before did not belong to her. He had told her of a broken engagement—to the daughter of a prosperous brewer in Ulm—but it could not have been the brewer's daughter who had taught him his accomplishments in bed. This—Meyer!—had been worth waiting for. Had her parents, her grandparents, or anyone else come together in such unabashed ardor and joy?

"Take my name but keep your own," Meyer said. "Distinguished women are doing it more and more these days."

"Rebecca Langer-Wolf," she murmured, and praised his gallantry.

Rebecca awoke one morning to wonder if they had been so self-absorbed, so drained with their love-making, that they had lost sight of the turning earth? Half a world away, a stock market had collapsed, emitting shock waves that were threatening the nascent prosperity of Europe. The main prop of the German economy, loans from America, evaporated (but Henry Ford kept pumping millions into the burgeoning treasury of the Nazis). Germany was not able to export enough goods to buy the raw materials and the food that were needed. Industries and small businesses were going bankrupt again. Unemployment was once more mounting into the millions. Samuel decided that the time was not appropriate to expand the line of paperweights or to start marketing in the Scandinavian countries.

Neither Rebecca nor Meyer was consumingly interested in politics, but the results of the national elections were dismaying. Adolf Hitler, the ranting Pied Piper with the breath of a basilisk, was now leader of the second most powerful party in the Reichstag. The Versailles Treaty would be ignored. Germany would stop paying reparations and start rearming. The money barons (*those* vermin) would be stripped of their wealth. "Pure-blooded" Germans, "the glory of mankind, the master race," would reclaim their inheritance . . . more Lebensraum, and banishment of the inferior, impure races. In the east, Stalin was up to no good.

All of Lübeck officialdom turned out for the inaugural festivities of Radio Lübeck. Meyer could now go from the administrative burdens to the creative pleasure of programing. But within days he had a surprise visitor from Berlin. Excessively polite, the chief of the broadcasting bureau asked to be shown around. The minutest detail interested him. Into a notebook he recorded Meyer's explanations. In taking his leave, he was profuse in appreciation of Meyer's cooperation and courtesy.

"It must mean something," Rebecca said.

"Likely not. Just bureaucratic red tape. Supervisors supervising other supervisors. It takes a big kettle to feed everybody. It's nothing to worry about."

Rebecca was not so sure there was nothing to worry about. Meyer might be trying to reassure himself as much as to persuade her. She said nothing.

The visit from Berlin faded into memory beside the stark realities at hand. The Depression was spreading. Paperweight Classics was in a slump, and Frieda Langer's health was seriously deteriorating. The raving demagogue became Chancellor.

And Rebecca Langer-Wolf was pregnant.

Rebecca's feeling about having a family had been ambiguous. She loved the *idea* of children but felt strongly that any child brought into the world should have the prospect of being a child of good fortune. "Times are almost always bad," Meyer had argued, "but the human race goes on. New generations always find the courage to face what they must face."

Incident after incident reinforced Rebecca's misgivings. A dim-witted Dutch Communist was accused of setting fire to the Reichstag, his head was chopped off, and immediately, personal freedoms were outlawed for the "protection of the people and the State." Citizens could no longer speak or meet or write or read as they chose. Private correspondence could be opened. Houses could be searched. The people and the State must be protected from the perfidy of communism. Hoist the specter of the Red flag and one could get away with any illegality!

"The destruction of all those books," Rebecca cried. "Stupid! Fatuous! Abominable! They even burned Helen Keller."

The new censorship came to Meyer's own doorstep. A directive from Minister of Culture Jolst ordered that forthwith and henceforth the works of certain poets could not be read or discussed on the radio. Among the proscribed were Heinrich Heine, Micah Joseph Lebensohn, Judah Lev Gordon, Hyman Naman Hislik, Yehuda ha-Levi, Abraham Shalonsky, and Isaac Lurie.

"Another bureaucrat trying to make an impression," Meyer said, hiding his hurt and embarrassment behind his sheepish grin. "Next week, somebody above him will rescind the directive to impress *his* superiors."

"I wonder," Rebecca said, "all those names have one thing in common."

"Not Heine. He converted."

"Meyer, you know the way they think. Once a Jew, always a Jew. Lest any of us forget, there will always be some gentile around to remind us." (Deluded Heine. Predicting Jews and Germans would create a New Jerusalem in Germany, "a modern Palestine that would be the home of philosophy, the mother soil of prophecy, and the citadel of pure spirituality.")

Meyer came home jubilant the very next day. "Every Christian at the station signed a statement protesting the ban."

"I'll wager Berlin ignores it," Rebecca countered.

Was pregnancy making her contrary and contentious? Of all times to be argumentative with Meyer. She deeply loved him, and they should be drawing closer. But it was hard for her to hold her tongue when he sounded naive or was downright dissembling.

Radio Lübeck relayed the premiere performance of Kurt Weill's *Der Silbersee*. The opera was fictional and set in a remote time. Its theme was the evil of power in the hands of ruthless dictators. Literally overnight, *Der Silbersee* was shut down. Weill was called a Jewish avatar of the alien influences poisoning Germany. He was declared an enemy of the people.

"To tell the truth," Meyer said, "it wasn't a very good opera."

"What are you saying, Meyer?" Rebecca screamed. "What does good-bad have to do with it? Kurt Weill is being muzzled because he's a Jew and dared to bring home some objectionable truths."

Berlin ordered a nationwide boycott of Jewish-owned businesses. Obedient Lübeckers kept their distance from this bakery and that bootery and those sundry confectioners, clothiers, tailors, and wine merchants.

"Goebbels claims the boycott is needed to calm passions."

"Do me one kindness," Rebecca snapped. "Please don't repeat anything so stupid that you, yourself, don't believe it for a moment."

The boycott lasted only three days. It was aborted by threats from abroad of a retaliatory boycott of German exports. But on its heels there was a fresh edict from Berlin: "Civil servants not of Aryan descent are retired . . . in order to restore a national professional civil service and to simplify administration . . . "

Meyer was spared. As a concession to the dying General Hindenburg, men of "tainted blood" who had served at the front were to retain their employment.

Meyer tried to put on a brave face. See, there was appreciation for those who had fought for the Kaiser. But he could not mask his devastation over the tens of thousands of loyal and competent citizens who were being stripped of their livelihood. Rebecca saw her husband's dispensation as only temporary. The intention of the latest directive was obvious: Fire the Jews and create full employment of "pure" Germans.

She walked on eggshells and held her breath. She became depressed. Out of the depression grew a vision of gray skies that would never break to let the sun shine through.

Bertha Pappenheim made a return visit to Lübeck. She was past seventy now but still soignée in her silver-fox coat and lace cap and cuffs. She confessed to a sense of failure. Rebecca listened affectionately to the lecture but found it irrelevant, dated.

"The J.F.B. should be preparing people to emigrate," Rebecca said to her mentor.

"Emigrate! Emigrate to where, pray?"

"To anywhere at all. Even Palestine."

"Palestine! Rebecca, what *can* you be saying? We are a cultured people. We cannot become peasants and live in the desert. We need the books. The journals. The concert halls. The paintings. We need to express ourselves, have exchanges with our equals. We are city people."

"This, too, shall pass"—Deor's Lament—was Meyer's rationale. *Less than one percent of Germany was Jewish.* With even a collective will or force, how could a handful of people subvert their own government, even if they wanted to? This thing, this anti-Semitism, always surfaced when a scapegoat was needed. During the horrible plague of the fourteenth century, Jews were accused of causing the epidemic and were thrown down wells, thrown off city walls, even though they were victims, too. But since Napoleon's invasion of Germany in the early nineteenth century, anti-Semitism had been mild and innocuous, something adopted as casually as the fashion of a beauty mark.

"Beauty mark? Is it just a beauty mark that Mr. Riegelmann up the street can no longer practice law? Is it only a beauty mark that people are pleading for visas to leave Germany?"

Even Rabbi Baeck lost his optimism. "We must think of emigration," he exhorted his congregation. "There is no future here. Even those of us who have economic security should consider giving it up to find some brave new world."

"Palestine?" Meyer sneered. "Is Rabbi Baeck about to give up his opulent synagogue and lead his flock to the sands?"

"Not fair, Meyer. Rabbi Baeck has always said he would be the last Jew to leave Germany. That is not clinging to opulence. It is how he conceives of his responsibility."

Most Germans were going along with Hitler. He had the support of the bourgeoisie and the civil-service racists and many of the best-educated people in the professions—even the Junkers, who jailed Hitler after his coup d'état had misfired in Bavaria, in 1923. The populace seemingly had a need, a craven hunger for a messianic figure who would tell them, "Follow me and all will be well. You will know greatness and become the masters of Europe. Tomorrow the world!" His speeches stirred genitalia and rattled ovaries.

"He is an extremist," Meyer reasoned, "and the German people are too solid and traditional to put up with insanity very long."

Rebecca thought differently. Inside her body, she felt the new life taking shape. It was having a movement of its own. In her mind an idea was taking shape as well. But it was an idea that could not be implemented in any foreseeable future.

Shortly after the death of President Hindenburg, Meyer received the news that Rebecca had known to be inevitable. Even those Jews who had been at the front would be severed from the civil service.

Meyer was shaken to the roots. "I don't understand, I don't understand," he repeated forlornly.

"It isn't the end of the world," Rebecca soothed him. But it was a world decidedly unhinged. "If it had to happen, the timing may be for the best. You can take over for me at Paperweights. I'll be too busy being a mother."

Esther arrived on a drizzly November morning in 1933. She was a delicious, lovely, warm baby with apples in her cheeks, a pug nose, bright black eyes, and a crown of black ringlets. She was loved idiotically by both parents, and she brightened the last days of Grandmother Langer. Esther's adoring mother saw her as the one good thing in a rotting world. Her father saw in his daughter affirmation for his belief in the durability and continuity of life.

"I never knew my mother," Rebecca reflected sadly in the carriage ride back from the cemetery. "I lived with her all my life. I could anticipate everything she would say or do. But I never had the dimmest understanding of what went on inside her head. I pray that my daughter won't say the same thing about me."

With Mama gone, the time had come to dispose of 17 Kurfeinstrasse. The time had come and gone when they could afford the luxury of trying to hold on to the past. Some new owner, more prosperous than they, would have to contend with the upkeep and repairs and with tenants who could not or would not pay their rent. That new owner, shrewdly assessing the Wolfs' inability to redress exploitation, paid them a small fraction of the market value of the house. Meyer rented a warren on the third floor of the modest frame house of the greengrocer Jäger. They took with them their china and silver and a few pieces of furniture and, for Esther, Samuel's peeling green rocking horse.

Esther replenished them. She blinded and anesthetized them. Rebecca asked herself if a small child really had the power to turn resolve into noodles. For a time she was too lost in the delight of this budding new life to dwell morbidly on the drift of events that should have kept the apprehension of both parents keen.

A beefy, florid-cheeked inspector snooped around the office on the Trave and asked Meyer, "Who owns this business?"

"We are affiliated with A. Reinhardt in Berlin," Meyer said, thinking quickly. A. Reinhardt, known to be a citadel of Christian respectability.

"Reinhardt associates with Jews?" the inspector sneered, but left without further comment.

One August night in 1935, Globus was savaged; like bee-stung bulls in a china shop, thugs smashed glass counters and looted jewelry, furs, and silver. It was a typically stupid act of terror; most of the employees of the department store were Aryans and now were without employment.

The Globus incident was an isolated act of hooliganism in Lübeck. But passage of the Nuremberg Laws a month later froze Rebecca to the marrow and reawakened her fears and furies. One man's bedeviled loathing had resulted in a revision of the laws of the nation. German Jews, no matter how long their ancestry in the Fatherland, were deprived of their civil rights, their very citizenship. Anti-Semitism was legitimatized and legalized.

"If we are no longer citizens," Rebecca cried, "we are dead. Woe to him, as Nietzsche said, who has no native land."

"Why have we become Jews and nothing else?" Meyer asked, more incredulous than outraged. "We are Germans first and Jews only by faith, by—by *nature!* Are other Germans first identified as Roman Catholics or Lutherans? We have been peaceful citizens here for hundreds of years. Our fathers are buried here. We are not nomads who pick up our bundles and flee from the Cossacks. Germany is our home."

"They would like us to pick up our bundles and flee," Rebecca said. "And if we don't, they'll keep shoving us."

"World opinion will not permit such behavior."

"Do not put too much faith in world opinion, Meyer."

In their postal box one day was a hand-delivered message from one Bruno Rudolph. The lieutenant begged permission to call upon them that evening. Trying to disarm them with politeness and pleasantries, the black-uniformed, black-booted officer said, "You must appreciate that this is a time of sacrifice for *everyone*. You are in possession of a Château Rose silver set for eight. It would be a mark of the highest patriotism if you would surrender the set. The silver will be converted into arms for defense of the Fatherland. Naturally, you will receive reimbursement . . . "

Reimbursement amounted to less than one percent of the value of the silver. The effrontery, the enormity, the *thievery!* Sacrificing for a Fatherland whose new legalities had rendered them powerless and invisible. And for what defense? No one was threatening to make war on the Fatherland. Stalin, for one, was too busy killing his own people.

A shift of national priority made breathing easier for a time—the country was putting on its best face for the '36 Olympics in Berlin. (True, the Army had just reoccupied the far flank of the Rhine, and, true, none of the liberal democracies had protested or even boycotted the summer games. "A grave violation," Meyer acknowledged, "but still, if I were a soldier today . . . ") Grosser racial insults were muted. The signs "Juden unerwuenscht" (Jews not welcome) disappeared from shops, hotels, restaurants, and beer gardens—Jews could spend money there again. The world converging on Hitler's hub could see how "clean and good and strong we are." But invincible? Racially superior? Not when the Negro Jesse Owens could streak to victory after victory in Olympic Stadium. (Later, another "American-African cannibal," Joe Louis, was to knock out the Teutonic titan Max Schmeling in the first round of a world heavyweight championship fight.)

But inevitably, the atmosphere turned heavy again with

foreboding. In Munich, the obdurate Cardinal Pacelli turned his gaze from the evils at hand to drone on piously about the poison of godless communism. Mussolini, disregarding the threat of economic sanctions, had raped and gassed Ethiopia; Haile Selassie, the Lion of Judea, discovered that the League of Nations had feet of clay. Fratricidal Spaniards were drenching their cities and countryside with one another's blood; Germany tried out new weaponry for Franco's victorious Nationalists. In England—the bastion of stability—an effete king abdicated; he could not reign without the "support" of his twice-divorced inamorata. And in America, Albert Einstein placed in a time capsule the message "Dear Posterity: If you have not become more just, more peaceful, and generally more rational than we are (or were)—why then, the Devil take you."

Rising, falling . . . hope and despair. Breathers and fresh assaults. Yesterday's smile from an old acquaintance was today's turned head. Yesterday's permission was today's revocation. What happened happened as if by divine sanction. German troops marched into Austria and were received with o-pen arms. Jews were tortured with one restricting injunction after another. They must abandon certain occupations. Doctors were now "medical attendants." All Jews had "Jude" added to their ID cards. Drivers licenses were revoked—but how many of them could any longer afford to have an automobile? And the business of first names! Beginning with the New Year, Jews not named Israel or Sarah would have to add these names. (Meyer) Israel Wolf. (Rebecca) Sarah Wolf. (Esther) Sarah Wolf.

Rebecca tried valiantly for an esprit de corps that she rarely felt. She strove to deaden apprehension with the dull rotations of domesticity . . . marketing, cooking, cleaning, sewing for Esther, altering her own clothes, patching the elbows of Meyer's blessedly durable suits. ("No one knows how to build a suit like those Savile Row tailors.") In front of Esther particular-ly, she strained for a cheerful countenance. Children, it was said, read volumes into an unguarded expression or word. But she doubted that she was concealing her terrors from that bright, blossoming tulip.

"JEW MURDERS! JEW MURDERS!"

Rebecca opened her eyes. The Berliner Express had slid into the North Berlin terminal. At the kiosk she bought a tabloid screaming JEW SHOOTS GERMAN AIDE IN PARIS. In the taxi she sat bolt-upright reading. Failing to gain access to the ambassador, a Jewish art student had instead shot—and probably mortally wounded—the third secretary in the German embassy there. Herschel Grynszpan declared that he was avenging the cruelty the Nazis had inflicted on his parents, who had been terrorized in their home and shipped in a boxcar back to Poland. Rebecca prayed that Ernst vom Rath, the Nazis' chargé d'affaires in Paris, would not die.

"Two years, Samuel," she exclaimed, hugging and holding her brother. "Much too long."

Papa. He was the reincarnation of their father. That same thin triangular face sloping to a chin as sculpted as a Vandyke. The fair skin, strong aquiline nose, full lips. The wheat-colored hair—with strands of gray now—rolling back from the lofty wide brow. The eyes, blue as wild gentians, alit with merry sadness. The grainy bisected mustache curling upwards like scythes from each side of his Cupid's bow.

"Except for the mustache, you could be Leslie Howard, Samuel."

"Not Papa?" he teased.

"Papa must have looked like Leslie Howard, too."

"Or Leslie Howard looked like Papa, to be sequential."

They laughed together easily, as they had so often in the past over some shared whimsy.

"Samuel, do you know what I was dreaming about on the train? July in Kolberg."

"Grandmother and Grandfather Langer."

"Remember how wonderful we thought it was and how much Mama hated Kolberg. 'Those Baltic winds can saw a person in half . . . blinding sands off the dunes . . . a surf so treacherous it's suicide to dip even a toe in the water.' We'd play those silly games. On those dunes we'd be Stanley and Livingstone meeting in darkest Africa. Or pretend we were climbing Mt. Everest."

"Bubbe Langer."

Bubbe Langer *was* their Kolberg. She smothered the children with kisses and hugs that sucked them into her voluptuous body. She cooked and baked tantalizing things that they never had in Lübeck. She taught them snappy jigs that all three could dance together. Her breathless laughter flooded the house. At bedtime, the children were tucked into those gloriously snug beds under arches in the wall and she cosseted them to slumber with embroidered tales of the Baron Münchhausen and the scary Grimms. Grandmother Langer died when Rebecca was eleven. Rebecca hollered and wept and refused to eat or go to school and could not be consoled with promises of being reunited someday with Grandma in heaven. Even then, she didn't much believe in heaven.

"And we never went back to Kolberg," Rebecca said.

"We'd have interrupted Grandfather's absorption in his peach roses. Or his rereading of Balzac."

"Everything looks the same," she said, gesturing to Samuel's high, white airy rooms.

"It does and it doesn't. I miss Karen and Anna doing for me. The last I heard, neither of them had found work anywhere else. Typically stupid law. My newest is a Mrs. Rutstein. She means well and tries hard, but . . . She said that until a year ago she didn't even know how to boil water. And still doesn't know much more."

"It could drive you to marriage."

"Yes, if worse come to worst."

"What if vom Rath dies?"

"He *mustn't.*"

"I said a prayer for both him and the boy."

"Is your mind completely made up, Becky?"

"Completely."

"Does Meyer know?"

"No."

"You make it sound like a matter of life and death."

"I think it is."

Rebecca let herself be seduced by Samuel's invitation to some "fun" before she went about her mission. They took greedy gulps of Berlin . . . strolls down the busy Kurfürstendamm and the luxurious Via Triumphalis . . . morning coffees at the Café König swathed in its streamlined art deco . . . a film (*Moonlight Sonata* with Marie Tempest and the great pianist— Poland's former president—Ignatz Paderewski) . . . dinner at the Drei Husaren . . . a moonlit sail on the Wannsee . . . a visit to Samuel's sculptor friend who had the studio in Tauenzienstrasse . . . an hour among the oaks, beeches, and horse chestnuts sloping in their November starkness in the lovely Lustgarten.

It was so sad, all the Gemütlichkeit and charm and beauty of architecture and the lively interest in the arts and all those intelligent people with their softer accents and love of cultivation and the good life. And none of it changed a thing—the arts and the amenities had absolutely no modifying influence on government or mass behavior. Rebecca knew that stomping black boots and the blood-red banners with fat black swastikas would prevail over Schnitzler and the splendors of baroque.

Rebecca and Samuel were home in Dahlem supping on Mrs. Rutstein's Spätzle and Sauerbraten when they heard the news from Paris on the Telefunken. Ernst vom Rath was dead.

"Verdammt!" An extraordinary expletive from gentle Samuel.

Rebecca was roused from her sleep that night by the sound of distant eruptions. A fire or bombs in the center of Berlin? She slept again and awoke in the morning to the horrors of the Kristallnacht . . . a night of incalculable savagery without precedent since the Thirty Years' War three centuries earlier . . . the glass fronts of ten thousand shop windows crashing into the sidewalks . . . hundreds of synagogues torched . . . innocent thousands routed from their homes and businesses, arrested and hauled off to concentration camps . . . crippled and consumptive children driven in their nightclothes out of hospitals and made to walk on broken glass in their bare feet . . . looting, raping, wholesale murdering. Walpurgisnacht.

The mayhem was engineered, orchestrated by the Minister of Propaganda as reprisal against the Jews for the murder of vom Rath.

"Being a Jew is not a crime," young Grynszpan had sobbed. "I am not a dog. I have a right to live. The Jewish people have a right to exist on this earth."

Rousing from shock, Samuel shook his head repeatedly and said sadly, "I no longer understand the world."

Rebecca agreed to stay put in Samuel's flat for two days; it might not be safe for her to venture into the downtown streets. The suspense and frustration were almost intolerable. She could not reach Meyer at the Paperweight office in Lübeck, and their blind landlady had no telephone. She sent a telegram with little expectation that it would be delivered.

Her heart sank at the size of the queue on Unter den Linden. At least a thousand people were waiting to get into the American consulate. They stood together, taking some solace in their common desperation. "Applications for visas will not be heard at this time," the notice nailed to the consulate gate announced. "At this time" could mean "or any time imminent"—a single U.S. State Department official, Breckenridge Long, had put both fists into the immigration dike. It was hopeless.

Rebecca wept convulsively.

"Becky," Samuel pleaded, "don't. It will be all right. Listen to me. I want you to come here and live with me. You and Meyer and Esther. We'll close the Lübeck office. We'll be safe here and we'll have . . . "

"*Safe?* Samuel, how can you say such a thing? Safe? We're the victims and we're being charged with 'abominable crimes.' They want the Jews to pay a fine of a billion marks for what *they* did to *us*."

"It's just an insane moment, Becky. One blind tick of the clock."

One blind tick of the clock? Samuel, her beloved brother. What was the flaw in his nature that he, too, must cling, rationalize, obfuscate?

"Listen to your Rabbi Baeck," Rebecca said, throwing at Samuel the name of the man he esteemed above all others. "Even he says that German Jewry is dead. The thousand-year history of the Jews in Germany is at an end."

"He's speaking metaphorically. What the rabbi really means . . . "

Rebecca left Berlin with the haunting premonition that she would never see Samuel again.

The return journey to Lübeck was interminable. The rickety building on the Trave was locked. Back in Mrs. Markheim's house she found her precious Esther—a whimpering, reproachful Esther.

"Where's Daddy?" Rebecca asked.

"Gone."

"Gone where?"

"Gone. Like you."

"Some men came a few nights ago," Mrs. Markheim explained, her crochet needles flashing. "They said Mr. Wolf should go with them. They said it was for his own good. He would be all right."

"Daddy said he would be back real soon," Esther sobbed. "But he isn't. What did you bring me for my birthday?"

Rebecca suspected the worst. Nocturnal knocks meant only one thing in these times. Many men had been taken away. Even the snooping Nazi Blockwart knew nothing. Nor was any other source forthcoming. The tension was unbearable for Kitty as well as herself: Two representatives of the State had also taken off Harry Rosenthal.

"I am safe and well. Please send winter clothing." The handwriting on the postal card, arriving more than a week after Rebecca was back in Lübeck, was Meyer's. The postmark was Buchenwald.

Thank God (*God?*) for that much. Meyer was alive, and she knew where he was.

"When is Daddy coming home?" was Esther's plaintive, daily cry.

"Maybe tomorrow."

Tomorrow and tomorrow creeping at this petty pace . . .

Kitty visited every day. They drank coffee and waited like wives of warrior husbands for news from the battlefront.

"You'll never guess where the Einhorns ended up," Kitty challenged Rebecca.

"Dachau?"

"Shanghai."

"Shanghai, *China?*"

"The only Shanghai. It's an open city, Becky. There are absolutely no quotas, no restrictions of any kind. They'll let *anything* in. Jack the Ripper, Haarmann, Al Capone, Mata Hari. No questions asked. Just get there and the pearly gates open. Susanne Einhorn writes that it takes getting used to, the slums and the begging and the terrible heat. In summer you think you're on the equator. John got a job with a pharmaceutical firm and Susanne says the whites live there like kings for next to nothing. And they're absolutely safe. The Orientals don't dare bother the whites."

"It's a long way to swim."

"You don't have to swim. If Berlin sees you're serious about going, they'll let you have enough of your impounded funds to buy steamship tickets."

Shanghai? What did she know of Shanghai? She had an image of millions of dirty people, opium parlors, brawling sailors, junks jammed together in polluted waters, scarlet-lipped temptresses, Marlene Dietrich and Anna May Wong in that movie about trains and bandits—and a naked baby crying her head off in the bombed-out shell of a railroad station. In seven years, she knew, Hirohito's German-trained generals had swallowed up the space equivalent in China of pre-Munich Germany and France combined and occupied the Chinese sections of Shanghai.

Rebecca poured over the brochures of the North German Lloyd Lines. The *Hannover* called at Southampton, Gibraltar, Bombay, and Manila, and the *Potsdam* called at Cherbourg, Marseilles, Genoa, Bangkok, Kobe, and Hong Kong. Both liners would deliver their passengers, sedated with sybaritic indulgences, to "the Paris of the Orient."

It was more a tap than a knock. It couldn't be *them* again; they did not make polite sounds. She waited. More light tapping downstairs at the front door.

"Who's there?" she called from the stairs.

Someone responded, but too feebly for her to make out the words.

"Who's there? Who's there?"

" . . . Mey . . . Mey . . . Meyer."

Rebecca flew to the door and threw it open. To stifle a scream, she put a hand in front of her mouth.

Meyer! *Meyer?* A ghastly apparition, a cadaver. In only four weeks, his face had become hollow and gray. His nose was bent. There were white patches in his hair. He was staring at her with the eyes of a dead soul.

In the days that followed, the story came haltingly. The very *idea* of being imprisoned in Buchenwald for no offense! No offense other than being who you were, a democrat or a communist or a socialist or a gypsy or a homosexual or a conscientious priest or an editor or a nightclub master of ceremonies. Or a Jew. Law-abiding human beings consigned to animal lairs of the most degrading filth and putrefaction . . . nearly naked bodies exposed to rain, sleet, snow . . . old men cleaning latrines with their beards . . . youths chosen by lot for a fifty-mile crawl and forced at bayonet-point to polish black boots in the snow . . . lugging blocks of granite from one end of the camp to the other and back again . . . digging craters into the ground with bare hands and refilling them with the same earth . . . trotting like dray horses hitched to one another in chain gangs . . . subsisting on swill.

For a whole week at Buchenwald, Meyer's bowels did not move. "Count your blessings," a fellow prisoner said. "It's slippery around that shit pit. If you fall in, you'll drown. It's happened to a few already."

The need to void his bowels returned. Meyer dreaded it more than he had feared the prolonged constipation. Having to squat on soaking clay alongside other men to perform this most private, this least esthetic of bodily functions, was excruciating for him. And just as painful was the indignity that followed. There was no toilet paper. Less fastidious men pulled up their drawers and trousers and shuffled off. Unthinkable for Meyer, who began disassembling his charcoal pinstriped suit. After each bowel movement, he cleaned himself with a swatch of sartorial splendor and consigned it to the sewage pit of Barrack 23. Strip by strip the jacket went. Next, the vest; then, the trousers. Soon, he would be naked.

Two work forces were commandeered to build a stretch of

road to nowhere. They were arrayed against each other like fighting cocks, "The Bolshie scum" and "the Jewish scum." One day, it was the whim of an SS officer to declare the Bolshies incorrigible loafers. "Into the ditch, Bolshies. Start digging, Jews. Bury them. Smother Stalin's rats. Dirt on dirt."

Meyer's group froze. They could not lift their shovels.

"You don't take orders, Jews? All right. Out of the ditches, Bolshies. Into the ditch, Jews. Bury the Jews, Bolshies."

The "Bolshies" fell to with a vengeance. They heaved soil on the Jews. The end, Meyer thought. He would be buried alive. The shoveled earth rose higher and higher. It covered his thighs, his hips, his torso, his neck, his chin, his mouth. He made a decision. He would not lift his head. His nostrils would not beg for one more breath of life. He would not cry out. Within a millimeter of suffocation Meyer heard the capricious order. "Enough! Dig them out."

Cradling the broken man in her arms, stanching his tears, Rebecca said, "It's all right now, my dearest. You are here. You are alive. You are home. Nothing else matters. For whatever reason, they let you go."

"For whatever reason did they take me?" he sobbed. "Becky, it is time for us to leave."

"It is time for us to leave." Something she never expected to hear from his lips. He had had enough at last. The Kristallnacht had unleashed a spate of new restrictions. They couldn't even go to films or concerts or the theater anymore. Or play with their daughter in the triangular park that had been a gift of Grandfather Herschel to the citizens of Lübeck. She could easily have said "I told you so," but restrained herself to a simple "Yes, I think you are right, Meyer. We shall leave."

"America," Meyer said. "We'll go to America."

Such naiveté! Even now, Rebecca could not confess that her real mission in Berlin, albeit a defeated one, had been to test her wits and charm against virtually impossible odds at the American consulate. "We must forget about America," she said. "We would have to wait five to ten years."

And they must forget about England and Canada and Australia and South Africa and Latin America. All had "exhausted quotas."

"Where is left, Becky?"

"There is only one place. Shanghai."

"Shanghai?"

"It is the only place. It is an open port. We can wait there."

"China," Meyer moaned. "The worst of places. The Yellow Peril. Millions starving. War. Thousands slaughtered in Nanking. China is a country of dangerous people . . . "

"Germany is a country of dangerous people, Meyer. What is our alternative? Follow the advice of Mahatma Gandhi?"

Gandhi, deploring violence as the resolution of any problem, had issued *his* modest proposal. German Jews, all half-million of them, should commit collective suicide. It would dramatize the horrors of Hitler's Germany and Nazism, and the whole world would rise in righteous wrath. The moral victory of good over evil would be secured forevermore.

"Shanghai," Meyer said, burying his face in her lap, "will be our coffin."

January—February
1939

IN TRANSIT

"So where will it be?"

Dora Mittendorf's tone conveyed her irritation. Really! Having one's valuable time taken up by a child. There were people waiting who *did* mean business. Where, the foolish boy was asking, could you buy passage to?

Miss Mittendorf put a hand on the illuminated globe on the counter and gave it a contemptuous twirl. "Take your pick."

The boy slowly examined the dizzily spinning earth and asked, "Haven't you got anything better?"

Meyer Wolf managed a thin smile, rare for him these days. It took a child to wonder openly if there wasn't some better place than anywhere in this world.

Miss Mittendorf's frown took in Meyer as well as the impertinent boy. She was a plump, clear-skinned, flaxen-haired woman in her thirties, a younger, crudely polished version of her sister, Hedwig. Rebecca had recalled that Dora worked at the Four Corners Travel Agency.

When Meyer introduced himself, Miss Mittendorf's expression brightened for a moment. "Oh, yes, yes, Hedwig always . . . " She broke off and nervously riffled some folders sandwiched in a ledger. Shanghai? Three lines were still calling there. Lloyd's, of course. And Italian ships. And a few Japanese. So many people all of a sudden wanting to go to Shanghai. She dropped her somber, professional mien to become personal and chatty. "My sister always held you and your good wife and Mrs. Langer in the highest regard, Mr. Wolf. She always said one could never find nicer people to work for. She said your home was such a pleasant place. Everything was in the best taste. She so admired the beautiful paintings on the walls, especially the oval one over the highboy in the dining room. The one of the dancer tying on her slippers."

"The Degas."

"Mr. Wolf"—reverting to the demeanor of the harried travel agent—"it's going to be very difficult. I shall do my best. Please, if you can, call back tomorrow."

"Who would ever have thought Hedwig had such an eye for fine art?" Rebecca laughed. What instinct had told her to hang on to the painting when she had disposed of so much else? "Take Miss Mittendorf the Degas, Meyer. She won't find out it's only a copy until she tries to sell it."

The *Hannover* sailed from Hamburg.

The port was on the eve of celebrating its seven hundred and fiftieth birthday and was straining for a festive look. But all the bunting and the gay lanterns could not mask the sinister façade of the city. The serried rows of swastikas lining the main thoroughfares, the ubiquitous military presence of SS men, police, and troops created an air of smoldering violence.

At Pier 101, the emigrating passengers were segregated. The men and the boys—"the Judickies"—were ordered to one side of a dark, drafty, dilapidated shed and the women and the girls to the other side. All cases and trunks were searched, and everyone was subjected to a physical inspection. To Meyer, dehumanized by the concentration camp, the ordeal of pulling down pants, bending over, and spreading buttocks was sufferable. With barely a wince, he could endure the smack of a riding crop because he had still not spread wide enough. Was he trying to secrete a ring or a bauble or Deutschmarks up there?

"Horrible, horrible," Rebecca sobbed, clutching Esther to her. It was her initiation to the violation of what properly should be inviolate. "Those gross matrons! They made one woman remove her artificial leg and they cracked it open on the floor. They tore the wig off the shaved wife of a rabbi and squeezed it like a dish cloth."

The band on the snow-covered quay played *Auf Wiedersehen*, and the *Hannover* sounded off with great echoing blasts. Many of the emigrants boarded the ship with tears in their eyes, but others shook their fists in fury at this last glimpse of their homeland.

The Wolfs settled comfortably into Stateroom B-66. It had

twin beds, a folding cot, a dressing room, and a fully appointed bathroom with water closet and luxurious toilet tissue. As the *Hannover* steamed through the darkening winter day—past snow-covered fields and villages along the canal and estuary of the Elbe—and plunged into the tempestuous North Sea and English Channel, life slipped into an aura of other-wordliness.

Captain Helmut Brandt welcomed the Shanghai-bound Jews most cordially. And why not? Had not his employer obliged all eighty-six departing Jews to travel in luxury class? And to purchase a return ticket, though there would be no return?

Courtly and aristocratic of bearing—his remote blue eyes had measured distant horizons during a lifetime at sea—Captain Brandt introduced his passengers to the facilities of the 17,000-ton liner . . . to the commodious decks and the grand salons and the deluxe staterooms. The Jews had only to ask for anything they wanted that they didn't see. The Olympic-size pool, when the voyage came under a benign sun, would be theirs during the sunniest, the best, hours; the non-Jews—the German nationals, the English, and the others—would have to swim earlier or later. In the Café Europa, with its wickerwork chairs and tables and freshly laundered pink linen and crystal, the Jewish passengers would have the second—the preferred—seating at each meal. The first-class social hall was converted into a synagogue to accommodate the religious—Orthodox, Conservative, Reform. The first-class smoking salon would be their private club, open around the clock.

Rebecca took to reading aloud the Lucullan excesses of the menu: " . . . and there's Beluga caviar, Gromitz oysters, pâté de foie gras, cream of barley soup, consommé, salmon mousse, roast squab and cress, duckling Bigarade, veal Marengo with buttered noodles, fried chicken with grilled tomatoes, cauliflower hollandaise, asparagus vinaigrette, creamed carrots and green peas, Parmentier potatoes, Waldorf salad, orange or chocolate ice cream, peaches in chartreuse jelly . . . "

"I want it all," Esther announced.

"I just had it all, my dear," an orotund, double-chinned man called over from the next table. "Weissenberger," he introduced himself. "Civil engineer. Danzig."

Rebecca smiled. The temptation to gorge was human. Who knew what was ahead? Anyone burdened with the memory of history going back five thousand years knew that after feasts came famines.

Too restless, too exhilarated for sedentary pastimes, she walked the promenades and inhaled the bracing sea air. She luxuriated in the suspension of care.

The time was beyond recall when she had felt so free, so unoppressed with impending crises. It was a time in limbo. China was a month away. This chapter of the Diaspora was to be savored. She had never been so effortlessly sociable. She saw in a softening light people she might once have found unattractive. They were, after all, quite literally in the same boat.

Esther was in wonderland. There was the kindergarten under the stewardship of that nice Miss Beimer. There was the sandbox fore and the sandbox aft. There was the inexhaustible magic of Rumpelstiltskin's Castle. There was Willie Stenger, a blue-eyed, dimpled, tow-headed six-year-old—Esther's first boyfriend.

Rebecca studied the heavens and said to Meyer, "You are my Northern Cross," but she could not cajole him out of his introversion. He would not join her on the decks, and he grimaced at her gregariousness. He was too much to himself, turning inward, brooding, nursing his hurt. "Why don't you meet some of the men," she suggested gently. "Many of them have been through what you've been through." Meyer wasn't interested. Except for meals, he kept to their cabin and his reading of *Der Untergang des Abendlandes, Umrisse einer Morphologie der Weltgeschichte.*

The young man was quite alone. He visited the library. From the bow he braved the Atlantic rollers. At table he sat with three much older men—cabinmates possibly, none of them seemingly his father.

Sometimes, in the Café Europa, Rebecca intercepted his glance—his stare—and he would look away, flushing.

He was handsome enough to catch any eye. He had an innocent beauty, a bit delicate and refined. His large dreamy eyes were a shade somewhere between violet and a deep brown, and his auburn hair was thick and wavy. He had a thin, sensitive pairing of lips and an appealing cleft in his chin. His smooth skin shone. He could not have been more than eighteen years old. If she were sixteen and high spirited, like those perambulating Jewish girls, Elsa and Inge, Rebecca would be setting her cap for him instead of pursuing dubious pastimes.

She found herself at the railing beside the young man. They gazed at the Jurassic limestone fortress looming before them. British passengers who had boarded at Southampton were disembarking and there was the frenzy of reunions and quayside unloadings.

"The Rock," Rebecca remarked. "After all those travel posters and geography books!"

He turned to her, the violet-brown eyes swimming with excitement. "It's stupendous. A three-mile tank."

"Leave it to the British. They know a good thing when they see it."

"And how to appropriate it."

Oh, he was sharp, too. She extended her hand, introducing herself.

"I am David Buchbinder," he said.

"I gather you are traveling alone."

He flushed and looked back at Gibraltar. "Yes."

"You are very brave," Rebecca said.

"Is it brave to be leaving one's parents to their own fates?"

"Where are they?"

"My mother is in Breslau and my father is in Dachau."

Forever would David Buchbinder's parents be fixed in memory as they set off for the Breslau opera one autumn evening. They paused in the foyer and turned to say goodnight to him. Mama was radiant in her white satin gown, black velvet shawl, and white satin slippers. Bedecked in long strands of pearls and a diamond-studded band around her head, she looked like Her Serene Highness. Her eyes sparkled and her black hair glistened. That special face with its ivory skin and exquisite cheekbones and sweet uptilted chin. She was a vision. Papa, too. He was Prince Charming in his evening clothes, cape, and silk opera hat, and he carried a silver-handled evening stick. He was so handsome. His dark hair rolled back in a pompadour off his smooth brow. His moustache was bushy but perfectly groomed. He was not a tall man, but he stood and walked in majesty. David was so proud of his parents, so filled with love for them that evening that his eyes were misting.

"The next time they perform *Die Hochzeit des Figaro*," Mama said, "you must come with us, David. It is very amusing."

David would have loved to have shared their passion for fine music. (Even as a boy he scoffed at operas for their silly plots and pompous posturing.) Breslau breathed fine music. All the great musical figures performed there. Caruso, Galli-Curci, Flagstad, Melchior, Schumann-Heink, Melba, and Mary Garden sang in the Staatsoper. What Papa, himself, would have given to have been a violinist in the Philharmonic. He at least stood on the fringe of that pulsating world through his printing company that specialized in orchestrations, sheet music, and primers for the piano and the harpsichord. On Thursday evenings, Papa and three friends would gather in the library and play the music they cherished. They played Haydn and Mozart and had a special fondness for Schubert's No. 29 in A Minor, and they would segue smoothly into the same-sounding "Andantino" from *Rosamunde*. "The Thursday Night Irregulars" claimed that they were not sufficiently virtuoso for Beethoven's late quartets or anything by Schumann. David was allowed to stay up and help turn pages. Sharing Papa's hours of greatest happiness made him feel so close to Papa.

The Buchbinders lived in a flat on Hindenburgstrasse that occupied an entire floor of the Heilbronner Mansions, a red-stone citadel with turrets and gables and other Victorian furbelows which was set far back from the road in the shadows of arching Lombardy poplars. The Heilbronner Mansions had vast stretches of lawn and a spacious private park. Behind the building were croquet and badminton courts. Each family had its own plot of garden and little apple trees. There was a pond on which regal swans and ducks and geese glided gracefully in the crepuscular light of a long mid-summer night's evening.

Breslau! There could be no other city so splendid as this capital of Lower Silesia. The magnificent boulevards were flanked by towering phalanxes of chestnut trees, and one brilliant park gave way to the next. Always he would see the Oder flowing through the city in soft curves, like the fluttering blue ribbon on a young girl's bonnet. Always he would recall the grandeur of dozens of buildings, some so distinguished in design that they attracted admiring architects from all over the continent. Visitors exclaimed over the magnificent churches —St. Elisabeth with its Renaissance helmet bathed in a green patina, the Romanesque St. Giles, the baroque cathedral of St. John the Baptist, St. Mary Magdalene with its proud Gothic basilica—and the ancient Market Square and the town hall with its Gothic portals and the statues of Christ and St. Hieronymus and the Olympic stadium and the flamingoes in the zoological gardens and the lilacs and rhododendrons and tamarisks blooming along the banks of the Oder in springtime.

David was never altogether satisfied with his parents' explanation of his being an only child. "You are all we could ever want in a family," they told him. Instead of siblings, David had Hanni, a cocker spaniel he adored to distraction. When Hanni succumbed to distemper, David was wreathed in grief. He dug a grave for her behind a row of hollyhocks in their garden and sat shiva.

Otherwise, David's early memories were sweet. One Saturday afternoon, when he was seven, he saw a Ken Maynard western at the Odeon and decided he would become a cowboy or join a tribe of Sioux Indians. His next birthday was celebrated with a two-gallon hat and a bow-and-arrow set. He devoured the novels of Karl May, who wrote so incisively about American Indians: David would be Old Shatterhand. Sunday mornings, he and Papa took long walks, hand in hand, that always ended at a Konditorei. ("Not a word to your mother," Papa would say. "She'd lay me out in lavender if she knew I let you have a cream puff before dinner." Their little secret, their conspiracy.) They would come home to find Mama on the tufted red leather settee in the library, a book propped on her stomach. She read to be entertained, not informed, she confessed. "That Mr. Pickwick," she would chuckle, "will be the death of me."

David was nine and a student at St. Rudolph's School when he discovered the world was not so sweet after all. Reinhold Fortwangler was having a birthday party and everybody in the class was invited—everybody, that is, except David and three other boys. Their teacher said to the four of them, "You know why Reinhold wouldn't ask you to his party, don't you? You don't? It didn't cross your stupid little minds that the Fortwanglers wouldn't have their home soiled by the oily heirs of usurers and war profiteers and Christ killers?"

Oily heirs of usurers and war profiteers and Christ killers?

"Dr. Hermann should not have spoken so discourteously," David's father said, sighing heavily. "People do not always become wiser, David, when they become bigger and older. Even some people who should know better. Sometimes, people are called bad names because they have a different faith. This is wrong, very wrong. All faiths say we should love God and our fellow man and be kind to one another. When times are bad, some people feel helpless and look around for someone on whom they can vent their anger. It is easy to pick on the ones who are a little different."

You might look like other people, go to the same school, play with one another, speak the same language, but you are not invited to birthday parties. Was that what it meant to be Jewish!

Though keenly interested in topical affairs, David's parents were careful to shield him from discussions that might be distressing to an impressionable young mind . . . massive unemployment, massive inflation, massive reparations, the impotence of the League of Nations and the abstention from the League by the United States, the rising National Socialist party. Chaos was swirling like the millions of wild geese that came and went in migration twice a year.

David had parental encouragement to believe that he was bright, special, and entitled to his opinions. At the *Gymnasium* he was of the strongest opinion that obligatory Latin was a waste of time. Why learn to translate "fiat justitia" and "errare humanum est" when "let justice be done" and "to err is human" were already mottoes in their own language? The Latin class met in early afternoon, and usually the professor came in with flushed cheeks and glassy eyes after calling on a nearby wine cellar. "Boys, boys, boys," he often bade them, dabbing at his eyes, "you must never, never, never forget the immortal words of Horace: 'Dulce et decorum est pro patria mori.' It is sweet and noble to die for one's country!"

David saw little sense, either, in Hebrew lessons. He looked forward to his bar mitzvah, after which he could stop going to Talmud Torah. Soccer practice was much more fun.

"A person must first and above everything be good in all of his personal relations," David began his essay on the meaning of citizenship, which took first prize in the contest sponsored by the Breslau City Council. He was also elated to have his father point out to him that he had written an explanation of Kant's categorical imperative. David's course was set. The other boys could dream about becoming cowboys or Autobahn engineers or Nobel Prize physicists; he would be a journalist.

A history class soon after the triumph of the essay contest provided him with a journalistic assignment. He and the other students were to review a textbook. " 'Just as one poisonous mushroom can kill a whole family,' " David's mother read at random, " 'so can one Jew ruin a whole city. . . . ' " She threw the book to the floor and kicked it across the room. "The author is an insane hatemonger," his father said. "You must write your review very carefully, David. You do not want to invite punishment, but you must not perjure yourself, either. It is like walking a tightrope. You will have to be clever in your way of phrasing things so that the teacher will seem to be reading what he wants to read. For example, you might write, 'The author is a man of the strongest convictions,' then use up considerable space quoting them. Or you could say, 'He writes with great vividness,' and give examples. The professor will read it one way, you will mean it quite another."

The geography instructor projected the future glories of the Fatherland. The Volk would be avenged for the "treacherous thefts" of their land dictated at Versailles. Tapping Berlin on the "temporary" map of Germany unfurled over the blackboard, he said, "Observe how close our capital is to those savages on the East. Let us ever be wary of the avaricious and detestable Poles. They are scum and they know it." A film called *Heldentum und Untergang unserer Emden* introduced a new lesson: "Never trust the English. Their attack on our ships off the Coco Islands was cowardly."

Even sheltered schoolboys could not close their ears to the word Depression or their eyes to its creeping manifestations. Businesses were closing, and more people were without work. Those who had been entrepreneurial and well-off were selling their sterling silver and gold watches and looking for any kind of employment and pleading for loans. Many people took to the streets to sell yarn, shoelaces, lumps of coal, pencils, even horse manure. Some crouched all day long at the side of the cobblestone streets, their hats upside down at their feet to receive a coin or two. The vendors and the beggars grew threadbare. People whispered of a despairing neighbor who had plunged out of a window or had hanged himself with a silk cravat or had never come home.

The director of the *Gymnasium* asked David and several other boys if each could bring an extra sandwich from home for the less fortunate scholars. He asked David's father if the Buchbinders would be willing to accept an evening boarder.

David's classmate Martin Schumann took dinner with them for almost a year. He was a pale, weak-looking boy, nearly as white as an albino, and his watery blue eyes were always red-rimmed, as if from crying. David's parents treated Martin like a nephew, never patronizingly. To David, he was too polite, too withdrawn, too shy to be easy with. Martin never brought much to the table besides a ravenous appetite.

After gratifying that appetite one evening, Martin announced abruptly, "I shall come here no more. Thank you for your kindness."

David was delighted. He had come to detest Martin and resented his presence. Yes, he was even jealous of him. Martin came between him and his parents, intruding upon familial intimacy and good conversation.

"Martin," Papa said, "we shall miss you."

"Yes," Mama added, "you will be welcome here always."

"Let us hope things are easier for Martin's family," Papa

said later. "It must be bitter gall for parents to have to send their children to someone else's table because they have only thin soup at their own."

Life was changing, constricting. Neighbors in the Heilbronner Mansions started to act strangely. Papa's business was still sound enough—Germans gave up music just before they gave up eating and drinking. But the Buchbinders stopped going to Bad Gattstein in the summer, nor would there be, *could* there be, any more winter holidays of ice skating, tobogganing, sleighing, and the good air in the resort in Czechoslovakia.

Marian and Clara, who were virtually "family," left them. Marian had lived in the maid's room and did general maid's work and laundry and some sewing. She rarely left the flat, except to attend Mass. She was slavishly devoted to her mistress. (Years later, David, in some amazement, put certain clues together and concluded that his mother had arranged a forbidden operation for Marian and attended her through the sordid affair. Marian the bony spinster!) Clara arrived early in the morning to prepare and serve breakfast, then cooked and baked the whole day long. She had the smooth skin, rosy plump cheeks, and taffy-colored braids of a milkmaid. Her high girlish voice trilled the hours away in a tuneless repertoire of hymns and folk songs.

Simultaneously, Marian and Clara were telling their employer that they must take their leave. Each had received a stern, threatening message. The two servants entered the breakfast room holding hands and wiping away tears. "Good people, good people," Clara sobbed. "It is not our wish. We must do as the authorities tell us."

The Fatherland had determined that Marian and Clara were too young to be working for non-Aryans. Henceforth, only women over the age of forty-five would be permitted. . . .

How would Mama manage without them? "I'll have to do the best I can," she said. "My two boys must be patient with me."

The Führer honored Breslau with a visit. Jews were not to be on the streets for the occasion, but one of Papa's friends risked it. "Gerhardt, I have had the dubious honor," Herr

Lachmann told him later, "of seeing and hearing the greatest criminal of this century."

The Führer addressed the nation on wireless: "The German people are restoring honor to themselves. They know that honor—and freedom—can be restored in only one way. That way lies in law and order, in discipline and obedience, in sobriety and cleanliness. . . . "

"He is a clown, my son," David's father said. "We should be free of him in six months."

In a park, David rescued a boy of eleven who had been beaten, violated, and abandoned. The head of the boy's circumcised penis was coated with iodine and on his chest was painted a brown swastika. At school, one of David's "best friends" asked him if it was true that "Jews eat the skin they cut off their pricks." Another good friend warned David that he would not be able to help him if anything should "happen" to David.

The broad avenues of Breslau burst into pandemonium. Drums dinned. Cornets blared. French horns cracked. Cymbals collided. Tubas boomed. Jackboots pounded. The "gutteral" rhetoric resonated. The New Order was audible long before it was visible.

The Brown Shirts swigged their beer and bawled the Horst-Wessel-Lied, the Nazi anthem named for an early martyr. Some sang, "Wenn des Judenblut vom Messer spritzt, dann geht's nochmal so gut" (When Jewish blood splashes from the knife, things go twice as well). To elderly citizens, they gestured obscenely and chanted, "Fee, fie, foe, fum, I smell Jewish scum." In sodden camaraderie they stomped the streets. They tied jurists by the robes and paraded them through the avenues, then forced them to their knees to clean up the droppings of dray horses. They trapped a rabbinical student in a revolving glass door and tried to asphyxiate him.

"Bierhops and hooligans," Gerhardt Buchbinder said. "Blockheads are always with us."

"Yes, but where were the police?" Gertrud Buchbinder asked, repeatedly, not realizing that many of the mob were police in civilian clothes.

Papa was so calm, so protective, so reassuring. But only in

Papa's presence did David feel calm and protected. The *Gymnasium* that he had loved was becoming a dreaded, fearsome place. Calling upon David, certain professors looked at him with a coldness that felt like hatred. When he was alone with one or another of his friends, it was the same as before. But if he tried to join a group, he encountered hostility. The others would have pained expressions that said "Don't try to be one of us. You understand?" By-and-by, he did come to understand it for what it was.

"I have met with some of the other fathers," Papa said quietly one evening, "and we have decided that you and Franz and Theodor and Ludwig are to wait for one another after school and all leave together."

"The Four Musketeers," David said derisively. He hardly knew two of the other boys, and disliked the third, and he was skeptical of the stratagem.

His skepticism proved well founded the very first week of this odd new confederation. Making their way along the looping macadam in Emperor Wilhelm Park, the four were fallen upon by a gang of twenty. A chorus of taunts went up from the bandstand: "Dirty Jews!" "Jewish maggots!" "Christ killers!" "Scheisshaufen!" The gang was a delegation of the New Manhood. The Four Musketeers were knocked down and pummeled and had their noses bloodied and their eyes blackened. David looked up to see Martin Schumann—their evening boarder for nearly a year—raising a cleated boot over him. Martin dangled the cleats close to David's face, then relented. He spat on David. The good friend who had told David not to expect help if anything untoward should befall him was squeezing Franz's testicles while another lout sat on Franz's head.

At home, David wept piteously. It was not the shock or the blows. It was the humiliation. Mama looked at Papa in reproach. Papa had no answers, only *his* pain, *his* humiliation. Later, as David tried to sleep, he heard the voices of his parents rising in dissension.

For David, Papa had been the authority, the repository of wisdom, the embodiment of all that was good and just. But now even Papa could not save him from danger. Papa was not infallible. Nor could he predict the future. School had turned into a golgotha.

One day David found a cartoon on his desk. "I want you to give Fifi a shot for rabies," the woman in the drawing instructed her veterinarian. "My dog's been bitten by a Jew." David guessed who the culprit was and sank his teeth into the soft, drooping lobe of the boy's right ear. "Die of rabies yourself," David screamed.

David became fearful and distracted, moody, introspective. A recurring nightmare began to obsess him. Somewhere, some day, alone, he would be ambushed by a pack of tormentors. They would beat him up, rip off his clothes, and castrate him. Hitler Youth—uncircumcised, like all non-Jewish Europeans—had a ghoulish fascination with the genitalia of Jewish males.

The insults were random.

"Bang, bang, Jews!" A crazed old man roaming the streets raised his alpenstock and aimed it like a rifle. "Bang, bang, Jews! Kill the Yid!"

He was glad to be graduated from the *Gymnasium*, but what now? Though fully qualified by academic achievement and aptitude for pursuing a doctorate next, he was forbidden to enter a university by another of the new laws.

"For the time being," Papa advised, "enroll for some business courses with the Tannenbaums. Typewriting and shorthand will help you in your career in journalism."

"What career in journalism?" David snapped.

"David, David, I know you are disappointed. I am disappointed for you. But I am sure these frustrations are temporary. And I must tell you how much you hurt me when you speak to me in that tone."

Shortly after David began his classes with the Tannenbaums, the Night of the Broken Glass shattered the uneasy calm.

The morning after the Kristallnacht, David went with his father to the printing plant. Every door and window had been slashed and broken. Sledgehammers had demolished the presses. Heavy black ink washed across the floors. Gerhardt Buchbinder went ashen and nearly collapsed.

David forgot all his recent resentment, spoken and unspoken, of his father. How many times had Papa soothed *his* hurts and injuries! Now David saw the traditional roles reversed. He must now comfort Papa.

"I understand murder," David said. "I would like to kill whoever did this. We'll get the presses repaired."

"They are beyond repair," his father said, rocking and holding his head. "And you're not to talk like that. The walls have ears."

As they helplessly surveyed the ruins, David and his father were surprised by authorities bursting through the shattered front door.

"Buchbinder?" one of the troopers asked.

"Yes."

"You are not permitted to reopen this shop."

"What are you saying? What have I done?"

"You are an agitator. You are guilty of a traitorous act. You printed the poster."

"Poster? What poster? I don't understand."

"You know. The one in adulation of that vermin Mendelssohn. 'Can a Fatherland of bovine Brunhildes marry without the Wedding March?' "

"I know of no such poster," Gerhardt Buchbinder protested.

"Please, Buchbinder, we have evidence."

Papa perceived his powerlessness and shrugged his shoulders.

"Papa, why didn't you demand to see the poster?" David asked later, gently. "You could prove that your printing mark wasn't on it."

"It would be a waste of breath, my son. Vengeance is theirs. They have their cunning ways. They would say that all the posters had been destroyed. They could not permit such sedition to be in circulation."

They came for Papa that same night.

It was the ritualistic middle-of-the-night seizure.

The Buchbinders had long since left the luxurious Heilbronner Mansions and were now in the attic flat of one Doctor Alben. It was he who responded to the pounding on the door. He feigned confusion.

"That's all right, Doctor Alben," Gerhardt Buchbinder

said, coming down the stairs. "They know I am here. I have nothing to fear. I have done nothing wrong."

"The hour is inconvenient," the representatives of law and order apologized. "But surely you know, Mr. Buchbinder, the work of the Fatherland never sleeps."

Again Papa saw the futility of protest, pleas, hysterics, the futility even of asking where he was being taken. He kissed his wife and his son and assured them that he would be all right.

David and his mother wept together, then rallied to support each other. Papa *would* be all right. For his "crime" he would be sent to a concentration camp. He would be back after a short period of "corrective detention."

Two weeks later, there was a terse message from Dachau, the converted gunpowder factory. Papa wrote that he was well, that conditions were fine, and that he loved Mama and David very much.

"Now that we have heard," Mama said firmly, "you must leave this country, David."

"Leave" meant Shanghai. Mama had a brother, who had lived in Stuttgart. They used to exchange greeting cards on the High Holy days but never visited each other. "With some people," Mama had said, "relations are better left to the postal system." Coming from the mildest of persons, that said volumes. Now Uncle Moritz was in Shanghai and brimming with tales of success and familial concern. Get out of that insane asylum, he implored them in letter after letter, and come to "paradise." Moritz Felcher would help the Buchbinders get on their feet.

"Go to your Uncle Moritz," Mama said. "You will be safe there and looked after."

"I can't leave without you, Mama," David cried. "We shall wait for Papa and then all go together."

"No! *I* shall wait for your father. That is as it should be. You go ahead. When your father and I get there, you will be our guide to 'paradise.' "

"How fortunate for you," Rebecca said to David, "to have someone in Shanghai who will receive you."

The fact that she could be so lightly apprehensive about the indeterminate fate that awaited her and her family actually bemused her. The Wolfs had no sponsorship. Nor was the prospect of life in Shanghai roseate. They had heard the starving dropped dead in the streets, and innocent people got caught in the cross fire of raging factions—the Communists, the Nationalists, the warlords, the Green Gang, the Red Gang, the international gangsters, the Japanese conquerors; knives slit unsuspecting throats and kidnapings were rampant; the police chief ("Frenchie") in the French Concession was on the take; and Europeans were particularly vulnerable to the pestilences that fermented the air.

Still, Rebecca had not felt so unfettered and hopeful in years. Perhaps it was the exhilaration of change, of having at last made the move conceived years earlier. Perhaps it was the hypnotic sway of the *Hannover* cruising through changing waters and the fresh and invigorating air. Perhaps it was the never-never-landness of shipboard, with its indulgences and its dispensations from care and responsibility. Carpe diem. Her mirror told her that she had shucked five years and regained a youthful glow. The crinkly lines at the corners of her blue eyes had vanished. Her hair looked as live and as fresh as new-mown alfalfa. Her color was schoolgirl pink again. (Kitty should see her now.) She rejoiced in her revived esprit. But she was saddened by the spectacle of the ones who were beyond resuscitation.

"Who is that woman?" Rebecca asked another new acquaintance, pointing to a raven-haired woman with translucent skin and the soulful dark eyes of a Hedy Lamarr. "I have not seen her before, Mrs. Winkler."

"My dear Mrs. Wolf," Mrs. Winkler responded, "you are asking the right person. Mrs. Schneider happens to be my cabinmate. And the reason you had not seen her is that she was keeping herself in the cabin. I even had to arrange to have her meals served there, though she rarely touched them. Yesterday, I became worried and took it upon myself to ask the doctor to look in on her. He talked to her sternly, I can tell you. He told her that she would suffocate in this heat if she did not get up and walk around. And he didn't want her telling him she didn't care what happened, she had to get out of bed and stop pitying herself. And there you see her."

Alma Winkler was a retired mezzo soprano, a childless widow from Berlin who was amply cushioned and had a turreted bosom. She had fine features and skin, merry gray eyes, and long ash-blond hair. She also had the liveliest interest in the passing scene. Rebecca had warmed to her good humor and compassionate worldliness.

"Mrs. Schneider is from Linz," Alma Winkler went on. "The Schneiders were in the leather business there, very well-to-do people. Mr. Schneider? The familiar thing, carted off to Dachau. The day they brought him back, they threw him off a moving truck in front of his home like a bundle of newspapers. The poor man was more dead than alive, and the Schneiders agreed that they had better leave Linz. Mrs. Schneider had heard about Shanghai but wasn't well informed. She thought you had to apply for visas. She filled out endless forms at the emigration bureau. When she tried to bring her forms to the clerk, she was made to stand behind a yellow stripe on the floor many meters from his wicket. 'Don't come any closer,' he called out. 'I don't want to inhale Jew breath.' Someone with a little decency saw what was going on and offered to present her papers to the clerk, who then said, 'Tell the Jewess she doesn't need papers for Shanghai. They let in the trash of the world.'

"While they were waiting to sail, Mr. Schneider was abducted again and Mrs. Schneider guessed that he was back in Dachau. She wrote the camp commandant a notarized and registered letter assuring him that she had ship's tickets for the Orient. Normally, this could have been sufficient to win the release of the prisoner, and by return mail she indeed received a polite reply inviting her to Dachau to fetch her husband.

"Mrs. Schneider was courteously received by one of the commandant's aides, who invited her into his office. She thought her husband would be brought to her presently. The aide busied himself with papers and the minutes became half an hour, then an hour. There was no sign of Mr. Schneider. You can well imagine her state of mind. Finally, she summoned enough courage to ask the aide if he had any idea what could be keeping her husband.

" 'Nothing's keeping him, madam,' the lieutenant replied. 'He's here. He's been right here in this office all along.'

"The aide found Mrs. Schneider's befuddlement amusing. She didn't know if he was trying to make a fool of her, or if this was a ruse to exploit her for some gift or offering. She was at his mercy, a puppet who would have to hang on the next twitch of the string. After the most excruciating procrastination, that despicable man opened a drawer in his desk and brought out a cigarette box. 'You'll find your husband in there,' he pointed. And that indeed is where Mrs. Schneider found Mr. Schneider. Or what remained of Mr. Schneider. His ashes. He had 'succumbed' from some 'mild discipline,' and cremation was the 'tidiest' way of disposing of him."

David Buchbinder shared an extra-large stateroom with three middle-aged men. They slept in double-decker bunks. The men were his father's age and they were to be shown respect and deference, but it was hard for David to show them much else. They were remote, sealed inside themselves. He could not reach them. None of them took an interest in him or in one another. They neither sought nor rendered warmth.

But David was at least journalistically curious. As he found each man alone, he would think of something pleasant or sympathetic to say that might draw him out. It was an interest that no one else, anyway, was showing in these men. Bit by bit, he had their stories.

Mr. Schenckbrunn was a slight, balding man from Vienna. His mouth was set in a fixed reversed U and he sucked on a thumb or munched the hairs of his wrists in moments of extreme agitation. His florist shop on Eugenstrasse had been trampled and every blossom, leaf, and fern hacked to shreds. After the Anschluss, hell. Two hundred—TWO HUNDRED!—suicides a day. Everywhere, vicious signs and slogans. DEUTSCHLAND ERWACHE; JUDA VERRECKE! (Germany, wake up; Jews, die!). DIE JUDEN SIND UNSER UNGLÜCK

(The Jews are our misfortune). Every day there were insults. A four-year-old pointed to him and asked his mother, "Is that a Jewish swine, Mommy?" "Yes, Hans, that is a Jewish swine." The Nazis pushed and kicked priests out of windows and hung banners in front of St. Stephen's that screamed "Clergy onto the gallows." They murdered everything nice. The flowers. His neighbors. Magda, his wife. Don't talk to him about the Kristallnacht in Germany. In Vienna, they burned *every* synagogue. Without the beautiful flowers, the good friends, the good wife, the old Vienna—who cared if the *Hannover* sank!

Mr. Gruber reveled in multilingual expressions of futility and finality. "Macht nichts." "What is the difference?" "N'importe." "Kaput." "C'est fini." He was an elongated man with sloping shoulders and eyes so hooded they were flickering slits. An architect in the Bauhaus School, he had stood at drafting tables in the pantheon in Weimar with Mies, Gropius, and Breuer. The school was shut down six years ago, and there were few opportunities for private practice. Through the good offices of a former colleague, he was invited to join the tutorial staff of a university in Barcelona. He believed that form should follow function, but he admitted enchantment with the Hänsel and Gretel gingerbread houses and peppermint sticks of Anton Gaudi. During the Spanish Civil War, Mr. Gruber decided that discretion was the better part of valor and fled to another post that had opened in Milan. But Mussolini gave him the jitters, and he secured papers for emigration to Ecuador, where he had family. Arriving penniless in Guayaquil, he was told that his visa was fraudulent. Cousins in Quito cabled funds but told him they had no influence—he had to return to Europe. In Genoa the authorities informed him that he had two days to remove himself from Italy again. Herr Professor Gruber became a man without a country. He paid a king's ramson for "the last ticket to Shanghai," purchasing it with the sale of his treasured set of silver drafting tools, a graduation gift from his four grandparents. "Shanghai? Singapore? Soerabaya? Macht nichts."

Captain Horn was a whey-faced man with a corrugated brow and bloodshot eyes. Twenty years ago, he was in the

Richthofen Staffel. It was the euphoric thrilling high noon of his life. In his Fokker he had duelled with Sopwith Pups, Camels, Nieuports, and the Lafayette Escadrille over the Zeppelin sheds at Tondern and over Saint-Mihiel. "Do you realize, young man, that it took the Americans fourteen months after declaring war to find the courage to fight us at Belleau Wood?" Captain Horn, who wore his flying helmet as a night cap, would not be drawn out about anything that had happened to him since that time of glory. He had a plaintive wail that was heard again and again. "Why? Why wouldn't they call us up again? Why wouldn't they let me fly for them again?"

David listened to the men in his cabin and observed other solitaries who hid or cowered or gazed fiercely at the heavens or mumbled threats and furies to nameless antagonists. Strung together, their recollections could form a ghoulish nautical version of the *Canterbury Tales.*

"Meyer, come and take a stroll with me. You have never seen a sky so blue."

"No, thank you. I have seen my share of blue skies. But please see if the library has *The City without Jews.*"

Stop it, Meyer. Why wallow in it! Who needs to read Bettauer's fantasy about a glittering Vienna whose anti-Semitism becomes so fanatical that its two hundred thousand Jews are driven away? For God's sake, fact is giving the truth to fantasy.

Meyer was the dark cloud over her shoulder. But for Meyer, she could laugh again with total abandonment and think of herself as not too ill-favored. Of course, it would be mindless to suppose that Meyer could throw off what had happened to him as if it were a mere bagatelle. He had never been the same since his severance from Radio Lübeck. How could anyone who had not personally experienced it, even a spouse, begin to perceive the nightmare of the concentration camp and the toll it had taken? But good sense suggested that there were some things salubrious for a depressed mind and other things that could only perpetuate depression. Solitude and immersion in distressing literature was not a prescription for a healthier perspective.

David blushingly confessed to Rebecca that he had stared at the Wolfs so much when they were at table because at a distance Mr. Wolf reminded him so much of his own father. "I had hoped you were staring at me," Rebecca said with a smile, and invited David to take his meals with the family. He and Meyer could talk about books, and, who knows, it might lift Meyer out of himself. It was certainly good for David. From the first evening it was clear that he was fascinated with Meyer's erudition and civility. Meyer, however, was only mildly susceptible. "A sweet young man," he said. "Sensible and well-bred. A good mind. But I may not be up to so much conversation. There is much to be said for pauses and silences."

Rebecca had somewhat better luck diverting Meyer with the capers of Elsa and Inge.

Much was hearsay. Elsa and Inge were said to be first cousins. They were said to be of the Rothschilds from Munich—only the south spawned such uninhibited spirits. They were said to be the shame of their families and had been abandoned to the fates. They could not be more than sixteen or seventeen years old. They were traveling alone. They were ripe as peaches, and their giggles vibrated along the companionways. From the beginning they had riveted attention, but they feigned unawareness of the notice they had courted. Nimbly, they eluded elders who might lay a restraining hand upon them. This was their season.

The pool, erected above the cargo hold aft on A deck, had been filled when, off the Algarve, the first warming sun embraced the ship. In bathing costumes, Elsa and Inge plunged into the salty water, romping like two squealing pup seals.

"Gertrude Ederle didn't have this big an audience when she set off to swim the Channel," Mrs. Winkler remarked to Rebecca.

From the gallery, two German nationals stood by a bulkhead and trained a field glass on the girls. Their flushed, bewhiskered faces, cantilevered bellies, and porky fingers advertised them as substantial men of commerce. But for the lascivious ogling, they could have been doting grandfathers watching their progeny at play.

"Would you look at those two overstuffed sausages," Mrs. Winkler laughed.

"They would never look that way at a wise, cultivated, mature woman of the world," said Rebecca, adding mischievously, "such as yourself, Mrs. Winkler."

"And who would have them?" Mrs. Winkler shot back. "Even if they were covered with strawberries and cream."

The nubile mermaids crawled out of the pool but prolonged their public performance. They dried their bodies sensuously and did a series of calisthenics that displayed their assets to advantage. They did handstands. They preened and stretched, then draped themselves onto chaise lounges to bronze under the midday sun.

"In five minutes," Mrs. Winkler predicted, "either Porky Number One or Porky Number Two is going to have a cardiac arrest."

The following day, the pup seals were joined in the pool by the two walruses, who honked and spewed water and later hoisted themselves onto adjoining chaise lounges.

"You know, strictly speaking, those men should not have been in the pool at this hour," Mrs. Winkler observed. "Milk and flesh together?"

Rebecca looked up to find David Buchbinder fixed on the spectacle. It was an unguarded moment. His expression was eloquent, mixing disgust with the ache of longing.

"As soon as you stop bawling, you can tell Mommy what happened."

"He—he hit me!"

"Who hit you?"

"Willie."

"Willie hit you? That is very naughty of Willie. Did you do something to Willie?"

"No."

"Now, Esther, you must have done something."

"We were flying a kite and I went back to his cabin and I

turned the picture around. I turned it, Mommy, so nobody can see it."

"Turned the picture? What picture?"

"The picture of the bad man."

"Oh, my honey. Now listen to me. Willie was wrong to hit you. But you were wrong, too. We don't ever, ever go turning pictures to the wall when we are in someone else's room. And here, Esther, we must be extra careful to be on our very best behavior."

In the writing lounge, David Buchbinder wrote a letter to his mother for posting at Port Tewfik.

"This morning, we took on coal at Port Said," he wrote. "The Egyptians are funny people. They keep laughing while their backs are breaking. We are in the Canal. Through a port-hole I can see Sinai. If Palestine is anything like that, I am glad I am not going there.

"In the dining room I sit with a nice Mr. and Mrs. Wolf from Lübeck. At first, Mr. Wolf, who was in Buchenwald, reminded me of Papa, but Papa, I think, would never allow himself to become so dispirited and detached. (I address this letter to you, Mama, but I am hoping more than anything in the world that Papa is right there beside you when you read it and that he has in hand two tickets to Shanghai on the next ship.) Mrs. Wolf is kind and beautiful and has much humor. The Wolfs have a fanciful little daughter who is 'almost six,' though her sixth birthday is ten months off. She calls me 'Uncle David' and sits in my lap and tweaks my ears and pulls my nose. She says that she plans to marry a boy named Willie, but her mother suspects that it's just one of those shipboard romances.

" . . . how easy it was for our government to dispense with so many decent citizens. I now agree with Mr. Wolf that most Germans—most people?—are born subjects [geborene Unter-tane] who depend on someone else for authority and direction. The Nazis are zombies—think of their mindless torchlight parades. And I am convinced that Hitler wants war . . .

"I think about you and Papa all the time and wonder if any other son had such wise and wonderful parents."

Meyer proposed to stop having dinner, and Rebecca felt her reservoir of patience ebbing.

"We may never, ever have it so good again, Meyer. The day may come when we can only dream about such food. It is sinful to turn up our noses at any meal."

"I don't need dinner. I have had a great sufficiency before then."

"Take lesser amounts at the other meals and save room for dinner."

"I prefer to forget about dinner."

"Is it David? The strain of an outsider? I can certainly ask him . . . "

"It's everything. It's the infernal clatter of dishes and cutlery. It's the chatter of a hundred magpies. It's that insipid dance music and the sight of tons of food being shoveled onto plates and down gullets."

Meyer was not the only one. In her endless strolls, Rebecca saw that many of the refugees were beyond the blandishments of an ocean voyage. Some slinked around and shot furtive looks as if they expected to see Gestapo agents lurking in every passageway. Others, acting out their label of Untermenschen, crept and hid like subhuman creatures in a jungle. Some wallowed in their guilt and grief for the Fatherland and for aged parents and aunts and uncles left behind. Doomsdaysayers presaged the same fate for the *Hannover* as the *Lusitania;* one fine dark night they would be gliding to the bottom of the Mediterranean Sea or the Indian Ocean or the South China Sea—they would never reach the sanctuary of Shanghai. Behind Captain Brandt's congeniality and rectitude some saw only insincerity and treachery. Rebecca felt like a Pharisee, thinking, "Thank God I am not like them." Too much had happened to them for hope or trust.

The *Hannover* steamed through a Red Sea that was as flat as a mirror. The sun lent the water a blinding white sheen. For days, the universe held its breath. The passengers sweltered, moaned, fell prostrate. The women had lighter frocks, but the men had only their heavy northern clothing.

Meyer could not be lured to the pool, but Rebecca was glad to find a responsive chord in him. As she rejoined him in their stateroom, he would put aside his book and give her a faint smile. He was waiting for her report.

"Meyer, I do believe we advanced to a higher plateau today. There was the usual splashing and ho-hos and cavorting. And the usual baking side by side on the mats, first Inge, then Porky Number One, then Elsa and Porky Number Two. As usual, they repaired to the Rheinkeller. You should have heard the giggles and hee-hees and ha-has. Usually, the girls come scampering out and go off to their next amusement. But today, Meyer, the four of them came out together and the billy goats baaed some noisy Auf Wiedersehens. Mrs. Winkler said that it was for our benefit, 'to throw us off the scent. Some Westphalian ham and honey sandwiches are in the making.' "

After relating the scene, Rebecca felt a shiver of remorse. Bertha Pappenheim had lectured that there was no higher good than saving errant girls from themselves. Instead of being amused by the antics of Elsa and Inge, shouldn't she be extending motherly arms to restrain those frivolous girls? Pinprickings of conscience jabbed at her, but she had lost some of her lofty righteousness and come to a baser understanding of the way the world worked.

"I do wish you would go with me to the lectures on Shanghai," Rebecca prodded Meyer.

Rebecca had no better luck with Mrs. Winkler. "It's Professor Spiller who's giving them? That windy pedant? You should have heard him going on for days about the battle of Teutoburg Forest and the powerful dukes of Lotharingia." She rolled her eyes skyward. "Pass the Nesselrode pie, please, Mrs. Wolf."

Rebecca and David were among an audience of fourteen. Professor Spiller was oblivious to the size of the turnout; he would have been content to release his pedagogy upon an empty chair. He was a stooped, sickly-looking man with skin as pale as dumplings. Behind copper-framed round glasses that sat at a severe slant on a broken nose, his opaque brown eyes focused on some point in the foyer leading to the first-class staterooms of the Aryan passengers. His long black hair fell unkempt to his shoulders, and his beard was scraggly. His black suit was dusty and unpressed, and his shirt was yellow around the collar. Who could guess his age? Forty? Fifty?

"We are approaching a country that is almost as large in area as all of Europe," he began in a high-pitched voice at breakneck speed, as if he feared there would not be time enough to impart all that he knew. "We are approaching a country with a long, distinguished civilization that gave the world many inventions and discoveries. It is China that first invented printing and the making of paper and the magnetic compass. China also was first with a system of weights and measures, the spinning wheel, the mechanical clock, the suspension bridge, cast iron, the collar harness, the kite, the fishing reel, and fireworks, as well as geometry and map-making and earthquake detection. The Great Wall, which was built in the third century before Christ, was a feat of construction that overshadows both the pyramids and China's one-thousand-mile Grand Canal.

"China is old and worn out, but Shanghai is young and dynamic—and not truly Chinese. Until a century ago, it was a sleepy fishing village. The modern, polyglot, enormously wealthy metropolis materialized out of the Opium Wars. A few thousand British marines and a few corrupt Chinese warlords humiliated the Chinese people and won the right to flood China with opium. It was like feeding poisoned milk to children. The white 'barbarians' were also allowed by treaty to carve out choice areas for themselves in Shanghai and in other port cities. It was as though Americans in cahoots with German businessmen had carved out extraterritorial sections of Hamburg, Essen, and Bremerhaven, and the German people had *nothing* to say about it—and we could not even live in *their* sections of *our* city.

"Shanghai is favored by its location at the mouth of the three-thousand-mile-long Yangtze River. The population of four million makes it the largest city in the East; one million of them are Chinese refugees from the war with the Japanese. By all accounts, Shanghai is a wicked and debauched city, where the grossest of appetites are gratified with impunity. Shanghai . . . "

The door to a stateroom opened in the corridor of the Aryan passengers. Elsa came out smoothing her frock. She undulated toward Professor Spiller's audience with the slow, exhibitionistic swivel of a professional model. She smiled sweetly and unabashedly—let others think what they would. Out of the corner of an eye Rebecca saw David's frown and flushed cheeks.

"Shanghai," Professor Spiller resumed, a vein in his temple pulsing with irritation, "is home to people of forty-eight nationalities, who enjoy the privileges and the laissez faire of the two enclaves known as the International Settlement and the French Concession. This neutral 'foreign territory'—nearly thirteen of Shanghai's three hundred and twenty square miles—is by far the most desirable in the city. It is also so sacrosanct that even the Japanese army dared not touch it when they captured Shanghai two years ago.

"Shanghai comes by its notorious reputation through being an open city and a safe haven for many types of people who are not welcome anywhere else. Shanghai receives one and all. Murderers. Thieves. Smugglers. Slave traders. Pirates. Rum runners. Gamblers. Political dissidents. Prostitutes by the thousands. But you should be gratified to know that . . . "

Another stateroom door beyond the foyer opened and the audience burst into spontaneous laughter. Again the timing seemed contrived. Now it was Inge's turn to pass amongst them with sweet-defiant smiles.

"Why?" David muttered. "Why do they do it?"

"For the money," Rebecca whispered. "They are but two waifs in a world they never made."

"You should be gratified to know," Professor Spiller prevailed, "that Shanghai has always been hospitable to Jewish people. Some of its most esteemed families emigrated there from the Middle East and India more than fifty years ago. They are Sephardic Jews with names such as Sassoon, Hardoon, and Kadoorie. After the Bolshevik Revolution, another tide of Jewish immigrants—White Russians this time—swept into Shanghai . . . "

In another letter home, David tried to spare his mother his confused feelings. He was restive with shipboard life, but what to expect when he set foot in Shanghai? What if his uncle and aunt did not find him to their liking? What, then, of the future beyond tomorrow? "Yes, German Jewry may be dead," Rabbi Ackermann said in his valedictory on the *Hannover*, "but it is your commandment to live."

"I'll pack my own, Mommy."

Rebecca looked from the intensely bright young face to the clusters of folded dresses, stockings, and undergarments that must fit into the small cardboard case. "Do it neatly, then," she said. "Press down tight, the way Mommy is doing."

Meyer was breathless from the exertion of his walk and the climbing of stairs. He had returned to the library *Four Hundred Million Customers*, an advertising man's delusion of the China "market," and he wanted assurance for the dozenth time from Rebecca that they would not be going to a shelter or charity home when they reached Shanghai.

Rebecca reassured him that they would not be herded into any communal lodgings—it would be too demoralizing to start life anew in some shed or dormitory. If need be, they would spend their last mark on private quarters. Please, Meyer, change may be terrifying, but it is not fatal.

A fist pounded on the cabin door.

Willie had come to say goodbye.

Rebecca gasped.

Esther's betrothed was dressed in a khaki shirt, and on each sleeve was the red arm band inscribing the swastika.

"I hate you," Esther screamed. "Go away, Willie."

Willie Stenger clicked his heels and threw out his right arm. "Heil Hitler, Esther!"

1939–1943

SHANGHAI

David Buchbinder smelled Shanghai before he saw it.

It stank.

It stank of decaying fish and rancid garbage and factory smoke and coal dust and raw sewage and dried spittle and millions of unwashed bodies.

Leaving the coastline of jagged green islands and the East China Sea, the *Hannover* nosed into the mighty Yangtze. It slid past the Japanese-occupied forts of Woosung and myriad waterside hovels housing the squalid poor. Twelve miles up the river, it wheeled into the broad curve of the tributary Whangpoo and heaved its anchor into the middle of the harbor. A tender came alongside to ferry passengers to the jetties and the Customs House.

"New York is bigger and taller," a steward said to David, sharing his field glass at the bow, "but Shanghai is more exciting."

The steward's sweep of arm embraced the river, the quays, the godowns, and the Bund, that celebrated drive along the shore. David's pulses throbbed. In the darker days ahead, he would recall these last moments at the deck railing—and recall thinking that this was a fresh beginning in a new city and an exotic land and that all things were possible.

David's eyes fixed on the phalanx of skyscrapers thrusting into the mist. The blurry outlines and muted lights were like a pointillistic canvas. There they towered, monoliths of global power and wealth. The insurance and the oil companies, the banks, the textile and the pharmaceutical manufacturers, the trading houses, the stock exchanges, the newspaper publishers, the hotels, and the shipping lines.

"That building with the columns is the Shanghai Club," the steward pointed out. "It's supposed to have the longest bar in the world. I wouldn't know; you have to be British and veddy veddy haughty to get in. And over there, the two big bronze lions guarding the Hong Kong Bank of China? You'll have good luck, they say, if you rub their balls . . ."

The south side of the Whangpoo was depressing in the extreme. Row upon row of squat windowless mills the color of dried blood were unfurling banners of sulphuric smoke and purple fumes of wood-oil vapor into a blackening sky. The hideous buildings stretched into infinity. The district of Pootong!

The harbor was a maritime wonderland.

David picked out ocean liners of eight nations sporting their flags like wash in the dismal February afternoon. The thrill of uncharted vistas! From this very port, people could board a ship that would take them to London or New York or Cape Town or Sydney or Tokyo or San Francisco or Manila or Rio de Janeiro or Havana or Marseilles or Naples or even back to Hamburg—anywhere, if you had the money and weren't a Jewish refugee!

Sullen men-of-war were flying the Union Jack and the Stars and Stripes—and the Rising Sun looking like the blood-stained dressing of a war wound. A behemoth of a freighter was wobbling under its mountain of coal toward a slip in Pootong. An armada of long, crude, motorized craft bursting with human cargo sped toward ports serving the fertile fields—the breadbasket—of the infinite Yangtze.

"Blood Alley, here we bloody come!"

The whoop and a-holler went up from a launch.

"Limeys on their way to shore leave," the knowledgeable steward explained. "To raise holy hell. They'll get into knife fights and drink themselves into a stupor. They're a rough lot. And they're fools. We Germans will beat them in the next one."

A flat-bottomed boat wreathed in white (for mourning) maneuvered through the dung-brown waters and came hardby the starboard side of the *Hannover*. An ancient Chinese man lifted skyward a bamboo pole with a net at the end. A porthole opened and garbage was thrown into the net. The Chinese lowered the net and turned it over on the sampan, where four pairs of yellow hands set about ravaging the windfall of table droppings—crusts, bones, rinds, homogenized swill.

"White garbage feeds half of Shanghai," the steward commented.

Hundreds of fishing boats and houseboats rocked and bobbed in waters agitated by the harbor traffic. Drab, brown vessels displayed on their stern a crimson phoenix, the fisherman's harbinger of good fortune. "A lifetime of bad luck doesn't shatter a superstition out here," the steward said. Still other boats were ferrying thousands of blue-clad workers toward grim confinement in the factories of Pootong; there, for twelve and fourteen hours, they would toil like zombies in the production of woven clothing, beer, fireworks, and curios.

David trained the field glass on one of the houseboats. A woman was stooped over a smoking brazier and several children were hopping about on the sloping deck. A naked tot wiggled out of its cheesecloth blanket and began crawling across the deck. It crawled and crawled, right off the boat, tumbling into the brackish waters. "Ba ba," the woman cried out. "Ba ba." A man rushed out of the shed at the stern. He picked up a rod with a straw basket at one end, leaned over the side of the houseboat, waved the rod around a bit, and scooped up the drowning baby from the cesspool. It was a gesture of such casualness that it could have been a carp or a starfish he was fishing up for the evening meal. The man rubbed down the infant with his blouse, wrapped it back into the blanket, and lashed it to the mast.

"A boy baby, no doubt," David's informant remarked. "They don't bother with girl babies."

And so the exotic fleet whirled around the port in the failing light of the weepy winter afternoon . . . the high-sterned junks, bulbous eyes painted on their prow to see them through safe waters with their loads of lumber . . . the tramp steamers . . . the dredgers and the scows . . . the tankers . . . the barges . . . the canal boats . . . the lighters . . . the liners and the launches . . . the tugs, the tows, the tenders . . . the ubiquitous sampans, houseboats, fishing boats, and ferries.

Presently, David was caught up in a rivulet of traffic flowing along decks, across a gangway, and onto the tender. Three hundred passengers were jammed shoulder to shoulder in the creaking boat. David looked in vain for the Wolfs. From the jetties burst the high-pitched coolie chant of "Kei, kei." The bewildered passengers stepped onto the masonry pier aswarm with concave, bare-torsoed, perspiring yellow men—perspiring in the raw cold!—scurrying like maggots. The backs of the coolies buckled under stacks of wood, drums of oil, bales of cotton, trunks of silk, crates of sausage casings, hides of seals, stoats, bears and leopards, bushels of coal, kegs of tea, blocks of cinder, and sacks of shoats. Slaves were still stoking China in return for a bowl of rice.

"Attention, refugees!" loudspeakers commanded. "If you have no accommodations, follow the guides. They will conduct you to the Embankment Building. You will be given shelter and supplies until permanent arrangements can be made. Attention, refugees! If you have no . . ."

David thought of falling in with the homeless. To be standing outside Customs, in a disoriented mob, in a strange city, with darkness upon them, was frightening in itself. He was all but destitute. Would the single mark left in his purse be enough to pay for a taxi to his uncle's home? Would he even be able to make himself understood to the driver? (Professor Spiller doubted whether any of them would ever achieve a command of any Chinese dialect. "If you don't speak Chinese by the age of five, you never will," he had said.)

"David Buchbinder! This way, David Buchbinder."

Clutching his case, David walked toward the voice and the muffled footsteps approaching. In the murkiness of the dark thoroughfare, he was being drawn into the embrace of a stranger. It was awkward and embarrassing—but so reassuring.

"Well, well, well, welcome to Shanghai. So this is Gertrud's little boy."

"Not so little, Uncle Moritz."

"No, indeed. A big strapping fellow."

Uncle Moritz bore no resemblance to Mama. He was bulky and coarse-featured. He had pinkish skin and beady eyes that glinted shrewdly, even in the dusk, from behind rimless spectacles. He was hearty and loud. He must also be prosperous— coats with astrakhan collars and sealskin hats cost money.

"Well, well, well, you are here, David. Come, we'll get you settled."

Moritz Felcher thrust two fingers into his mouth and whistled. A pedicab was upon them in a flash. He haggled with the cadaverous prune-faced cyclist, who moaned and raised his eyes to some failed deity, and restrained David from hoisting his case onto the luggage rack. "No, no, no, my boy. Your first lesson. That's the Chinaman's job. None of them wants to see white people doing menial chores, we would lose respect in their eyes."

"Is that true?"

"And I am telling you, David, the pedicab and rickshaw fellows have it better than most. They're all licensed and compete for the privilege of pulling us around town."

David had seen magazine pictures of rickshaws and pedicabs. But being here and being borne through the streets by some exhausted human beast of burden was something else. It was so shaming, so unnatural. But here they were, ragged hordes of thousands, as disposable as toothpicks, clop-clopping and puff-puffing under mountains of white flesh and the appendages of white flesh.

"This is the only way to get about, David. The trams are murder on the nervous system. Listen to that screeching. Never ride them myself anymore. Someone's always falling under the wheels, and people are goddamn lucky to get off with what they got on with. A doctor I know had the side of his leather medical kit sliced open right in the middle of a packed car, and all of his surgical tools were stolen. Listen to what happened to yours truly. I had a doctor's appointment and I was to take along a urine specimen. The nearest thing to a specimen bottle your Aunt Sophie had was an empty jar of Cretchley & Hartridge's ginger marmalade. Well, someone snatched the jar right out of the rattan handbag I was carrying and ran off. I only hope the thief had a nice refreshing drink of 'ginger marmalade.' A friend of Sophie hid her change purse in her brassiere, but that didn't stop them . . . Ever see a fellow as tall as that constable over there? He's a Sikh. The British brought 'em in for a bit of class, a special tone. They're all that coffee color and have those long beards curled up at the end and they have to be at least seven feet tall—the red turban makes them look even taller . . . and now we're leaving the International Settlement and coming into the French Concession. That's where we live. We have our own police and laws and ways of doing business. Some people say it's more French than Paris."

They had crossed an unmarked boundary and were rolling through streets that seemed quieter, suburban, and indeed Gallic-looking. Moritz Felcher barked some mumbo jumbo—pidgin English—and waved his arms semaphorically at the pedicyclist. After a few leisurely left and right turns and another quarter of an hour, they arrived at a stucco and timbered three-floor house on the Rue Robespierre. It was stately and newly painted and the lawn was freshly seeded and there were flower beds and shrubbery. Uncle Moritz's property was surrounded on all sides by a white brick wall topped with spikes, shards of glass, and coils of barbed wire—"just to be on the safe side."

"Here he is, Sophie!" Moritz Felcher called out, leading David into a cathedral foyer. "Our nephew from Breslau."

Out of a recess a woman appeared and came into fuzzy focus. "Welcome," she said breathily, offering a fluttering hand. "You are most welcome here, David. I am so happy to make your acquaintance."

David had entertained no notion of what Aunt Sophie would look like. He saw a vague, birdlike woman with skin pale as parchment and a nimbus of fluffy white hair. Her eyes darted from her husband's face to David's and back again as she floated away in her trailing tea gown.

They sat down to coffee in a dining room so solid, heavy, and somber it might have been transplanted from Stuttgart. A grinning Chinese serving-woman brought in a tray of pastries. "She baked these especially for you, David," Uncle Moritz said. "Chinese pastries are too sweet by far—almost all sugar. Don't feel you have to eat them."

"Is there any news from home?" David asked.

Sophie's left hand flew to her mouth and her watery eyes beseeched David's forgiveness. "Just yesterday. In your room." She was up the stairs and back in the next instant. She handed him an envelope stamped "Via Trans-Siberian Railroad."

"Read it aloud, David," his uncle commanded.

Mama, David thought with a wince of displeasure, would

never have commanded that someone else's letter be read to her.

Editing out the endearments and the expressions of concern for his well-being, David read, "I wish I had good news for you about your father, but I have heard nothing. We must continue to hope that he will return soon. I am well, and managing. Doctor Alben and his wife invite me downstairs to have a light supper with them two or three evenings a week. If the afternoon is nice, we take a long walk together. So you see, I am not confined.

"You must thank your uncle for his generous offer to send money for my transportation. But, of course, it is unthinkable that I could leave without your father . . ."

David was relieved and happy that the lines of communication were reopened after his long voyage. But on rereading the letter, he became sad, almost to the point of tears. Mama was so helpless. Who was going to rescue her?

"Such a sweet letter," Sophie commented. "Isn't it, Moritz?"

"Sweet? More like stupid. My sister is stuck on a suicide course."

David stifled his surge of fury. "My mother takes her marriage vows seriously," he said defensively.

"Misguidedly, I would say. If I am not mistaken, it was your father's stalling and wishful thinking that got them into their pickle. I'll never understand people who refuse to see the handwriting on the wall when the handwriting is bold enough for the blind to read."

Crimson blotches came to his uncle's ruddy cheeks, and David knew that he himself must be flushing. The beady eyes, the color of mahogany, were challenging him, and David could think of no logical rebuttal. He studied his uncle's head—the reddish-brown swirls of hair that had been coaxed just so to minimize his near-baldness. Uncle Moritz must be vain, as well as haughty and opinionated.

"Just two years ago," his uncle recalled, taking a softer tone, "I was playing first violin in the dance orchestra in the best hotel in Stuttgart. I had been major-domo of that orchestra for fifteen years, if I do say so myself, and they had the stinking gall to hold auditions under my nose and then tell me that I was being let go and they were replacing me with another violinist—a lousy one into the bargain. That let me know what the lay of the land was. But what was I to do? Get a monkey and become a street fiddler and hold out a cup? To make a long story short, David, I had an acquaintance who had moved here, and what he was writing me was enough to sell me on Shanghai. I sent him some small sums to deposit so that I could make a start when we arrived. I began with a tiny restaurant— a hole in a wall in a back alley. You needed a map to find it, but people did find us. Sophie here did all the cooking. People said, 'Felcher, you're too good for this. Expand. Branch out. Get a nicer place.' Things happen like greased lightning in Shanghai if you've got something people want."

Uncle Moritz was glowing with self-complacency. He looked to David for some word or gesture of approval, and David nodded. "Just the same," Uncle Moritz said, "I will hold your father accountable for what happens to my sister. Now back to the salt mines."

"David," Aunt Sophie said, "if there is any way we might serve you . . . "

"Serve *him*? He'll be serving us. David, keep tomorrow for yourself, shake your sea legs, then I want you to come to work for me in the café."

David had never known any city other than Breslau, and his first twilit glimpses of Shanghai had filled him with the wildest curiosity. He would make the best use of his free day. He would go back to the Bund and wander where his feet took him. He was without fear—even the fear of becoming lost.

It was a day of unflagging wonderments. How could one begin to absorb this . . . this . . . phantasmagoria? When he came to sorting out his impressions, David found that they could be classified into two groupings—those he would write home about and those he couldn't.

He could describe to Mama the vivacity and the picturesqueness of the street carnival. Vendors with frayed white beards peddled the quaintest of wares . . . parakeets and orioles and hysterical macaws in rattan cages . . . nervous piglets in cord bags . . . strings of firecrackers and clusters of paper lanterns . . . flaming sticks of incense . . . bolts of silk . . . Mah-Jongg sets. Would she believe that he had bought—and eaten—a *thousand*-year-old egg? He could tell her that here, in the shadow of stupendous wealth, was poverty beyond anything she could imagine. He saw the homeless sleeping in doorways and in gutters, with discarded newspaper pages for warmth. He saw a wizened woman jab a knitting needle into a child so that its screams would arouse pity—and fetch a coin or two. He guessed that the man was a professional letter writer composing a love letter—full of flourishes and literary expressions—for an illiterate Chinese swain, and wondered if its recipient would need to hire someone to read the letter to her. He could try to describe for Mama the pathetic sight of fifty authentic hunchbacks humping back and forth in front of a movie theater to advertise the premiere of *The Hunchback of Notre Dame*. He was never to overcome his disgust at the spectacle of copper-skinned coolies spitting up their lungs as they hauled drays inhumanly weighted down with billiard tables, and ice boxes, and pianos, and marble-top desks. He stood transfixed as a Chinese funeral cortege marched by to blaring Strauss waltzes and Dixieland jazz.

But those other things! He could not tell his mother that he had seen a spider-webbed man lying in a doorway with his throat slit or a severed head nailed to the storefront of a chemist's shop or that corpses of babies were piled up on the streets awaiting the sanitation cart. He would not alarm her with mention of the illicit opium dens where people escaped to dreamland or with the newspaper headlines about the shocking epidemic of kidnapings or the billboard advertising the erotic boy bathhouses (frequented by Auden and Isherwood, as the only English steward on the *Hannover* had told him). On Yates Road, "the street of lingerie," he ogled lovely young women of all races modeling silky undergarments in the windows of luxurious shops. On Foochow Road, a luscious girl of no more than sixteen—perhaps a French-Korean hybrid—smiled sweetly at him and purred, "For you, no pay, only fun." He ached to go with her.

"Our possibilities are going to be slight," Rebecca said after the decision to sail for Shanghai had been made. "We had better go knowing how to do something basic."

"Like taking in washing?" Meyer sneered. "Or peddling opium?"

"Shanghai is a city of commerce. Typewriters are always breaking down. Perhaps if we knew how to repair typewriters . . . "

Meyer went to an office equipment sales and repair shop in the center of Lübeck and bought a typewriter on the condition that Mr. Haupt, the owner, would visit their flat in evenings and teach the Wolfs how to clean and repair it. Charging them exorbitantly for his services—he had pointed out that it could be "dangerous" for him to be there—Mr. Haupt taught them how to remove the roller and replace broken characters and the shift lock and to realign the carriage and to douse the mechanism in cleansing fluids and to install the ribbon.

"Here's a good place to hide your rings," Meyer said, unwinding the knobs of the hollow roller.

"It's not worth the chance," Rebecca said. "Please, Meyer, believe me. I don't care about the jewelry. All I want is our lives. Sell the jewelry and use the money to buy repair tools. And, Meyer, you, too, must make your sacrifices. I know how much it means to you, but I think you should obey the law and turn it in. Or get rid of it."

Meyer offered no resistance. He disassembled his prized souvenir of the war, his Luger, and made a little game of its disappearance. Esther was his St. Christopher's figure. They set out at dusk for a stroll together along the Trave. In the dimness he surreptitiously slipped a piece of the pistol into the river night after night, and then the bullets from three full boxes. Ping. Ping. Ping.

"We'll get someone in to help in the shop," Rebecca now said. "We can afford it and things will be easier on you."

"As you wish," Meyer said.

If only he would defy her, or protest! But this passivity was insufferable. Whatever she proposed—he assented. If she had suggested, "Let's sell the business and open a noodle factory," he would say, "As you wish."

One of the replies to her advertising notice in the *North-China Daily News* touched and amused her. "You will see I am honest boy," Teng Wun Gon wrote. "I am clean boy, wash much. I am schoolboy, no experience in commerce. You teach me typewriter, make me man of full experience. I am afraid with foreigners, you will see. I can write or be at telephone. Good with hands. You may reward me at your choice. Waiting your honored reply, I am for you humbly . . . "

Teng Wun Gon materialized as a sweet, shy, excessively polite young man of nineteen. His pale skin shone, his jet hair was parted neatly in the middle, and his black almond-shaped eyes snapped with intelligence and suppressed humor. He wore a blue tunic and shapeless muslin trousers. At first glance, Rebecca thought he must belong to the New China that people were talking about—the New China she took to mean the emerging middle-classes, who were finding niches of respectability and security for themselves somewhere between the starving millions on the bottom and the gangsters and the mandarins on top. Teng Wun Gon lived with his family in Chapei, and his father sold birds and birdcages in the Old City.

"You teach him," Rebecca asked of Meyer.

Meyer's instruction was terse, but Teng proved to be a keen student, quickly mastering the rudiments of typewriter repair. In quick order he knew all about pawls, ratchets, wheels, and platens and could replace a roller or fix a collapsed or stuttering space bar. He was fascinated by the inner workings of the Smith-Coronas, the Wellingtons, the Royals, and the hand-stenciled, beflowered Sholes & Glidden. His ancestors may have invented movable type, but it was the "barbarians" who had made machines that could hammer out ninety words every single minute.

"Missie and Master pleased with this boy?"

"You are our Number One Boy," Rebecca said, and Meyer nodded.

Teng was soon relieving, then virtually replacing Meyer at Wolf Typewriters—Repairs and Sales.

By noon, Meyer's energies flagged. He yawned compulsively, his fingers trembled, his breathing became labored. He sighed heavily, and complained about a chill even after the weather had turned scorching hot. He had nightmares, shouting out, "Bury the Yids."

"Now that we have Teng," Rebecca said to Meyer, "you go home and rest in the afternoon." There, hours later, she would find him stretched across the sofa nodding over Boethius' *Vom Trost der Philosophie.*

But for Meyer's receding energies and elusive diagnosis, Rebecca could have been content. "In Shanghai," someone had said, "you can wake up and find yourself either rich or dead." Their fortunes had picked up right away. The business was prospering. They were comfortably situated in the French Concession. Esther was happily enrolled in the Shanghai Jewish School. And the bitterest of memories seemed well behind them.

Rebecca could trace Meyer's further slippage to that first night in Shanghai. She had overruled him and said that because of the lateness of the hour they must spend the night in the Embankment Building near the wharves. The contrast with the *Hannover* could not have been more cruel. Each of the refugees was given a hand towel and a shard of white soap by volunteer women who had the air of moving among lepers. At long, bare wooden tables they sat down to a supper of sinewy stew, stale rolls, and cold tea. Meyer dutifully kissed Rebecca and Esther, and they went to their respective dormitories. The sexes were separated for the night, families notwithstanding. But the expression in his eyes! That look of anguish, abandonment, betrayal!

"Why? Why is he accusing me?" Rebecca asked herself as she lay cold and sleepless on her cot under the soiled sheet and blanket.

The next morning, Rebecca tried to infuse Meyer with an enthusiasm exaggerated for his benefit. Look! An extraordinary city! It was so huge and bustling and colorful, such a wondrous blending of East and West. Meyer looked. His eyes fixed on mothers nursing babies curbside. He saw a Japanese sentry bayoneting the buttocks of a peasant who hadn't bowed low enough, and he turned away from coolies defecating on the sidewalks and honking green mucous onto the roads.

The market for second-hand fur coats is limited,"
P. Bostwick, Furriers, informed Rebecca. "So many of our customers have left. The uncertainty of conditions everywhere,
you know . . . " P. Bostwick gave her a seventh of what she had
paid for her Russian sable coat in Lübeck a decade earlier. But
the sale of the coat enabled them to move into a three-room flat
in a Gothic-spired house on Avenue François Gautier and to
rent a square one-story cinderblock building on Boulevard St.
Honoré. They began business with only the typewriter that
they had brought with them. When a customer told them that
the big insurance companies bought new machines rather than
fixing their old ones, Meyer arranged with United Assurance
to buy its discards. The Wolfs repaired, cleaned, and sold the
overhauls for a substantial profit, primarily to middle-class
Chinese families that had daughters entering secretarial
schools.

"We are on our feet again," Rebecca observed, "and are
living better than we have since either of us can remember."

Meyer said nothing.

It seemed to Rebecca that the sea change had reversed
their philosophies. She was now the one who was excusing
inconveniences and finding causes for optimism and Meyer
was the one who was disgruntled and preoccupied with the
deteriorating conditions in Europe. "But we're here, Meyer,"
she reasoned in vain. "Our lives are here for now. Let's make
the most of it."

Some departing Americans, who had sold them an Under-
wood for ten U.S. dollars, offered to turn over their lease for a
seven-room floor-through apartment completely furnished, in
the Maison Charlevois on Rue Bonaparte, if the Wolfs would
pay a modest sum for the furnishings. "Shanghai is a city of
passers-through," the Americans said. "You come and you go
and you don't want to take anything with you." The rooms
were large and filled with light furniture—rattan, wicker, Dan-
ish blond—reminding Rebecca of Kitty Rosenthal's home and
long-ago good times.

"Good food, good service, a big welcome, and a little
schmaltz," Moritz Felcher boasted. "I never have a bad night."

"Tout Shanghai dines with us," Prince Litvinoff sniffed.

From the first, David was impressed, and he looked at his uncle in amazement. The Café Moritz could have held up its head in Paris. The restaurant, a red-brick building on the stylish Avenue Joffre, had a green awning with white piping, and its entrance was a halfmoon of graveled driveway. Gilded mirrors graced walls of regal red damask. Patrons sat on imitation Louis XIV chairs at tables with starched pink linen, matching serviettes, and vases of fresh-cut flowers, and they ate and drank from gold-rimmed china, gleaming silverware, and tinkling crystal. On the main floor there were three crescent-shaped dining rooms. A red-velvet carpeted stairway led to private upstairs dining rooms.

David saw the cosmopolitan mix that found its way to the Café Moritz night after night as ever-changing characters in a long-running theatrical production. They all came. The taipans who ran the city . . . British bankers and insurance magnates and their wives, dressed to the eyeballs on even the hottest nights. (Uncle Moritz had refused to pay "squeeze to a bunch of bandits" to have air-cooling installed.) . . . Compradores from Jardine Matheson's and Butterfield & Squire's with their concubines . . . Chinese mobsters Croesus-rich from opium or prostitution . . . American Marine officers, usually loud, usually laughing, always drunk . . . Obsequious, bespectacled Japanese rear admirals with their Malaysian, Burmese, and Korean mistresses . . . visiting film stars with their entourages of sycophants . . . aging gentlewomen bestowing coquettish airs and smothering attentions upon escorts-for-hire . . . the directors of the hotels Cathay, Park, and Palace with their parties . . . the Far East managers of the Chase Bank, the Glenn Line, and Sumatra Chemicals and their parties . . . nabobs from the Race Course and the Sportif Français . . . soccer and polo champions with that night's sultry sirens . . . swindlers and smugglers and confidence men and cardsharks and blackmailers and thieves and black-marketeers . . . a Portuguese antiques dealer who everybody "knew" was a Nazi agent . . . the warlord who had shipped two hundred thousand coolies to do donkey work in France during the Great War . . . a retired Norwegian ship captain with his tantalizing and vibrant Eurasian wife . . . the orange-haired owner of the gambling casinos Ambassadeurs and Crockford's with a gaggle of singsong girls . . . the Christian missionary from America who always converted his quota of one Chinese a year . . . a shabby "contessa" or a "grand duke" who could only afford the soupe du jour and let a charming smile pass for the gratuity . . . Mr. Publisher (a passport faker), Mr. Loan Shark, and Mr. Evidence Remover (the abortionist) . . . a quartet of elderly gentlemen with tinted hair and rouged cheeks who drank much too much champagne and giggled and patted one another's hands . . .

"Scratch a Shanghailander," Uncle Moritz put it, "and you get dirt under your fingernails."

Of all the parade of characters David found his uncle's imperious maître d' the most colorful. Prince Litvinoff was so decorous, so gracious, so grand. He was tall, thin, and lithe of movement; and he had a lean elongated face and a pointy nose with nostrils that were always sniffing—the food, the wine, the staff, the guests. His dyed black hair was combed back in a pompadour from an extremely high brow. He was immaculate, always in tails and white gloves, and he sometimes would raise a monocle to his left eye. He toadied to favored patrons, and when he had a spare moment he related anecdotes from his youth in Imperial Russia. "Madame, we *always* passed some weeks in Yalta in summer . . . " "The family was at table in our dacha, which was no more than forty kilometers from the Imperial Palace, when we got the news . . . "

"Prince, my arse," Uncle Moritz snorted to David. "An imposter and a fourflusher. The town's full of these White Russians. To hear them tell it, every last damn one of them is descended from the czar or a grand duchess. Even those strumpets over on the Street of Sweetest Joys. I'll say this for Litvinoff, he earns his keep. He has the grand manner, he sets a tone. People like to think they are being welcomed by royalty, and Litvinoff does it to a turn."

As an embryonic waiter, David came under the tutelage of the prince. He found the stern dicta of the training course ludicrous and had no intention of honoring them. "A good waiter has eyes in the back of his head . . . Service plates are removed immediately the order is given . . . Dropped silverware is replaced before it hits the carpet . . . Matches at the ready before ladies have the cigarette in holder, and no twitching of nostrils when they blow smoke in your face . . . If memory fails—and it must not!—refrain from asking, 'Who is having the côtelette à la Kiev?,' but say, 'I believe Madame ordered the côtelette—am I not correct?' . . . Loyal friends of the restaurant are to be greeted by name and complimented on looking in excellent health, however they look . . . No chitty-chitty-chatter with clientele . . . No overfilling of wine glasses . . . No daydreaming . . . No claspings of hands behind the back—good waiters mourn that they have but two hands to serve their patrons . . . "

David slouched and daydreamed and clasped his hands behind his back and thought two hands were two too many to be devoted to this type of service. He did not have eyes in the back of his head nor did he have the quickness or the coordination of movement, the concentration on serving and pleasing, or any of the other hallmarks of the "good waiter."

"Dah-vid, Dah-vid," Prince Litvinoff sighed, shaking his head, "you are a bee-oot-iful boy, and in-dub-it-ably you have great riches to give the world. But in ten thousand years, a fine waiter you will never be. You lack the finesse, the je ne sais quoi. . . ."

Dah-vid did not argue. He would not be there at all except for his uncle. At night, he would wait for Uncle Moritz to close the restaurant, and together they would return to Rue Robespierre, where Sophie had hot chocolate waiting for them, whatever the weather. She listened reverently while her husband recounted the triumphs and frustrations of the day. Besides such tales of excitement from the world of glamour, how puny were her tidings about the Szechuan peaches that Li Hing had discovered in the market or about Wa Wang's sister having to shave her son's hair off and douse his head with kerosene to get rid of the lice.

Mornings and early afternoons, David wandered in the dense, bewitching metropolis. He brooded about his parents—still no word from his father, and his mother was letting down her guard of cheerfulness . . . "and they've arrested Rabbi Baeck."

In his wanderings, David was sad to see so many Jewish refugees, some of them his own age, idling in the streets. They were ill-clad and listless. They gathered in circles but took no joy in companionship. One day, he crossed the Nanking Road to avoid meeting one of his cabinmates from the *Hannover*—the bitter ex-fighter pilot still in his flying cap—and embarrassing himself, if not Captain Horn. David asked his uncle if he could not provide employment for at least a few of the drifting refugees.

"Look, David," Uncle Moritz said. "I wouldn't have these ragamuffins sweeping out my kitchen. Not that I haven't tried it. I had a dishwasher who was so busy crying for the good old days and quoting Kierkegaard that he couldn't see the dirt on the plates. Whiners and philosophers I don't need. I'm not the only one—you have seen the advertisements for furnished rooms: 'No refugees.' 'Will not let to refugees.' Who wants to take in tramps? No, I'll stick with my kitchen coolies. They laugh like hyenas while they chop-chop and scrub-scrub, and they don't steal any more than the next one."

David did not argue with him. He had come to a grudging admiration for his uncle's uncanny knowledge of people. Monsieur Lafitte, who had had his own restaurant in Frenchtown until an addiction to drink drove him out of business, was a case in point. "I'll make a deal with you, Lafitte," Uncle Moritz had said. "You be my chef and stay sober until the last meal is served, and then you can help yourself to the Schnaps." And there was Karl Koschner, "the best pastry chef in Shanghai." His cakes and tarts had made Dobrin's famous in Berlin. New Zealand had promised him a visa if he would spend a day in a gentile bakery in Berlin and prove he could bake to please Aryan palates. Karl Koschner passed the test, but then His Majesty's Government reneged. A cable informed him that he would not be welcome in Auckland "at this time."

Sometimes in the late hours, Uncle Moritz—in response to a special request—would pick up his violin. Otherwise, a succession of White Russian chanteuses would sing for their supper, going through repertoires culled from the operettas of Romberg, Friml, Stoltz, and Herbert.

One autumn evening, Madame Alexandra was complying with a request for *Two Hearts in Three-Quarter Time* when a drunken diner uncorked his bottled-up agitation. He was a sales manager for a Liverpool manufacturer and had been in Danzig when German trucks, horses, Stukas, and, yes, grocery wagons "counterattacked" Poland and Hitler inexplicably shared the loot with Stalin. "Wake up, everybody," he cried, waving his magnum, "we're sitting on another world war. The Bolshie hater goes to bed with the Redkie and Johnny Bull goes to bed with the Polacks—we're all sick in the noggin." The bibulous prophecy corroborated David's own grim foreboding. How blasé everybody was over Hitler's treacherous invasion of the east. By treaty, the British had declared war on Germany, but they had not yet fired a shot—Warsaw was too remote to defend. Paris, naturally, was going about its business on the terrace of Maxim's.

Mail was still getting through, and Mama wrote that all seemed quiet, no one wanted war, at least in Breslau, but there *was* more and more rationing. Hitler was raving on and on about "English warmongers and capitalist Jews," and there were disturbing reports of unnecessary SS brutality in Warsaw and Cracow, as if *any* brutality were necessary. Things must be heating up all over the continent. If the English or the French or even the Americans had raised their voices when the Führer goosestepped into the Saar, Austria, and Czechoslovakia, he would have drawn in his horns like the bully he was. David recalled reading somewhere that Albert Einstein, lamenting man's "lust for hatred and destruction," had asked Sigmund Freud in the early 1930s if he thought that mankind could somehow evolve out of its predisposition for war, and that Freud had replied, "In some happy corners of the earth, where nature brings forth abundantly whatever man desires, there flourish races whose lives go gently by, unknowing of aggression or constraint . . . " Neither Europe nor China, at least today, was one of those corners.

Thinking of Mama and Breslau, David asked his uncle, "Will the British bomb German cities?"

"Why? And what with? Churchill's stogies?"

David resigned himself to the likelihood of not seeing his parents again soon. In Aunt Sophie and Uncle Moritz he had surrogate parents whose shortcomings were irritating but not unendurable. Aunt Sophie was more shadow than substance, and she deferred slavishly to her husband. She had no opinions that didn't come from him, and she swooned when he paid her the mildest of praise for parroting him correctly or for doing well in a bookkeeping course. ("She picked it up overnight.") With three servants to market, cook, clean, sew, and do the laundry, she was free to keep the Café Moritz's accounts and pay and submit bills. Uncle Moritz accepted her abject servitude as his proper due. At home he could be irritable, abrupt, cynical, and sarcastic. But the Café Moritz saw only a beaming, bowing, slightly unctuous proprietor determined to please at all costs—"If that is what you suggest, Prince . . . Lady Cavendish, what a delightful honor to welcome you here again."

If David sometimes felt "family" was too much with him, he had only glancing contact with the others who also lived in his uncle's house. The Felchers had the first two floors. Downstairs, the entrance foyer gave way on the left to a parlor and on the right to the dining room. French doors swung into a large kitchen-pantry. A central staircase led to the two upper floors. The Felchers and David had their bedrooms on the second floor, and Sophie used the third room there for her bookkeeping. In two rooms on the third floor were the Wittens and their two small daughters. "We met on the *Conte Biancamano*," his uncle told David. "Witten's from Mannheim and found a job here the second day off the boat. He works in a fine haberdashery on the Avenue Foch—see, there are places for people who want to work."

The other third-floor room was occupied by a widow.

"Mrs. Keyser and her husband used to come to my old place," Moritz Felcher explained. "Würzburgers. They weren't here six months when just like that, no warning, he went pop, poof, heart attack. The widow said it was too much sun. Poor woman, the sun seems to have gotten to her, too."

David did his best to avoid Mrs. Keyser. She was so embarrassing. A woman of her age—older than Mama and as old as Aunt Sophie—behaving so foolishly. There could be only one Mae West and someone should tell Mrs. Keyser. What must they think of her at Mlle. Marie's, the milliner's shop where she worked, wearing that blond wig and those slinky gowns and clanging bracelets and rolling her eyes and undulating her hips.

"Hiya, young, dark, and gorgeous," she cooed to David, blocking his passage on the staircase. She swiveled her hips and rolled her eyes insinuatingly over his body. "Why don't you c'mon up and see me sometime?"

"Well, I'm quite busy, Mrs. Keyser, and . . . "

"C'mon up and I'll peel you a grape."

David closed his eyes and yearned for the girl on Foochow Road: "For you, no pay, only fun."

"You see," Rebecca said, "it's been all for naught. Your incessant monitoring of the wireless. There's no real war going on."

She meant it as a rebuke. It had been a month since she and Meyer had so much as gone out to a neighborhood restaurant. His vitality couldn't be that low, but his spirit was. He had been countering her suggestions for an evening out with the rationalization that they had better keep an ear to the wireless "to hear when Hitler blows up Europe." So their lives were circumscribed, unnecessarily so she felt. She was carrying the burden of the shop and came home to quiet evenings to listen to the Classical Hour on the B.B.C. in New Delhi. Always there was the refreshment of Esther. ("Miss Niemeyer says the mosquitoes that bite me all day have forty-seven teeth . . . Grace heard her mother tell her father that our teacher has a past. What's a past, Mommy?")

Just now, Rebecca had the domestic burden of trying to teach Li Hing, their live-in housekeeper-cook, the basics of European cooking. Li Hing, sorrow's child. In pantomime and pidgin English, she limned her tale of horror. Through her province, Japanese soldiers had slashed, shot, raped, pillaged, burned, and decapitated their bloody way. Li Hing fled, carrying on her back an elderly aunt with golden lilies. She ran through sorghum and millet fields to a stream miles and miles away, leaping from rafts to barges to junks and ending up in Shanghai with the great tide of homeless, hopeless refugees inundating the city. Yet she wore a perpetual grin!

Meyer was rarely out of Rebecca's thoughts. During the long afternoons that he rested at home and she and Teng minded the shop, she wondered about him. What was the cause of his unwellness? How much of it was real? To what extent was any of it avoidable and self-induced?

"I do think you would feel better if you smoked less," she suggested.

Always a moderately heavy smoker, Meyer had escalated his dependence on cigarettes alarmingly. She did not like to be a snoop or a scold. The three and four discarded packets of Gauloises and Players every day told the story.

"Even your skin is getting to look nicotinish," she told him.

"Sympathetic adaptation. When in China, look as the Chinese do."

"Ah, so that explains how I married a Caucasian and awoke one morning to find myself in bed with an Oriental."

Meyer smiled wanly and lit still another cigarette.

At her insistence, he visited a kindly old doctor who had moved from Bonn to Shanghai in the early '30s. Doctor Finkelstein diagnosed "Shanghai ague" and prescribed a tonic and vitamins. He, too, admonished Meyer about his smoking.

Everything contagious came Meyer's way. A head cold or a chest cold built up no immunity against the arrival of the next one. Late in the autumn, something called "Peking virus" was going around and, predictably, Meyer came down with it. The fever subsided, but he was chronically debilitated.

One night in bed, Meyer became lachrymose. His weeping was soundless, but Rebecca felt the vibrations. She reached out to touch him, gently rubbing his chest. "What is it, Meyer?"

"Nothing."

"Please, Meyer, I am your wife."

"I'm—I'm—I am not your husband."

"Meyer, what are you saying?"

"I am not a real husband."

"Oh, Meyer, Meyer, Meyer." She shushed him, cradled him in her arms, and kissed his tear-drenched cheeks.

She knew only too well what he was saying. How long it had been! Not since he had come back from Buchenwald! Instinctively, she had known then that she must restrain herself and not send out signals to which he could not respond. She must wait for him to regain his health and strength. She had hoped that the air of the long ocean voyage would be restorative, the mild aphrodisiac that would prompt the resumption of physical relations. One night in their stateroom, after Esther was fast asleep, Rebecca had begun a certain caress that Meyer always had found maddeningly exciting. But he stopped her. "Don't," he had pleaded. "Don't start something I can't finish. It's not there yet. I am sorry." Since then, nothing of that nature had passed between them.

"You are my husband," she consoled him now. "You are all the husband I will ever want. Stop this foolish talk."

With remorse stinging her, Rebecca heard herself speaking less than the truth. How wild and enrapturing it had been in the beginning. That summer and autumn ten years earlier. It did not seem that a lifetime would be sufficient to satisfy their ardor. Through circumstance and a perverse collaboration of the body and the mind, passion had died in Meyer. It had not in her. There were days when she seemed to be consumed with sexual longing. What Meyer was telling her now, she had known for a long time. The deepest part of the bond with her husband was dead forever and she wanted to cry out, "It's not fair. I'm still here. I won't be deprived."

David was in his reading period. The unexpected harshness of winter in a semitropical city and the darkness of the days had discouraged his matutinal roamings. He was stretched on his bed with the lending library's copy of *It Can't Happen Here* propped on his stomach when he heard Aunt Sophie call to him, "There's a letter for you, David."

Somehow he knew. After all these months and months and the many letters from Mama, he knew this would be the one. It was. "By the time this reaches you, I will have lived with my sorrow for some weeks. But only now do you learn that your good father is dead. I can only pray that you have been preparing yourself for the worst. The camp merely informed me on a postal card that he had died of pneumonia and 'complications.' Let us live with that. You are not to worry about me. I do not feel strong enough to think about traveling anywhere just now, but we must both hope, my beloved son, that you and I will be reunited soon, soon . . . "

David wept and keened and wailed. The tears of a lifetime, manfully suppressed when he said good-by to Mama and when the *Hannover* sailed, poured out of him. Uncle Moritz and Aunt Sophie cried with him. Uncle Moritz patted David's head and caressed his cheeks. "There, there, that's right. Get it all out. Don't hold anything back."

Another of David's intuitions became grounded in fact. The letter telling of Papa's death would be the last he would receive from Mama. Europe's half-hearted or "phony" war had indeed turned into a threat to Western civilization. At the end of one of the continent's bitterest winters, the Russians conquered Finland and the Nazis stormed into Denmark and Norway and, skipping right by the Maginot Line, blitzed the Low Countries. After only eighteen days, the French threw up their hands and threw down their arms. The British Isles would be next.

David could not distinguish where personal grief left off and universal Weltschmerz began.

"You are not Atlas," his uncle chided him gently. "You cannot carry the woes of the world."

But David could not shake his despondency. He knew that he was worrying Uncle Moritz and suspected that Uncle Moritz brought Ignatz Stern into the picture partly to distract him from his languors.

"He's just off the *Conte Verde,* David. You know how all the refugees coming in these last months had to put up four hundred dollars for a notarized passport card. Well, young Stern lost his or had it stolen. No tickee, no landee. This was one fellow who was not about to be shipped back to the Fatherland. How's this for chutzpah? He collars one of the coolies wrestling with the trunks and packing cases and shoves him into a water closet and uses sign language to get across the idea that they should exchange clothing. It's happy Chanukah for the coolie. He can sell Stern's woolen suit and feed his family of nineteen for a year. Our boy shimmies into the coolie's stinking rags and sandals and soaks the wrappings from a cigar butt and rubs them all over his face and puts on the coolie's conical hat and there he is, Lo Mein Stern, just another coolie breaking his gonads with the luggage."

David liked Natzie immediately, and Natzie liked everyone indiscriminately. What a brash, funny, irreverent fellow! "Natasha can't sing for rotten cabbages," he whispered of the chanteuse during the first night they waited tables together, "but who's listening with those knockers." Giggling, David almost tipped a tray of near-boiling mulligatawny on Lord and Lady Covingtree (China Cottons, Inc.) and their anemic triplet daughters.

Natzie found a room in the house of an English widow in Yuyan Road. He had responded to a notice in the *North-China Daily News* that said "No Chinese, no refugees, no children, no pets" by ringing up and asking, "Would you take in a nice, clean, cuddly koala bear?" "You're daft," Mrs. Parrington hooted, "come on out."

Natzie was a year older than David, but infinitely more worldly. A few weeks in Shanghai made him a Shanghailander. If he had been set down in the Gobi Desert or in the Australian Outback, he would have taken root there just as well, thrived. He was so self-assured. David came to wish he could be as certain of one thing in this baffling universe as Natzie was of almost everything.

Natzie, too, was an only son who had left two parents behind. His father had operated a perfumery; after it was shut down, he began peddling a line of home-made cosmetics from door to door to a vanishing circle of customers. "They're stuck," Natzie said. "They couldn't leave that damn house and the heirlooms, for God's sake. They're believers. This is no world for believers."

Natzie meant to be noticed. He had a pencil-line mustache that thickened into dashing fillips at the ends and a luxuriant mop of chestnut hair that flashed under thick coatings of pomade and curved around at the temples, Napoleonic style. His eyes were dusky, and gold flecks sparkled out of chocolate depths; their expression was merry, questioning, suggestive. He had a dimpled chin and a faint rash of freckles on his forehead and rounded cheeks. Prince Litvinoff wrung his gloved hands over Natzie, declaring him "a buffoon," and despaired over the "slipping standards" of the Café Moritz. "Jewish boys are not made for waitering," he sighed.

"A brilliant observation, Prince," Natzie said. "Waitering is for the cockatoos."

David glowed in the warmth of this new friendship. How long since he had had a friend! (Were his former schoolmates Kermit and Oscar mopping up Dunkirk? The Balkans? Poised to spring into Piccadilly Circus?) Natzie made him laugh and expand his point of view on many things. Natzie had planned to be a lawyer—"Until the Nazis threw a wrench in that!"— and he indeed had skills of disputation. David saw those skills admirably demonstrated at a debating evening that they went to on a night off. David sat in the broiling auditorium of the Shanghai Jewish School and listened to his friend debate— with a persuasiveness that would have gotten mass murderers off scot-free—a large-framed, homely Ashkenazic girl. Natzie argued that Zionism was a retrogression, the last refuge of provinciality and parochialism. How many Jews who had made it to the desert of Palestine before the unexpected White Paper had stopped immigration cared a carrot about establishing a Jewish state? They would be just as content, if not more so, in the desert of the southwest United States, Natzie contended. Zionism, Miss Baronoff countered, was the only permanent resolution of the Diaspora, the only protection against the forces imperiling the future of international Jewry. Their voices rose. They raged. They insulted each other's intelligence, and they even resorted to name-calling. The debate was gallantly called "an even match," though Natzie was clearly superior. He grinned and grabbed Miss Baronoff by a hand and led her out of the auditorium, a blanket flung over his shoulders.

"Loud arguments are the biggest come-on," Natzie explained to David the next day. "The louder a girl debates, the harder she fucks afterwards."

"Are you a communist, Teng?" Rebecca asked bluntly.

They had had so many theoretical conversations of late

about the future of China—if China was to have a future—she thought she could take this further step. But she caught his suspicious sidelong glance and felt him retreating into his former cocoon. He was right, of course, to be cautious, even annoyed with her. Why should any yellow-skinned person completely trust a white-skinned person? Particularly one who came from a country where communism was deemed a crime even greater than Judaism?

"We admire many of Mao Tse-tung's teachings," Teng replied evasively. "In the summer of 1921, do you know, Mao wrote down those teachings in a house just a few blocks from this shop. He said the future of China was the peasant."

"We" was Pioneers for a New China. In her innocence Rebecca had asked if Pioneers for a New China had anything to do with the New Life Movement she had heard about. The vehemence of his reply startled her.

"The New Life Movement! It is stupidity—the opiate of Chiang and his parasitic Madame. Tell the people to be prompt and button their collars and brush their teeth and kill rats and attend their house of worship, then keep them drugged and quiet for another two thousand years. Pioneers for a New China want the people to wake up and claim their rights as human beings. We say good-by to Confucianism and ancestor worship. We say stop looking backward and forget Lao-tse, who would have us believe that it is in our nature to suffer and do nothing. We say that a man's place in the universe is not fixed. We can improve our destiny. Confucius has kept China asleep for twenty-five centuries. Napoleon called China a sleeping giant but said that some day the giant will awaken and the whole world will tremble."

Could this be the same youth who had come to their employ only months earlier so meek and genuflecting?

"Please stop calling me Missie," Rebecca had said irritably to Teng one afternoon months earlier. "It sounds so servile. I do not regard you as a servant but a colleague."

The change was immediately apparent. Teng relaxed the excessive politeness and became less guarded. His English improved. He dropped the awkward syntax and misusages. So he had known better all along, as she suspected. The quaint manner of speaking was his protective armor and way of reassuring the Wolfs that he knew his place. She had read about American Negroes who resorted—for survival's sake also—to "nigger talk" in the presence of whites.

Often when she and Teng were alone in the sales-repair shop, with its plaster walls and hemp-bladed ceiling fan, Teng would talk about himself. He had hoped to enter a university, but with an older brother studying medicine and times being so bad . . . On his own he had never stopped reading and learning. Listening to him, Rebecca felt that she might be coming nearer to gaining some tangential grasp on the conundrum of China. "Democracy" was Teng's catch-all word. Democracy would bring justice for everyone and end the hunger, brutality, and other indignities inflicted by a corrupt and venal oligarchy. Democracy meant that anyone who grew rice would own the land it grew on. No longer would the peasants be broken by the burden of taxation. Democracy promised an education for everybody. Democracy would rid China of the white man . . . the red-faced British, the obnoxious French, the autocratic Germans, the loud-mouthed Americans, the murderous Japanese. "Chiang would rather fight Mao than the Brown Devil," Teng complained bitterly. "He murdered a half million of his own people right here in the streets of Shanghai."

Rebecca was relieved that Teng could be anecdotal and gossipy as well as polemical. Death was frequently a theme. He told her of the funeral of a baby cousin. The parents placed a doll into her coffin so the spirits would think that both of their daughters had died and would not return for the living one. His grandmother had spent the last two decades lacquering her own coffin, which sat on a trestle in the parlor. Teng described the house of his superstitious godfather whom he and his family had walked ten miles into the countryside to visit. There was a mirror over the front gate, so that the spirits would see their evil reflections and fly away. Spirits, Teng had to explain to Rebecca, flew only in a straight line, so the walls of the entrance were curved. When the godfather's sister-in-law died in his house, her body was carried out through a window and firecrackers were exploded to confuse the spirits.

Neither the business nor Teng could distract her from the disheartening reality of Meyer. His "Shanghai ague" seemed to have reappeared, and in a more virulent form. He no longer had the energy to go to the shop at all. Rebecca returned home to find a husband mired in a sea of lassitude that was like a breathing death. Nothing tempted his appetite, and she had to begin spoon-feeding him like an obstinate child. The books she bought him went unread. He yearned only for his cigarettes. Was it the nicotine alone that had brought on that dreadful cadmium-yellow complexion? Even the whites of his eyes had turned yellow.

"Daddy is sick," Rebecca said to their daughter. "He loves you very much, but you must let him rest until he feels better."

Prevailing over Meyer's feeble protest that nature was the best healer, Rebecca brought him again to the old German-Jewish doctor. This time, Dr. Finkelstein was not so sanguine. "It's jaundice," he told Rebecca privately. "Why didn't you call me sooner?"

"Jaundice?" Rebecca said numbly.

"Yes. I'm certain. It's quite common out here, and never pleasant, of course."

"Doctor Finkelstein, you examined my husband months and months ago and he has not been well since. One thing gives way to the next, and overall his general condition gets worse and worse. Excuse me if I tend to think whatever ails him is part and parcel of one illness that hasn't been properly diagnosed."

"No, Mrs. Wolf. You are quite wrong. His symptoms may be all of a piece to you. But this is jaundice. I assure you that he did not have jaundice when I examined him previously."

"In any event," she said, her voice rising, "as you imply that I have been negligent, what is to be done now?"

"Something he will not like. All of his teeth must be extracted. They are badly decayed and are feeding bacteria into his system. They add to the poison already in his bloodstream."

"Can that be absolutely necessary?"

"It is absolutely necessary."

"I don't know how I can even suggest such a thing to him."

"You had better do more than suggest. Otherwise, his liver will collapse and he will die."

Toothless! Meyer toothless! This man whose only foible had been his vanity about appearance and his fastidiousness with his wardrobe! And now someone who had made a complex ritual out of cleansing his teeth must be told those teeth would have to be extracted. Rebecca waited for the darkness of night and bed to tell Meyer what Doctor Finkelstein had said.

Meyer turned his back to her and faced the wall. He wasn't even going to answer her. Rebecca became infuriated.

"Meyer, I was not speaking rhetorically."

"I heard you."

"Then you heard me ask you something."

"The answer is no."

"Then you will die."

"So be it."

"Damn you," she cried. "I am not going to stand by and let you die. This is one decision that is not yours to make. Teeth can be replaced. *You* cannot."

Erika Zuckerman stepped through the door and Prince Litvinoff moved quickly to conduct her upstairs. He preferred to keep lone diners out of the spotlight.

"No, thank you," she said. "I wish to be seated down here."

The Americans, the Prince sniffed loftily, were becoming as imperious as the British.

Natzie winked at her in passing and she winked right back. "Eager lady, Davie," he whispered. David saw a quite plain-looking woman of perhaps thirty-five. She was expensively dressed and flashing bangles, baubles, and beads. She had owlish green eyes and a squarish chin, a large aquiline nose, and a sensuous mouth. Her hair, the color of apricots, was drawn back and gathered in a chignon.

"Refugee?" she asked, looking inquiringly at David.

He bridled. The word had such a shaming sound.

"Don't take on so," she smiled, patting him impulsively. "Refugees are my life. Thank God you're one I don't have to worry about."

Without consulting the menu, she ordered a filet mignon and tucked into it strenuously when it came. Tonight, at least, she couldn't be worrying about *anyone*.

Later, as he refilled her wine glass and served her a charlotte russe and numerous cups of black coffee, David learned quite a lot about this singular and voluble woman:

"I'm from the Windy City. Chicago. The City of the Big Shoulders. I'll stop you before you ask. Yes, I have seen real-life gangsters. Well, two anyway. Al Capone one night in a restaurant. And John Dillinger coming out of a movie house—no, not *Manhattan Melodrama*. Have you heard of Marshall Field's? My father was sort of a bigwig there. We lived in Highland Park—people called it the Jewish suburb—and I must say I never wanted for much. I went to college—a kind of sweet small-town college in Ohio called Oberlin. I am not telling you how long ago I was graduated, let's just say it was the year that Lindy flew the Atlantic and Babe Ruth hit those sixty whatever they were. And it could have been [winking] a couple of years before that. I went back to Chicago and put some time into social work. Then I worked in Mexican-American neighborhoods in San Antonio, Texas. Got hired away from there by Co-op Funds of American Jewry. They needed someone proficient in Spanish to go to the Dominican Republic to help with the Jewish refugees starting to pour in there from Europe. The Dominican Republic was a sort of way-station where the refugees could cool their heels while hoping to get into the States. *Then* everyone started coming out here to Shanghai hoping that *this* would be their way-station to the U.S. The State Department asked me if I would go out and help them cut the red tape. I said I would be glad to if someone would tell me where the hell Shanghai was. I thought my job here was going to be clerical. How green was my valley. I could write an encyclopedia on the mess that ended up in my lap."

There was no time to describe that "mess." She was due elsewhere—"by popular demand." She left a lavish tip, tapped him on a shoulder, smiled warmly, and said, "Hasta luego, chico." David thought about her and decided she had become more attractive in the two hours or so that he had been in her service. She was so animated, so certain of herself, like the modern, unconventional heroines he kept seeing in the movies from Hollywood. A well-bred woman on her own—so far from home and family—in Sin City. Exactly what was she doing here? Was she lonely to be talking so much to a waiter? Or just naturally friendly?

"I thought she was going to eat you for dessert," Natzie kidded him.

The encounter with Erika Zuckerman was unsettling. She had reminded him of his refugee status. As if he needed still another reminder, he had it in a newspaper editorial a few mornings later.

"The word 'youth' generally is associated with a happy time," the *Shanghai Times* opined. "But for a certain class of youth, life is full of problems that seem beyond solution. We refer to the young Jewish refugees who arrived here from Germany and Austria, many of them destitute and without parents or guardians. They must look for work at a time when Shanghai is undergoing severe economic crises and uncertainty is in the air. We are saddened by the spectacle of boys idling in the streets. There is the foreboding that these youths may grow desolate in a serious and irrevocable manner. . . . "

David was not one of the street idlers, but a desolation had been growing in him. Time was passing—all the months and months of mindless dish-shuffling—and he was standing still. "It is *you*, not time, that is passing," the Chinese philosophers would say. "The life of a man is briefer than the dew on the grass in the morning sun." Chinese philosophy was no comfort. And Natzie's impatience was unsettling, too. "There has to be something better than this," Natzie said repeatedly.

David could not have guessed that Mr. Ledbetter would be

the instrument of his liberation. He must have served this quiet, ashen man—always filet de sole anglaise and a boiled potato—a dozen times without their eyes ever meeting. Mr. Ledbetter was more interested in his crossword puzzle than in his dinner. His pencil streaked across the empty squares of the puzzle from some dated issue of the London *Times;* he usually finished it before remembering to eat. But this night he was stuck and his pencil was poised in midair. David couldn't help but see that "67 across" was stumping him: "Licensed, nonregular univ. prof.—Ger." Twelve letters.

"*Privatdozent,* sir," David whispered.

Mr. Ledbetter looked up, startled, hazel eyes blinking behind horn-rimmed bifocals. "How's that again?"

"*Privatdozent.*" David spelled the word slowly—"z, sir, not c"—as Mr. Ledbetter filled in the spaces.

"Yes, quite. Thank you veddy much."

It was exhilarating to have even this smallest exchange with the financial editor of the *Shanghai Tribune.* Some other evening, now that the ice had been broken, maybe David could be helpful again and perhaps there would be an opening for him to ask a question or two. Meanwhile, Erika Zuckerman came back to the Café Moritz—again to his station, again alone—and before she took her airy leave he heard himself being invited to lunch—the Cathay Hotel on Wednesday at one. "I'll tell you about all my sad refugees," she promised, "and you'll be the second best expert in the world on Erika Zuckerman and her cast of thousands." As if to resolve his befuddlement, she added, "I'm a fool for a handsome young man."

David's feet sank luxuriously into the amber carpet of the black marble-pillared lobby of the Cathay. He waited at the glass-doored elevator beside an ancient Chinese man impeccable in a white silk suit and a Panama hat. Just as the doors swung open, a bellhop in a red fez interceded and directed the man to the lift in the rear. To be Chinese here was to suffer a thousand stabs a day. An age of justice had to be coming when they would rise up to avenge every last insult of the white race.

On the eleventh floor, David saw a dozen people sitting on

two black leather settees in the corridor between the elevator and Erika Zuckerman's suite. Some of her "cast of thousands," her refugees, no doubt. Through the open door he looked into a large room lavishly furnished with divans, glass tables, Persian rugs, and a Steinway grand piano. Behind a gold-inlaid mahogany desk Erika Zuckerman was listening to a man who crumbled a battered felt hat in his moist hands and shifted from one foot to the other. He and the other supplicants waiting in the corridor must have walked miles and miles from the heims, the Hongkew poorhouses, to beg favors of the one person who might be able to help. She made notes, rose, promised to do what she could. The man bowed, thanked her effusively, and shuffled out.

"It's you, it's you," she greeted David, holding out both hands. Erika Zuckerman was dazzling in her lime-green brocade dress encrusted with a Janus-headed dragon breathing fire and smoke from both mouths. She had subtle coloring on her cheeks and she smelled flowery—jasmine? bougainvillea? She looked even more feminine by daylight than by candlelight.

"You look very nice," he complimented her.

"A girl tries," she said, slipping an arm through his. "Come, we'll go to the roof garden."

To the refugees in the corridor, she said, "Please be patient. I'll be back in an hour or so." To their grumbles and moans, she said, "Now, now," and to David she explained in the lift, "They would suck you dry if you opened a vein to them. They have to realize that I must keep up my nourishment or I won't be of any use to them."

From the roof garden, on the eighteenth floor, the views were awesome. Behind the façade of towers on the Bund the streets were like a thousand crooked seams. Under the pale yellow sky Shanghai sprawled to the curve of the earth. To the northwest were quandrangles of infernal mills and the chimneys of Chapei. To the south were the spidery webs of the Forbidden City. Jessfield Park was a patch of green the size of a billiard table, and the Race Course in the very center of the French Concession was an oval miniature. Beyond the Western Districts and suburbs, lush plots of farm and garden flowed in manicured procession to the shantied shores of the Yangtze. Over the rim of the horizon were lotus lakes, purple mountains, mists like silk, cities sparkling like orange juice, and great white clouds like oceans of milk. In the Whangpoo the swing-sailed junks were a flotilla of brown beetles, and Japanese warships—their long gun barrels like so many bent fingers—waited for the other shoe to drop.

"When the view is great," Erika Zuckerman said to David, "the food is usually comme ci, comme ça. But first something to perk up tired taste buds."

Captain Charles, fawning over her like royalty, dispatched a waiter to bring Tom Collinses. ("No maraschino cherries, Charles, remember. Only papaya wedges. And be sure we get frosted glasses.")

She knows what she wants and how she wants it. Was there a single woman in Breslau who would go to a public dining room and order cocktails with such specificity?

"To better days, come what may," she toasted David, clinking her frosted glass against his.

David sipped the unfamiliar lemonadelike beverage and felt a warming nip in his stomach.

"Refreshing?"

"Mmmmm."

"I have been thinking about you, David," she said, the owlish green eyes studying him sympathetically. "Such a waste. You should be in journalism somewhere, but you're here. It can't look hopeful that anything is going to be over very soon, not with Europe flat on her back."

"England alone can't stop Hitler," David said testily. "What would have to happen for America to give up its posture of isolationism?"

"Public opinion would have to change. But public opinion can be manipulated and we happen to have a master manipulator in the White House. I do not believe for one minute that my country has lost its innocence, its idealism and decency. Almost every single American, remember, has ancestral roots in the Old Country, and you can bet we are not going to stand by and let Hitler cut off Europe's genitals. Lend-Lease was a clever stroke, and I'll wager Roosevelt has many others tucked up his sleeve. Oh, David, we had better go with the 'special.' Anything else may be most unspecial."

The veal marengo arrived and the sommelier poured Bollinger '26 into champagne glasses. "It's 'Erika,' *puh-leez*, David. Now, where were we? Oh, yes, you were worried about all those poor people downstairs coming to this ritzy hotel and seeing all this frou-frou. Well, let me ask you this. How would you feel if you were a lowly private in the army and stuck in some dreary, overcrowded barracks and they built some splendid recreation center where you could occasionally get away from it all? It would give your morale a tremendous boost, I can tell you. The same with my people downstairs. They get a big lift just being in such a posh place and seeing smart-looking people. Those shrewd moguls who run Hollywood—and most of them, you know, are Jews who came out of the ghettoes and pogroms of Eastern Europe—knew what they were doing when they made all those pure escape movies in the depths of the Depression. People could go to their Lyceum or their Orpheum and forget their troubles while watching Rogers and Astaire dancing cheek to cheek or Hepburn and Grant cavorting in a Fifth Avenue mansion. For a dime they could leave their cares and woes behind and bye-bye blackbird, fly to the moon on gossamer wings for a couple of hours."

Did she really mean what she was saying? Or was it a self-serving rationalization? Or merely a romantic appraisal of the situation? "It is the female prerogative," Natzie had said of a debating adversary, "to be irrational." But why look a gift horse in the mouth? Just now, anyway, in the middle of this delicious lunch with this fascinating American?

"These refugees, let me tell you, are my constant heartburn," Erika said, spearing another sliver of veal. "Oh, not the refugees in themselves, though a few of them have turned into professional whiners and loafers, but let's face it, it's hard to start life anew when you are no longer young and just plain bushed. I came out here, as I told you, thinking I was going to help process visas at the American consulate and then beat it back home on the next Clipper. I can't begin to tell you what I found at the consulate. Feet-dragging, chaos, total disaster, Gallipoli. I have never seen so much incompetence, apathy, and downright callousness. Only a handful of Jewish refugees were getting the visas they were entitled to. I don't blame the consulate entirely, not when they were being told these people were the dregs of humanity and not the kind of immigrants that America wanted. And guess who was feeding the consulate that canard? None other than the committee of Shanghai Jews to whom my organization back in New York had been funneling money to help the refugees here! Fat-assed local Jews blocking the way of other Jews to the Promised Land!"

David bit his lips to keep from smiling at her outburst. He must have made her defensive, but indignation over the abused rights of outcasts seemed a little absurd in this setting. "Who is on this local committee?" he asked.

"Don't get me started," she started, "but I'll tell you who's on it. The chairman is a senile pot of lard and a pathological liar to boot who thinks there's something to be gained by kowtowing to the Japanese. The head of the medical board is an Austrian with phony degrees whom I wouldn't let take my temperature—he thinks a Chinese veterinarian is good enough for a sick refugee. There's a German Jew who came out here in '32 and is on the committee strictly for the publicity and the parties. There's a tyrant of a White Russian who would make Rasputin look benign. I could go on and on with this confederacy of knaves and nincompoops. The prize S.O.B. of them all is the guy running the heims. With friends like him, who needs Hitler! He used to be a big-game hunter in India and for years was in charge of the loading operations on the Whangpoo wharves. He kept the coolies in line with whips, clubs, and kicks to the nuts. He thinks the refugees should be treated the same way! 'Coolies, refugees—all the same.' Believe me, I'm gunning for his head on a pike. Bastards, one and all!"

She shook her right fist in the air and with the other hand summoned the wine steward to refill their glasses from a new bottle of champagne. David smiled. Her eyes were giving off sparks that seemed to touch his cheeks with pleasant prickly sensations. Indignation became her.

"Why?" David asked. "Why are such men on the committee?"

"Because they are regarded as Somebody and if you are Somebody you serve on committees."

"There must be some nice people who would like to serve."

"You're nice," she said softly, "and so lovely to look at."

A hand, cool and scented, was caressing his, the long fingers tapering to nails of purple crescents. His groin transmitted a quiver to his hand and Erika smiled knowingly.

"See that woman with the black-dyed beehive," Erika gestured, "and the miles of pearls around her neck?"

David welcomed the distraction.

"She calls herself the Baroness de Queenswyth. That's who she *might* have been. Here's a story for you, David. She's actually a retired madam. She ran the greatest fancyhouse in Shanghai during the 1930s. Once upon a time, it seems, she was a pretty but humble English lass, who was seduced by the Baron de Queenswyth. He persuaded her to join him on a voyage to Shanghai, promising to marry her when they got here. The baron, it goes without saying, had no such intention. He tired of her long before they landed and promptly deserted her. Time passed, but not her vow of vengeance. She came up the hard way, literally and figuratively, and by-and-by became the famous Madam Magdalena. Every male who could lay hands on a fiver made it to her establishment—even the baron found his way to Madam Magdalena's on one of his many trips to Shanghai. Outwardly, she welcomed him like a long-lost friend and told him that she had someone special for him. Oh, not one of those twelve-year-old virgins from Canton all the old geezers wet their pants for. No, this was someone very special and very experienced, someone born to please. Very special, indeed. Actually, it was someone Madam Magdalena was about to take out of service because an examination had shown her to be syphilitic. The baron in good time became infected and died a slow, agonizing death. And there was this added touch. It wasn't until the baron had taken his pleasure that Madam Magdalena told him that the special girl was their daughter."

David, mesmerized by the tale of sexual decadence, stared

hard at Madam Magdalena, and heard himself saying fatuously, "Ah, Shanghai."

"The city of four million stories, quoth the *North-China Daily News*."

"Not like that one."

"Who knows? You might be surprised. I think anyone who *intentionally* comes here must have a screw loose or be hiding from something. Even if you're only half nuts when you get here, Shanghai will finish you off. It's Sodom and Gomorrah. All hedonists, cannibals, and profiteers. It never crossed anyone's mind to try for some minimal beauty here. There are no fountains or squares, statues or gracious boulevards. Nobody cares what the place looks like. All anyone cares about is chasing the bitch goddess. Sooner or later, most of them take their bucks and pounds and francs and go back to the places that *are* beautiful—and clean. Everybody's here on lease. But knock it all you want, this city has drama, an ambience, a divine laissez faire that I've never found anywhere else, and I've been around. Shanghai and I are made for each other."

Over "digestive" cognacs, Erika confessed with a sheepish smile that she was still the object of parental concern. Yes, at her age. Must she be as far away from Chicago as she could get without falling off the planet? Social work might be praiseworthy but how much happier for *her* her parents would be if she were married to a nice doctor or a nice lawyer and living in some affluent suburb like Shaker Heights or Brookline or Squirrel Hill or, best of all, Highland Park itself. But that, her Ouija board was telling her, was not the sweet destiny that God had laid down for her.

The brandies were finished and Erika said, "You like views? Come back to the suite with me and I'll show you another."

The waiting refugees roused expectantly. "You'll have to be patient a wee bit longer," she told them, and closed the door. She led David down a foyer and into a bedroom. She drew him to the louvered window. "There!"

He had an aerial view of Soochow Creek. Sampans and barges were jammed together bow to stern, starboard to port in the putrid brown water coursing through the city. On the edge of one sampan a naked boy was urinating against the bow of the next sampan. Women were bent over cooking pots or scrubbing clothes that had been soaked in the creek. One woman was nursing two babies simultaneously.

"People live their whole lives in that cesspool," David mused.

"Let's live a little right here," Erika cooed.

Two hands were on his shoulders, turning him around, drawing him close. Then he was in her arms and their lips were meeting. His eagerness responded to hers. In his tipsiness, his embrace was brutish. She bit him on the lips and his knees buckled.

"When in Shanghai, David . . . "

Erika removed a barrette and her loosened hair tumbled down her back like a spreading flame. She felt his excitement and her fingers went to the springs of it, touching, pressing, fondling, as she undid the buttons of his trousers. She unleashed the straining tumescent organ and fell to her knees.

"Oh my, oh my," she trilled. "Look what we have here."

David knew very well what they had there. But all he could see was a lustrous mane of carroty hair.

"It's beautiful. A prize. I'm mad about these things! And such a big red knob. Yummy."

The fingertips stopped their feverish exploring and teasing. A moist mouth enclosed him like a sheath and a hot tongue flicked him with darting nips. Her lips began to move across and down and up, from tip to base. "Whoa, whoa . . . hey, not so fast," she implored. David fell back across the fluffy king-size bed, moaning. He lay there blissfully, passively allowing himself to be undressed.

Should he be doing the same for her? He had never undressed a woman. He reached tentatively for a clasp at the back of her dress, but she shook him off. Later, when he recalled with pleasure and amusement that amazing afternoon, he thought that if ever there were a marathon for women shucking off their clothes, Erika Zuckerman would win by twenty-six miles.

Erika drew him inside of her. He felt the wetness, the readiness, the command, and he lost himself in the most natural of miracles. His body melded into hers and they gyrated and thrashed and undulated and gasped as one. She screamed. He nearly screamed.

They lay back on the drenched sheet.

"We're on a fast track here," Erika smiled, reading his mind. "So it's our first date and it's not even three o'clock in the afternoon. Do you realize that in this very hotel it took Noël Coward only four days to write *Private Lives*?"

Blissfully, David studied the mounds and rounds and valleys and softnesses of her body. A Rubens. How could he have guessed that those stylish but loose-fitting clothes were concealing so much delight? He rested his head between the hillocks of her breasts with their taut mauve cappings and he stroked the auburn furze between her thighs.

"So Lord Chesterfield was right," she sighed.

"About what?"

"Older women. Having our uses. Being ever so much more experienced and knowing how to show our appreciation."

David rolled back on top of Erika.

"No," Erika said. "No more."

David's excitement drained away and he was close to tears. "Why? You said you liked it."

"I *loved* it. And you're absolutely adorable."

"I don't understand."

"You don't have to understand. This is the way it is, and don't try to psychoanalyze me. I've got rid of the itch and the curiosity. When we meet again, we shall be friends and nothing more. What a catch you'll be for some girl your own age, though. You are sweet and dear and very handsome and you will be a terrific lover."

Hopping out of the bed and reaching for her clothes, Erika said, "And now, after the pause that refreshes, back to my suffering Jews. 'Miss Zuckerman, Miss Zuckerman, the heim expects me to work two hours every day in the kitchen and my feet can't stand it.' 'Please, Miss Zuckerman, if we could only have some coupons, my wife has no coat for the winter. . . . ' "

Shanghai was, in Erika Zuckerman's phrase, "winding down." Lifelines to the rest of the world were being severed. Things were visibly going from bad to worse. People feared that if there were all-out war against the white man in the Pacific—Lord knows, the peace talks in Washington were going nowhere—Japanese troops would take over the International Settlement and French Concession. More Shanghailanders were in flight. "We're packing it in for now," businessmen said. "You can't deal when you have nothing to deal with. We'll be back. . . "

Some of the leave-takings were uninhibited, even for Shanghai. Formerly quite proper people became noisily drunken in restaurants and had to be escorted to water closets and taxis. In the Café Moritz one evening, a most favored patron in his cups had to be restrained from taking off all his clothes. Another patron with a purple perm grabbed David's crotch and gave his testicles an agonizing squeeze as he was placing a fingerbowl in front of her.

Moritz Felcher was hired to cater farewell suppers. On one October evening, David assisted him at a party held in a Tudor mansion in the Western District. Eight middle-aged British couples were at play in the large drawing room, where the buffet was to be set up. They offhandedly greeted the arrival of the foodbearers and went right on with their games. The monocled men went behind a floor-to-ceiling silk bedsheet in which eight holes had been cut side by side. Soon, eight penises were poking at half mast through the holes. The object of "Who's Dickie Is It?" was to see which of the women could identify the most concealed men by their pee-pees. One woman named all eight correctly, prompting another woman to squeal, "Why, Emily, what a tart you've turned out to be." In "Going to Stratford-on-Avon," two teams enacted charades of Shakespearean titles. One of the men teased his penis to a throbbing erection. *"As You Like It,"* one of the other men purred, only to be topped by Emily's jeering *"A Midsummer Night's Dream."* A copulating couple fell asleep before reaching orgasm. *"Love's Labor's Lost."*

"I'm sorry to have exposed you to that, David," his uncle said apologetically.

David felt a hundred years older than his innocent and affronted uncle. And he couldn't throw cold water in Uncle Moritz's face by revealing, "You should only know what I've been exposed to."

Sallow, sunken, perspiring, Meyer Wolf lay abed with his eyes closed.

"Meyer, I know that you are resting," Rebecca said. "But hear me out. Please. For all our sakes. The bed rest and the quinine alone aren't going to make you better. They are only palliatives. There can be no cure unless you agree to do what the doctor said must be done."

Meyer said nothing, feeding her exasperation with him. In the past they had had their disagreements and differences of opinion, and their voices had risen sometimes. But neither had ever used the insidious tool of silence.

"Speak to me. I demand that you talk to me."

"No," Meyer said. "How many times do I have to say it? Is there no end to this nagging? No. No. *No.*"

Something snapped inside Rebecca. There would be an end to the nagging. She would save herself immeasurable anguish as well as wasted breath. The Judaic ideal of the deferring wife was not appropriate to the occasion. How depressing, even repellent, it was becoming to return home night after night to this supine, yellowing invalid who so stubbornly refused to be cooperative.

She bided her time for another three days. "Meyer," she then said casually, "inasmuch as you are not feeling better, Doctor Finkelstein would like you to go into Shanghai General for some stomach tests. This time, I'm not asking or cajoling, Meyer. An ambulance will be here in the morning."

Meyer issued a sigh of resignation.

Doctor Finkelstein had been a reluctant conspirator in her subterfuge. "We don't need to open him up," he said. "But—if that is the only way. . . . "

Under general anesthesia, Meyer had all of his teeth pulled out.

Rebecca stood at his bedside and watched the first flickering of his eyelids. He ran the palms of his hands over his stomach. There were no bandages, no bag. He looked at her, then closed his eyes and kept them closed. He knitted his brow. After the longest while, the tip of his tongue found the gauze on his gums and darted from side to side like a frantic windshield wiper. His eyes snapped open in horror. From his mouth issued a blood-curdling, mucousy roar. And another. He then clamped his lips shut.

"I am sorry," Rebecca said softly. "But I had to agree to it. I couldn't bear to lose you. We'll get some new teeth, Meyer."

He shook his head, and she felt the chill of icy hatred.

He closed his eyes and ignored her entreaties to say something—anything.

Rebecca took him home after four days, and he still had not spoken a word. She begged him to eat, but the food on his tray went untouched. She instructed Li Hing to spoon-feed him, forcibly if need be. The warm beef broth drooled out the sides of his mouth and down his jaw and neck. Rebecca was sick with guilt and foreboding. To inflict through artifice a toothless mouth on a vain man was no small matter to have on one's conscience. What if he were to persist in this perverse revenge? What if he should take a permanent vow of silence? How far would he go in his refusal of nourishment?

"Was I wrong, Teng?" Rebecca cried out.

Meyer's deepening illness had been the unseen presence between her and the Chinese youth. It drew them into a quiet intimacy during their hours in the shop. "Medicine," Teng mused. "My grandparents in Guandong followed only the ancient practices. When they became ill, they went to the herb doctor or the acupuncture man. If people had sore throats or backaches or headaches or a woman was not fertile, they were given medicines that had come down from the time of Ch'in. Moldy bean curds or powders made from musk or rhinoceros horns or potions of a baby's urine. . . . "

Teng's response was elliptical but Rebecca did not pursue it. She began to dread going home. At the sound of her footsteps Meyer would feign sleep so that his eyes as well as his lips were sealed to her. She would never have guessed that even in illness and debilitation Meyer could show such a streak of sadism. This man who was so sympathetic with the quivering waiter who had splashed coffee all over him on their first evening together.

At the limit of her frustration she became, in a maneuver that startled her, almost physically abusive. She thrust a pencil into his right hand and a pad into his left. "I know you are not sleeping, Meyer. I know you don't feel like talking. But will you please write on the pad anything, anything in the world, that I can get or do to please you."

He was awake. He was listening. Her heart quickened to see the bony, jaundiced hand moving across the pad. He was managing to write something without opening his eyes. He dropped the pad on the bed. Rebecca picked it up eagerly and read, "Leave me alone."

She refrained from comment and quietly left the bedroom. She was stricken and furious. How dare he write her a message like that! Illness made some people charming and tractable—Meyer's was making him insufferable.

The next evening, she took a deep breath and tripped into the bedroom affecting a cheeriness and bantering tone. "I wasn't too enamored of what you wrote yesterday, Meyer." Again, but more gently, she slipped the pencil and pad into his hands. "Do you have something nicer to say to me today?"

Again he was writing with his eyes closed—and this time he managed to underscore what he wrote.

Rebecca picked up the pad and read, *"Leave me alone."*

Meyer turned on his side and faced the wall, his back to her.

Rebecca told herself, in despairing intuition, that this was not the whim of a week or a month. Her husband intended never to speak to her again. Nor even to Esther.

"Er—er—I say, waiter . . . "

Mr. Ledbetter was looking up, summoning him, and David hurried to be of service.

"Could you er—er—give a chap another lift? Not strictly sporting, but one hates to leave off with any blanks. Look here, this '26 down.' "

This time Mr. Ledbetter was asking for help. "Gothic letters, older Ger. alphabet, seven spaces."

David pondered—as if to suggest he must reach into the deepest recesses of memory—and said thoughtfully, "I believe the word is *Fraktur*, sir."

Mr. Ledbetter tapped out the spaces with his pen and said, "That's it, by Jove. Splendid fit. Thank you veddy much." He returned to his puzzle, then looked up at David again. "How do they call you?"

Mr. Ledbetter nodded in recognition. Ah ha, the pieces of another puzzle were coming together. "Yes, oh yes. Bloody shame for all you young chaps. Messy disruptions. Educations blighted. Future up in the air. All that sort of thing."

Mr. Ledbetter addressed him again when David served the coffee. "I say, lad, what would you be studying if you were in university and had your druthers?"

"Literature and political science, probably. I wanted to be a journalist."

David wondered if he had said the wrong thing. Mr. Ledbetter stiffened, looked at him suspiciously, and seemed to be dismissing him with a "Yes, yes, of course."

Unpredictable actions and reactions did not warrant much scrutiny in unpredictable times. Everything was askew. In Europe, British Lancasters were smashing Berlin and Bremerhaven and Lübeck and Essen and Hamburg, but not, not yet, Breslau (to David's knowledge). Uncle Moritz lamented that the Japanese were outnumbering Anglos at the Café, but there was Erika Zuckerman smiling and winking with a handsome American Marine officer in tow. Natzie had quit—for nowhere specific—humming, "Fish gotta swim, birds gotta fly," tossing everyone a farewell kiss, and leaving David feeling bereft and betrayed. Aunt Sophie was humped over a card table hours on end with her thousand-piece jigsaw puzzle of the stately homes of Britain. Florenz ("Mae West") Keyser, becoming bolder, again trapped David in the foyer, surveyed him with her rolling eyes, vamped around a bit, and drawled, "Say, big boy, is that a pistol in your pocket or are you just glad to see me?"

And then, amidst all the unpredictabilities, Mr. Ledbetter was offering David a job.

"Well, if a chap's got journalism in mind, well, the thing is, um, er—er—well, a chap's got to make a start. Young bloke with us, an Aussie, can't cut this climate and he's back to Perth. Humph! A chap could come with us. Not much of a spot. Copy desk, bit of research, that sort of thing. Still, er, a beginning. . . . "

David thought that he would leave his skin. Even to run errands for the *Shanghai Tribune!*

"Here's your chance, David," Uncle Moritz beamed. "You go and watch and listen and work hard and you'll make something of yourself."

David warmed to this expression of pride and generosity. In the beginning he had thought Uncle Moritz rough-cut, smug, and unsympathetic—he still called the drifting refugees "the sweepings of the dust bin"—but David had come to see him in a softer light. They might never speak to each other from the depths of their soul, but he could now grant that Uncle Moritz had a soul and was doing the best he could. Uncle Moritz adapted to the world he had to live in, and he adapted without losing a basic decency and sense of fairness.

"The thing is, the only thing is," Uncle Moritz fumbled, "I hope this doesn't mean that you will move out. Your Aunt Sophie, you know, it would make her feel very bad."

David impulsively kissed his uncle on both cheeks. "I'm not moving. You and Aunt Sophie are my family."

But the words sounded hollow in his own ears. The day must come when he would cut this cord, too.

The stench in Meyer's room was beyond disinfectants and room brighteners. Rebecca steeled herself to sit with him a couple of hours each evening, but he neither acknowledged her coming or going nor her presence. She did not press him to speak or to write. She, herself, took up the pad and left a bright little message—"Can Meyer come out to play with me before dinner?" or "I would like some [write in flavor] ice cream"—but there was no sign that he even looked at her "cheerup"s.

Rebecca asked Li Hing to sleep on a cot in Meyer's room and he appeared to ignore the intrusion. He rallied briefly and his skin seemed to be a shade or two lighter. Li Hing reported that he had been signaling for cigarettes. Rebecca said he might have one when he signaled for it, but not to leave the packet within reach. Another night, Meyer was demanding blanket after blanket as his body burned with new fevers. From his room came meshed moans and whimpers.

Doctor Finkelstein now said that Meyer was in the grip of "tropical disease."

"Tropical disease," Rebecca exploded. "What next? First it's Shanghai ague and then it's Peking virus and then it's jaundice and now it's tropical disease. Do you ever cure anybody of anything, Doctor Finkelstein? You could be a medical Cook's tour director of the Orient. What's left, leprosy?"

"Your husband must go back to hospital," Doctor Finkelstein said wearily.

Rebecca hardly needed to be told by an attending doctor there that Meyer had very little resistance left. But she was overcome to hear that the end was so near—three or four days at most. She should keep in close touch.

Meyer was conscious the whole time. His eyes were open and glued to the ceiling. Never once in the eleven hours that it took him to die did they turn to Rebecca. She tried to arrest his stare by standing over the bed, but he stared vacantly through her. His were the eyes of death, sunk deep in their sockets. The lids seemed stuck to the skin behind them. He never blinked. The eyes of a man mummified.

"I love you, Meyer," she wept. "I meant always to do the right thing. If I didn't, please, please forgive me."

Was this how it was to end? Would the union that had begun in the white heat of love and passion pass into nothingness without a murmur from him acknowledging that it had ever been?

"Please, please, Meyer," Rebecca pleaded. "Tell me you forgive me."

She waited. Each breath might be his last and he would leave her without answering.

"Please . . . say . . . you . . . forgive . . . me . . . Meyer."

The limp hand holding the pencil crossed over, slowly, as a bow in an adagio strain, to take up the pad. He scrawled, "You and God."

"I don't mean to stare, fella, but it's the kind of thing that bugs me. I've seen you somewhere, but where?"

David had been unaware that he was being studied. He looked up from the cuttings that he was compiling and saw an American Marine officer, handsome as a model for a recruiting poster, sitting across from him in the periodicals reading room of the *Tribune*. He recognized him as the Marine who had been with Erika Zuckerman.

"The Café Moritz?"

"That's it, that's it! That was some night."

The American grinned, and David grinned, too.

"Now I remember. You're 'the refugee youth with the excellent mind.' "

David blushed. "The refugee part is true anyway."

"Well, anyway, it appears that you are working here; that's a step up in the world."

Was it really a step up in the world to be snipping trivia from old issues of *Life* magazine ("Dottie Lamour No. 1 Pin-up Girl of U.S. Army," "Triple-Threat Rita Hayworth") and *Collier's* magazine ("Leopard Falls from Plane onto Kilimanjaro," "Baseball Manager Lifts Catcher Rather than Rapped Pitcher")? Was this how the great journalists began their careers?

"Cut out anything from English-language magazines," Jocelyn Ainsworth, the features editor, had instructed David, "that we might use for the Home, Sweet Home page. Hollywood gossip. Romances, marriages, divorces, suicides, murders. Stuff on the Royal Family. Anything at all about the princesses, even their favorite flavor of ice cream in the bomb shelter. Anything on the latest fads and fancies of the rich and the idle. Tiresome, regurgitated rot, to be sure, but our readers eat it up."

"I'll have to start getting here before you do," the lieutenant said, holding up a mutilated copy of *Life*. "You're sure an eager beaver with those clippers."

"Sorry. Almost everything in that issue was trivial enough for our readers."

The Marine hooted and David felt a pang of disloyalty toward his employer. Trifling as his present duties were, he liked being there—the atmosphere was Victorian England—

and he liked everyone to whom Mr. Ledbetter had introduced him.

The *Tribune* was at the eastern end of the Bund. On the ground floor of the brick building were the publisher's suite and the business offices. Sagging wooden stairwells led to the upper floors. On the second floor, the editors and reporters worked in glass-walled cubicles. On the third floor, the *Tribune* was put together with clacking linotype machines and bluish-purplish photoengravings and muscular make-up tables. On the top floor were the morgue, the back-issues stalls, and the periodicals reading-room, which was open to the public. Matrixed impressions of the pages of backward type were carried to an adjoining building, where they were cast by stereotypers into lead cylinders. Coolies hoisted the heavy plates onto the rotary press.

David especially liked Mr. Ledbetter. This kindest of men was always chugging up the stairs to look in on his protégé. "It was crumbs from humble pie," Mr. Ledbetter was recalling. "The humblest. Back in Birmingham. I was a lad of twelve when I went to the *Advocate*. An 'inker,' they called me. Like a little monkey I was. Climbing all over the press with my big black soaking brush. Getting as much ink over me as on the rollers. I'd come through the door at home and Father would call out, 'Mother, did you invite a little blackamoor to tea?' . . . "

The American was studying David again with amusement. "You know," he said, "if you make light of *Life,* you make light of its publisher. Mr. Luce is no less than Chiang's Number One Boy in the United States. You could be playing a very dangerous game."

David smiled and snipped "Queen of California Wine Discovers Perfect Way to Drink Champagne."

"I have to be off," the officer said. "But hey, as one Jew to another, how about having dinner with me tomorrow night?"

This giant with the bristling brush of blond hair and eyes as blue as the Pacific and pink cheeks and gleaming white teeth . . . *Jewish?* In a black instead of a forest-green uniform he could pass for an SS officer!

"I know what you're thinking. We come in all shapes,

sizes, and colors. The skin of the Persian textile men who came here a thousand years ago eventually turned yellow. In Yemen we're short and dark brown and in Ethiopia we're pitch black. I can imagine two pygmies meeting in darkest Africa and one saying to the other, 'Jewish, I presume?' "

David was impressed. Transported.

First Lieutenant Joseph Stone Gordon of the U.S. Fourth Marines had access to the American Club. In the vaulting ebony bar with the "whorehouse-red" walls and the oil paintings of reclining nudes, his host ordered gin fizzes. "Your health," Joe said, clicking glasses, "and better days."

The days were still good enough for the men crowding this privileged sanctuary. They laughed and slapped backs and refilled glasses and their voices commingled in a thunderous din of hearty male camaraderie. David was reminded of prosperous German burghers loud with drink in their taverns and Weinstuben.

"That man over there with the walrus mustache," Joe pointed out, "is Clinton Thorndyke—big mucky-muck in Shell Oil. The bald fossil in the corner dozing over his ninth martini—William Williamson IV, a cotton broker who sailed out here before Marco Polo. The duffer with the constipated look at the next table is Patrick S. Stanhope, of Chase Bank . . . "

"Nice to see you, lieutenant." A florid-faced man in elevator shoes playfully punched Joe's shoulders. "May I buy you and your friend a drink?"

"No, thank you, Mr. Seligman, we're set."

"Driven to drink," Joe said. "Edgar Seligman. A real brain. Became a Baptist so Lambert Minerals would promote him, which they did. The minute he filed *the* definitive report on China's geology, Lambert had no more use for him and gave him the sack."

Someone else was offering drinks, and again Joe was declining. It was heady and confusing to David. He could not quite believe his presence in such a setting, and he was amazed that his new friend should be receiving (and *spurning*) attention from distinguished older men. "People show you so much respect," David observed.

"Why shouldn't they? We're out here to save their butts. Look what happened four, five years ago. We nearly went to war for Socony when the Japs bombed those tankers and the *Panay* in the Yangtze."

That self-assured, somewhat boastful air sounded a lot like Erika Zuckerman. Was it the gift of all Americans to be so un-guarded and sure of themselves and their value? It was a diffi-cult thing to ask, especially here in the American Club, but the thing that he most wanted to learn from Joe right now was what it was like to be a Jew in America. David was in Shanghai, after all, because he had been a Jew in Germany.

"Are you asking me if there's anti-Semitism in the good old U.S. of A.? Does the North Pole have ice? You show me a land that can put together a minyan and I'll show you a land with anti-Semitism. The virus didn't die at Ellis Island. But it hasn't germinated into a lethal contagion, either. We have our Ku Klux Klans with their motto 'Down with Koons, Kikes, and Katholics,' and our Father Coughlins and our Gerald L. K. Smiths, but mostly it's the unwashed and the unread who feed on their garbage. As you go up the socioeconomic ladder, you still have bigotry, but it gets a little subtler. Unwritten quotas for getting into the best colleges and universities—you do a fan dance, and then some, to get into the top law or med schools. There'll be a Jewish President about the same time that you see white smoke signaling the election of a Jewish Pope. We, too, have restricted hotels and resorts, and the membership rolls of our country clubs aren't 'sullied' by Greenbergs, Cohens, and Leibowitzes. Real-estate operators know how to preserve choice residential areas from 'contamination.' Jews are exclud-ed from gentile banking and brokerage houses and the board rooms of big corporations, which, by the by, were the ones that brought on the big Depression. And who of us has not listened to a few thousand rotten little jokes and slurs and been called a sheenie or a Hebe or a kike or heard someone whispering, 'Is he one?,' or 'They've changed their name, but who do they think they're fooling.' The great thing about America is that there is always some new minority group for everybody else to look down on and kick around. If you think we've got it bad, how would you like to be a 'nigger' in America? But until some-body invents something better, it's still the best damn place on earth."

Joe Gordon was born and grew up in the Squirrel Hill district of Pittsburgh. Grandfather Garfunkel had landed in Pennsylvania as a penniless youth from Düsseldorf and went from house to house sharpening knives and scissors. He worked long and hard, saved his pennies, invested in a hardware business, and prospered. ("Unlike the wretched Chinese immigrants in the American West, David. They broke their picks building railroads for Wall Street and ended up with nothing to show for it.") Joe's father made paints and struck it rich, too. Other than the "usual father-son beefs," Joe had a happy and fortunate boyhood. The Depression pretty much by-passed the Gordons. (Yes, Garfunkel was "sanitized" into Gordon—"not a very imaginative switcheroo, every third Jew in America was changing his name to Gordon.") Joe went "the preppie way" and became the "token Jew" in Lawrenceville, the expensive preparatory school in New Jersey. He went on to the college of Dartmouth "for the skiing and the she-ing," but in truth was enough of a "grind" to win a Rhodes scholarship. Oxford would have to wait until he was through with the Marines. As for the Marines—well, he had had a low draft number and it "sure beats dragging ass in the infantry." He hoped to enter the foreign service some day. He should be a shoo-in alongside the "fractional intellects" who were representing Washington in the chancelleries of the world.

"Ambassador Gordon," David said. In his mind's eye he could see this magnificent man presenting his credentials to the Court of St. James. And maybe changing his name back to Garfunkel.

"Come, I've got the mother of all hungers," Joe said. "Let's eat German. You pick the place."

Café Louis in the Bubbling Well Road was run by Louis Eisfelder, of Berlin. He, too, had a nephew working for him— Fritz, a couple of years older than David. Uncle Moritz and Louis Eisfelder would occasionally eat in each other's restaurant as each other's guest.

"In the custody of the United States Marines," Fritz greeted David. "What has he done, general?"

"Developed an appetite," Joe beamed.

Dinner was on the way. But first, gentlemen, observe the woman in the confectionery area—the big one peering at the rows of sweets through her pince-nez. "Such a difficult decision," Fritz whispered. "Will it be the bonbons or the marzipans or the Berlinkranzers? It may be closing time before she'll decide that tonight a marzipan will be just right for Bubelah."

Bubelah?

"Her two-hundred-and-fifty-pound, thirty-five-year-old son."

David and Joe feasted on Sauerbraten and dumplings, red cabbage with caraway seeds, and slivered cucumbers with dill. Their palates were refreshed with goblet after goblet of Berliner Weisse, a Café Louis specialty made of raspberry syrup and beer fermented in the bottle.

"The Far East's a powderkeg, David," Joe contended. "Japan has been empire-building for years: Formosa; the southern half of Sakhalin; the islands of Hainan, east of Hanoi, and Spratly, near Singapore, which are miles from Tokyo; not to mention taking over Korea. F.D.R. is doing the best he can, slapping embargoes on scrap iron and steel, junking trade agreements, shutting off their oil, lobbying to get 'em booted out of Indochina—all the while pouring Fort Knox into Chiang's pockets. Tojo's one tough customer, not some little buck-toothed, grinning, slow-brained strutter with horn-rimmed glasses and a silly grin on an inscrutable face. It's anyone's guess what he'll try to pull next. G-2 tells us that their military is itchy-itchy, but then Yamamoto makes a big speech saying that taking on Honorable Uncle Sam would be national hari-kari. I've argued that that could be a clever feint to throw us off-guard."

"They wouldn't *dare* start something with you," his incredulous companion blurted.

"Don't be so sure, David. There could be an 'incident' in the Philippines—remember, it was an 'incident' at the Marco Polo Bridge that ignited their invasion of China, just as there was that fabricated flare-up in the Polish Corridor, German soldiers masquerading as Poles. The Fourth Marines have been in Shanghai since the Boxers, but we've got bigger fish to fry now. Our shipping orders read 'Manila.' "

Shipping orders? Joe was leaving? Minutes ago, David had been rejoicing in this serendipitous comradeship. A few pleasant hours together could not forge a firm bond, but the promise of a developing friendship had grown in his mind. Joe was someone he could respect, he could emulate, he could grow to love. In time, he might even have learned from him how to be Jewish without apologies or apprehension. Again, the stab of loss, of denied fulfillment. Was it indeed true, as the Chinese proverb prophesied, that every meeting was the beginning of a parting?

David felt himself slipping into one of his heavy, dark, Wertherian moods, and it must have been apparent enough for Joe to ask, "Why so triste, my friend?"

" 'There is hope,' " David said softly, " 'but not for us.' "

"Kafka? What the hell brought on Kafka?"

David could not tell him that he had just had a frightening intimation that one of them would soon be dead.

"Come, boychick. 'Let us go then, you and I, when the evening is spread out against the sky, like a patient etherised upon a table.' Come, let us have the quintessential Shanghai experience." Joe inhaled dreamily and closed his eyes. "The Great Smoke."

A rickshaw deposited them at the low doorway of a produce shop in a moon-beamed lane in Chapei, and they stooped to pass through. By the light of an orange lantern swinging eerily in the windless air David made out a room strewn with heaps of soybeans, rice, smoked meat, fish, and tobacco. They walked through the store and into a backroom. Nine or ten people dozing there took no notice of the strangers. With red paper arrows pointing the way, David and Joe passed through a small courtyard that reeked of decaying garbage. At the far end was a doorway with a torn dragon-shaped pennant flapping above it. They entered a storeroom filled with tubs of turnips, cabbages, bean curd, and dried fish stinking as horrendously as the garbage in the courtyard. At the back of the storeroom was a wardrobe. Joe opened it and confronted a ladder. He began to climb, and David followed so close behind him that his hands grazed Joe's legs.

In the darkness they climbed perhaps fifteen squeaking

rungs. Joe bumped into something and swore, then pushed an opening through a pair of tattered parchment screens. A different kind of odor, not of rotting vegetables or fish or human waste, assaulted them. David was nauseous. Childlike, he reached for Joe, who gave his trembling hands a reassuring squeeze and drew him beyond the screens and into the gauze of a smoky interior. David's heart pounded wildly with a nameless terror.

A coolie's life was not worth living, it was said, without the smoke that brought dreams, and so there were thousands of these illegal dream parlors throughout Shanghai. Periodic campaigns by university students and society women to shut them down were no match for the "smoke lords," who justified their profiteering on human misery by claiming that it was inhuman to deny the wretched their only consolation in life. But where was the "humanity" in the spectacle of a coolie starving his body to buy fumes that would bring an hour of sunlight before he dropped to the road in front of his rickshaw—to lie there attracting flies until the Blue Cross Benevolent Society carted his carcass to the furnace?

In the vaporous void David discerned wooden platforms rising in tiers to a peaked roof. The platforms were covered with straw mats; on some, three bodies stretched out side by side, ragged, somnolent, disconnected. Only a cough, a moan, a sob punctuated the spooky silence. In one corner, two naked urchins were stirring a kettle on a flame over an oil lamp. From boiling fluid drifted swirls of steam.

David and Joe were led to a top tier by an old man in a grimy nightshirt and paper slippers. His skin looked like untanned leather and his eyes were as vacant as a blind man's. Joe slid onto the matting as though it were a canopied fourposter in the Cathay. David lay down reluctantly beside him, thinking "Lice—Typhus." His hands were ice cold. The two young men placed their heads on "pillows" of concave square wooden blocks—decapitation blocks? An oppressive heat mingled with the smoky whorls. David was still quaking. "Relax," Joe whispered, holding him in a powerful embrace.

The ghostly host padded back to them with paraphernalia. He handed each of them a bamboo pipe with a long stem and a tiny bowl and pantomimed how they were to use the pipes. He placed between them a saucer of the substance that had been boiling in the cauldron. The mixture had cooled somewhat and had the consistency of molasses; it looked like an Indian-rubber ball that had melted.

Joe deftly dipped a silver skewer into the gluey mess and took up just enough to twist into a ball the size of a pea. With an air of casual elegance, he stuffed the ball into the bowl of his pipe and passed the skewer to David. With a shaking hand, David managed to get some of the mixture into the bowl of his pipe. The old man gave them foot-long wooden matches and palm-leaf fans, and shuffled off.

They lit their pipes and fanned the small flames.

"Inhale deep," Joe said. "Take it down your throat and into your lungs. Breathe in hard."

Inhaling did not come naturally to David. He had never even tried to smoke a cigarette. ("Promise me you'll never smoke," Papa had said, "and I'll never ask anything more of you. Cigarettes are an insult to your body and brain, and disgusting to those around you.") David tried to do what Joe was doing, but he was so frightened, so rigid. He could feel he was holding on, holding back.

Finally, a taste started in David's mouth. It was an unpleasant taste, like sweetened kerosene. Nothing was yet coming into his nostrils. He heard Joe rhythmically sucking on his pipe, then exhaling. Sucking, exhaling. Sucking, exhaling. He heard Joe begin to dream.

"To get them down," Joe dreamed. "All of them down. The exact shadings. The hues. The haunting hues of Shanghai. A canvas of the haunting hues of Shanghai. The vermillion of sunset. The pomegranate sun of an autumn afternoon. The silver of electric signs flashing against cobalt heavens. The scarlet lips and aquamarine eyes of ladies of the evening. The cerulian blue of the harbor under a starry blanket. The winds from the east, wafting scents of Saigon cinnamon and cloves and ginger and frankincense. . . . "

David giggled at the narcotic fantasy. The true colors of Shanghai were piss yellows and dull grays, slimy greens and shit browns. The honest smell was of excrement.

David sucked fiercely, desperately. And then it began. It began to happen. His eyeballs were spinning like Ferris wheels. His skin was burning. His heart was pounding. His insides were in convulsion, threatening to erupt. In an instant he would explode. His end was near.

David came to on a cot in the Marines barracks near the Race Course. Vaguely, he remembered vomiting into the piles of decomposing fish and that his whole frame was racked by coughing. He remembered crying because he wanted to go on and on vomiting and there was nothing more to throw up.

Joe was testing David's brow for fever and showering him with apologies. "The first time can be rough," he acknowledged.

David knew there would be no second time. Last night was his hello and good-by to opium.

Woozy and unfocused, David was still angry with himself for submitting to an experience that he had been instinctively avoiding, when a note arrived for him at the *Tribune*. "Listen," Joe Gordon wrote, "here's something to consider if you're not browned off with me. My family is giving me a farewell dinner on Sunday, and I'm authorized to bring a nice, clean, deserving landsman."

This was the first time David had been invited to anyone's home since he arrived in Shanghai, and Joe was explaining, "Uncle Aaron is not really my uncle. Aunt Marilyn is my mother's first cousin. Mother didn't think too much of Aunt Marilyn's catch. But Uncle Aaron, as they say, made something of himself. He's in the movie biz. Warner Brothers. Out here he's big latkes. They live in the Broadway Mansions, that should tell you."

Broadway Mansions was a sixteen-floor red-brick building that the fourth estate called the ultimate in luxury and the Shanghai of tomorrow. Its thick glass entrance, framed in bronze, was decorously guarded by burly American Negroes fastidiously groomed in top hats, white ties, and tails. The lobby sparkled with chrome and gilt-edged mirrors and a crystal chandelier as large as the iceberg that sank the *Titanic*. In the flower shop off the street, a trick cascade of water streamed *up* the plate-glass windows, keeping the air moist for the orchids. To go to gaming tables, residents of the Broadway Mansions really in the chips had only to cross the street to the flamboyant Tango Club, which flourished night and day.

Except in the movies, David had never laid eyes on anything like the thirteenth-floor flat of the Balabans. He beheld a moonscape of blinding whiteness. Everything was alabaster white—the long divans, the easy chairs, the ottomans, the tables, the deep shaggy carpeting, the grand pianos—even the telephones and the table-model radios in every room. High-ceilinged rooms spilled into other high-ceilinged rooms, up a step or two here, down a few steps there.

Aaron Balaban was as broad as he was tall, which was no more than five feet three. He had two chins—and the beginning of a third—and they bounced when he laughed (rarely) or was in violent disagreement (often). He had sharp black eyes and oily, reddish kinky hair. Tiny ears pressed close to his head. He directed a mesmerizing scene, dominating the conversation and making sure that it never strayed far from his monomaniacal interest—the movies. Movies in the works. Movies that were dogs. Movies that had gone through the roof. Movie people.

"Errol up to the usual, Herb?" he smirked.

"They say he's tapering off, A.B. Down to one starlet and one fifth a day."

"And Little Miss Marker?"

"Says she's had it up to here with those goodie-goodie two-shoe bits. Wants to do a stag. 'If it's good enough for Crawford . . . ' "

Herbert Simon, vice president of world-wide exploitation for Warner Brothers, was calling at Shanghai for the first time. He was tall, taller than Joe or even Gary Cooper, and handsome enough to be acting in movies. He had a square earnest jaw, a cleft in his chin, laughing blue eyes, a deep sun tan, and thick wavy black hair.

"Too bad the Clipper didn't get you here in time for *Moon Over Miami*," Marilyn Balaban said. "They turned the Majestic into Florida and everybody but everybody was there. They even got out the Marine Band to play."

"It stank to high heaven," Aaron Balaban snorted. "Is there anyone sappier than that Robert Cummings? The business gives Garbo, Crawford, and Brooks a hard time and lets that idiot make anything he wants."

"Oh, Aaron, just because it isn't a Warner picture."

Marilyn Balaban had been a Warner starlet and was almost beautiful. With her olive skin, dark flashing eyes, high and sharp cheekbones, and black hair parted in the middle and pulled back into a bun, she looked Mediterranean. She was slender, almost a head taller than her husband, and at least fifteen years younger.

"The new year ought to be socko, A.B.," Herb Simon boomed, "between *Yankee Doodle Dandy* and *Now Voyager* alone."

"Why are you being shipped out, Joe?"

At last she was speaking. The beautiful girl. David hardly looked at her for fear that he would stare and never take his eyes from her. He had seen thousands of beautiful girls in Shanghai but none so breathtaking as this goddess down the table from him. She had eyes the exciting green of jade. Her long burnished copper hair was curled up at the ends. Her fine and firm eyebrows were of the same rich copper color and winged. She had a small straight nose, a tiny mouth, and lips as delicate as the stroke of a calligrapher's brush. Her neck was long and sculptured. She was wearing a simple sleeveless frock the same shade of green as her eyes, those captivating eyes that missed nothing and ignited with mischievous, mocking laughter.

Joe, who had been coasting along with the conversation, said, "I don't know exactly, Rosalie. The Japs are getting antsy, and I guess Washington wants us to have our dukes up."

"Those runts better not start anything with us," Aaron Balaban snapped.

"I wouldn't underestimate them, Uncle Aaron. They are more formidable than . . . "

"Crap!"

"Jack Warner was in New York for a U.J.A. board meeting last month," Herb Simon put in. "He says the East Coast has a bad case of war jitters. We just can't keep turning the other cheek when those U-boats sink the *Kearney* one week and the

Reuben James the next. Back there, they feel that we're already at war with Germany."

"I keep thinking of those people who never made it out of the Old Country," Beatrice Dubinsky said. "Did they make the same mistake my family almost made? I remember how we argued about the samovar—worth its weight in gold or diamonds—and the heirlooms and whether . . . "

"We've heard it a thousand times, Bea," Aaron Balaban cut in. "The point is, you got your tuchis out of there."

Mrs. Dubinsky, Marilyn Balaban's mother, was also visiting, and would be going back to Los Angeles that week. She was out of the pogroms of Galicia ("where Freud's mother was from too, David"). Before being chopped off by her son-in-law, she had recounted the tale of fleeing to America as an eight-year-old girl with the family jewelry sewed into the hem of her innermost petticoat, which she never took off during her grueling odyssey. She was a chunky woman in her late sixties, with a towering pyramid of honey-colored hair. She spoke slowly and breathed laboriously, making a long story longer.

"Now it's too late for the Jews to get out of Europe, Aaron," Rosalie said. "They're trapped."

"This fellow's here, isn't he?" Aaron Balaban pointed to David.

"I was very fortunate, sir," David said, and almost amended it with "*am* very fortunate."

He was fortunate, above all, to be alive and in the presence of Rosalie Balaban. She couldn't be a typical American girl—or typical anything. She called her father by his first name and talked back to him. ("That's a crock, Aaron.") She shimmered and radiated in center stage. She caught him staring at her and stuck out her tongue at him impishly, sending him back to the contemplation of his plate—a plate filled with food foreign to him: smothered chicken with a thick cream gravy, mashed rutabagas, cranberry sauce, and watermelon pickles.

A collage of white and jade-green and burnished copper danced in his head. The colors metamorphosed and he was sitting on a white silk-cushioned window seat beside the enchantress. A hand soft as silk itself had led him there. He had some dim perception of the other men disappearing into the library for brandy and cigars. Like the silent corps of Chinese servants who had passed food and drink and cleared away plates and glasses, Marilyn Balaban and her mother had disappeared as well.

"We have Joe in common anyway," Rosalie was saying. "I absolutely adore him. He was so funny about you. He said that when he first saw you, he felt some 'ancient, atavistic stirring of blood brotherhood.' But he decided that was rubbish. He picked you up because you were a 'sweet, sensitive guy' and 'very intelligent.' Are you?"

"I don't know," David blushed. "I try not to think too much about myself."

"Baloney! Everyone thinks about himself all the time."

"Just now I was thinking about you. I mean, you're all so different."

"We're not all that different, believe me. Aaron was transferred here when I was nine years old. I am nineteen now, which means I have lived in Shanghai one year longer than I lived in Los Angeles, but I still think of the States as 'home' and I hope to go back there some day. I happen to think it is kind of depressing to live in a place where you have a few haves and several million have-nots. I love the Chinese and despise the Japanese. You've seen my parents—they're what they are. I go to St. John's. Okay, had enough?"

Enough? How could he have enough of *her*? And so he asked, "What are you studying?"

"I'm majoring in anthropology."

"Anthropology?"

"Why not? If it's good enough for Margaret Mead." Rosalie gave David a sly smile. "I'd love to do just what she does— maybe go to the Tobriand Islands and study the sex customs of the natives."

David nodded soberly. The mention of "sex" was titillating. Her hand, magnetic to the touch, was drawing him across the parlor to the grand piano. She plunked him down beside her on the bench, her thighs grazing his.

"I'm surprised to see black keys," David smiled, "in an all-white flat."

"You're a sharp one, David," she smiled. "Hey, do you know *Elmer's Tune*? It's number one on the Hit Parade in the States." She flipped open the sheet music and, accompanying herself, sang, " 'The hurdy-gurdy, the birdy, the cop on the beat . . . ' "

She sang with a lilt and a bouncing gusto. Did he like it?

He would have liked it if it had been—God forbid—the entire score of *Die lustigen Weiber von Windsor.*

"Listen to this, it's absolutely delicious." And she launched into another merry tune, singing out refrain after refrain that everybody and everything under the moon up above was "doing it." At one of the more suggestive lyrics—"Even little cuckoos in their clocks do it"—she nudged him gently in the ribs. His whole body tingled. He felt the familiar swelling, the embarrassing localization of his pleasure. Quickly, he lay a page of sheet music on his lap and studied and studied the chordings.

"Gotta fly," Rosalie said, bouncing up. "Playing acey-deucy with the girls. See you." She gave him a swift peck on the cheek, matter of factly wondered aloud "What *is* the use of moth balls?" and was gone.

That night, David dreamed about Rosalie Balaban ("Oh, Rosalie, rare, Rosalie, divine . . . ") orgasmically.

Rebecca buried her husband in the new Jewish cemetery on Columbia Road. A stranger and afraid in a world not of her making, she tasted the vile phlegm of bitterness. She had been abandoned to fend for herself and their child. Meyer was dead, they lived. Must she add to her woes the burden of guilt?

"Do you forgive me?" she had asked him. In a fair world— had there ever been such a thing?—should he have not beseeched *her* forgiveness? It was his obdurateness, his blind trust in Iron Crosses and war records and other dishonored emblems of franchisement that had left them with no choice but this sanctuary in the Orient that he had found so disagreeable. And now Meyer was gone, to be mourned, to be regretted—and yes, to be forgiven.

When the numbness wore off, Rebecca saw that she was not totally bereft. With such a daughter, who had dealt with grief frontally and sprung back, she could not declare herself emotionally bankrupt or superfluous. Still, she could not live just for and in Esther—Esther had no such need of her. What next? She had the dulling perception of time suspended, of dark passages with no exits.

Now that she was free of the oppressive demands that Meyer's illness had made on her, she should make more of an effort to be a social being. Where to start? She regretted having lost touch with the two people she had become attached to on the *Hannover*. It was stupid of her not to have asked David Buchbinder for the names and the addresses of his uncle and his uncle's restaurant. She had placed two advertising notices in the *North-China Daily News* inviting Alma Winkler to be in touch with her. There had been no response, and Rebecca worried that Mrs. Winkler might be one of the majority of refugees who was faring badly.

The association with Teng had grown into tender comradeship. He was keenly sensitive to her circumstances and in a politely teasing way tried to be helpful. Did she know that the ladies of the International Art Theatre were scheduling a debate at the American Club on birth control for China and that the I.A.T. wanted more European women to join? . . . If she just had a little yen for gambling, she could go to the Columbia Club and put a small sum on one of the Mongol ponies . . . Teng could just *see* her in a long chiffon dress and wide brim hat at one of those garden parties on Hungjao Road having her picture taken for the social columns . . . Had she seen a Monkey play? Might she be interested in lessons in kite-flying? Lantern-making? Calligraphy—she need not learn all one hundred thousand ideograms?

Teng, beneath the bantering suggestions, was telling her that she needed more of a personal life than books and Gramophone records and the care of a child. The thought chilled her that one day soon she might have to tell him she could no longer afford his employ. Business was sliding badly. The Japanese presence was becoming more dominant by the day, but the Japanese were no boon to business—they had their own machines and their own mechanics. Besides, new parts and ribbons were now hard to come by.

Teng intercepted one of her troubled glances and said, "Reduce my wages. You can compensate me when conditions return to normal."

Sweet Teng. It was doubly dear of him. In his revolutionary heart he had no wish or conviction that conditions would ever return to "normal."

David had often thought he was becoming neurotic, obsessional, so much was s-e-x on his mind. Shanghai's unbreathable stench had to be laced with aphrodisiacs. At every turn there was female beauty to sizzle the senses, and there were many turns. In fantasy, he passed his life in brothels. Only fear had restrained him from following seductive street walkers into their neon-lit houses of assignation. In fantasy, he had coupled with every last one of them, in the safety of a solitary embrace that left him drained and terribly frustrated. The new face, that special face, the face that now filled his dreaming, cast all others into ebbing shadows.

The day after dinner at the Balabans, he was told at the *Tribune* to spend mornings on the copy desk, leaving only afternoons for his scissors and the latest word on Clark Gable, Carole Lombard, conga lines, and victory gardens. As assistant copy editor, he was to check for inaccuracies in stories turned in by feature writers. It was a promotion of sorts, and it brought a modest raise.

Projecting a future rich in sexual abandonment, David summoned his resolve to make the painful separation from Uncle Moritz and Aunt Sophie. ("I don't see the sense of it," Uncle Moritz grumbled, "trading the home you have here for a dingy room under a staircase way out in Digwell Road.") The dingy room was in the house of an amiable English widow, and he had to share a water closet with the four other tenants. "Invite your friends to visit you," Mrs. Barnstable said. "But, please, no overnight guests."

All of Shanghai turned out in freezing rain to give the U.S. Fourth Marines a tumultuous send-off. A washtub band of Chinese orphan children banged out the Marines' Hymn and the Marines' own band blared out John Philip Sousa marches. Down the Nanking Road rolled a sea of white caps and long blue coats. In their wake wheeled Chinese bicyclists waving "Godspeed" banners. The leathernecks swung into the Bund and came to a snappy halt, one-two, in front of the Customs building. "You are taking with you much of the life and soul and heart of this great city," the mayor of Shanghai intoned. Military formality fell out and there was pandemonium.

In vain, David strained for a last glimpse of Joe Gordon. He was well beyond the outer fringe of a surging mass of hysterical sweethearts and girl friends from the amusement parlors, who were giddily showering their American lovers with kisses and tears. A whistle blew. In single file the Second Battalion marched onto the pontoon bridge and aboard tenders taking them to the *President Madison* and the *President Benjamin Harrison*, which were anchored near Japanese cruisers in the Whangpoo. (Two weeks from now, "much of the life and soul and heart of this great city" would be shattered by Japanese gunfire in the Philippines.)

Minutes after David was back at the *Tribune*, there she was, breathless from the sprint up the stairs. Her lovely face was glistening from the cold, late autumnal rain. She was enclosed in a canary-yellow slicker with a hood that covered her glorious hair. She was like an adorable China doll. He longed to wipe dry the raindrops one by one.

"I'm fagged," she panted. "Cut classes to see Joe off. I had to shove like a fullback to get near him, but it was worth it." She gasped for another breath. The extraordinary green eyes, having swept the antiquated trappings of the newsroom, fell on him forlornly. "Look, we're all in a blue funk over Joe. Even Aaron. Marilyn thinks it would be nice to go out tonight. And *I* think it would be nice if you would come, too. Please."

In a sheltered roof garden overlooking a hidden mews the dinner foursome picked at ducks' tongues with bamboo shoots, sharks' fins, fried fish swimming in an undecipherable brown sauce, and fowl stuffed with lotus kernels. Below, wiggly rain-smeared streets gleamed in the twinkling of red, blue, green, and white lights. Searchlights swept the river, soared into the sky, and fell back on the junks, the warships, and the distant shore of Pootong. The sounds of Shanghai, so shrill at street level, blended and drifted up in a muted hum.

Aaron Balaban set the restless pace and tone of the evening. He was subdued, distracted, bored. David found himself preferring the loud and arrogant man he had met the previous Sunday.

"Journalism, eh David?"

"Yes, sir. It's not really an apprenticeship, but I think . . . "

"You wanna starve? They pay peanuts. Newspaper guys are a dime a dozen."

Under the table David felt a sympathetic tap on a knee, and shivered.

"Oh, Aaron," Marilyn Balaban said, "where was I reading how much Walter Winchell makes a year?"

"I don't know, but whatever it is, it is too much. Talking about a sally in my alley. He never gives us a goddamn plug. And that Lotte Eisner of yours, David! Every time she reviews a Warner picture, the gross in Germany sinks another five hundred thou. Tell her to stick to Nazi pix."

"I don't know what I would do back in the States," Marilyn Balaban tactfully changed the subject. "Mother says the servant problem there is not to be *imagined.*"

David almost laughed. Shanghai had to be the only place left in the world where people could talk of "servant problems" as civilizations crumbled.

"Then let's not imagine it," Aaron Balaban said.

Rosalie flashed David a glorious grin.

"Come on," her father said, "let's blow."

On the wave of his whim they migrated to Seventh Heaven in the Wing On department store. A circus was unfolding. Jugglers and acrobats and fire-eaters and merlins and conjurers and illusionists and dancing girls and unicyclists moved frantically against a gaudy backdrop of paper flowers, lanterns, banners, and moving screens. In a second theater, actors were putting on what was obviously a lewd comedy to the squealing laughter of the Chinese patrons crowded together at the apron of the stage.

"Christ!" Aaron Balaban said, and it was on to the Club Soerabaja, where every heart would be "drunken with blissful happiness." They sipped Veuve Cliquot while watching willowy Chinese and Korean taxi-dance girls vibrating to the raucous thumping of a Filipino band on a floor of Technicolor-neoned lightning flashes. Aaron Balaban was soon bored. At the Blue Angel, young German men with slicked-back hair, cheeks hollowed with gray maquillage and eyes rimmed with kohl were dancing cheek to cheek. ("Holy Jesus! And the krauts think they're going to win the war?")

Aaron Balaban said that they would ride for a while. Joining his Siamese chauffeur in the front seat of the Bentley, he barked the route. David sat between Rosalie and her mother in back. Under the sable lap robe there was that thrilling touch of thigh again, and her cat's eyes glowed in the dark. They said almost nothing directly to each other all evening, but he had been aware of her every single second. Once he caught her staring at him, and she said simply, "Sorry."

"Foochow Road," Aaron Balaban called back through the blower.

As if David didn't know! (His first day in Shanghai—the lovely temptress offering herself to him free.) But he had never seen it at midnight. Music from the three-floor dance halls cascaded into the street and meshed contrapuntally in cacophony. Their skins greenish in the garish light, the prostitutes were more numerous, various, and brazen than by day. Some of them were mere children. Pimps hawked their wares: "Girls go 'round the world." "Glorious virgins from Fukien." "Boys! Boys! Boys! Juicy boys! Juicy little boys! Juicy big boys!"

The magnificent chariot of Aaron Balaban wheeled soundlessly out of the tawdry thoroughfare, headed west, and picked up speed. As it swung into Digwell Road, Rosalie's hand reached for David's under the robe and he squeezed it hotly. "Soon," she whispered. "You are something different."

David's head swam with champagne and the delirious intimation that he was falling in love.

You are something different.

Later, when he asked her what she had meant, Rosalie said, "You *are* something different. Something exotic. The low voice, the British English. Shy on the surface, but underneath . . . Krakatoa. I never thought of myself as Queen of the May, but Jesus, Joseph, and Mary, the wrestling matches I've had with guys I wanted no part of—most of them Joe's Marine buddies. They come on hubbahubba and think they are God's gift to womanhood. What girl can resist them? They want to hit the hay before even saying hello. They think it is owed them. All I was really saying is that I was getting the hots for you."

"Soon" could not be soon enough. She was never out of his thoughts. But he would let a week pass before contacting her, and then invite her to have dinner with him. Before the week was out, Rosalie phoned him at the newspaper office. She wanted to do his portrait. "I have to bring in something to Professor Belmont on Monday. Can you come here on Sunday and sit for me?"

"There must be someone else who . . . "

"No, there isn't. At least no one as gorgeous as you."

He flinched at "gorgeous." It was a sensitive area. References to his looks embarrassed him, and this went back to earliest childhood. "You have a beautiful little boy, Mrs. Buchbinder," people gushed to his mother. "When you grow up, David," they said, "you are going to break the hearts of all the ladies." They also said, "A young man with your looks should think about going on the stage." They meant to be complimentary, but it sounded to him more like praise for an adornment than for a human being. If one must be loved, the lady sonneteer wrote, let it be for naught but love's sake alone. He promised himself never to grow up to be one of those vain young men, comb and brush in hand, always staring into the looking glass.

But there he was, "sitting" for her—and sitting regally in a white velvet Louis Quinze chair in the library of the Balaban flat. He was posing. To be the object of such scrutiny! To have those lovely green jewels fixed on his face!

"Don't look at me, David. I want your head at the angle that I set it."

Rosalie sprang from her high white stool, and her hands were resetting the pose. She went back to her easel. Stroke, stroke, stroke, the stick of charcoal moved across the vellum. She contemplated her subject. Stroke, stroke, stroke. He heard a little girl's sigh of contentment and turned his head to catch her smile of self-approval.

"David! You've done it again. You've moved."

Yes, and deliberately. Just to feel those long caressing fingers on his face again, tilting his head just so.

"A little like Kafka, I think," she said. "Only much, much

handsomer. Your ears don't stick out like his. Men's ears can be so-o-o sexy. Especially the lobes. Your eyes are a cross between mauve and pumpernickel. When you sit perfectly still and don't fool around, you look saintly. Not one of those pinched, sex-starved early Christian martyrs. I mean *saintly*. Like wise and good and serene . . . "

David affected a coughing spell. Reaching for his handkerchief, he was again out of pose. "Saintly, hell, you've got the devil in you."

They kissed for two hours.

As with his earliest memories of Breslau, David was to remember that long afternoon in the Balaban library as belonging to an innocent time. The Innocent Sunday before Black Monday.

David went directly from the Balabans to the *Tribune*, where he was substituting on the night shift for a colleague on holiday. At a significant moment in history, he would tell Rosalie later, he was reading a feature on prognostications for the coming year by prominent Shanghailanders and was smirking at the contribution of a professor of political affairs at her university: Madame Chiang Kai-shek would move to the United States permanently, probably as early as early 1942. If true, David was wondering, who would wipe the Generalissimo's nose? When the shattering blast came. Then another. And another. The booming resonated like thunder. Thunder? In *December*? It couldn't be. From the third-floor windows he saw that the sky was clear and softly lit by the Milky Way.

"An oil tanker must have exploded," a copyboy speculated. "Funny business in the godowns again," someone else said, pointing to flames rising from the Whangpoo.

A few minutes later, an off-duty reporter in tuxedo was leaping up the stairs with news of what really had happened. A motor launch flying the flag of the Rising Sun had approached H.M.S. *Petrel* and demanded its immediate surrender. The *Petrel*, which "looked more like Beaverbrook's yacht than a gunboat," told the bastards where they damned well could get off. Damned if the Japs didn't go back to the cruiser *Itaki* and damned if the *Itaki* didn't unload. Four cannonballs ripped the *Petrel* apart and all those blokes went right to the bottom—the very same *Itaki* that sneaked up on Port Arthur forty years ago. But the Yanks on the *Houston*—they knew how to save their ass—they couldn't hoist the white flag fast enough.

A five-bell flash exploded on the Reuters ticker carrying the cataclysmic news:

JAPANESE BOMB PEARL HARBOR . . . U.S. PACIFIC FLEET SUNK . . . THOUSANDS PERISH.

Character by character, the details raced across the scroll of the Teletype: ". . . 8 U.S. Battleships . . . 9 Cruisers . . . Many Destroyers . . . Fighter Planes Bunched on Hickham Field . . . "

The *Tribune* staff stood in paralyzed silence over the clatter. When the gruesome details were exhausted, everyone babeled at once.

"Where the bloody hell's Pearl Harbor?"

"Invading Russia from the rear, yes, that would have made sense. But this—?"

"Stark, raving bonkers. Insanity."

"That's one way to get the Yanks in. Hallelujah."

"Collective suicide."

"Pipsqueaks bestriding Colossus."

The night editor said quietly, "Let's roll up our stockings, gentlemen. Kill everything: 'Japan Ambassador's Peace Plea in D.C.'—that's one for the archives. 'Manila Builds Up Air-Raid Shelters.' 'King Leopold Marries Commoner.' 'Reds Rout Nazis from Moscow.' Yes, even 'Royal Navy Sinks Nazi Raiders.' The whole front page. It's now WAR IN THE PACIFIC!"

The white man's Shanghai woke to find itself occupied. Before dawn, the inviolable sanctuaries of the International Settlement and French Concession had been seized without the firing of a shot. The Emperor's representatives were at every corner.

When the first bales of the "Emergency Edition" rocketed into the street for waiting trucks just after six o'clock, a patrolling soldier entered the *Tribune.* He clomped up the stairs, his bayonet soaring above him, and commanded the attention of the editorial crew and compositors. His sign language and fragmented English were explicit. No more newspapers. Nobody leave. Stay. Wait instructions. Behave. No trouble. He opened and slammed shut file drawers and doors, and, with a shrug, clomped back to the street.

Sit still, be patient, shuffle papers, keep your pecker up. Papa. Papa could have run away. Papa let himself be caught. The smashing of his presses was a clear warning that they were not done with him. Printers and printing presses are mortal enemies of despots. These despots will come back and accuse us of publishing lies.

Panic gave wings to David's feet. He flew down the stairs. There was no one on the ground floor. The door that gave onto the street was frosted, but he could make out a dark figure pacing in rhythmic cycles—the Japanese sentry.

The soldier took longer to patrol in one direction—to the Bund and return—than in the opposite direction to Doyers Street and back. David counted in the way that he had been taught to measure seconds: "A thousand one, a thousand two, a thousand three . . . " Fifty-six seconds for the soldier to patrol from the opaque window to the Bund, to about-face there, and march past the window again—ten seconds longer than his steps to Doyers and back.

As the soldier passed toward the Bund, at the beginning of the fourth cycle, David put a shaking hand on the brass knob of the door and began to turn it slowly. His thumping heart counted: "A thousand eleven, a thousand twelve, a thousand thirteen . . . " A thousand twenty would be his cue. Enough distance for him not to be heard, and with a few seconds to spare before the soldier would about-face and turn back.

". . . a thousand seventeen, a thousand eighteen, a thousand nineteen . . . " David sucked in an enormous breath and slipped into the street, leaving the door ajar. The tips of his toes sped into cobbled Doyers and then Petticoat Lane. A shot tore through the dawning day. David ducked into an alley thronged with merchants and mendicants. He was grateful for the mazes of Shanghai and that a frantic running figure attracted no notice.

The sky had become overcast and etched with streaks of red from flames dying in the harbor and Pootong. People were going to work as usual. The only discernible difference between this and other mornings was the prevalence of Japanese soldiers, who were marching in units of three and four, their rifles held parallel to their bodies. Behind the bayonets and the rifles were raw recruits thudding around in outsized rubber boots—operatic buffoons playing at being the Japanese Army.

David was in a fretful sleep when his landlady called him to the telephone. The awful confirmation was delivered by Mr. Ledbetter. The *Tribune* was shut down. "By Orders from Supreme Headquarters in Tokyo. Er—er—sorry, David."

Devastated, David wandered the streets aimlessly. It meant little to him that he was free to do so while the British, the Americans, the Dutch, and the others were now "enemy nationals" and restricted to quarters. He remarked the irony that as a stateless person he had more freedom and mobility than yesterday's most powerful Shanghailanders, but it was an empty irony.

From a garbled loudspeaker on a cruising military truck David learned that brave sons of Nippon had bombed Clark Field in the Philippines and the American islands of Guam and Wake. Was Joe safe? How were they, *she,* the Balabans? He telephoned. "Madness and mayhem," Rosalie reported. "There are dozens of soldiers out front. Aaron's apoplectic, Marilyn's wearing earplugs to muffle the screaming. I wish you were here, but don't try it yet."

At loose ends, puzzled at what to do next, David went to the Café Moritz. He half expected to see the restaurant closed or languishing. Business was flourishing.

"Well, well, well, stranger," Uncle Moritz greeted him, twinkling up at him and giving David's cheeks a pinch. "I was thinking about you. Too bad, too bad, terrible, terrible, terrible. But look on the bright side. The Americans will take on the Nazis, too. This whole thing will be over with before we know it. I'm sorry to hear about the *Tribune,* David, but we won't let you starve. Want to eat a little something now? Are you hungry?"

Someone was waving at David. To his surprise he saw it was Erika Zuckerman. But of course. She would find some way around the quarantine. She was more than waving at him, she was commanding him to join her party and directing Prince Litvinoff to draw up another chair.

"At seven o'clock they announced we could breathe and go forth," she explained, "and we breathed and went forth and here we are. Jesus bejemus, what a tsimiss. I'm still in shock."

"You don't look it," David observed.

"Well, you know, a girl has to try to pull herself together."

She introduced him to her friends, three American businessmen and their wives and her escort, a touring cellist from Chicago ("We go way back to the Second Punic Wars, don't we, Isaac?").

David was amazed that the conversation was so light-hearted—the universal crisis was all but buried under the froth of gossip and japing. He said to Erika, "Will you be able to carry on as before?"

"I should certainly think so." She gestured for a refill of the champagne glasses. "I'm going to take each day as it comes. If I've learned anything at all, it's that living well is the best revenge. Quote, unquote."

Erika. *Americans.* War breaks out, they dine out. Was this their variety of stiffupperlipness? Of keeping their pecker up? Or was it insensitivity or superficiality? Or some innocent conviction that all dangers were lickable? Mr. Ling, who had been a compositor at the *Tribune,* would have an opinion. He detested Americans with a passion. "Their wealth is an obscenity," he had once said to David, "but they are the poorest, the most unhappy of peoples. They worship money, speed, and power. But they do not know what the humblest coolie knows . . . that it is good to be alive and that man is but one of a billion things in the universe. The world is all of a whole. Heaven and earth. Yin and Yang. Men and women. Humankind and plants. Light and darkness. Life and death. It is meant for all of us to live in harmony with the whole. More than anyone else, Americans violate the harmony of the universe . . . "

But could Mr. Ling swear that these people here did not know it was good to be alive? How much laughter had Yin and Yang ever produced? How much music? Nevertheless, the high spirits of Erika's friends grated on David, and he mumbled something about having to meet a friend.

"I have something for you, David," Erika said to him as he left, "if you want to come by tomorrow afternoon."

She was as good as her word. "Look, the Chief Samurai is enthroned in Sassoon's penthouse upstairs. Some heinie sent him a summary of his tome. He can't read German and needs someone to read it to him. Like most of the brass, he knows some English. It's none of your beeswax how I know him, I know him. Don't put your nose out of joint. Just get up there and translate it for him and you'll get your money."

David found Commander Takayo sitting in a tooled black leather armchair studying with a magnifying glass a globe that sat on a cherrywood end table at his side. He was a slight, bald, bespectacled, scholarly-looking man of perhaps fifty years. He was in full parade dress, with ribbons, braids, and medals covering the breast of his mustard-green uniform. He pointed to a booklet on a black leather ottoman, bade David sit down, and spread out his arms for the translation to begin. He had not spoken a syllable.

It took David two hours to translate the digest of *Jewry and Science*. Sometimes the letters swam and his voice almost broke as he read. He had not been aware of this particular work of smut and slander. The author, Wilhelm Mueller, a professor of science at Technical College, in Aachen, accused Jews of sabotaging scientific inquiry. Einstein was the archvillain of the international conspiracy. If Jews were allowed to remain in the sciences, good Germans would be castrated and reduced to slaves and imbeciles.

Commander Takayo kept his eyes closed during most of the reading, listening intently, nodding frequently, and murmuring, "True, true." (True, true?) David turned the last page and said pointedly, "This book was published in 1936, sir, and is already dated, sir. There are no Jews in the sciences in Germany today, and Einstein is in America." He wanted to add that the exile of Jewish scientists had sealed Nazi Germany's doom. He stifled his rage until he saw Erika Zuckerman, then lashed out at her for sending him to "read Nazi slime to that . . . that . . . baboon."

"You got paid, didn't you?"

"Erika," he cried, "money isn't everything. There are a lot of things I wouldn't do for money."

"Stop being so self-righteous. In the first place, I didn't know what the hell he wanted read to him. In the second place, what can he do with bilge?"

David was not mollified. The thesis of the book per se was the issue—its pervasive slander. It was a poison that the Japanese, as partners in blood of the Nazis, could adopt and spread.

"Oh, David," Erika said, wrapping her arms around him. "It was a mistake, but let's not have harsh words. We're good friends. And please remember, you're not the only one who's sensitive to anti-Semitism."

He saw that she was genuinely sorry and he forgave her. Her day hadn't been pleasant, either. She had spent hours in a queue of enemy nationals registering with the gendarmerie in Hamilton House. The Japanese military had harangued them with messages from both sides of the mouth. The Japanese were imbued with "peaceful intentions," ah so, but let all Americans and Europeans be warned that there would be repercussions if any of them engaged in activities contrary to Japanese interests. The tanks patrolling Mohawk Road and the numerous platoons of Japanese soldiers billeted in the former barracks of the U.S. Marines on Ferry Road were a subduing influence. She loathed the idea of wearing an armband with an "A" for American on it. When they came to confiscate her wireless, she remonstrated so strenuously that they let her keep it, "with the admonition," she laughed, "that I don't listen to any lies and propaganda emanating in Chungking, Delhi, or San Francisco."

David went directly from the Cathay to the Broadway Mansions, and he was warmed by his reception there. Rosalie squealed, and kissed him long and hard. She held up her snowball French poodle, which also licked David's face long and hard.

"Look here," she said, pointing to the red, white, and blue ribbon tied in a double bow on the dog's left foreleg. "I've registered Vodka. He's an enemy alien, too."

"That's cute," David said, "and so dear." The anthropologist anthropomorphizing a dog!

"Hear that?" Rosalie asked him.

The world could have heard it. Aaron Balaban was bellowing into a telephone. ". . . the goddamnest crud ever put on the screen. The pitchas all take place in the *ninth* century and all you see are these runty cowboys playing with their swords in front of some tight-assed Madam Butterfly. And starting Monday they're going to have propaganda newsreels playing the whole Asia circuit. Not a laugh in a barrelful."

David approached Rosalie's father after the phone had been slammed into its cradle and said, "I'm sorry, Mr. Balaban."

"Yeah, yeah, kid. We sure got caught with our *gotkas* down."

"That's how wars start. Somebody always does something sneaky."

"That goddamn cripple in the White House must have been asleep at the switch. Goddamn it, look at us here, at the mercy of these little sons of bitches."

"At least, Aaron," Rosalie said, "they're going to let the movie houses open again."

"What good's that? No new product can get in here and all we have in the can are turds that won't draw flies."

"Daddy"—David recognized the salutation as the address of appeal—"isn't there something you can give David to do? He's out of a job for no fault . . . "

"There damn well isn't. They've got me up to my neck in horseshit already. Out with my people and in with theirs. 'Within seven days, most respected sir, it is required that you provide ten vacancies on your staff for which we shall supply replacements. Fill out these forms, please, honored gentleman.' If you wanna shrink to half your size, David, and throw some brown gunk on your face, I'll see what I can do."

"The least you can do, Aaron," Rosalie said, "is to take us out for dinner."

During jellied sturgeon and chicken Pojarksy at KavKav, David knew that he was indeed in love and that from the pressure of the hand that met his (oh, delirium) his love was reciprocated. But he resolved he would not see Rosalie until he was working again.

The Japanese seized the *President Benjamin Harrison* en route to Chinwanto to rescue U.S. Marines fleeing Peking and Tientsin, and they also seized every ship in the Whangpoo except the *Conte Verde, Pelikan,* and *Pluto.* In deepening thrusts into the Philippines, Indochina, and Malaya the "yellow bastards" were meeting little or no resistance. The white man was in retreat everywhere.

Shanghai, far from the fields of strife, nevertheless felt the strictures of war. Coolies queued for rice, water, and chips of coal. They queued for cans of gasoline. Automobiles and motorized taxis all but disappeared from the streets. There were further cuts in bus and tram service, and ferries were terminated. Without transportation, the night life fell into abject decline. Farren's—once the most popular nightclub but now unreachable way out on the Great Western Road—shut down. The dance halls, bordellos, and bars on Yu Huen Road which had been popular with the U.S. leathernecks fell on hard times. Tea dances at the Palace were suspended. Enemy nationals could not withdraw more than six hundred dollars from their bank accounts. Laundries and dry cleaners begged understanding for their deteriorating performances. Bakeries stopped making fancy cakes. Electricity was rationed. Crime was escalating, with robbery commonplace and reports of rapes and even axe-killings frequent.

Only the Russian places on Moscow Road—conveniently located in Frenchtown—were prospering. The Balalaika, the Renaissance, and DD's still pulsated with gypsies, sword swallowers, Georgian folk dancers, coloraturas throbbing through *Two Guitars* and *Nights in Moscow,* and impromptu wild performances of drunken patrons, many of them Sons of Heaven.

Dotty English gentleladies, in letters in the Japanese-controlled *Times,* gamely tried to spread cheer. Wasn't it nice of the Japanese to let the Shanghai Racing Club continue to run its events—a little wager gave life its tang. All Shanghailanders should rejoice over the surprise snowfall that was "whitewashing" the filth of the streets. Wasn't everyone feeling a mite perky to know that the poor little rich girl in America was going to find happiness at last by marrying that dear Mr. DiCicco?

Teng beamed when the tall, well-dressed European brought in his Blickensderfer, and he begged to be of service. The springs for the letter keys O and T were broken, and the carriage was sticking at the right-hand margin. Could the gentleman have the machine back tomorrow? He had much typewriting to do.

Rebecca recognized the ginger-bearded stranger as a countryman. However, she was not able to place the locality from his accent.

"You must speak with him when he returns," Teng said to her.

"Must I now?" Rebecca said mildly.

Hugo Raschenbaum was delighted to discover that they were compatriots. "Lübeck? Ah yes. A magnificent city."

"You've been there?"

"No, no. But people I know have been, and they said such fine things."

"And you? Where are you from?"

"Someplace not so grand as Lübeck, I am afraid. A little town, Ebingen. It's in the far southwest. The Swabian Jura. I am sure you have never heard of Ebingen."

"Wasn't Ebingen where Goethe fell in love with the mayor's daughter?"

"You are remarkable. Yes, the master did visit and pluck one of our flowers. It is extraordinary that you should know that."

"And I think it is extraordinary that you have much typewriting to do. It is my impression, Mr. Raschenbaum, that nobody has much business left to handle."

"It is my profession," he said, adding with a rueful shrug, "here."

"Nor was I always in repair and sales," she smiled.

"I could see that. Let me tell you that the most intelligent thing I ever did was to take night classes in typewriting. That was in Frankfurt, where I was a salesman. Here, who was looking for another salesman? I had to turn to something else. I advertised myself as a professional typewriter, and I had precisely one response. A professor at Aurora wanted a thesis done. It was a start. One night, I went to a restaurant that was very crowded. A woman who was alone invited me to share her table, and I soon learned that I was in the presence of fame. This lady was none other than Ernestine Hersch, who wrote that popular novel about Shanghai which was published a few years ago. She said everyone thought that she must have been living in Shanghai since its swamp days. Actually, she had moved here from Berlin only a year before she wrote the book. Now she is doing a biography of the Soong sisters. Before the meal was over, Miss Hersch asked me if I would like to do the typewriting of the manuscript, and I was most happy to accept. She is easy to work for, and most generous."

"If she tells the truth about the Soongs, can the book be published without inviting a visit from their tong?"

"Oh my. Miss Hersch is on chapter four. The Soong girls are sailing off to school in the American south."

"That's innocent enough, I guess. But they now happen to be three of the most influential women in the world. The Generalissimo's wife, I know, is Mayling, the Dragon Lady herself. But I get the other two mixed up. Is Chingling Sun Yat-sen's widow and Eling the banker's wife or is it the other way around?"

"I probably won't find out," he smiled, "until I get to chapter thirty-eight."

Hugo Raschenbaum struck Rebecca as chatty and a touch naive and more than a touch lonely, and she regretted expressing her cynicism about the Soongs. In good time, perhaps long before chapter thirty-eight, he would learn for himself. It was unlikely that the ladies could pull the wool over the eyes of the incomparable Ernestine Hersch.

He was also a pleasant and gentle man, a few years older than herself, and certainly solid and conventional enough to be a marrying man. But there wasn't a hint of a "we" or a Mrs. Raschenbaum in his conversation. Had he, too, suffered some terrible loss in the sea change that had brought them all to Shanghai?

It was a little disconcerting to look at him. The scar at the right side of his mouth twisted his lips into a frozen lopsided smile. He was pale and squinted a lot—perhaps he was myopic and should be wearing glasses. He was obviously fastidious—his beard was well trimmed and his thinning hair (that same ginger color flecked with gray) was neatly slicked from right to left across the crown of his head. Not handsome, but interesting looking. And so well turned-out.

She didn't think that she had in any way encouraged him, but she was hearing an encapsulation of his life. He was eight years old when he was permitted to bicycle all alone through the rutted streets of Ebingen to the marketsquare. It was one of those epochal experiences. He was bedazzled by the rows of shops selling everything anyone could ever want. Some day he, too, would work in the marketplace—but a marketplace far bigger than Ebingen's. As a young man, he went to Frankfurt and became associated with a manufacturer of women's gloves of the highest fashion. He traveled the Rhineland with the line: Cologne, Düsseldorf, Bonn, Koblenz, Karlsruhe, Wiesbaden, Mainz, Mannheim. "Believe me, Mrs. Wolf," he said, "I was received with courtesy by the managers of some of the finest shops in Germany."

"I believe you," she said. A refined and unassuming man should be able to gain entree to the best emporia. She imagined that her own father, who had also traveled with women's garments, had found the same easy welcome.

"A sledding accident," he said.

Rebecca blushed. She must have been staring at the crimson comma that pulled his lips into that askew smile.

"It's all right," he said. "I did not turn the sled fast enough and my face struck a sharp-edged rock."

Rebecca felt Mr. Raschenbaum would have been there until closing time if another customer had not come in demanding her attention. She also knew that he would be back. When he did return a few days later (she was grateful that Teng was not in the shop at the time), it was to ask if she had typewriter ribbons.

"Mr. Raschenbaum, I can't remember when I last saw a new typewriter ribbon."

He looked neither surprised nor disappointed. "I have been thinking of our remarkable conversation," he said, "and I have been thinking how much pleasure it would give me if you would be my dinner guest one evening soon."

"I do not know what to say," she hesitated.

"Say yes."

"Mr. Raschenbaum, may I ask you one thing?"

"Anything."

"Are you married?"

He smiled, the arc of scar stretching his mouth into a curious grin. "Yes. I *think* I am married."

"That's a little confusing."

"Yes, I am sure. Do you really want to hear any more about me?"

"I think I had better hear this."

"I married 'out'," he began, sighing softly. "Gerta and I had known each other for a long time. When I moved to Frankfurt, my flat was in the Sachsenhausen district, where she lived with her family. It was a small community, and it was not peculiar that I should make their acquaintance and be invited to their home. They were Protestants but not observant of religious practices. There was an attraction between Gerta and myself. Her parents liked me well enough, but they opposed the marriage. Bastardization of good blood and all that, I guess. But Gerta had a mind of her own. We married and her parents became reconciled to it and everything was fine for a while. Gerta stood by me even after everything in the country went sour. She swore that if I had to leave Germany, she would leave, too. Her parents regarded her decision as misplaced loyalty. Why should she have to turn her back on her family and her country and everything else that had been dear to her? Even as the wife of a Jew she could stay on in Frankfurt and not be mistreated. But Gerta was like Ruth: 'Whither thou goest, I will go; and where thou lodgest, I will lodge.' We arrived here three Julys ago. July, the worst month, you must agree, unless it is June or August. It did not take Gerta long to realize that she was not Ruth. Everything was so punishing, so difficult. She could not bear the heat. She could not bear the filth. She could not bear the people. She disliked all types of Orientals— even the Eurasians. To her, Shanghai was a nightmare. We had no children to consider and Gerta gave way to her strong feelings. 'I am sorry, Hugo,' she said, 'but if I stay, I will die.' She had her return ticket, of course, and she went back on the *Hako Zaki Maura*. I had a few letters from Frankfurt. She sounded cheerful but so very far away. And then she wrote, 'I wish you all good luck, Hugo, but I believe we should not continue corresponding. I hope you will understand.' One never stops wondering about someone one's been married to. But for long periods of time I don't think about Gerta at all."

In a back room, David sat at a bench with seven other men and fixed bands to Panama hats. For ten hours a day they twirled the bands into triple loops and pinned them to the white straw. One hour it was navy-blue bands, the next it was Robin Hood greens, then scarlets, then canary yellows, then Black Guard plaids. The men toiled mostly in sullen silence. David tried to reach them, especially the middle-aged Austrian refugee named Kassel, but they preferred to stay mute inside their shell of stupefying tedium.

H. Steinwig, Hatmaker, occupied a reinforced concrete building on the Avenue Pétain. Pedal-driven machines in a factory in Chapei dyed and wove the straw and assembled the hats and a truck carried the hats into the city. Three Chinese seamstresses, sisters who lived in a tenement near the factory, made the bands, and each morning an inordinately tall coolie arrived at the Avenue Pétain workshop with bundles of them lashed to his chest and back. The finished Panamas were stacked into crates for delivery to Sukihama Exporters. On the busiest days, as many as two hundred crates would be shipped to Bangkok.

Hermann Steinwig was a spare, wrinkled, wiry man, a dynamo in his seventies. He vibrated constantly on a circuit circumscribing the factory in Chapei, the office and workshop in the Avenue Pétain, and the shipper on the Bund. When he alit anywhere, he could not stand still. Hop, hop, hopping. Hum, hum, humming. Whistling. Chuckling over some private matter. Fussing and checking. Passing up and down the work table—a derby hat falling to his eyebrows—patting heads or shoulders and bestowing compliments.

"Excellent! Excellent!"

"The touch of an artist."

"A thing of beauty. As the poet said, a joy forever."

Trailing his affection and appreciation were his lamentations. "Such costs, such costs." He slapped in the direction of his brow, striking the front of his derby and making it flip into the air. "Costs seen and unseen. Everybody with the hand out. Slipee here, slipee there. Everybody on the squeeze. Squeeze, squeeze, squeeze. The cobras squeeze you to death. I can't breathe."

Mr. Steinwig had been an esteemed hatter in Mainz. He arrived in Shanghai with little more than the clothes on his person and a hat blocker. For piece payment he blocked fedoras and homburgs for haberdasheries. In Siam the Japanese conquerors had decreed that the country must become "civilized." A hallmark of civilization called for men, when in public, to wear a hat. The call from General Songgram went north to Shanghai: "Send us Panama hats." Mr. Steinwig convinced the Japanese exporter that he was a Panama-hat-maker par excellence.

"You're off to a splendid start," Mr. Steinwig told David, handing him his first pay envelope.

David glanced at the pittance and wished he were off to a splendid finish at H. Steinwig, Hatmaker to Siam (long on praise, low on pay). But at least he could now invite Rosalie to dinner. Fortuitously, his uncle invited him to a meal at the Café Moritz and to bring his American friend along.

Rosalie sailed past Prince Litvinoff and rushed to David's table. She kissed him generously on the mouth and gushed, "Oh, how I've missed you."

How he had missed her! She at least had her classes. He had had little to fill his head with but daydreams of her, and now he feasted his eyes on her. The cold winter evening had brought peach blossoms to her cheeks. Peach dust danced in her jade eyes. She threw a soft heathery coat carelessly against the back of her chair and placed both of her hands on top of his. She had swept back her hair and tied it in a bun. Rich amber flowed from her face. Her ears were like two delicate teardrops.

Uncle Moritz beamed on Rosalie as something fresh,

lovely, and choice, so many cuts above the crowd. "Order any-thing," he said, hovering over them like a mother hen. "Have what you want. Get a bottle of nice wine."

The Café Moritz, the war notwithstanding, still bustled. The clientele now was mostly Japanese military and Chinese people of dubious classification.

"I don't know how you do it," David said to his uncle. "This food is as superb as ever."

"A wise man has his ways, sonny boy," Moritz Felcher said, winking at Rosalie.

"There's a lot of Aaron in your uncle," Rosalie commented to David. "There must be a word for it. Just now I can't think of it."

"Embarrassing?"

They both giggled.

"How are you, really?" he asked tenderly.

"Not so great, since you ask."

"Yes?"

"Something's eating me, I don't know what."

"The same things that are eating everybody else?"

"Who knows? I used to love school, David. Now I open a book and the print turns to spaghetti. I can't concentrate."

"You should be grateful you have studies to distract you."

"Thank you, Dorothy Dix. And just don't ask me who Dorothy Dix is."

"I wasn't about to."

"To change the subject, my dear, somebody has been ogling you for the last half hour, you might like to know. An *older* woman. Back there at the corner table."

It was *she*.

He had never stopped thinking about her, and had never dreamed that Shanghai was so immense people sooner or later would not run into each other. He had thought of her and her ailing, withdrawn husband and saucy daughter. What had happened to them? Now there she was smiling at him, and she rose as David approached. They embraced.

"David, I have thought of you a thousand times."

"And I you. Hello."

"It's been nearly three years."

She looked older and tired. A few strands of gray had crept into her flaxen hair, but her smile was as warm as he had remembered it.

She answered the question that hung between them. "Meyer is dead, David."

"I am so sorry," David said, recalling the man he had wanted to cling to on the *Hannover* but who politely rebuffed him.

"It was for the best, I guess—if anything is ever for the best. David Buchbinder, this is Hugo Raschenbaum."

The man in the sharply pressed navy pinstripe suit and the robin's-egg-blue shirt with French cuffs rose and extended his hand to David. David waited, but Mrs. Wolf did not volunteer anything more about her companion, and so he said to her, "How's my little girl friend?"

"Too darn well, thank you. Growing like a weed. And getting sassier by the day. She speaks only English and pretends not to understand when I slip into German. Yesterday, she was cross with me and asked if a child had to have *no* parents to get into an orphanage."

David chuckled and said, "That's our Esther. How are you getting along, Mrs. Wolf?"

"Not very well. I have a typewriter business that started to slip even before the war began."

"This is my uncle's restaurant. I used to be a waiter here. But I have found my real calling—I now stick bands on Panama hats in a closet on the Avenue Pétain."

"Oh, David," she laughed. "I can see that we're both setting the world on fire. But our day will come. Please, now that we have found each other, let's not lose touch."

The Princess Alana was bathing in a jungle lagoon. Downstream a man-eating crocodile raised its long ugly head and swam silently toward her. A carnivorous mouth opened to sink a million teeth into her voluptuous nude body. To Alana's rescue, with barely a split second to spare, rode the elephant boy Carbu. He swung into the water, snatched the languorous maiden from the jaws of death, and flung her onto the embankment. Carbu turned his back and shielded his eyes with a lily pad as Alana slipped back into her sarong.

"Look at her, Carbu," Rosalie yelled at the screen. "You shtupenagel."

David laughed and stroked the back of her neck.

Carbu climbed back on his elephant and rode off into the sunset and the lights came up in the Majestic. A pair of hands clamped around David's neck and a voice buzzed, "The crocodile's got you."

"What in the—Natzie!"

David was absurdly happy to see the ear-to-ear grin and the freckled face with the twirling mustache and the thick waves of brilliantined hair. Remembering his reunion with Mrs. Wolf, he vowed in a trice that he would not lose Natzie again. When they had so little of anything else, what could be more important than friendship?

"Hey, hey, Davie. A girl friend. And a looker. Rosalie? Bee-oo-ti-ful name . . . "

Same old Natzie, picking up as if it were only five minutes since they had seen each other, plying him with questions but cutting off the answers, moving in and taking right over. In the café behind the movie house, Natzie unfolded, confident of the insatiable interest of his audience of two.

"I tell you, Davie, you're lucky to have caught up with me tonight. It's rare I take any time off. I'm working my butt to the bone. Listen to how things get started and one thing leads to something crazier. I was looking around for something to peddle that they didn't have here. I came up with peach nectar, but the real thing. All I could find in this whole damn city was some syrupy, ersatz horsepiss—cut my tongue out, Rosie— that came out of some chemistry lab, so that gave me the idea. I found a wooden press no bigger than a nutcracker—sorry again, Rosie. What I do is take my peaches and I press all the juice and a little of the pulp out of them and pour the stuff into rainbow-striped bottles and call it Sunbeams. I tell you I can't lay hands on enough peaches to keep up with the screaming for Sunbeams. Anyhow, that's how Stern Trading Corporation Unlimited got going. Then I noticed there wasn't anything like Düsseldorf mustard here, and you know there are certain things that don't taste right without Düsseldorf. So what I did was mix some dry mustard with water and sizzle it up with pepper and horseradish. Success number two! But that isn't all. The thing that really drives people out of their minds is my Deluxo. 'Better than butter' it says on the label, but just between us girls Deluxo is lard . . . "

"And you're bananas," Rosalie said.

"What can I say, a boy has to hustle."

Natzie looked eagerly from one to the other of his companions. He basked in their approval and fascination, and embroidered his own exploits.

"Natzie," David said, "you'll end up either owning Shanghai or going to jail or both."

"Davie, what am I dreaming about?" Natzie exclaimed. "Dump those hats and come work with me. There's more than enough to keep both of us busy. And move in with me. Save all that rent and tram money. Ja?"

"Yes," David said without a moment's hesitation. "There isn't enough room in my room for both me and sunlight anyway."

"An inspired idea," Rosalie chimed in. "I can't wait to see you up to your knuckles in *trayf*, David."

Stern Trading was a one-floor stucco building on Museum Road. There were two boxy rooms and a shallow cellar. The front room was the office and it had a telephone. A drape of gray shantung silk separated the office from the bedroom with its two cots and low chest of drawers which Natzie shared with David.

"You're not in my way," Natzie assured David. "I never bring girls here. I have to get up and get going too early in the day. Whenever I feel the urge, I just invite someone to the park and spread a blanket. Let me know anytime you want the place to yourself."

Still half asleep, David would hear Natzie sponging and dressing in the darkness. By the time that David was up and dressed himself, Natzie would be back from market and slipping chips of coal under pots in the airless "factory" downstairs. They cut the pig fat into thumb-size pieces and flipped them into the pots, then squirted in yellow dye to give a buttery color to the mess. They mixed, squeezed, bottled, and loaded the jars of Sunbeams, Duchy of Düsseldorf, and Deluxo onto the sidecar of a bicycle. David wheeled off to make deliveries in the extraterritorial enclaves while Natzie stayed behind to catch up with his "Mount Everest" of paperwork ("You even need a notarized authorization to pee in this town these days").

David wondered, but not aloud, if there would ever be any good news. (Discussion of the war irritated Natzie.) With each disheartening development, David despaired of a turnaround. The Japanese bicycle corps had surprised Singapore from the rear while the British long-range guns—frozen in place—were aimed impotently out to sea. The Japanese conquered Burma, the Road to Mandalay, Malaya, and the infinite natural resources of the south Near North. They overran Manila and forced the death march of U.S. forces north from Corregidor and Bataan. They captured the seven thousand islands of the Philippines. They inflicted blow after disastrous blow on the Allies west of Midway and north of the Coral Sea. They sank the U.S. aircraft carrier *Lexington* and crippled the flattop *Yorktown* and sank the British behemoths *Repulse* and *Prince of Wales*. They took Guadalcanal and forced the Aussies to abandon Darwin on the northern coast of Australia. In cold fury, David listened to the purring, insinuating voice of Tokyo Rose on the English-language radio station as she asked, night after night, "Where are the brave United States Marines hiding? Where are you, boys? Come out, come out, wherever you are."

Rosalie visited Stern Trading and promised herself, "Never again." Pinching her nostrils and pointing to the white globs of pigs' fat swirling in the kettle, she said, "P.U. Dis-gust-ing. And there are people who put that goop into their mouth? Ech!"

"Now listen here, college girl," Natzie chided her, "nobody likes a Fräulein Weisenheimer."

"Even the label stinks," she persisted.

"Who cares? The stuff sells itself."

Nevertheless, Rosalie took it upon herself to design a new label for the Deluxo jars. She sketched placid livestock lounging and munching in fields waving with golden grain. Natzie was delighted, and had a printer run off huge quantities. He bought orchids and a gargantuan heart-shaped box of John's' chocolates and said to David, "For the artist, and tell her they're from you."

David was bemused by what he observed on his delivery rounds. He could not understand the complacency of the enemy nationals—the Americans, the British, and the others. They grumbled about privations and inconveniences but were not apprehensive. The Japanese would not dare start anything with *them*, the privileged whites. They were in nobody's way and somehow still managing to maintain their independence and feed themselves.

But then what he had seen as inevitable, but had tactfully refrained from predicting to others, came to pass. The British and the Americans were going to be incarcerated. Quietly, almost apologetically, the Japanese military headquarters was announcing that in time of war "regrettable but necessary measures" must be taken. Lists of enemy nationals would be posted, and those people listed must be ready in seven days for internment. Any resistance or pleas for exemption could only result in mutual embarrassment.

"May I call Mr. Raschenbaum 'Uncle Hugo,' Mommy?"

"You may not."

"Why not?"

"Because he is not your uncle. You have a real uncle. Your Uncle Samuel."

"But Uncle Samuel is far, far away, Mommy. It's not like having an uncle."

Esther was testing her again. She was a wise and sly one. Those dancing black eyes had a glint of mockery, challenge. Esther was prying for information, or at least for a sign. She had her sign now and Rebecca saw the shadow of disappointment crossing that sweet face.

Oh, my precious, if you only knew how you wound me when you say things like that. Yes, your Uncle Samuel is far, far away. But don't ever think it's not like having an uncle. But dear Samuel, how terribly far away it does seem, all the more so now that letters can no longer come through. I almost dare not to think of you, to let myself surrender to grim speculation.

Rebecca would not be pressed or hurried—certainly not by an eight-year-old child. Were she one to see conspiracies at every turn, she would suspect that there were those who were breathing as one, aligned in some pact to smoke her out. Subtly, each of them—Esther, Teng, Hugo—was propelling her in a direction that she was not ready to go. Each had his little stratagem. But she held back, telling herself one step at a time, even a half step. Act in haste, repent at leisure.

"You are happier," Teng noted. "It is good to have a dear friend to spend the evening with."

Hugo observed that they had much in common. Gentle and polite as he was, he was also shyly persistent and purposeful. He would ask a question, a question of such artless simplicity, who could deny him an answer? "You, too!" he'd then exclaim. "That is precisely the way I have always felt." An expression of hers, a gesture, the tilt of her head, the merriment of her laughter would put him in mind of someone else— invariably a breathtaking beauty of the stage or the cinema. He had a way of suggesting that they were two of a kind, marooned in a vast desert but somehow finding each other. She began to think him appealing, and that was her hint at the potential of more than friendship. Unless she kept alert, she could be swept away with the incessant tide.

Where were they going? What was going to happen to them? Much as she might wish things to stay just the way they were, life pushed one along. Nothing ever stood still. Human relationships, particularly between men and women, were never static. Friendship, undemanding, sustained on a comfortable plateau, was rarely attainable.

At times, she felt stirrings of cautious hopefulness. There was nothing in the air that called for optimism. But still . . . it was good at least to imagine the possibility of better times. That she was beginning to feel like a live, whole person again she had Hugo Raschenbaum more than anyone else to thank. What she might feel for him, as a woman for a man, could never be what she had felt for her husband in that pristine, unclouded springtime of their lives together. That she even gave Hugo that kind of thought, however passing, disturbed her. Hugo, she did not have to remind herself, was a married man. She did not remind *him*—that might suggest that she was speculating seriously on the future of their relationship—but again, uncannily, Hugo seemed to read her thoughts.

"If the mails were coming through," he said seemingly out of nowhere, "I am sure I would learn that Gerta has divorced me."

"If comfort means so much to her," Rebecca said, "she may be having second thoughts. With all the bombing and the rationing of everything in Germany, she must now be finding Frankfurt more unbearable than even Shanghai."

"It seems like only yesterday," Hugo mused, "that I was a young man so full of dreams and telling the years what they should do for me."

Rebecca heard him as really saying, "We are no longer young. What sense can there be to playing the waiting game?"

Nothing overtly stated, proposed. But there was that intimation of benign pressure edging her toward a precipice.

"Don't hurry me!" she yearned to cry out. "This is enough for now. Let there be a little more time—time for me to grow into the wisdom of what I should do. Let me dance to my own rhythm."

The Balabans were on the list.

The news crashed around David's ears like a funeral knell. His heart ached as he listened to the weeping, laughing, half-hysterical girl at the other end of the telephone.

" . . . no, no, I'm all right, I'm telling you . . . Aaron's wild. He's charging around like a bull in mating season. Keeps bellowing, 'Those slimy fools can't do that to us.' But they have, David. They have."

"Remind your father," David said gently, "they're only doing what the United States has done to the Japanese in California. And there's a big difference—those Japanese are American citizens."

"Aaron would hit the roof if I told him that. He'd say they're all sons of bitches wherever they live and ought to be rubbed out."

"How's your mother?"

"All a-twitter. Hands fluttering like Zasu Pitts."

Rosalie laughed and the laughter dissolved into more tears. Then she thought imprisonment would be a "grand adventure"—meeting all kinds of new people, drifting and letting the mind go blank, learning how to do without so many precious conveniences—and then she thought, *knew*, that it would be totally hideous.

David's distress was leavened with an absurd image, and he laughed in spite of himself.

"What's so funny?"

"Something I just thought of."

"What?"

"I was thinking with you gone I'll have to tell Natzie I can't discharge my duties in the pig-fat factory without the help and support of the woman I love."

"Very funny."

"How much time is there?"

"We're going early. The day after tomorrow. Aaron thinks that if we volunteer to go with the first batch, we'll get a jump on the best quarters."

"I have to see you," David said desperately.

"Tomorrow night. I'll come over. Why don't you tell Natzie to am-scray."

David trembled with the promise of bliss. There could be no misinterpreting her intention. It was inevitable. It was the terminus of the honeysuckle path that they had been strolling since the first day when she had tinkled the piano for him, thrilled him and excited him by a touch. (What *is* the use of moth balls?)

"Your parents?" he asked huskily.

"I'll think of something to tell them."

He prayed that if he slept he would not spend himself in anticipation.

The May evening was warm and scented with lilac and oleander. Rosalie paused a moment, framing herself in the doorway. She was wearing a light pleated navy-blue frock with a scooped neckline. She stood perfectly still. Was she only a mirage created out of his feverish longing?

"Hello."

"Hello."

"You're here."

"I'm here."

"Do they know?"

"Half of them knows. Marilyn."

"Yes?"

"There were no hysterics or histrionics. She said I was almost twenty and that I had always been headstrong and nothing she could say would stop me from doing what I was going to do anyway. And that was that."

David embraced her and kissed the top of her head, inhaling the fragrance of her clean shining hair.

"Hungry?"

"Ravenous."

"Likewise, I'm sure."

"Oh, we're eating Chinese."

From a street vendor, David had bought large portions of fried noodles with baby shrimp, shredded chicken, salty cakes stuffed with bean sprouts, and chopped greens. They sat thigh-to-thigh at the candle-lit card table that was otherwise Natzie's desk. They washed down the sharply seasoned, oily food with cup after cup of the potent rice wine that Rosalie had brought. Through the small window above them a breeze from the west flickered the candlelight and brought the lovely face into bewitching shadows.

"Is there a curfew?" he asked.

"Dawn."

Some curfew."

"My last night of freedom. Let's drink to that."

They clicked cups and he put a hand on top of hers. He stared into her eyes.

"Finish the wine, David," she said.

He threw it back in a gulp. His head floated and his heart pounded. He closed his eyes for a moment. He opened them and saw that she was undressing. The frock was coming up over her head. As he had been obsessively aware, there was nothing underneath. He had visualized them a thousand times, what they must be like, their precise contours, dimensions, texture, shadings. Beauty imagined paled beside beauty perceived. The twin, taut milky cones dipped in amethyst beckoned to him in exquisite invitation.

David sucked the milk of female perfection. He sucked, he gulped, drinking dry the lovely vessels of their inexpressible sweetness. He moved to her lips. Without breaking the kiss, he scooped her up and carried her across the bare concrete floor. He arranged her gently on the fresh bedding and tore off his clothes. Rosalie shuddered as David lay down beside her and whispered, "Don't be afraid."

"Look who's talking," she smiled, and ruffled his hair playfully.

Their union, their ecstatic joining, would come later. There was time to explore, time to discover the secrets and sweetnesses of their magnificent beings. There was no place that his fingers and tongue did not touch and probe. Heaving, afire with her own curiosity, she reached out to stroke him, and was no longer fearful. "Now," she implored.

They were like frenzied mountain climbers ascending peak after peak, each headier and more precipitous than the previous. He gently cupped a hand over her mouth to muffle her cries. She begged him: Faster. Deeper. Harder. Again. Again. They gave themselves riotously to the long, too short night of rapture.

The perversity of malignant fate! What purpose would their forced separation serve anyone! Throughout the history of man, billions of people had mated to perpetuate the species. But how many of the couplings had been so rare, so canonized? "When two souls that are destined to be together find each other, their streams of light flow together . . ."

Rosalie left in her wake a mooning manboy of twenty-two.

"I'm fine," she wrote to him after a week in the internment camp in Capei. "You *have* to know how much I love you, but please do not try to see me. It could be dangerous for all of us . . ."

Feeling disconsolate, David went to visit his uncle. He was pleased to discover that Erika Zuckerman was there. She was giving her "swan song" dinner party. She, too, was going into internment. "Sing no sad songs for me, David," she chirped. "They're letting me take my custom-built bed and my good hard mattress and my eiderdown quilts. I'm stocked up with Dundee marmalades and Colombian coffees and my favorite Major Grey Lapsang Souchong and my tins of Beluga caviar and Loch Lomond salmon and Bay of Fundy shortbreads. I can tell you one thing, I ain't volunteerin' for nothin' except kitchen and garden duty. When the chips are down, the first rule of survival is to stick close to the sources of sustenance."

"What about the refugees?" David asked her.

"Well you might ask. No funds are getting through from the States. The old Shanghai Jews are going to have to cough up or see other Jews starve."

These daughters of Sarah. How formidable they were! Rosalie "fine" in internment and Erika going there like the Queen of Sheba, high of heart and bearing luxuries. Mrs. Wolf widowed and alone in an alien place. Women! The strong sex, the sex of survivors.

For more than a month, David did not hear again from Rosalie. Mail from the camps had been shut off abruptly. He pined like a star-crossed lover. How lonely and empty life was. He was peevish and quarrelsome, and even managed to get Natzie's goat.

"What's eating you, Davie? Is it Rosie? If you itch, scratch. Go haul your ashes somewhere."

The prickly, soaking heat of summer became the prickly, soaking heat of autumn, and the news was as oppressive as the weather. Allied commandos were slaughtered when they tested Nazi defenses in the Atlantic fortress at Dieppe. In the East, the German army had captured Rostov and oil fields in the northern Caucasus. Hitler was vowing that Stalingrad would fall before the first snows. The Americans *were* back on Guadalcanal—but that was just one dot of land, with millions to go.

In his bleakness and hunger David eventually took Natzie's advice. He went to Foochow Road late one afternoon and spent a fast, furious ten minutes with a Japanese-Korean girl who called herself Scarlett O'Haya. A week later, he passed an inflamed night in a bordello on the Street of Happy Meetings.

"Come again," Lotus Delight said with a lewd grin. Satiated, David held himself in disgust and resolved to quit his whoring around.

Out of the mists of that stagnant season a buttermilk-skinned courier in white silk shirt and trousers stood opaquely before the door of Stern Trading and said, "Meesta Boo-binder? I Ah Chang. Meesta Ballyband Number One boy in office. Missie say wait he write I take back."

See?" David read. "Love will find a way. (See? There's no cliché like an old cliché.) Ah Chang found where they had stuffed us, and things already are looking up—a smidgen. Daddy's Old Faithful will smuggle things in and out for us.

"How the mighty have fallen. From twelve snow-white rooms in the Mansions to a bituminous nine-by-fifteen-foot cubicle for the three of us. The Fall of the House of Balaban. We are lodged in the ruins of a former seminary. So much for Aaron's hunch about the advantages of coming here early. We slept on rushmats over the concrete floor until our beds arrived. A bedsheet—'the walls of Jericho'—separated parents and scion (before I moved on; more about this anon).

"We are a cast of thousands—all extras. Mostly Americans and British, a few Dutch, Canadians, Indians, Eurasians. Doctors, lawyers, dentists, bankers, professors, salesmen, missionaries, importers, exporters, a movie magnate (one guess!), shopkeepers, teachers, journalists, adventurers, a professional tea taster, a tobacco expert, jazz musicians, Sinologists, customs officials, priests, nuns, monks insurance representatives, shipping executives, mining engineers, dope addicts, lighthouse keepers, soccer players, artists, stenographers, nightclub singers, travel agents, stranded tourists, a jai-alai team, and some very bratty children.

"Class distinctions are out the window. Everybody stokes fires or cleans toilets or cooks or tends garden or repairs things (*every*thing!) or collects garbage or works in the clinic or teaches school.

"I have been moved into a women's dormitory with nine Carmelite nuns! They line up like penguins to pray at dawn and at vespers. Everything is 'Sister Helena' this or 'Sister Evangeline' that or 'Sister Cecilia' when they speak to one another. We've also got an honest-to-goodness ex-whore in our dorm—your Mrs. Keyser would say that 'goodness has nothing to do with it'—she used to make 'house calls' at the Cathay, the Palace, and the Park. She says she cured more lower backaches, migraines, and depressions than all the acupuncturists and chiropractors in Shanghai laid end to end—which wouldn't surprise her in this town. Do I shock you, David? In the spirit of the place she refers to herself as 'Sister Sadie.' You should see the Carmelites go tight-bottomed when they hear that. 'What the hell,'' Sister Sadie laughs, 'we're all sisters under the skin.'

"Wish you were here. Or wish I were there. If a cow can jump over the mooooooon, why oh why can't I?"

David read and reread the letter, all but forgetting that Ah Chang was waiting to carry back word from him.

"You have made a brooding soul so happy," he wrote. "I think and think of one night in May and I swear to the truth of a homemade (mine) aphorism: Abstinence makes the heart grow fonder.

"*You* are something different. You are so brave to be wearing such a cheerful face.

"News from the outside: Money is so scarce that people are turning to barter. Natzie exchanged a carton of rusty tins of sardines for some Mason jars and he says that that carton will keep moving from one pair of hands to the next until someone hungry enough opens the tins and then there'll be a stink that will carry all the way to Chapei.

"The Japs have let the Nazis know who the masters are here. The German counsul in Tientsin came down and ordered the Nazis here to a meeting in the German School. The kempeitai spies heard about it and asked to see the permit, please, honorable gentlemen, for the meeting. There was no permit, so there would be no meeting, and the consul went back to Tientsin on the next train. Some allies!

"Uncle Moritz has discharged Prince Litvinoff. He suspected Litvinoff of being a Nazi spy and I said just because the Japs see a spy hiding under every table was no reason for him to. He laughed and said, 'Who needs that faker anyway with the crowd I've got coming in here now.'

"The Huns do it, the Sons do it, in internment camps even the nuns do it—let's do it!"

David would have been reluctant to admit to himself how keenly he awaited her letters. It seemed somehow less than manly to be hanging on the arrival of a courier. Her temperament was so much more sanguine than his. She was like some Frances Trollope or Jane Austen of the internment camp. Her sharp eye was always alighting on something amusing. Her days went from one to the next in cheerful monotony—work, sleep, a little reading, lots of observing.

He laughed at her imagery. Her father's face was "redder than the light in a harlot's window" when the gaffe was exposed. She explained: "We're committeed to the eyeballs—Housing Committee, Laundry Committee, Discipline Committee, School Committee, et cetera, ad nauseam. Daddy appointed himself chairman of the Co-ordinating Committee—thinking that was the top post in the camp—and told the chairmen of the other committees to meet with him in Kitchen #1 after 'dinner.' The commandant hit the stars. 'There is some mistake in the translation,' he said. 'We should have said Miscellaneous Committee, not Coordinating. So sorry.' That's how Aaron got to be in charge of the sewing section, the barber shop, and the canteen."

She, everyone, was learning Japanese, one word a week—the password, in case they were caught out-of-doors after curfew. The new password was "benjo," Japanese for toilet. The horn player with the colored jazz quartet from the States was keeping company with an English nurse. After having his pulse taken by the nurse in the pea patch one midnight, Smitty was tiptoing back to his dorm when he was stopped by a guard. Smitty couldn't remember the new password—only that it sounded like a musical instrument.

"Guitar?"

"Password!"

"Cello?"

"Password!"

"Mandolin?"

"PASSWORD!"

"Violin?"

Like a great a cappella choir, a thousand voices boomed into the night, "*BENJO*, you bloody fool."

David tried to be her eyes on "the real world," but so much of what he saw and heard was not likely in turn to induce smiles. The Japanese paraded captured U.S. Marines in open trucks through rainy streets, all the while threatening to strip them and make them walk naked along the Bund. ("Look," they seemed to be saying to the Chinese, "the yellow race is mightier than the white. When you come to your senses, you will welcome our partnership, and together we shall humiliate the white man, then kick him out of this continent. Asia for Asians, the way it was meant to be.") Jimmy Doolittle's bomber fliers who had surprised Tokyo and crashed into occupied China were captured and a few beheaded at the Bridge House. The Japanese military had appropriated the Shanghai Club and were proving that they could be as drunken and as obnoxious as the British red-faces. Two Americans (collaborators?) who called themselves "Mutt and Jeff" were performing satirical sketches over the German radio station, portraying Roosevelt and Churchill as bungling dunces. Everywhere you turned there was another swastika armband. A refugee doctor whose wife had died of cholera threw himself off Big Ching's clock tower and broke into a hundred pieces. A mob on the Bubbling Well Road wagered over which of the four hunger-maddened mongrels would be the first to chew off the arms of a dead baby. Cheery news upon cheery news.

David then had a slight but curious adventure, and something of narrative content to write to Rosalie.

On Sunday afternoons he would take a book to Jessfield Park and sit on a bench by the circular pond, reading and occasionally watching the graceful gliding swans. He became aware this day that someone had sat down on the same bench and was staring at him.

"After many a summer dies the swan," the stranger murmured.

"Pardon me?"

"Huxley. Aldous. His latest novel."

The stranger smiling at David was slim, handsome, and a few years his elder. His hair was as golden as an autumn sun and parted in the middle and slicked down. He had fair skin, eyes as blue as periwinkles, good cheekbones, a firm mouth, and a strong chin. David wondered idly what this superior young Teuton was doing here? Why was he not shooting down Spitfires over Dover or commanding a tank corps in the Heer?

"May I ask what you are reading?"

"Fame Is the Spur," David said.

"Ah, yes, Howard Spring. I know of Howard Spring. After *My Son, My Son* was published, people started to call me Oliver. Hardly a compliment. But they said no, they meant I just looked like Oliver."

David felt uneasy, not knowing what to say.

"Christian Boehm," the stranger introduced himself, switching to German. "From Berlin—the city of the Hollenzollern, by way of Heidelberg, the city of wayward students."

Breslau? A charming city. So much culture. Ideas, too. The city of the unionist Ferdinand Lassalle, correct?

David heard these pleasantries as patronizing. But they could be merely the overtures of someone trying to strike up a friendly conversation. He was discomfited, too, by the insinuating eyes that were boring through him.

"I think I can guess who you are," Christian Boehm said. "Not personally, please. I should guess you are one of those who are in Shanghai under duress."

David could more than guess who Christian Boehm was. He had seen myriad Christian Boehms, but he was not about to ask why this one was in Shanghai. "You are right to be wary," Christian Boehm went on. "I know—I think I know—some of what you must be feeling, but we are not all cut by the same die, you must know. I personally have always liked Jews. I am magnetically drawn to them. I feel an *affinity* with them. I am in good company—the great Thomas Mann calls himself a philo-Semite. I, too, am a philo-Semite. Perhaps it is something weak and wavering in me that I gravitate toward their strength and their—their intensity and their—their cosmic humor."

It was a little late in the day for professions of Jew love from *that* source, David thought. For whatever reason was Christian Boehm hoping to be taken for one of the "good" Germans? Maybe David was being overly sensitive. But didn't the situation itself demonstrate that loathsome Aryan arrogance and superiority—that right to demand and to command? Christian Boehm, in following one conversational gambit with another, was operating on the infuriating assumption that David would really rather be talking with him than reading his book.

"I think you would find me an amusing companion," Christian Boehm said. "I think we could have interesting dialogue. The light is failing and it is colder. If you are unengaged, I wish you would come to my flat and be my dinner guest. Wo Lang is preparing venison for tonight, and I always have a good Moselle chilling."

"I politely declined," David wrote to Rosalie. "Why the invitation? Loneliness? Curiosity? Guilt? Not the hope of friendship, certainly."

Rebecca was skating on thin ice. Imminent impoverishment and dalliance were her Scylla and Charybdis. The unequivocally forbidding poised against the forbidden. The forbidden what? Desire? Wolf Typewriters was dribbling to a dead halt. Hugo Raschenbaum pursued and persisted but never quite explicitly said, "It's not important whether or not I am technically married. If you feel only a fraction of what I feel, that is more than enough for my happiness. Will you live with me?"

The year turned without the promise of resolution, and her spirits lifted somewhat. Someday, sooner maybe than anyone could predict, the evils of this tormented world might be routed and one could dare to think of a new life. Churchill and Roosevelt had met in North Africa and agreed that Germany and Japan must surrender unconditionally. Hitler was not invincible. He had boasted that Stalingrad would be his by the first snowfall, but German armies were in retreat across a three-thousand-mile-long front. Leningrad might be starving, but it was holding on. In North Africa, Generals Montgomery and Eisenhower were tightening the vise on Rommel. Yes, the new year *was* beginning hopefully.

"You are smiling, Mommy," Esther observed.

"My darling child, isn't that something I do quite often?"

"No."

"Then you'll just have to remind me it's time for another smile."

February 18, 1943.

The Jewish refugees in Shanghai could not have escaped the directive had they been floating in a junk on the Yellow River. It was published on the front page of every newspaper, broadcast from every radio station, barked from loudspeakers, and nailed to trees, telephone poles, stanchions, and kiosks. It was everywhere, dinning their ears, assaulting their eyes, seeping into their pores.

PROCLAMATION

Concerning Restrictions of Residence and Business of Stateless Refugees:

(I) Due to military necessity, places of residence and business of stateless refugees in the Shanghai area shall hereafter be restricted to the undermentioned area in the International Settlement:

East of the line connecting Chaoufoong Road, Muirhead Road and Dent Road; West of Yangtzepoo Creek; North of the line connecting East Seward Road and Wayside Road; and South of the boundary of the International Settlement.

(II) The stateless refugees at present residing and/or carrying on business in the districts other than the above area shall remove their place of residence and/or business into the area designated above by May 18, 1943. Permission must be obtained from the Japanese authorities for the transfer, sale, purchase, or lease of the rooms, houses, shops, or any other establishments that are situated outside the designated area and are now being occupied or used by stateless refugees.

(III) Persons other than stateless refugees shall not remove into the area mentioned in Article I without permission of the Japanese authorities.

(IV) Persons who violate this Proclamation or obstruct its enforcement shall be liable to heavy penalties.

    s/ Commander in Chief of the Imperial Japanese Army in the Shanghai Area

    s/ Commander in Chief of the Imperial Japanese Navy in the Shanghai Area

Villainy hiding behind euphemisms! "Stateless refugees" meant Central European Jews who had arrived after 1937. "Designated area" meant ghetto. The Jewish refugees living peacefully in the International Settlement and French Concession would have to surrender their homes and employment and move into a ghetto—a ghetto within a slummy native quarter!

"Scheisse! Arschlöcher!" David raged.

"Let the shitheads proclaim all they want," Natzie scoffed, "there's always a way to get around things."

"Wake up, Natzie. This is Tokyo talking, not some local Pooh-Bah. These shitheads are our jailers."

Rebecca was speechless. Then incredulous. Then infuriated. Then strangely becalmed. Either the order would be rescinded or things would not be, *could not be,* as bad in the designated area as the more hysterical Cassandras were painting them to be. The business she must leave behind was now a business in name only. But to have to move out of her light, spacious flat!

Hugo was only mildly nonplussed, and it had irritated her. He reasoned with her sweetly. He pointed out that some "conciliatory, faintly imitative gesture" by the Japanese must have been required to placate their bloodthirsty ally. More welcome, somehow, was David's reaction. Paying an impromptu visit, he ranted and cursed and shook his fists and finally buried his head in her lap weeping. At the Café Moritz, Rebecca asked David's uncle if he thought the Japanese would go through with the directive, and he answered gravely, "Yes, I am afraid they will."

"Oh, Mr. Felcher," she sighed, "it can't mean this lovely restaurant, too."

"Five years," he said, tears welling in his eyes. "Five years, it's been my life. But they mean business. It's like back home all over again. I'll be lucky to walk out of here with the shirt on my back."

"I couldn't be sorrier."

"I never thought—here," he said brokenly. "And all of us will once again respond to authority like mindless robots—our German upbringing will be the death of us."

Rebecca had developed a vague aversion to Moritz Felcher. She was uncomfortable with the obsequiousness that he bestowed on those compatriots he regarded as his betters. But in this unguarded moment, when he was exposing his vulnerability, she saw him in a kinder light. Stripped of his glad-handing persona, he was seen as someone who had struggled against the stream more valiantly than most and who soon might be stripped of everything he had striven so hard to achieve.

The weeks passed without a whisper of revocation or relaxation of the Proclamation. Rebecca could not bring herself even to visit "the designated area," and Teng supported her in this. "It will be time enough," he said, "when you must go."

One evening in early April she went with Hugo to the Café Moritz for the last time. She had tried, against Hugo's insistence, to avoid the occasion.

"Hugo, it's expensive. We don't need that."

"I am still employed and receiving good wages."

"I think you should be hoarding every penny. The future doesn't look bright."

"I am placing my hopes on Miss Hersch. She says she will make every effort to see that I am exempted. I am sure that they will listen to such a prestigious person."

Here was another man who dreamed. There would be no exemption. If one refugee went into the ghetto, they all would go. She was sorry she had said anything that could lead the conversation toward intimacy. But she had, and Hugo went on and on about the prospect of exemption. Underlying his jubilant hopes was the innuendo, "Of course, the exemption would include you, Rebecca, and Esther, if you were living with me."

Characteristically, Moritz Felcher all but ignored Hugo.

"Mrs. Wolf, you are looking at the ex-owner of the Café Moritz. No, no, no sad faces, no tears."

"But here you are, Mr. Felcher."

"Until the tenth of May. The deal is set. Some deal! Grand larceny!" He gave a harsh little laugh and Rebecca clucked sympathetically.

"They say it's your friends you should watch out for, you always know the enemy. I have this 'friend'—a refugee like ourselves—and he made like he was handing me the Cathay Hotel by saying he had a buyer for the café. When I heard what the buyer was prepared to pay, I laughed and told my friend he was quite a joker. That's it, he said, getting hot-headed, take it or leave it. You won't get any better offer. If you don't take mine, you'll end up with nothing."

"Your friend carved out a fat fee for himself," Rebecca guessed.

"You said that, Mrs. Wolf. I'm not one to speak ill of a good man." Moritz Felcher winked slyly and went on. "I did about as well in disposing of my house. I traded my beautiful place on the Rue Robespierre for a shack in Hongkew plus enough coins for tram fare for Mrs. Felcher and me to get there."

"Mr. Felcher, you make it sound so—so final."

"It is final. And, Mrs. Wolf . . . "

He was interrupted by the sommelier and strode briskly toward the large closet off the rear dining room that served as the wine cellar. Rebecca said to Hugo, "I can't quite see this as the Café Fujiyama."

Rebecca observed Hugo's sudden moroseness. It had to come from something other than Mr. Felcher's curt notice of him. Perhaps it was Mr. Felcher's acceptance of a reality that Hugo at last perceived might include him, too—an intimation that there would be no exemption!

She was wondering what Moritz Felcher had been about to

say to her when Hugo abruptly paid the bill and steered her out of the café. Really, Hugo—an abrogation of good manners.

"He dislikes me," Hugo said. "I can't think why. Well, anyway, it isn't as if anybody's going back to the Café Moritz."

"Yes, seeing is believing, Hugo. By a conciliatory, faintly imitative gesture, as you put it, Mr. Felcher has to give up his restaurant—and we have to give up our freedom. It would seem that Hitler's arm must be ten thousand kilometers long."

1943

SHANGHAI

"What is a Jew?" David Buchbinder cried.

Hath not a Jew eyes? Hath not a Jew hands, organs, dimensions, senses, affections, passions? . . . If you prick us, do we not bleed? . . . if you poison us, do we not die?

Who are these children of Abraham and Sarah who are called the Chosen People? Chosen? Chosen for what?

It is our duty, our commandment, to live.

Duty to whom? Live for what? To endure agonies without end?

In suffering, strength and pride.

Where do the helpless find strength and pride?

Jews will haunt the conscience of the world forever.

Conscience? Slavery under Pharaohs . . . Babylonian captivity . . . Roman massacres . . . Inquisition and Expulsion . . . pogroms . . . the *Konzentrationslager* . . . and *this*. In five thousand years, when had the world shown a conscience?

Patience. Patience.

But where does patience leave off and mindless passivity begin?

Jewishness is that which must in times of dependence and weakness retreat into its shell, conserve its resources, endure in silence—and wait for better days. This Jewishness is hope and pain, Messianic dreams and other-worldliness.

Pain, yes; hope, no. Where is that other world?

God? Who is He?

Where is He?

Who has seen His compassion?

God asks that Jews believe in His kindness. Yet we see only His indifference and vengeance.

"I the Lord thy God am a jealous God."

Jealous and spiteful, demanding everything, giving nothing.

Who is this God Who breaks His covenant time and time

again and boasts, "I am omniscient and omnipotent. You must put no other gods before Me."

You, God, have abandoned Your foolishly adoring servitors, who were made in Your image.

If we survive, we will owe You nothing.

What is a Jew?

A Jew is the last, the least, the lowest, the lost.

Rebecca wept when she saw it. Nothing had prepared her.

Moritz Felcher had surprised her with a call at the typewriter shop the morning after that last dinner in the café. "Suddenly you were gone," he said. "I didn't have a chance to say what I wanted to."

"My friend was not feeling well"—only partially a white lie.

"Mrs. Wolf, I spoke of a house I had acquired in Hongkew."

"A shack," she corrected him, smiling, "unless I misheard you."

"Yes, well, compared with what we have had. Still, the best I could do. What I wanted to say last night is, if you have not made other arrangements, Mrs. Felcher and I would be pleased if you and your daughter would come to live in our house. My nephew, David—your friend David—is moving in with us. I think it is better if our people lived together. We would not be comfortable living with Chinese people. And none of us would want to go to the heims if he could avoid it."

Rebecca was grateful and relieved. She had reconciled herself to the inescapable. A major problem was being resolved with no effort on her part. Moritz Felcher was assuring her that with some luck they would adapt and get back on their feet.

"But, Mrs. Wolf, I must warn you, it will be very, very primitive."

There had to be some stronger, more accurate adjective than "primitive" to describe 22/158 Kimpei Lane, Hongkew.

It was not so much a house as a pile of junk, a collage of refuse slapped together with—with what? It was a haphazard laying-on of chipped bricks and rocks and chunks of concrete and cement and clay and bits of frame and corrugated zinc and broken glass panes. It was two wobbly floors tall and scarcely fifteen feet wide and thirty feet long. It had a more or less parabolic roofing of torn tarpaper over crisscrossing planks of flimsy lumber.

This house of jackstraws was assembled two years earlier by a Japanese pharmacist. Moritz Felcher had subdivided the floors identically. The square front room went from wall to wall. Behind the front room were two small rooms separated by a narrow, precarious stairway. A ceiling-to-floor sliding parchment screen divided the larger room in front from the rooms behind.

Moritz Felcher was maddeningly absurd, welcoming his tenants as grandly as if they were guests arriving at his hunting lodge in Bavaria. "I would much prefer to put you and Esther in the big room upstairs over ours," he said to Rebecca, "but I must try to get reasonable rent for it so I can start business again. If you can manage in here, I'll ask for just a little from you."

The tiny downstairs room in the rear left was smaller than a linen closet in the house on Kurfeinstrasse. There was a single bed with a shrouding of musty mosquito netting. One tatty chair, an open wardrobe of sorts against a wall, a catch-all table. The brick floor was partially covered with blood-red splotches of linoleum—Rising Suns? There was one window, and it had a zigzagging crack.

"Is this going to be my room, Mommy?"

"It's going to be *our* room."

Esther wailed.

Rebecca threw herself into hyperkinetic activity: scrubbing, sweeping, scraping, pounding, dusting, mending—immunization against slipping into a paralyzing depression. She poured boiling hot water over the bedding to kill the bugs. She stripped off the yellowing newspaper pages that decorated the walls and saw that the plaster beneath was moldy in many places. "You are the artist in this family," she said, handing Esther some gaily colored construction paper. "Make some

flowers and trees, and I will paste them over those ugly spots."
Rebecca wrapped a golden paper lantern around the weak electric bulb that dangled nakedly from the ceiling. "Like the garden in the Café Kranzler, Mommy." (The powers of memory
and the resiliency of children! Esther could not have been more
than four years old when her parents took her that balmy evening to the restaurant on Dieterstrasse.) Under the mosquito
netting that exuded a noxious odor of spray repellent, Esther
fantasized that they were captives in a sandy-colored tent flapping in the desert and Arab sheiks on black stallions with ban-
daged noses were galloping to their rescue.

Moritz Felcher was holding court in what he had grandly
referred to as his courtyard—a pathetic patch of angry red clay
enclosed by a bamboo fence bordering the lane. A few orphaned shoots of grass struggled for air. Under the scorching
sun prospective occupants of the three remaining cubicles in
the house were waiting their turn to be scrutinized by the for-
mally attired (spats!), formal-mannered landlord. "I must be
careful in my choices," he had confided to Rebecca.

"You say you are a comedian," he addressed a bulky middle-aged man with a harried expression. "Make me laugh,
Feinstein."

"If I tell a joke, I'm going to pass the hat your way."

"You do that and you can pass your keister right out that
gate."

Hermann Feinstein's mouth worked soundlessly. He
could be reciting Kaddish or squelching insults with language
that did not bear airing. "Joke? Okay, joke," he muttered with
transparent hostility, and began rocking, as though in singsong
prayer. "'Such a gentleman I had last night,' one streetwalker
said to the other. 'When I woke up, I found two hundred marks
on the chiffonnier.' 'That's nothing,' her companion said. 'I
had the Führer last night. When I woke up, I found his mustache on my stomach.'"

"One more crack like that, Feinstein, and you'll definitely
be out of here on your keister. We have ladies living here. Take
the rear right room upstairs. And if it rains, you'll just have to
sleep under your umbrella."

When Rebecca went into the courtyard to start the fire under the clay pot for supper, she saw the hunched, pasty-faced man with the watery red-rimmed eyes behind thick horn-rimmed glasses. Where had she seen him before? The disheveled black hair, the scraggly black beard, the dusty black suit, the grimy shirt—they were all familiar.

"Stop right there," Moritz Felcher said irritably. "I don't want to hear about any history of Jews in China. Do you have a livelihood? How do you propose to pay your rent?"

"I am keeping a bookstore on Thornborne Road."

"Good, you have a business!"

Professor Spiller. Of course. From the *Hannover*. Such a co-incidence. He would be in the room next to hers.

A woman of perhaps thirty-five, quite plain, with large thyroid eyes, coarse features, and ash-colored hair streaked with gray was presenting credentials. She was doing all the talking. Her husband stood beside her in silence, his eyes transfixed by the ghostly staircase winding out of the ruins in the next lot.

"We have a little saved up," she was explaining. "I worked as a waitress on the Nanking Road. My husband sold throw rugs from door to door. Our educations in science prepared us for something quite different, but I needn't belabor . . . "

"Yes, yes, but have you work now? Will you have income?"

"We both have employment, sir," the woman replied. "Mine is half days. I work in a clothing shop on Poatling Road. Mr. Schiff works nights. He is a watchman in a factory that makes knitwear and he is . . . "

"Front room upstairs."

The house was fully let. Downstairs, the Felchers in the front room, Rebecca and Esther and Professor Spiller in the two small back rooms. Upstairs, the Schiffs in the front room, David in the room above Rebecca and Esther, the comedian Feinstein in the room above Professor Spiller. To the aerie with a porthole that he had coolies construct on top of the annex, Moritz Felcher had assigned a woman named Ada Hurwitz. "Surely you have heard of the Mozart Pâtisserie, Mr. Felcher," she gurgled during her interview. "People stop me and say, 'Mrs. Hurwitz, you are the centerpiece of Chusan Road. You are queen of Little Vienna. Your éclairs and Sachertorten are beyond comparison.' I am not so foolish to have my head turned by that kind of flattery. It cannot be as it was in the real Vienna, where we had the best of everything. It is so difficult here with all the shortages . . . "

"That room over the annex isn't the Schönbrunn Palace, but it's yours if you want it."

Rebecca smiled for the first time since moving to 22/158 Kimpei Lane. The image of a dirndl-skirted middle-aged woman—whose ample proportions testified to heavy consumption of her own confections—huffing and puffing rung by rung up a ladder and then shoehorning herself into that cubbyhole was amusing. And threatening. What if, as she lay down her heaving frame, she crashed into the annex!

The annex. It was but a shed measuring about eight feet by ten feet that jutted back from the house and into the courtyard like an afterthought. Miraculously, it had been sectioned off to provide three communal rooms, cabana-style, each with its own door. The combined wash-up room and kitchen-pantry had a wooden sink and two slanting shelves. The middle room had a square tub so small that only Esther could use it. The third room was the Throne Room with its bucket and round wooden seat. The Throne Room, a mortification of the flesh, the cruelest of adjustments.

In pain, shame, embarrassment, and awkwardness, the inhabitants of 22/158 became an entity, if not a family. And the house *was* sturdy in spite of its looks. Like all of Shanghai, it merely needed a bath.

"You made the fire yesterday, Mrs. Wolf. You should not . . . "

"No, no, it's quite all right, Mrs. Felcher. I am not so busy as you."

What to make of this frail, fluttering woman with her chalky face and halo of soft white hair? She was a spindle without curves or swellings, as though God had had second thoughts about creating her a woman. How could such a bony creature generate so much energy? She never stopped. She was forever scouring, sweeping, swabbing. Always the obedient vassal, she jumped to her husband's commands. "Sophie, look for veal in the market today." "Sophie, you do my shirts. The laundries over here are stingy with the starch . . . "

It was dreadful in the extreme to live under one another's armpits. To hear every syllable, every breath, even thoughts. The very marrow of human dignity was violated. There was no hiding place. Even darkness provided no cover. Night, in fact, yielded eloquent revelations.

Moritz and Sophie Felcher never came together in conjugal embrace.

David Buchbinder, sulking by day, tossed and fretted, and calmed himself with compulsive masturbation.

Justin Spiller scratched on a writing pad until all hours, mumbling all the while that it was easier to work by the moon-light.

Hermann Feinstein moaned and snored in his sleep and unleashed his anger through the rat-a-tat-tats of flatulence.

Joseph Schiff, shuffling back at dawn from his watchman's duties, never answered his wife, whose whispers were franti-cally beseeching.

Ada Hurwitz had dreams—nightmares?—calling out, "Bitte, Herr Professor."

Esther alone slept the sleep of the righteous and greeted the new day with untroubled eyes.

How long? How long was this humanly endurable? A new order was being forged out of painful ruptures, the filth, the decay.

Within these mean forty square blocks the new residents (refugees) must learn to cope. The odors were asphyxiating. The summer sky was nearer, and the summer sun slammed down with unrelenting venom. The cries in the streets were sharper: the yelling of the hawkers, the begging of the hungry, the keening of the babies. The wet heat of day was like a sauna, and it merged into the wet heat of night. To sleep, perchance to dream, but on waking to remember to shake the bugs with the hundred feet out of the shoes.

If they slept, they woke to the matutinal cry of the honey-pot man. "Myah kai, myah kai."

The grinning coolie has a wispy goatee and wears ragged khaki shorts, yellow reed slippers, and a feces-stained sleeveless tunic. He pads into the Throne Room and lugs the bucket out to his wooden cart stinking up the lane. With a bamboo rod he scrapes free any droppings cloying to the bucket. His wife swabs and scrubs the honeypot in yesterday's dishwater with a coarse brush and returns it to the Throne Room.

"Mrs. Hurwitz, you have been in there fifteen minutes," Moritz Felcher banged on the door. "I go first in the morning. Get the hell out. You're not Anna Held taking a milk bath."

The rites of the Throne Room. Sophie Felcher flits in and out, light as a feather, apologetically. Hermann Feinstein is constipated and telegraphs the news with grunts and groans. Professor Spiller must be reminded that it is not a reading room. Moritz Felcher is up twice in the night—kidneys? prostate? Miriam Schiff tries to make a secret of her visits, slipping in only when she thinks no one is around. Rebecca, too, bides her time for that elusive moment when everybody, however briefly, is out of the house. Esther, sometimes, for the smiles it brings, wears a stocking over her face, heeding her promptings without inhibition. Joseph Schiff and David Buchbinder find outlets elsewhere. The Throne Room—the w.c.—the toilet—the crapper—the loo—"our Water-loo."

While Moritz Felcher is in the Throne Room, Sophie Felcher must have the kitchen to spread his hard roll with prune preserves, tap the shell off his hard-boiled egg, and pour cold tea for him. Esther has her oatmeal (cooked the night before while there were still sparks under the pot), though she balks. "I even hate hot oatmeal, Mommy." She totes to school her lunch of cooked banana and apple. Providing even hard-boiled eggs, cold oatmeal, and "mushy" fruit necessitates the rediscovery—and the laborious scouring—of two basic elements: water and fire.

For safe water, Rebecca must go to a yard in the next lane. There, water boils around the clock in a huge, high, claw-footed vat that sits in a broad U-shaped iron cradle hovering over fire spewing from gas jets. Wooden steps lead to a platform overlooking the steaming cauldron. With an elongated wooden dipper a coolie ladles water into a tin sluice. Customers hold their containers to the mouth of the sluice.

"This water is not boiling. Stoke the fire."

"Water is hot, lady. Plenty hot."

"I want boiling hot. Boiling."

"More boil later. Go back in line, lady."

Backyard chimneys begin to puff in the late afternoon. Matches are touched to a few dead leaves or twigs or newspaper pages in a shallow pit, and a spit of flame is born. Fan, fan, fan, the sputtering flame becomes a fire hot enough to heat the "black eggs," the ingenious briquettes compounded by tubercular Chinese of the baked sweepings from coal wagons and cinders, ashes, straw, sand, and water. Into the pot goes everything at once, the whole meal. Pieces of scrawny chicken cook with potatoes, carrots, cabbages. ("Honest chicken, lady, honest." He is not one of those short-changing merchants who stuff sand into the belly and sew it up.)

"One hour of electricity per day per room," Moritz Felcher legislates. "One bulb in a room. Only twenty-five watts. Every house is rationed."

The most persistent sound in the night is the scratching of a pen.

"Spiller! Turn that damn light off in there! This instant!"

Teng surprised Rebecca with a visit. His was a welcome smile from "the free world." They sat sipping tea in the courtyard. She could anticipate the real purpose of his call. She had turned over to him what was left of the business, taking only a typewriter with her. There was an informal agreement to share any revenues he took in.

"It's finished, isn't it, Teng?"

"I am so sorry."

"I expected as much. I am so sorry for you. Close the shop."

Teng looked into her living quarters and the young Oriental face was solemn. He was concerned. He was worried about her. She had become one with the four hundred million others who belonged to his idealized constituency. "You are really in China now," Teng said gently.

Rebecca was hanging wash on the short hemp line that had been strung from the back of the annex to the bamboo fence when Miriam Schiff came tripping out of the house. She was almost diaphanous in a chiffon frock as white as a calla lily. At the gate to the lane she stopped and looked back at Rebecca. She seized the glance that they exchanged as her cue to stop and speak.

"You think *this* is terrible, Mrs. Wolf?"

"I *know* this is terrible."

"I hope I won't sound tiresome if I say you should have seen Hongkew when Joseph and I first came here. It was horrible, a wasteland. The Chinese soldiers running away from the Japanese had burned everything to the ground. If you think you are living among the ruins now, it was like Herculaneum then. All we could afford was a room where there were blood-bellied rats as big as cats. Joseph kept spiking at them with a bayonet. I never got over being petrified." Her hazel eyes clouded with sadness.

Rebecca, sensing that the reminiscence was intended to break the ice, said, "Mrs. Schiff, I have a feeling that I would like to get to know you."

"What is there to know?" she asked skittishly.

"All of us have a book inside us, they say."

"A book? I wonder what mine would be. *Simplicius Simplicissimus*?" She laughed grimly. "Is there a novel in our story? Joseph and I met at the Kaiser Wilhelm Institute in Munich. We were in cancer research and thought we were going to be the reincarnation of the Curies. Then the edict struck us down. There was no longer any room for Jews in science or research. It was a mortal blow. We came out here and barely existed and became obsessed with the idea that we had to go on to America. I have a cousin in San Francisco, and she sent affidavits assuring the United States consulate that we were honest and hard-working and would not become a public burden. We were interviewed, fingerprinted, examined, indexed, and approved for America, and were told to come back in two days and pay a fee of eighteen American dollars. We immediately appealed . . . "

"Eighteen American dollars!" Rebecca ejaculated. "A king's ransom."

"Yes, a fortune to us. We appealed to a Mr. Elias Mendez, a member of the committee helping Jewish refugees. What was eighteen dollars to him? A trifling sum, nothing at all, shoeshine money for the day. But he said he could not make a loan without collateral—what could we offer him for security? My husband spoke up and said that all we had was a cedar chest and our linen, and Mr. Mendez said that would be fine. But the chest and the linen were wedding presents from my parents and I refused to part with them. Fortunately, an English woman who was a patron at the tea shop where I worked learned of our plight and lent us the money without a single string attached. We returned to the consulate in great excitement. We had already filled out miles of questionnaires, but now there were new questions, inane questions. Had we belonged to a debating society? Did we plan to apply for scholarships in the States? Did we consider ourselves 'political' people? What were our pastimes? And on and on."

Rebecca could approximately intuit the rest of the story. The Schiffs were denied their visas—"under advisement." They were given no explanation except, oh yes, there had been a call about their case from an "interested party." There could have been only one interested party—Elias Mendez.

"This has caused trouble between you and your husband," Rebecca said. She didn't pose it as a question. She could not help knowing. The whole house could not help knowing. They heard the imploring whispers: "We must talk, Joseph. Say something to me. *Anything.* Don't ignore me. Tell me I was wrong and I will beg your apology. We all make mistakes." Rebecca had heard it with a heartsickness—what was the aural equivalent of déjà vu?—that evoked the awful silences that had haunted her last days with Meyer.

"Yes," Miriam Schiff said. "Joseph blamed me for everything. He called me every vile name and said I had as much as signed our death warrants. And then he stopped talking. But you see, it wasn't the cedar chest and the linen. I've long since had to sell them. It's just that I refused to conspire in the usury of that rich Mr. Mendez so we could leave Shanghai."

His treatment of his wife aside, Joseph Schiff had been arousing a cold fury in Rebecca. He was but marginally civil even to her. "Good morning, Mr. Schiff," or "Good evening, Mr. Schiff," she would say pointedly, and in response receive no more than a stiff nod, if that. He was a phantom presence shuffling to his watchman's job. He resembled some long, lean, slack-jawed Ichabod Crane, a stickfigure with a pinhead. His thick-lensed, shell-framed glasses were taped at the bridge, and he had the peculiar habit of stroking a tuft of his brown-gray hair, which rose like a coxcomb from his brow. There were moments when Rebecca would have liked to have implanted a foot in his derrière as he went up the stairs to inflict sadistic silence on his helpmeet.

"I have been tempted to say something to him," she said to Miriam. "When we live in a goldfish bowl, one can't help noticing certain distressing things. I am sure he'd only tell me to mind my own business—if he said anything at all."

"Don't trouble yourself, Mrs. Wolf. But thank you just the same."

If nothing else, now that Rebecca "knew" and was sympathetic, Mrs. Schiff might relax the brittle and artificial cheerfulness that must be so wearing. Every evening, she came home from her part-time work at Löwen's Thrift Shop armed with an anecdote meant to be amusing. A pint-sized lady of eighty-two had used language that would make a Hamburg dockhand blush when Mr. Löwen refused to accept a pair of shoes with holes as big as saucers in the soles in exchange for a blue serge suit for her husband. Another day, "a real harpy" of fifty wanted to "borrow" a stylish lime-green bathing costume so she could enter a beauty contest on the Halcyon Roof Garden; should she be crowned Miss Hongkew of 1943, she would share the prize of ten Shanghai dollars with Mr. Löwen. Recounting these tidbits, Miriam always laughed, but the laughter did not camouflage her underlying distraction.

"I'm glad we've talked a little," Rebecca said.

"Yes, I'll be all right. I have found I can live without love. It's just this, this—vindictive funeral hush."

She gave Rebecca a fluttery wave and was out the gate.

David deemed it his inalienable privilege to be miserable. It may have been his only remaining privilege. But it was impossible to be miserable in private. He couldn't just lie there wallowing in misery. If there had been a pill that obliterated consciousness for a year, he would have taken it gladly. Even two of them. He worried others, and that compounded his misery and self-disrespect.

"David, David, what is it?" Rebecca asked.

"It's so hot," he said limply.

"This is what, our fifth summer here? Are you like this every time the weather turns this hot?" It *was* hot—the kind of hot day on which the colonials would hire coolies to play tennis for them.

He must exert himself and seek work. "Try for a pass," people urged him, as if permission to reenter the Shanghai from which they had been banished was a passport to employment and gratification. Natzie was starting up with his pig fat again, his uncle was scurrying around for his new restaurant, Professor Spiller was consumed with his scribble, scribble, scribble, that sour Mr. Feinstein went somewhere every night to tell his jokes, and even that creepy Schiff fellow—somebody employed *him*. But where, David asked himself, was there a place in this godforsaken ghetto for him?

This is a shithouse. Life is a shithouse.

"How can you be so sanguine?" he asked Mrs. Wolf.

"I am anything but sanguine, David. But with a young daughter it would not do for me to lie down and give up."

Mrs. Wolf was reproving him, and he turned to his uncle. "Why? Why are we here, and living like swine?"

"I don't know why," Uncle Moritz said irritably, "but I can tell you one thing, my boy. If I kept asking myself that question, I would never get anything done. And I can tell you another thing. If you keep raising your voice, you could get into a situation worse than this."

He was surprised to see that others did not share his total despair and paralysis. Did he know something the others didn't know? What good was all that intelligence and reflection, Uncle Moritz as much as said, if all he could do was ask troubling questions and make himself wretched?

But on the deadliest of days—a day that recorded eighteen deaths among the refugees from heat prostration—David had one of his mercurial mood alterations that made him wonder if he would ever begin to know what was inside his own head. Ah Chang's arrival at 22/158 Kimpei Lane was certainly a factor.

"The hardest thing," Rosalie wrote, "is to count your blessings on a day that you are convinced you don't have any. I'm still laughing at everything except calculated bitchery or bastardry. Right now, I feel a monograph coming on: 'Sex in an Internment Society.' The f_____ that goes on in this place! Moppets are playing Advanced Doctor and Nurse. The attitude of some parents is that it's better they f_____ than __ight.

"Enter the Colonel's Lady. She's let everybody know that she's in Debrett's Peerage and was presented at the Court of St. James. The colonel is off Union Jacking in someplace like Tobruk or Rabat. So the other night what happens is, the colonel's lady gets 'presented' in a cabbage patch. Caught in flagrante delicto. There she lay, bare-assed and spreadeagled under the lighthouse keeper from Ningpo. She was speechless, but what *could* she say—that she was flat on her back stark nekkid because she was trying to pick out the Big Dipper?"

David laughed, felt ill with longing for the sight and touch of her, and resolved to try for a pass.

Rebecca, like mad dogs and Englishmen, went forth into the midday sun. She thrust herself into the teeming vertebrae of Hongkew. She wandered through the maze of streets and inhaled the rancid air, steaming and salty as beef broth. She observed and brooded and marketed and waited for a sign.

"Capture the children. Freeze them. Immortalize them."

She listened to the arresting spiel of the ambulatory photographer—Lipsky of Cracow—who carried a bulky, telescoping Zeiss and a wooden tripod in one hand and some children's garments in the other. A little boy you have? Dress him up in this sailor suit, say cheese, a picture you'll have of something cute enough to eat. A girlchick, a budding beauty? Slip this fluffy green dress on Little Miss Sweetheart, watch the birdie, you'll be framing a princess forever.

Rebecca haunted the Chusan Road blocks known as Little Vienna. Viennese refugees during the past five years had ingeniously recreated the aura of a corner of back home. There were coffeehouses and beef markets and veal markets and poultry markets and frock shops and booteries and stationers and jewelers and apothecaries and wine cellars and beer halls and roof gardens housed in framed two-floor structures with balconies rounded at the "corners" and cantilevered to create shaded arcades below. Nothing evoked the grand Vienna of the Ringstrasse or the Hotel Sacher or the Prater, but still it was good ersatz slumtown Vienna.

At the insistence of Ada Hurwitz, Rebecca stepped into the Mozart Pâtisserie one afternoon and was welcomed profusely and offered a prune roll at a little table. Ada Hurwitz apologized for the smallness of her place—only these four tables—and the leanness of her cupboard, "Ach, without the ingredients, there is no magic."

Ada Hurwitz. Rebecca felt more affection and amused tolerance than friendship for this formidably proportioned woman with her high amiability and harmless pretensions. Mrs. Hurwitz put Rebecca in mind of a middle-aged Shirley Temple gone to butter and fudge. She had a girlish complexion of peaches and cream, her blue eyes twinkled in animation, and her head was a profusion of blond ringlets. Her father, she said, was a "prominent furrier" who had claimed the best clientele not only in Vienna but from as far away as Salzburg, Graz, Linz, and Innsbruck. "Prominent furrier," in the grandiosity of the Viennese, could mean someone who skinned animals in a backstreet garret, just as "civil engineer" could signify a supervisor in an amusement park, or "distinguished doctor" a male nurse in a hospital ward. By "Viennese inflation," the merest Mister became General or Director or Chairman or Maestro. The atmosphere was always a little headier, the wine more exhilarating, the music a bit more sublime in Vienna than anywhere else.

At an early age, Ada Hurwitz—if she did say so herself—

demonstrated musical genius and was encouraged by a series of teachers to set her sights on grand opera. She was in the wings of the Staatsoper, so to speak, awaiting her cue to go on when, ach, the Anschluss. Fortunately, she had—as if by osmosis—acquired the art of pastry-making from the family chef, one of the greatest culinary artists in Austria. Everyone who tasted her confections urged her to open a Konditorei. With time running out, it wasn't until she arrived in Shanghai that that was possible.

Her generosity to Esther endeared her to Rebecca. "Für mein Schatzi"—had she had children of her own?—"an apricot palanchinka . . . for Queen Esther, an apple strudel." Did Esther like stories? Wonderful. She must come sit in Aunt Ada's lap and hear one. "' . . . oh, my, never in my whole life did I see such a tinder box,' the soldier said. 'I have only to strike it with a flint and my dog brings me my wish.' We must give the dog a name, Esther. What shall we call him? . . ." Ada Hurwitz committed body and soul to the telling of every tale, her voice rising and falling, her eyes dilating in surprise, contracting with suspicion. Her curls plopped and her tummy shook. She mimicked and grimaced, scowled and scolded, and she clapped her hands a lot.

"Mommy, why don't you act out the parts the way Aunt Ada does?"

"Well, Esther," Rebecca said, responding with a ridiculous twinge of jealousy, "we are reading *Black Beauty* now. Would you really want to hear your mother neighing like a horse?" Esther said she would have to think about it.

Rebecca couldn't help but think of a whale when she saw Ada Hurwitz struggling on the ladder and heard it squeaking under the blubber. She smiled thinking of this posturing woman who hinted of memories and associations too beautiful, too painful to be recalled. How much should anything that Ada Hurwitz said be taken at face value? Pondering the whereabouts of Mr. Hurwitz—he had never figured in his wife's recollections—Rebecca was caught, embarrassingly, staring at Mrs. Hurwitz's ring finger. "I had to sell my ring, Mrs. Wolf," came the explanation. "It's what Mr. Hurwitz would have wanted me to do. I needed the money to start the pâtisserie. I don't have to have an eighteen-karat gold ring on my finger to remind me that I was married to the most wonderful man in the world. "

"Where, if I may ask . . . "

"They took him away. 'Somebody has to stand up to all those lies,' Mr. Hurwitz kept arguing. How dearly he paid for his idealism."

War news reached the community as through a filter, diluted and dimmed. The Japanese had suffered a devastating shock. With the approval of President Roosevelt himself, P-38 Lightnings over Bougainville ambushed and shot down Isoroku Yamamoto, Hirohito's naval commander in chief. ("The sword of my emperor" had masterminded Pearl Harbor, then argued that Japan should immediately negotiate peace with the crippled Americans. His was only the second State funeral for a commoner in the history of Japan.) In the West, the Allies had driven the fascists out of North Africa and were poised for invasions of Sicily and Italy and maybe southern France—a Second Front at last. And the Americans had regained some islands near Alaska.

These events, though encouraging, were happening so far away and paled alongside the urgencies at hand. What was best for prickly heat? What was this about a Jewish Pao Chia? Was it safe to approach Chief Examiner Minobe again if he had once turned you down for a pass out of the ghetto? Did the Japanese have ulterior motives in corralling the refugees into this "designated area?"

Intimations of looming concentration camps in Manchukuo sent shivers into the stifling air.

Impeccably dressed in a three-piece lemon-colored linen suit, a long-sleeved white shirt with starched collar, polka-dotted tie, and his familiar spats, Moritz Felcher prepared to brave the heat. He teased the moist mahogany strands of hair to work their deception and he polished his spectacles. He dabbed his baby-pink cheeks with cologne and patted his shrinking stomach approvingly.

"I am seeing Schneidermann in thirty minutes," he told

Sophie (but was really making an announcement to the house-hold), flicking shut his pocket watch. "It will not do to keep him waiting. That man has connections, I can tell you. . . . " Unburdened with memories or backward glances, he hustled and bustled. Conferences here, appointments there. Always on the move, rushing.

"Sophie, David, Mrs. Wolf, everybody listen. There will be a new Café Moritz. The Café Moritz rises again! On Seward Road. It's not the Avenue Joffre, but it's a new start. There's a place there that I can rent for bird seed."

Rebecca looked for an opening for herself in the dense, vibrant tapestry. She scanned the bulletin boards and looked in shop windows for notices of help wanted. She must find work, but where was work to be found?

She strolled into Thornborne Road one afternoon. She had never visited Professor Spiller's bookshop, and was disap-pointed to find the door locked and the shade drawn. She mentioned it casually to him that evening, and he became sharply defensive. "Yes, yes," he said. "One cannot always oblige the public."

By degrees, she had learned a little of his background. Jus-tin Spiller was born in the Romanesque city of Trier (the oldest city in Europe, older even than Rome), a few doors ("Shhhh") from the birthplace of Karl Marx. He was the only child of soci-ologists, who had taken advanced training at Columbia Uni-versity, in New York City. Professor Spiller's mother was still another victim of the Great Influenza. (Surely Mrs. Wolf was aware that it took the pandemic merely one year to kill as many people as had been slaughtered during the four years of the Great War.) His father, during the 1930s, lost his teaching posi-tion at the University of Cologne and was shipped to Dachau for "promulgating traitorous concepts." Since then, not a word from his father. Justin Spiller thought that he, himself, must have been born with a history book in his mouth—nothing else had ever interested him. He entered university at a preco-cious age, took honors, won scholarships to complete his doc-toral studies at Grenoble, became a professor of history at

Tübingen, and was dismissed for the same "crime" that had landed them all here. But he would always believe that it was a mere coincidence that he was terminated on the day after he matter-of-factly had mentioned to his graduate students that when Germany, like any nation, embraced Christianity, it perforce embraced anti-Semitism. He was now thirty-eight years old—not the fifty or so that Rebecca had thought—and he estimated he would be at least sixty before he completed his history of the Jews in China.

To placate him (if she had upset him unwittingly), she inquired politely of his work in progress. "How far back does Jewish history in China go, Professor Spiller?"

"Centuries, Mrs. Wolf," he lit up. "Centuries and centuries."

His watery eyes focused on her in delight. Why, there were Jews in Kaifeng at least five centuries before the Polos set foot there; in fact, the Venetians met Jews in the court of Kublai Khan. In the eighth century, more than a thousand Jews from Persia and India had settled in Kaifeng at the invitation of the emperor of the Sung Dynasty. China's textile industry was suffering from a shortage of silk, and the Jews were skilled in the manufacturing and dyeing of cotton fabrics. Within a century there was a flourishing Jewish settlement in Kaifeng, then the eastern capital of China, with as many as a million inhabitants; it was conceivably the largest city in the world. The Jews were free to build synagogues and follow the customs of their forefathers. Splendid temples were constructed and great fortunes were made. And something extraordinary happened. The Jews became assimilated into the Chinese population. They intermarried. Their physiognomy became Oriental. Their eyes narrowed, their cheekbones broadened, and their skin turned yellowish. They took to wearing pigtails and to binding their feet. The commitment to Judaism and to knowledge of the most rudimentary rituals and customs of Jewish life all but disappeared. Today in Kaifeng only a solitary stone marks the site of the last synagogue. There is scarcely anyone alive there who has any awareness of a Jewish ancestry.

"How perfectly fascinating," Rebecca said in all sincerity.

"So close, Mrs. Wolf. Sometimes I feel I can reach out and

touch Kaifeng. It is only two hundred miles from here. If one only were free . . . "

Moritz Felcher set a date for the opening of Café Moritz III. Sophie Felcher discovered Banzai, a miracle powder that promised instant extermination of ants, roaches, centipedes, and all other pests. Dyspeptic Hermann Feinstein, who slept the day away, roused himself to see a doctor and learned he had ulcers—wasn't Jehovah ever satisfied? ("Feinstein, you may be a lot of laughs at the Café Blaue Donau," Moritz Felcher said, "but around here you're a barrel of sour pickles.") With squeals of laughter, Esther and her friend Lyng Huan, who lived in the next lane, floated a paper airplane into the pot cooking veal ragout and they fantasized the freestanding staircase in the next lot into Dr. Frankenstein's castle. Miriam Schiff began to rouge her cheeks and wear becoming clothes borrowed from the thrift shop; there was color in her lips, and the dark quarter moons under her eyes were in eclipse. Joseph Schiff slunk and slouched, his head digging deeper into his chest. ("So the Schiffs hate each other," Hermann Feinstein quipped. "At least they're not anti-Semitic.") By candlelight, Professor Spiller's bony, liver-spotted hand moved across his rarefied work. David used colored pins to trace the progress of the war on the flat Mercator map of the world over his cot and felt a grand idea taking shape. To a doddering old gentleman sitting with her in the courtyard Ada Hurwitz trilled of acquaintanceships with Berg, Schönberg, and Weber, and hinted at "a very special friendship I must tell you about when I am in exactly the right mood." And Rebecca said to herself, "I must visit a heim and satisfy my social worker's curiosity. And I must, must apply for a pass."

The heims were created out of missionary compounds or military barracks or schoolhouses. They took their names from the road on which they were situated—Ward, Seward, Wayside, Alcock, Chaoufoong, Pingliang. Many of the refugees had gone directly from luxury liners like the *Hannover* and the *Conte Biancamano* to these forlorn-looking buildings in Hongkew because they had no place else to go—and then they had not budged; for them, the filthy, pestilential poorhouses were the only home that they had known in Shanghai. Since the Proclamation, more than half of all the Central European Jewish refugees were in one or another of the heims. Rebecca had heard stories of two hundred men and women sharing one toilet bucket, of people so despairing they gave up on life. She had heard the irascible complaints of the midday feeding—the one real meal of the day—"More on this plate," "White beans today, red beans tomorrow," "You cooks eat all the sausage yourselves." One look at any of the heims was enough to remind her how much worse off she could be.

Rebecca paused in the gravel areaway before the Pingliang heim. Straitened as her own circumstances were, she must not appear like some Lady Bountiful or a Major Barbara come to bestow a crumb or a word of cheer. How would she explain being there? That she was looking for a neighbor from Lübeck?

"Guten Abend, gnädige Frau," she was greeted by a sallow, middle-aged woman fanning herself on a rush-bottom chair near the screened front door.

Rebecca stepped into a dark, narrow dormitory. She could barely make out the double-decker beds jammed together in two parallel rows touching the windowless walls at either end. It was only eight o'clock in the evening, but many of the bunks were already occupied. Body smells commingled with stale cooking odors, and there was a piteous medley of coughing, hacking, spitting, nose-blowing, whimpering, and moaning.

"Gott im Himmel! Gott im Himmel!"

A fragile man with a great beak of nose and yellowing white hair shambled along the corridor separating the bunks. He was holding his head in his hands and wailing. "Gott im Himmel! Gott im Himmel!"

Everything was out in the open, exposed. There were no attics, closets, cellars, or wardrobes. Clothing hung from nails in the walls. At the far end of the room, three women stood under a dim light bulb waiting their turn at a one-bowl latrine. In the corner opposite from the water closet someone had put a white tablecloth and a vase of paper flowers on a card table—an absurd amenity in this grimmest of settings.

From the kitchen, another old man, with a limp so tortured that his right foot dragged along the floor, carried a tin cup of pale fluid. "Tea," he whispered. "For him." He pointed to a catatonic figure on an upper bunk and said, "Too proud to get it himself. Look at him. Potato sack for a nightshirt. Sandals cut out of the inner tube of a bicycle tire. He hides up there."

There was an outburst. It came from the card table under the weak bulb hanging on a piece of frayed string. A two-handed card game ended in a geyser of cards.

"Sorehead! Sore loser!"

"Cheat!"

"Scumbag!"

There was another commotion, this one coming from a lower bunk that was enshrouded in a white sheet. A clever piece of engineering, of wrapping and tucking to create a four-sided cocoon. From within came the thrashing sounds of love-making.

Rebecca took her leave of the Pingliang heim—her visit had been a scant ten minutes—with a roaring headache.

Pao Chia.

Protect the home.

How shrewd of the jailers.

Police yourself, they were saying.

Let Jew keep Jew in place. The Jews would be more vigilant, keep a sharper eye on one another's comings and goings than would any Japanese overseers. Who better than these trapped refugees could appreciate the consequences to *all* if *one* should transgress?

All men between the ages of twenty and forty-five must enlist for duty in the Pao Chia. They would be policemen without arms or uniforms or the authority to arrest. They would stand at the passage points in and out of the designated area and inspect passes. They were to see that no one left without an authorized pass and to report anyone who returned after its date and hour had expired. Each man must serve three hours once a week.

"It's nice to be twenty-three, Mrs. Wolf, like my nephew," Moritz Felcher said. "But there are also advantages in being forty-nine."

Or fifty-five, Rebecca smiled to herself, having heard the truth from David.

The dreaded ordeal of going before the ugly Chief Examiner Minobe had yielded Rebecca permission to leave the ghetto by day. ("You get pass. Be sure you fix typewriters.") But she procrastinated. "Pretty-boy" David was denied a pass ("Not today," the dwarf had screamed, "not ever . . . Married ladies. Unmarried ladies. Make them pay."), and he was neither surprised nor disappointed. He dropped hints of a mysterious mission and borrowed Rebecca's typewriter.

The days of deadening summer wore on and Rebecca rationalized, "Maybe tomorrow." Only in the cloak of darkness, in the sleepless hours of night, could she admit to herself, "I procrastinate because I am afraid."

Moritz Felcher passed along a ticket that a patron had given him for the *White Horse Inn*. Rebecca had seen the original production in Berlin with Samuel and they had both liked the Benatzky-Stolz music and words. As for the plot, well . . . A diversion would divert her, at least momentarily, from the gnawing anxiety of having to produce income soon.

The heat inside the Eastern Theater was intolerable. Wretched as she was in a thin cotton dress, the man in the row in front of her was beside himself. Little wonder. He was wearing a vested blue worsted suit, a high starched collar, and a French-cuffed shirt. He was fanning himself fitfully with his program, mopping his face and neck, and moaning softly. When the lights came up at the interval, she saw that it was Doctor Pincus.

A few weeks earlier, Rebecca had taken Esther to Doctor Pincus for inoculations against typhus. He had been so gentle and playful with Esther. ("Let's pretend the needle is a sword and we're using it to slay a big bad dragon that's about to breathe fire on you. One little touch and you'll be safe forever.") Rebecca had also been impressed by his house— imposing by Hongkew standards, with its glassed-in veranda, smooth stucco walls, twin brick chimneys, and grassy lawn—and by the commendations gracing the walls of his office.

"Good evening, Doctor Pincus," she addressed him now.

He looked at her vaguely, distraught in the effort of recall. "Good evening, Mrs. . . . "

"Rebecca Langer-Wolf."

"Yes, yes, now I remember. The mother of Little Miss Bright Eyes."

"And tart mouth," Rebecca laughed.

"I have a tin ear, Mrs. Wolf. How does the performance sound to you?"

"Since you ask me, I think the proprietress could do with some singing lessons."

If he had a tin ear, what was he doing at the operetta? And why was he alone? Where was Mrs. Pincus? Most women married to such an attractive man would not let him out of their sight—particularly in a place where attractive men were in such short supply. He must be taller than six feet, and every inch the distinguished physician. How old—fifty-two? fifty-three? His head was handsome. He had close-cropped steel-wool-gray hair, gentle green eyes, a firm mouth, a clipped mustache, and a cleft chin. And just the hint of a paunch.

"Whew!" he moaned. "You could grow orchids in this hot-house."

"You might wear lighter clothing," she suggested, and was surprised by her brashness.

"I am a doctor, Mrs. Wolf," he replied, his eyes glinting with amusement. "If I were to wear as little as I liked . . . "

"You are permitted," she blushed. "Back in the Concessions the most respectable men put their heavy clothing into mothballs at the first hint of warm weather and put on tropical things."

"Perhaps I am too respectable for my own good."

The curtain parted again on the Tyrolean Players, but Rebecca's attention drifted from the silliness of the Emperor Franz Josef, Leopold, and the chatelaine of the inn to Doctor Pincus. Again she was sitting behind an attractive man alone at a cultural event. He was panting and swabbing, and shifting his position to avoid becoming glued to the chair. As Leopold dissolved inevitably into the arms of the innkeeper, Rebecca had a thought. She could do something for Doctor Pincus and at the same time do something for herself.

In the backyard, David typewrote on a blue stencil.

"What are you doing?" his uncle asked.

"I find the *Shanghai Jewish Chronicle* so boring. All that Zionist stuff doesn't mean much to most of us."

"That doesn't answer my question, David."

"I want to surprise you."

David had Frankenberg Stationers mimeograph two hundred copies of *The Hongkew Reporter*, and he ceremoniously presented the first two copies to his uncle and Rebecca.

David's newssheet was a page printed on both sides, a compendium of oddments—bulletins, ghetto features, and smiles. A census had revealed that the Hongkew refugees numbered 13,511 Germans and Austrians, 1,234 Poles, 212 Czechs, and 385 "miscellany," 15,342 Central Europeans in all. The mean round-the-clock temperature in August was 36.2°C, or 97.2°F. ("Very mean, indeed.") It took less than an hour for a rumor to travel from one end of the ghetto to the other—at eleven twenty, someone at a sidewalk table at the Café Marguerite whispered, "I heard all the women here will be required to take a course in welding," and it was repeated as gospel truth in the Foo Baths by noon. David had worked his uncle and Hermann Feinstein into the contents. The Café Moritz had received a supply of Colombian coffee—"the finest coffee in the world"—and Hermann Feinstein's joke graced the upper left-hand box on the back side of the sheet:

Doctor: Stay away from that Chinese rice wine. One thimbleful and you'll be out cold for a week.

Patient: Know where I can get a gallon?

David previewed *The Chopped Liver Heiress*, a comedy that the Shang Hy Players were preparing for the stage. The plot centered on an enterprising lady from Warsaw who had introduced Mother Lillian's Chopped Liver to Shanghai. Nobody can tell what makes Mother Lillian's chopped liver better than any other chopped liver and Mother Lillian isn't telling either. Only when she believes that she's dying does she confess to the rabbi—one of her best customers—that the chopped liver isn't, well, strictly kosher. Liver being so dear, she has to stretch it with a bit of something else. And what is that something else, my Liebchen? Well, rabbi, p-p-p-p-p-p-p-pork. The rabbi has a heart attack. But believe it or not, the play has a happy ending.

And there was this ominous bulletin framed in black borders:

By order of the Commander in Chief of the Imperial Japanese Army in the Shanghai Area and the Commander in Chief of the Imperial Japanese Navy in the Shanghai Area, all stateless males in the designated area thirteen years of age and older must report for a physical examination in September.

The Hongkew Reporter was an immediate success—all the copies, selling for a penny each in Frankenberg's, were bought in two days, but praise for David's effort was somewhat deflected by the announcement of the physical examination.

The men in 22/158 reacted variously.

"Who knows what they're up to," Moritz Felcher snorted, "with all that time on their hands."

"Just as long as they keep their hands off my nuts," Hermann Feinstein groused.

Joseph Schiff said nothing.

"Life is but a dream," Justin Spiller mumbled irrelevantly. "Death is the awakening."

"In Germany," David said, "they never bothered with physical examinations."

The heims were rife with doomsday prophets.

"They'll stick us in a tent with anopheles mosquitoes and call it malaria research."

"They'll ship the fit to slave-labor camps in Sumatra and New Guinea—and they'll find all of us fit."

"Banzai attacks! We'll be the first wave."

"They need us in Manchukuo to build railroads . . . in Kobe to assemble rifles . . . on the rubber plantations . . . in the coal mines. . . . "

Surely the doddering Mr. Spitzenberg would be spared the physical examination. Ada Hurwitz all but carried the antique man from the Chaoufoong heim to sit audience for her in the courtyard. As she lay in her bed (tomorrow *must* be the day), Rebecca wondered if Mr. Spitzenberg was even too weak to interrupt or comment on Mrs. Hurwitz' monologues of reverie; her visitor never opened his mouth.

" . . . I'm not going to tease you one minute longer, Mr. Spitzenberg. You are wondering how I met my illustrious friend? I can tell you to the minute when it was. That meeting occurred at precisely eleven thirty-eight in the morning of March the ninth in the year of nineteen hundred and thirty-three—a Thursday. It was one of those days—well, I needn't tell you, Mr. Spitzenberg, you are Viennese yourself, what March weather is like there. One moment spring is in the air and the next a frigid blast blows in from Hungary. I awoke thinking Fasching was past and there is nothing to look forward to until the Heurige. Then I remembered that it was the day that I was to go to Salzburg to be with my cousin Magda. Now if I am taking the train to Salzburg—or to anywhere else—I absolutely must be in the railway station an hour before the train departs. That day was no different. I purchased my ticket and went to the brasserie to sip a warming cup of chocolate. The chocolate recharged my energies, and I decided to stroll about the terminal a bit. My attention was arrested by a most distinguished-looking man standing near one of the ticket windows. Rather an elderly man, mind you, in his seventies, I should say, but still handsome. I was much taken with his elegantly trimmed Vandyke, and oh, he was well turned out! The Chesterfield coat with nice velvet collar and navy-blue Homburg. But such a puzzlement he seemed to be in. He was frowning at a timetable and removing his spectacles to wipe them and then frowning some more over the fine print. I stepped a little closer. Could this be the great man himself? Could it really be? Yes, it could be. It *was*. Well, Mr. Spitzenberg, you can imagine my excitement. I am not a bold or a forward woman, but I could not resist the opportunity. 'Excuse me, Herr Doktor,' I said. 'Could I be of some assistance?' Now, you will have to admit that this is humorous in itself. Me, humble Ada Hurwitz, daughter of Schiller the Furrier, offering assistance to Herr Doktor, whose profession is to help the most burdened and distressed people. You might not believe this of him, but he was an extremely shy man. He became ill at ease, agitated, with my attention. His glasses fogged and his eyes darted in all directions. He mumbled something about the timetable being confusing. I was determined to be of assistance. In bits and pieces I managed to extract from him the information that he was on his way to Bologna to deliver a series of lectures at the medical center there. 'What a pleasant surprise for me, sir!' I exclaimed. 'We shall be traveling on the same train. I disembark at Salzburg, but you must remain on the train all the way to Innsbruck. At Innsbruck you change for your connection to Bologna. . . . ' After I had completed all my explanations, Doctor Freud said to me, 'Thank you, madam, but it is tomorrow that I travel. I am here today only to make inquiry.' But the strangest thing, Mr. Spitzenberg, Doctor Freud was carrying his valises. That's when I realized how much we must have in common. We both have difficulty with travel. I must be at the railway station an hour before the train departs. But here was one of the world's greatest men who came with luggage to the railway terminal a whole day before he intended to travel. . . . "

Rebecca had been listening on two levels, to both the ridiculous reminiscence and to the breathing from the other chair that had deepened. There was a series of startled snorts, the sound of the old man's sudden waking. Rebecca giggled into her pillow.

At the passpoint of the humpbacked Garden Bridge, Rebecca struck terms with a rickshaw driver who would take her, wait for her, and bring her back. She stifled her guilt pangs at being borne through the streets by a bag of bones weighing about forty kilos. He freed one hand, then the other to sweep the sweat from his narrow strip of brow. He made weird gurgling noises—"Ai-ya! Ai-yee! Ai-ya"—but whenever he looked back at her, he grinned his eagerness to please and to serve. Could her fare be saving a dozen or more Chinese from starvation?

A gust of wind lifted the puller's ragtag blue shirt, and she saw in pity the severe corrugation of naked ribs. And he was grinning! What could be going on in that head? Did he never,

never, as he trotted mile after relentless mile every day, every day of the year, question a universe that had made life so harsh for him? Did he ever compare the luxurious quarters of the Concessions with his abode? Was he envious of the Japanese who could spend an entire day arranging three flowers in a vase?

Teng had once limned a portrait of a hypothetical rickshaw puller. After running across the streets of Shanghai from dawn to dusk, he would trot miles more to his village outside the city. He lived in a thatched hut through whose perforated roof the rain and sleet plunged. The hut was one long and narrow room with an earthen floor strewn with a few strands of straw. It stank to high heaven with rancid cooking oils, filthy bodies, stale urine, and steaming dung. The sooty walls crawled with spiderwebs. A kerosene lamp flickered on a lopsided wooden table, and steam drifted from a black pot heating on a crude grill. Piled in a corner were a few broken stools and a pair of soiled mattresses with protruding coils. The coolie's wife, looking ancient as a mummy, sat cross-legged on the floor tending the cooking pot and mending clothes that had been remended and remended. At least eight children would be darting in loops and chasing, pinching, tickling, squealing, laughing. The coolie would grin in contentment, as if to say that all this was his—the hovel, the slaving wife, the noisy children—and he pitied any man who had less. "Happiness is inherited ignorance," Teng had sighed. "The curse of Confucius."

Liberty! Rebecca's first taste of it in three months. Rattling through familiar streets, she was dismayed at how much tawdrier everything was. The teeming life had vanished from the monolithic towers. The French Concession was now a fortress: Japanese patrols, barbed wires, sandbags, machine-gun nests, antiaircraft guns, tanks. Spasms of distant rifle fire punctuated the air.

"White people never go to the Forbidden City," she had always heard.

"Why not?"

"It could be dangerous."

"How so? It is virtually unheard of for a Chinese person to harm a Caucasian."

People spoke vaguely of labyrinthian mazes that would

trap an outsider forever, of odors that would suffocate, of stampedes by surging masses of humanity, and of evil spirits whose hexes could strike the white man as well as the yellow. Everything she had heard now fed Rebecca's dread. But nothing so much as the dread of deception and its consequences.

The Forbidden City. The Old City. The Walled City. Nantao. The birthplace of Shanghai. Here, a millennium ago, a cluster of fishing shacks sprang up from the primordial ooze. Eventually, a black brick wall with four thousand archer loopholes and twenty guard houses had encircled the settlement, protecting it from invaders. There had been a moat, too. The wall was long since gone, and the moat had been bricked over to become a lively commercial artery.

Rebecca paused at the vaulting stone gateway that led to the native quarter and, taking a deep breath, walked under the low arch.

She had a moment of panic. A sea of human flesh pressed around her like an undammed flood. The noise beat into her eardrums like nails. She was terrorized by the sudden darkness and feelings of claustrophobia. Flimsy tenements tilting five and six floors blotted out the sky. The narrow, densely packed lanes wove in all directions like a haphazard army of caterpillars.

With a fixed uncertain smile Rebecca stepped into the pulsating Oriental bazaar. Red banners strung between tenements flapped over the streets, their gaudy gold characters advertising wares in the shops below. Lines of laundry were floating in the dank air. The barkers were as shrill as the banners: Ducklings. Lily buds, dragon eyes. Silk from the loom of the Spinning Goddess. Peaches sweeter than the nectar of Soochong. Snow peas to make the Gardens of Heaven blush.

Rebecca turned into a twisting thoroughfare. She passed a queue of young men waiting their turn at a barber's curb-side chair to have their head shaved to the skin—Buddhists? the new fashion? delousing? Around a dentist's chair a crowd was admiring specimens of gold teeth dangling from a rod. A blind storyteller was spinning a convoluted yarn—a love story from the Middle Kingdom?

Craftsmen bent at their trade worked in open stalls with

ivory and porcelain, brass and gold. Some of the young people in the crowd were wearing cloth fetishes on their blouses and shirts to ward off evil spirits. A toothless man in a filthy night-shirt pointed to crickets fighting in a matchbox—a gift for the lady if she would make "small contribution" to the four tots clinging to his legs.

Two boys stripped to the waist lay side by side in the road. An obese, bald prestidigitator in a mandarin robe planted a plump bare foot on the chest of each boy, giving him the eleva-tion of a stage. From his left ear he plucked a wand and waved it over two tin cannisters poised on a purple cloth he was hold-ing in his other hand. "Hai-u," he chanted. The lids of the bowls sprang into the air. The audience squealed and applaud-ed. No one "caught on" that the magician's wand was magnet-ized.

Rebecca passed an infinity of shops, each a specialty shop selling only one thing. Lumps of coal. Ningo pewter. Calen-dars with Chinese starlets. Silks. Bamboos. Mats. Sandalwood chests. Jade earrings. Colored papers. Marbles. Clogs. Sandals. Ivory tusks. Chopsticks. Lutes. Flower drums. Samisens. Tra-ditional kimonos. Modern gowns slashed to the thighs. Birds and bird cages. (Could one of those purveyors of parrots or mynah birds be Teng's father?)

Another galaxy of shops dealt in food specialties. Carp from Soochow. Turtles, bamboo shoots, and pigs' entrails from Canton. Silver thread rolls and salt sea cucumbers from Shan-dong. Ducklings from Peking. Hot chili peppers from Hunan. Pock-marked bean curd from Szechwan. The odors of burnt oil and garlic coming from the back of the food stalls overpowered Rebecca, stifling her appetite. Expert opinion held that Chinese cuisine was the most complex and healthiest in the world. But how few of them, the Jewish refugees, had been tempted to do much sampling of it! It was lamentable, perhaps, that their pal-ates were so unadventurous.

Beyond a footpath that zigzagged over a rock-strewn brook was a quaint teahouse with a pagoda roof of red slate. Rebecca pushed herself into a lane that looped back on itself like a horseshoe. Before her, improbably, incongruously, rose a glorious temple glistening with a façade of diamond-shaped stonework and enameled medallions. Next door, there was a house of soft blue tiles with gold-leaf trimming—a house that opium had built? a palace of concubines? A few steps further brought her to the stalls of haberdashery. There she touched, inspected, and held to her eyes various articles of clothing from leaning stacks of merchandise. She haggled and made her bargains, and calculated that shopping there had cost her a quarter of what it would have elsewhere. It had been worth the ordeal.

Doctor Pincus fingered the contents of Rebecca's package. He held one of the beige short-sleeved cotton shirts against his physician's smock and nodded. The matching thigh-length shorts seemed to be the right size, too. The long white cotton stockings—to lend a dressed-up touch—were admirable. He was regarding her with amusement.

"I kept thinking of our chat in the theater the other night," Rebecca explained, "and thought these might do for you."

"Maybe they will. Perhaps I should slip on the shorts to make sure."

"You don't have to accept any of these things," she said nervously, embarrassed at the intimacy of his suggestion, "if you don't want them."

"Oh, I want them, I want them," he cried gaily. "But you forgot one thing."

"What is that, Doctor Pincus?"

"A pith helmet."

That night, Rebecca dreamed about pith helmets and awoke to find Kimpei Lane cordoned off by Japanese soldiers. No one must leave—not even the schoolchildren. There were no explanations. For one dazed moment Rebecca thought she might have brought down the restriction by her unauthorized use of her pass. She had not been stopped at the passpoint, but you never could tell about the Japanese. They were everywhere and nowhere. They were visible, they were invisible. Before Shanghai, her impressions of them could have been put into a teacup. Mr. Moto. Madama Butterfly. Hirohito. Harikari. Flower arrangements. Bowings and scrapings. Shoguns. Samurai—and its code of Bushido. (To die in war is the greatest honor. To be taken prisoner is the ultimate disgrace. To commit suicide under certain circumstances is a glorious act of true valor.) The Japanese proclaimed their civilization the most exquisite of all and their Emperor descended from God. But Rebecca had looked in vain among the Japanese she saw for exquisiteness of behavior or divinity. In remote temples or in mountain retreats of Japan, cultivated souls might very well be extracting fresh beauties out of Shintoism or nurturing botanical gardens to new perfections or bringing higher refinements to the haiku or creating even more complex maneuvers for the game of Go. The Japanese character within her purview was a mass of contradictions. These Sons of Heaven groveled with inferiority feelings while their arrogance knew no bounds. One minute they were choking with sycophancy and the next they were slicing a sword across the neck of a Chinese who had not bowed deeply enough. They would rape any woman they could mount, but they would never take for a wife someone who was not Japanese. They were too proud to steal or bargain, but they were not above the most rapacious extortion. The soldiers who plodded through these lanes looked harmless enough, but they belonged to a military whose treachery had surfaced again and again . . .

Shortly before noon, a voice on a loudspeaker told them that they could go and come. Again, no explanation, no apology.

David basked in the acceptance of *The Hongkew Reporter*, but was appalled by the general apathy toward the progress of the war. "Pinpricks on the Map" informed his readership that eight hundred thousand Hamburgers had been left homeless by a British bomber blitz and that the Americans had liberated Sicily and that the Russians had regained Kharkov and that the Japanese airstrip at Munda had been destroyed. The noose was tightening, but there still was no Second Front in western Europe, no matter how much Stalin begged for it. Was it Churchill's plan to let Hitler kill off millions more Russians before diverting the panzers? No bulletin aroused much comment, let alone emotion, and to David such insouciance was as baffling as it was exasperating. Could not the European refugees appreciate that bombs might also be decimating other German cities, where they still had loved ones? Could they not see that their own futures were totally dependent on the outcome of the war?

"You're not interested in anything happening even a mile away from here," David accused Natzie.

"Look, Davie, the war will be over when it's over and there isn't a damn thing we can do about it here—except to stay alive."

A letter from Rosalie, intended to amuse, devastated David.

"About five hundred of us in the Chapei and Pootong camps are being shipped home," she wrote via Ah Chang. "In exchange, five hundred Japanese civilians caught in the States will be sent back to Tokyo. Cabin fever has given way to repatriation fever. Aaron has every confidence we'll be on the list. He expects to return to Hollywood like a conquering hero. 'The Studio will be pumping me for script ideas about the war in the Pacific,' he predicts. 'They'll promote me into world-wide distribution.'

"Sister Sadie is a riot. She's champing at the bit to get on the list. She says as long as she's stuck in this camp she hasn't a prayer of selling what so many others are cheerfully giving away. She says God should show some mercy to a girl who only wants to get back to work. I wished her good luck and she said she's keeping her legs crossed."

Rosalie repatriated? Abandoning him? Going off without him? Maybe never never *never* to see him again?

It was foolish for three pots to be working for supper. The women of the house, in the late days of summer, began to share the chores of marketing and cooking. Sophie Felcher, who was always in the new café, was not party to the arrangement, and Rebecca, for one, was relieved. Sophie Felcher would have insisted on doing everything herself every day.

Rebecca was toting chicken wings and carrots in her string bag when she spotted him. It was on the northern end of Chusan Road. He was behind a stand comprised of three cardboard boxes. She hardly recognized him in his frayed shirt-sleeves and unpressed trousers. The dapper amanuensis looking like that—and peddling in the streets.

He hadn't seen her yet, and she was of two minds whether to go to him. There could be no question of anything starting up again. She had not seen him since that last dinner at the Café Moritz. Moritz Felcher's invitation to live in his house in Hongkew had come like divine intervention to resolve her quandary. She had felt herself being pressured to the edge of commitment, and she had been resentful. Suddenly, it became quite easy to tell him that she thought it best if they didn't see each other again—at least not until she was settled in her new arrangement. He had been hurt and disappointed. Perhaps she had been wrong in the first place to encourage him to fill the vacuum of her loneliness. She liked him, but not ardently enough for romance. "I'll feel so ordinary again," he had said. "You made me seem like somebody new. I like me when I am with you." She had thought about him, wondered that their paths had not crossed, and now she had her corroboration that the famous novelist had not saved him from the Proclamation.

"Hello, Hugo."

"Rebecca!"

Hugo Raschenbaum was glad to see her—very glad. His smile—that strange scar twisting upwards—flashed and waned and recovered feebly. He looked at her hungrily, but saw something that restrained him. An awkward moment passed and a bridge was crossed.

"Miss Hersch tried," Hugo said, "but they were terrible to her. They said she should thank her stars that she was a Jew who had come to Shanghai before 1938 and didn't have to move into the designated area herself. So here I am, back in commerce." With a self-deprecating laugh, he waved a hand over the scarves, blouses, cotton anklets, and parasols displayed on top of the boxes.

She told him of her foray into the Forbidden City.

"How brave of you!" he marveled. "How lucky for you to have a pass."

It seemed strange but comfortable to Rebecca that they could be standing in a wretched street talking quite impersonally of prosaic matters. Did he have to have a license to be a peddler? Where did he get his merchandise? Was it only other refugees who bought from him?

"They bargain like they grew up here," Hugo said. "But I guess they have to, they—we—have so little."

"What are the things you have the most calls for?"

"Oil lamps. Raincoats. Blotting paper. Sun visors. Underclothing. Water canteens. Needles. Watch chains. Mezuzahs. Shoe polish. Inks. Razors. Mirrors."

"Hugo, what if I were able to get these things a lot cheaper than you can here? And tell you how much I must have and let you sell them for what you can over that?"

"A business partnership? Is that what you are proposing?"

"A business partnership."

It may not have been the kind of alliance that Hugo would most have prized, but it could be something that would benefit each of them.

The impending physical examination of the refugee men was generating gnawing tension. Rumors proliferated. Whispers of subterfuge and stratagems buzzed on the bamboo telegraph. Rabbi Bernstein was impelled to intercede from the bimah at Rosh Hashannah services. "It would not be wise for our men to avoid or subvert these examinations," he warned. "Thus far in the association with our 'hosts,' to put it politely, we have not been badly treated. We would be courting danger if we do not comply with orders. If we are cooperative, let us hope that God will find a way to protect us."

Hoping for help from Him again, David scoffed.

And he scoffed at a rumor that Hermann Feinstein brought home. You thought that was a cigarette factory around the corner, where the coolies slave away in shifts night and day? Guess again. It is an arsenal—they're in there making bombs. We are a sitting duck.

David was edgy and morose, and snappish even at his Aunt Sophie and Rebecca. What did it matter if someone was ten or ten thousand miles away if you couldn't see her? He was in no mood to be reasonable. At his most despairing, Erika Zuckerman breezed through the gate like a brisk wind from the East China Sea. She was being repatriated.

"It'll be no picnic, chéri," she said, patting David lightly on the crotch. "Five hundred of us jammed in a junk not big enough for Baby Leroy. The swap's at Goa in the Indian Ocean. We'll board the *Gripsholm*, where, thank heavens, there will be a few amenities, and the Japanese from the U.S. will board the junk we were in and paddle back to Tokyo. New York, here I come!"

She was breathless with excitement, radiating that vitality that was as pungent as perfume. Her hand on his groin evoked for a second their feverish episode of love-making in the Cathay Hotel. As he looked at her now in her tailored red coat, fox fur, heavy tweed suit, fine hosiery, and black velvet cloche—so smart, so charged with high expectations—he felt infinitely older than she.

"How did you find me?" he asked, a little embarrassed.

"Oh, I have my G-2."

"So you're really leaving?"

"I'm really leaving. With a few regrets, I might add. I just visited the heims, and I could cry. They're starving while those fat-fannied Shanghai Jews who have been in the Concessions forever ride their horses around the Race Course every morning and say they've given all they can."

"I'd like to stowaway on your junk," David said.

"Don't I wish, my love. I bet you'd rise to the occasion."

On the heels of Erika Zuckerman, Ah Chang arrived with his portentous missive from Rosalie.

"We did not—repeat—NOT make the list.

"Aaron is in a coma. He screamed, 'Merchant seamen and ribbon clerks, bakers and candlestick-makers get sprung, and we get f____d!' And then fell mute. I pray he snaps out of this snit and starts screaming like his old self.

"I amuse myself with definitions of happiness.

"1. Happiness is walking out of the front gate of this prison.

"2. Happiness is one good hot meal.

"3. Happiness is two months in bed with the Mad Lover of Breslau.

"On second thought, scratch the first two.

"P.S. Even if we had made the list, I would not have gone back with them. So *there*, ye of little faith!"

David yelped and beat his chest. "You silly goose," he told himself. "You are up and down like a seesaw. Your moods shoot and fall like skyrockets. You are worse than a pregnant woman."

David yelped again with the news that Italy had surrendered. Unconditionally. The ghetto suffered rumortism, but this was what Erika Zuckerman would call the real McCoy.

"Terrible news," his uncle snapped. "Those cowards and bunglers were more help to the Allies than to the Nazis."

"Uncle Moritz, how can you . . ."

"How can I say such a thing? It's the truth, that's how I can say it. Listen, my boy. Mussolini botched things so bad in the Balkans that Hitler had to go in and finish the job, so the German army didn't get to Moscow before winter and that was the end of that. No, better for the Allies if the Italians were still in."

"You are a fast man with a wet blanket, Mr. Felcher," Rebecca observed.

The day that Italy fell, the *Conte Verde* was scuttled in the Whangpoo, where it had languished since Pearl Harbor. The crew had opened the seacocks—they didn't want the Japanese to get her. Within hours, this jewel of the Italian passenger lines—seventeen thousand tons of luxury—went to its watery grave and now lay belly up in the harbor.

"The *Conte Verde*," Ada Hurwitz blubbered, "it's like losing a loved one. She brought me here, and I nourished every faith that someday she would take me home. The Italians have such flair, oo-la-la. They did everything so beautifully. The attention! The courtesies and the compliments! One of my acquaintances who wasn't fortunate enough to be so much in the middle of things as I was said to me with true envy, 'Mrs. Hurwitz, you seem to be a permanent fixture at the captain's table.' For our grand gala we put on a performance of *Die Fledermaus*. You never saw such spectacle! I can't begin to tell you. I leave you to guess who was asked to play the demanding role of Rosalinda."

"How can we guess?" Rebecca said. "We don't know who the other passengers were."

"You are a fast woman with a wet blanket," Moritz Felcher smiled.

Yom Kippur. New Year's. The beginning of the year 5703.

In a hundred Yom Kippurs the residents of 22/158 Kimpei Lane would never become a true family. But this Day of Atonement, the holiest day of the year, kept them physically close to one another within the house and, in the avoidance of blasphemy, some semblance of harmony and cohesiveness prevailed.

At sundown, Moritz Felcher went to the café and brought back light refreshments and two bottles of sweet wine to break the fast. He savored his role as the quasi-patriarch. In the courtyard in the pleasant evening he beamed, refilled glasses, listened to gossip and forebodings, and tried to mollify and reassure.

"And now," he said, "we shall play a little game. I am going to ask all of us to guess where he or she will be next Yom Kippur. The oldest and the wisest goes first. I guess . . . I guess I'll be right here. And I am guessing that the rest of you will be here, too. Now, now, none of that groaning. Sophie, you're next."

"Right here."

"Mrs. Hurwitz?"

"In the city of my dreams. Wien, Wien."

"Mrs. Wolf?"

"Somewhere over the rainbow," Rebecca said flippantly.

"Esther dear?"

"In Oz, with Mommy. Right, Mommy?"

"Mrs. Schiff?"

"America, I hope."

"Professor Spiller?"

"In China, I should say. Preferably some place with an old Jewish settlement where I can . . . "

"David!"

"Either Hammerfest or Tierra del Fuego."

"Feinstein?"

"Dead."

Not one of them had a stitch of clothing on. They stood shivering in long queues in the drafty common room of the Ward Road jail with its warped wooden floors, trapped fetid odors, and moldering Paris-green walls. They stood in four alphabetical formations waiting to be examined. It was embarrassing, pathetic, humiliating. The older and the weaker men, particularly, tried to hide their nakedness with clumsy posturing. The younger, sturdier men tactfully averted their gaze from the vistas of spindly legs, washboard ribs, sagging flesh, stomach scars, and shriveled genitals.

"At least nobody's shoving a riding crop up our asshole," the young man in front of him in the A-E queue remarked to David.

His name was Hans Ackermann. He was twenty-six, tall and powerfully built ("an hour a night with bar bells"), and had a curly mop of mustardy hair. He was from Salzburg, a fact subtly proclaimed by the tiny bass clef tattooed on his left shoulder blade. He was cocky and disdainful—the concomitant, perhaps, of someone with a pass to go to the Bund every day for his regular employment with a Swiss pharmaceutical firm. He was flip, with an answer for everything.

"Funny," David said, "I've never seen you before."

"And now you're seeing all of me."

"Why are we here? Why are they doing this to us?"

"They're playing Nazi, but they're only two-shilling Nazis."

"Why aren't they using their own doctors?"

"When you've got Jewish doctors around? Who's ever heard of Japanese doctors, anyway?"

"It doesn't take a Berlin doctor to do what they're doing. Anybody, a—a veterinarian could do it."

"Who knows, Buchbinder? Maybe they're afraid of confronting a circumcised prick head-on. They may have fears of contamination. They're all shmucks."

Could that be the thinking? They were in some way unclean, hygienically unclean, in the eyes of the Japanese—the Japanese who, historically, had made a fetish of cleanliness? Was that the reason for the compulsory examination? Still, if they were so curious, so suspicious, why weren't they doing this themselves? The two sentries positioned at either side of each of the four tables where the examining doctors were seated might be seeing everything. But how much could they hear? Understand? Nothing. Only the next in queue could hear, understand.

"Mr. Ackermann? Doctor Pincus."

Doctor Pincus? The Doctor Pincus whom Mrs. Wolf had mentioned? The one she had done some shopping for?

"Ever had any serious illnesses or injuries?"

"Never."

"Any history of weaknesses or certain predispositions in your family background?"

"None."

"Childhood diseases?"

"The usual. Measles. Mumps. Chicken pox."

"Can you think of anything at all that could have any negative bearing on your obvious appearance of good health and fitness?"

"Nothing."

"Mmmmm. Well, let's see what we see."

Hans Ackermann submitted, as had the others before him, to the tongue depressor, the stethoscope, the eye-ear-nose tools, the hammer tapping on the knees, the band wrapping and tightening around an arm to check for blood pressure. He coughed while Doctor Pincus held his testicles, then turned around and spread his buttocks to the probing physician.

Doctor Pincus shook his head and wrote on the report of H. Ackermann: "Hiatus hernia."

"What are you writing? Hiatus hernia? What the hell is . . ."

"Nothing fatal, fortunately, if you show caution. I advise you not to do any heavy lifting."

"Hiatus hernia? Doctor, what are you . . . "

"Hiatus hernia. Next, please."

Hans Ackermann tapped a temple—he's crazy, Buchbinder—and David was responding to the same earnest but irritating interrogation. No history of mastoid trouble? No allergies or postnasal drips? No diabetes in the family? Strokes? "Sports, Mr. Buchbinder? Did you engage in sports?"

"I played soccer."

"Aha. Ever get hurt?"

"The usual. A few bumps and knocks here and there. A sprain or two."

A few bumps and knocks and a sprain or two? Was David sure that was all? Doctor Pincus, frowning, pressed and massaged, his fingers progressing carefully from David's upper thighs to his feet. Again the handsome, gray-cropped head was shaking gravely.

"It's a little more than that, my young friend. You have a chronically disoriented fibula."

Chronically disoriented fibula? What did it mean? What kind of medical mumbo jumbo was that? David opened his mouth, framing a challenge, but was silenced with a wink.

And so it went.

Moritz Felcher learned that he had a distended testicle. Hermann Feinstein had a duodenal ulcer. Professor Spiller was legally blind. Natzie was "impotent by reason of hormonal deficiency." Natzie, the lover man, impotent!

And every other man had his private affliction to bear. If it wasn't pes planus, first degree, it was gastrointestinal congestion. Or pernicious anemia. Or incipient cataracts. Or hemorrhoids. Or peritonitis. Or rheumatoid arthritis. Or sciatica. Or diverticulitis. Or bursitis. Or acute myocardial infarction. Or emphysema. Or mumps. Or gallstones. Or kidney stones. Or astringent astigmatism. Or chronic somnabulism. Or diabetic acidosis. Or vertigo. Or hepatitis. Or cirrhosis. Or incapacitating climacteric. Or paranoid schizophrenia.

It was a horrendous reflection on the health of Jewish males that there wasn't a fit man in the whole ghetto.

Autumn banished the killing heat, but it was hardly a season of mists and mellow fruitfulness. Life in the ghetto settled into its monotonous rhythms and routines. If one day differed from the day before, it was because it brought a firmer grip on harsh realities and lessening expectations. If anyone had told Rebecca that she could *survive* these conditions for even a week, she would have thought him demented.

The evidence of how much crueler that fate was for so

many others was always before her. Hop Ng pulled her on shopping excursions to the Native City and told her gory detail upon gory detail of the famine in the province of Honan, where the wind broke backs. Hop Ng's cousin had just arrived from there, covering the three hundred miles to Shanghai on foot. Even for China, it was a devastating plague. A million people had already starved to death. To walk in any village was to pick your way around a human wasteland of corpses. The most horrible crimes against nature were being committed. Parents were cannibalizing their own children. Or bashing out their children's brains to stifle their cries of hunger. Dogs gnawed on dead humans until they were caught and eaten themselves. For one last meal, families bartered the rags off their backs and then slit their own throats with a sharpened stick. Babies suckled at the breast of their dead mothers.

The paper-thin-skinned Hop Ng grinned and kept ting-ting-tingling on the bell under his finger on the groaning rickshaw, its axle never greased, as he breathlessly described the many faces of human attrition. His cousin said that there should be no famine at all. There was grain enough in the provinces surrounding Honan to feed everyone. But against politics and so much greed the peasants had no chance. The Generalissimo cared only about the warlords who ran those provinces. He would never force them to feed the starving when they could sell that grain elsewhere and siphon off some of the astronomical profits for Chunking. Peasants were an expendable crop, but grain was something of value.

"Look for a cloisonné vase," Hugo Raschenbaum had instructed Rebecca. "I have a buyer." Another day it would be ladies' gloves. Or eightpenny nails. Or sewing needles. Or celluloid collars. Or Mont Blanc fountain pens. ("Chinese businessmen think they're somebody if they can show off a Mont Blanc fountain pen.")

Simple trading was keeping a flow of sorely needed coins in her purse, but she never set off without twinges of guilt or made the return journey without mounting anxiety.

"Next month you will be having a very important birthday," she reminded Esther.

"Is ten very important?"

"I think it is."

"That's good. Because I want a lot of things. I want a jump rope. I want a panda bear. I want silk bloomers. I want purple fingernail polish. I want a boy's bicycle so I can ride with Lyng Huan. I want . . . "

"Maybe we'll have to settle for a nice second-hand copy of *Anne of Green Gables*. Mommy's very poor."

"You should have married Mr. Raschenbaum."

"He's very poor, too."

They were all accommodating themselves to one another, to what now passed for "life." There were two exceptions. Hermann Feinstein, whose accommodation was shallow, and Joseph Schiff, who was not accommodating at all. Miriam Schiff had given up her beseeching and placating and was humming along in a mysterious serenity. Moritz Felcher had opened Café Moritz III and complained that he could fill three times as many tables. ("Nothing fancy, of course, like the old place, but for *here* . . . ") David was busy and only intermittently fretful and mooning.

Professor Spiller, in a rare social overture, buttonholed Rebecca and David. "Do either of you happen to know what holiday the Americans are celebrating today?"

"Columbus Day?" David guessed.

"Correct. And is either of you aware that Columbus was Jewish?"

Professor Spiller tried David's patience. Those quixotic theories and speculations put him in a combative mood, but contending with Professor Spiller was a waste of time and breath. "If that were true," David responded, "it would not have taken five hundred years to come to light."

"But supposing it were true," Rebecca temporized, "and the Americans did know? I wonder if they would be celebrating Columbus Day as a national holiday."

"It is true, it is true," Professor Spiller insisted vehemently. "I have the proof."

They had to hear him out. Columbus' family lived in Genoa, and like many other humble Jews they were in the wool

business, combing and weaving. The boy could quote the Jewish prophets and mystics, and his early exercise books (as well
as his later letters) displayed a style of writing much influenced
by the Old Testament. He was an ambitious and imaginative
youth and was determined early-on to become a sailor. The
natural thing for him to do was to go to Portugal and Spain,
whose empires were expanding—and none of the Italian states
were sponsoring exploration and discovery. It could be in-
ferred that when Columbus reached Spain he became a conver-
so, a convert to Christianity, as did so many Jews. After waiting for many years for the financing needed to sail west to the
Orient, Columbus postponed setting sail for a whole day beyond the scheduled embarkation—a most significant fact: The
original sailing date coincided with Tishah B'ab, the Jewish holy day of fasting and mourning to commemorate the destruction of the First and Second Temples of Jerusalem. "There are
many other circumstances that support my conviction that Columbus was Jewish. For example, in his last letters to his son,
he used beit-hay, the Hebrew symbol 'Praised be the Lord,'
and his will adhered to Jewish traditions in disposing of worldly goods. Also, it could be argued that Columbus was not looking for a new route to the spices of China and India but really
was trying to find a homeland for the Jewish people, who had
been expelled by the Spanish monarchs."

Professor Spiller cocked his head in triumph. The red-
rimmed eyes behind the copper-framed glasses blinked fitfully.
He awaited their applause.

"I must say," Rebecca said, "it sounds convincing."

"I can see where all the textbooks are going to have to be
rewritten," David teased. "What is the term for that, Professor
Spiller? 'Revisionist history'?"

The days were shorter, but they began as early as ever for
22/158 Kimpei Lane, thanks to a human alarm clock.

"Six o'clock, Mister Felcher. Six o'clock."

In the predawn darkness, Moritz Felcher rose, quickly
went through his matutinal rites, and was off and running—
haggling over his purchase of coffee beans, teas, flour, sugar,

and the black-market butter from Henri the Hungarian, firing the oven to bake rolls, and washing fruits and vegetables in huge wooden tubs. Still ahead of him were twelve hours at the café.

A mechanical alarm clock would have served just as well, but it would not have alerted the whole neighborhood to the importance of Moritz Felcher. His time was so valuable that he had to employ The Crowing Cock. "You have to let a Jew live," he rationalized. "The old man wakes me up and comes around to the café a couple of times during the day and I feed him."

"Six o'clock, Mister Felcher. Six o'clock."

David knew that voice. It couldn't be who he thought it was, but it had to be. No one else could sound like that. He shook off his early-morning grogginess to get up and see for himself one day. Through the barely breaking light he made out a derby hat bouncing on top of the little man retreating out the lane. Mr. Steinwig. H. Steinwig, the hatmaker. Hermann Steinwig. Stripped of his booming Panama-hat business and reduced to cock-a-doodle-dos at dawn.

The days as well as the nights were becoming chillier. The residents would have to struggle through the winter without fireplaces or Dutch tile stoves or furnaces.

"We'll have our love to keep us warm," Rebecca sang, hugging her curly-topped, leggy daughter.

"Fire would be better, Mommy."

Miriam Schiff had a luxurious Canadian beaver coat to keep *her* warm.

"Such a beautiful coat, Mrs. Schiff," Ada Hurwitz cooed, her eyes wide as plates.

"Yes, isn't it. And so warm."

Ada Hurwitz said to Rebecca, "That coat didn't come from the thrift shop, I can tell you. But where did she get it?"

"You all but asked her. If you want to know that bad, you'll have to come right out and put it to her."

Rebecca was just as curious. Miriam was blooming. She had gained some weight. Her troubles with her husband apparently were resting lighter upon her. Joseph Schiff had not gone to his watchman's job for three nights. He remained in

their room in the quiet of the dead. Miriam used this with-
drawal as a spur to be away each evening until nearly midnight.

"Is your husband ill, Miriam?"

"Not that I know of," she airily answered Rebecca. "Why
do you ask?"

"Well, why is he not going to his work?"

"He no longer has work. He was dismissed."

"Shouldn't he be . . . "

"I don't think he'll be looking for anything else. He just
wants to bury himself in his beloved *Steppenwolf.*"

Was Hermann Hesse going to pay the rent? Miriam must
earn only tiny sums from her part-time work. Moritz Felcher
would not be a lenient landlord.

"I know what you must be thinking," Miriam said.
"Which brings up something that I wanted to ask your advice
about. I have a friend. A new friend who wants to help."

"How nice, Miriam."

"He is a White Russian with a furrier business on the Rue
Clemenceau. We met when he came to the shop with clothing
that he had collected for us. He has been back several times
with more clothing, and we have become friendly. He is kind,
charming, and forthright. He talks openly about his family and
his devotion to them. He does not try to seduce me with promises of a home or a future. Still, I am attracted to him."

Rebecca knew something was expected of her, and Miriam
meant to say more. The pause was a challenge. "Well, Miriam,
that's your private . . . "

"He would like to find a room or a flat for me and see me
there. But I could not move out on Joseph. I—I tell you all this
as a way of asking if you think it would be all right if I entertained my friend here? In my room upstairs, I mean?"

Rebecca's first impulse was to lash out, "How dare you lay
this at my door. Do what you will, that's your business, but
don't try to make me your conspirator or defender." But she
counted to herself until she had simmered down, then said,
"What about your husband?"

"He'll have nothing to say about it."

"I mean, he's here all day."

"He'll just have to clear out when my friend comes to see me."

"You seem to have made up your mind. Why are you asking me anything?"

"I do have Mister Felcher to think of."

"Are you asking me if he will approve? Will he permit it?"

"Yes, something like that."

"Mr. Felcher is a man of the world. I guess it would be all right as long as he is not here and privy to any of your 'entertaining.'"

Refugees were hungry, some of them literally starving. It was one thing to be amused by the ingenuity of the Jewish doctors who had found a way of declaring every last male refugee unfit without inviting Japanese reprisals. It was something else again to look at all those naked bodies that day and see how many of them were conspicuously unfit. Men in their forties looked like seventy, like survivors (barely) of a death march. Mostly, they were ravaged by hunger.

A growling stomach was not a vexation that David shared with the many. He had a hot meal standing up in his uncle's kitchen every day ("I can't put you out front—I might need the table") in exchange for doing some of the early morning marketing for the café or for an advertising notice in David's newssheet. But how could David not know about the thousands in the heims who were subsisting on beans? He saw the meager rations going into the cooking pot at home and he listened to the obsessional talk of food—how bad the food was, how little of it there was, how dangerous it was to eat *anything*. It was unfortunate that the refugees couldn't make a virtue of privation and pretend that they were like those religious ascetics who managed to live year after year on a bit of gruel and a crust of bread. At a free performance ("donations accepted") of *The Threepenny Opera* he heard the audience stomp and hoot at the choral couplet, "For even saintly folk will act like sinners / Unless they have their customary dinners."

David raged impotently. Was there a lesson here? Was God using hunger for some divine metaphor?

Rosalie was more comic relief than philosophically inquiring on the same subject.

"They've clamped down here," she wrote. "No more contraband food sneaking in under the running boards of trucks. No more chickens thrown over the walls by peasants.

"So we're eating dung. But how these people *torture* themselves! We have our plate of dung and someone's recalling a great dining experience. 'Maxim's, yes, for spectacle and ambience, but for the very best food you go to the Grand Vefour.' 'Not if you want pressed duck—the only place for that is La Tour d'Argent.' 'We always booked Oscar Wilde's table at the Café Royal and ordered the entrecôte béarnaise with shoestring potatoes and green beans vinaigrette.' Ad nauseam, ad infinitum. . . . "

"Now, Joseph," Miriam announced for everyone to hear, "I expect you to be out of this room by one o'clock and not back before three. Otherwise, you will be considerably embarrassed, I can promise you. This will be our routine on Tuesdays and Fridays."

"Men's fur-lined gloves. Sweaters. Woolen mufflers. Long johns. A tea cosy. A teakwood medicine chest. Two lead soldiers—for a Chanukah present."

In less than an hour in the Native City, Rebecca had all the items on Hugo Raschenbaum's shopping list, then was back in Hop Ng's rickshaw and clop-clopping on the return journey. A wintry darkness was descending; it hung black and brooding. Shanghai was starving for color. A hooded candle in each fender of the rickshaw eerily illuminated the barricades of steel pilings, the sandbags, the clanking tanks and overstuffed trams, the squat foot soldiers, and the ragged hordes hunched over bicycle handlebars.

No warmth, no cheerfulness, no healthful ease,
No comfortable feel in any member—
No shade, no shine, no butterflies, no bees,
No fruits, no flowers, no leaves, no birds—
November!

"Lookee, missee," Hop Ng called to her. Rebecca saw a freshly severed head of a Chinese youth precariously perched on two strands of barbed wire, a cigarette dangling from its lips. To Hop Ng this was a sight, a diversion to relieve the monotony of the journey. Rebecca shut her eyes tight and meditated on the coolie's indifference to violent death and mutilation. "It is fate," the Chinese shrugged. Was it merely their infinite numbers—their expendability—that led them to place such low value on human life? Or was this fatalism another lingering legacy of Confucianism? Oh, Teng, you must have explained this, but did it go in one ear and out the other? Teng, Teng . . .

Rebecca must have dozed. She must have dozed through the backward dip and the forward thrust of the rickshaw as Hop Ng pulled her home over the Garden Bridge. He had stopped abruptly on the bridge, some yards from the wooden guard post of Pass Point #3.

"What is it, Hop Ng?"

"Bad, lady."

"Bad what?"

Hop Ng nodded toward the two sentries guarding the passageway into the ghetto. All armed soldiers looked menacing to Rebecca, especially at dusk, these no worse than others.

"Another way, lady. I take you. One cent more. Believe."

Hop Ng pulled her along Hongkew Creek toward East Yuhan Road and in a few minutes they were at Pass Point #5. This access, a narrow arc in a rotting planked fence, was being guarded by an unarmed Caucasian. Rebecca recognized the Pao Chia black sleeve band and name badge, and in the next instant, without a word, a tall, brawny, brutish man of about thirty in a navy-blue greatcoat had snatched the pass from her hand and was scrutinizing it.

Polish, she judged, from the incivility, the stone-faced expression, the mop of oily black curls tumbling out of an imitation sealskin hat perched at a cocky angle on his head. He was taking himself and his duties very seriously. He squinted and scowled at the pass, examined and reexamined the few facts of identification. He brought his head close to hers and stared at her suspiciously, matching her face with the blurred photograph on the card. He fingered the entire surface of the "passport" and then the four edges, as if in search for incriminating grooves, notches, or bumps. What kind of information did he suspect could be concealed in that harmless scrap of cardboard?

"You repair typewriters?"

"As it states. Yes."

"I am not asking what it states. You repair typewriters?"

"I repair typewriters, Mr. . . . Puchinsky. Have you one in need of repair?"

Stonily ignoring her sarcasm, he asked, "A busy day?"

"I am always busy, Mr. Puchinsky."

"Busy repairing typewriters?"

"Repairing typewriters."

"How many today?"

"Oh, let me see. One—two—three—and the one on the Avenue Foch. Four altogether."

How easily the lie tripped to her lips when she was jousting with someone beneath her contempt. She had lied to the Chief Examiner to get her pass and she thought nothing of lying to keep it. But her prejudice must be showing. She would not be speaking in this fashion to a German, whatever the impertinence. But a loutish Pole? By some ancient, uninterred bias, Polish people were of a lesser breed. The Polish Jews— unpolished and impoverished, fugitive from pogrom after pogrom—who poured into the Fatherland had not been like the German Jews. They were an alien lot, crude, vulgar, usually bearded, unbathed, and not readily assimilable. The socialistic ideologies they noisily espoused, Rebecca had often thought, had played a strong hand both in reawakening dormant anti-Semitism in Germany and in nurturing Nazi pathology in its hatred of all Jews. Not that exotic or politicized Jews were to blame for Hitler or that Hitler was to be "understood" or forgiven a thing. She was grateful to Hermann Feinstein for at least one of his jokes: "I'll tell you how dumb the Poles are—a Polish Shylock lent everyone money and then skipped town."

"Are those tools in that satchel?" the sentinel was asking.

"No, I keep them in the shop where I do the repairs."

"Where is that shop?"

"In the Boulevard St. Honoré."

"What do you have in the satchel?"

"Personal shopping."

"Give it to me."

"*Give* it to you? Are you presuming to appropriate . . . "

"I must see it."

"Is the Pao Chia authorized to conduct searches?"

"If there is reason for suspicion. Give it to me."

Pao Chia Puchinsky whistled and looked at her insolently. "You *were* busy today. Four typewriters fixed. And time to get all this? Do you wear men's underthings, Mrs. Wolf?"

"No, but the men in my house do."

"You must live with many men," he jeered, riffling through the mufflers, gloves, long johns, and woolen tam-o'-shanter.

Rebecca glared at him icily and said nothing. Hauteur was the only tactic in dealing with toy gendarmes like Leo Puchinsky. It might work. Confusion or apologies or objections, for a certainty, would not work.

"You can go this time," he said, throwing the card and bundle of clothing into her lap. "But next time could be trouble—much trouble. I shall be talking to authorities. I shall ask about people who are using their pass suspiciously."

There would be no next time. Rebecca knew that the Leo Puchinskys would do anything to ingratiate themselves with officialdom. She had heard of refugees spying on other refugees. There were rumors of a Jewish underground that reported directly to Nazi headquarters at the German consulate. "It's not worth the risk," she told Hugo Raschenbaum. "I have a daughter to think of, as well as myself."

"It's getting so cold," Hugo said. "People rush by. I'll try to sell what I have, then leave the street."

The days were thin wedges of gray between the thick black bookends of night. Today was colder than yesterday. Rain turned to sleet and sleet to a fine sheath of snow. The temper of the community was overstated despair. The tunnel did not have a bend, much less a flashing beacon at the end.

22/158 buckled with the freezing temperatures. Its residents crawled into caves of layered clothing. The amenities wore thinner. Joseph Schiff sulked out of the house to make way for his wife's afternoon lover. Ada Hurwitz lost her grip on the icy ladder to her loft and had her left foot consigned to a cast. "Keep moving, Sophie," Moritz Felcher advised, "and you'll stay warm." Professor Spiller became even more engrossed in his history of Jews in China, writing now with his mittens on. "I pass the hat," Hermann Feinstein raged in the middle of the night. "I go to the kitchen for a glass of seltzer and I come back and find the hat's passed right out the door."

Paraphrasing Hans Fallada, Rebecca asked herself, "Little lady, what now?" and David suggested, "You, too, should be using your typewriter. Offer your services, Mrs. Wolf."

Rebecca laughed.

"What's so funny?"

"When I learned to use the typewriter, back in the Bronze Age, I was a social worker. I learned to typewrite so I could pass along the skill to wayward girls who would otherwise end up in prostitution. Now you are telling me to get to my typewriter. Is it that or face the fate of wayward girls?"

David was serious. He pasted black paper patches over the keys of her typewriter to keep her from peeking and urged her to "practice, practice, practice" her touch typing. Rebecca tried:

The qkuci brown foc jump over t dog

Teh quick bowrn fox hmps

voer

The qucki rwbown fox mumps . . .

After a week of "practicing," she let David test her. Deducting for errors, she had a speed of nineteen words a minute. "The quick brown fox better get a little quicker," she remarked, and David, smiling, touched her typing fingers and kissed them in the courtly Continental style.

"I think Moritz Felcher hates every man in this house," Ada Hurwitz speculated, "except his nephew. He may have had a sadistic father."

Ada Hurwitz and her eternal analyzing—so Viennese, so owing perhaps to her fateful meeting with the Supreme Analyzer in the railway station. So rubbishy.

"Mrs. Hurwitz, please," Rebecca responded. "Mr. Felcher is a certain type of man. When you appreciate that, you know exactly how he would feel about Joseph Schiff. He would see him as a lazy layabout and cuckold. And Professor Spiller as a lost dreamer. Hermann Feinstein, you must agree, is hardly ingratiating, and he misses no opportunity to play Mack the Knife with Mr. Felcher."

Chanukah came. As best they could, they celebrated the Maccabean rededication of the Temple of Jerusalem. The menorah had only one candle, which they relit each of the eight evenings of the "festival of lights." On the last night they exchanged little gifts of a sort and they all laughed at Esther's antics. Moritz Felcher poured Schnaps from a bottle he had saved from the old Café Moritz.

"I have a new joke," Hermann Feinstein said.

"We don't want to hear it," Moritz Felcher snorted.

"There was this *other* pigpen. [Pause for connections to be made.] This other one was in a shtetl in the Pale. A candlemaker came crying to the rabbi because nineteen of his bride's relatives had moved into his two-room hut and he couldn't breathe. Move the goat inside with the family, the rabbi told Bodinsky. The goat? Bodinsky did, and came back crying even harder to the rabbi. Now move your chickens into the hut. The chickens? Bodinsky shooed them inside, and came back howling to high heaven. Now, now, calm down, Bodinsky, the rabbi ordered, and do what I say. Put the goat back outside and tell me how things are. Bodinsky had to admit that things were a bit better. Now put the chickens back outside. Bodinsky did, and told the rabbi that conditions inside the hut were now like paradise."

There was laughter and clapping of hands. Moritz Felcher pointedly emptied the bottle of Kümmel before it reached Hermann Feinstein again. Be it ever so humble, no one called his home a pigsty with impunity.

The tension was relieved by Esther. She alone had a way with Hermann Feinstein. To her, he showed his clownish, appealing, warm side—making faces, turning his eyes into his head, wiggling his ears, twisting his nose out of joint, and pulling the corner of his mouth down like an English bulldog's. Once, he crowned her with the henna toupee that he wore at the Blaue Donau.

"You got bigger ears than Dumbo," Esther quipped.

"That's because I got them at the Elephant Hotel."

"There's no hotel for elephants."

"Ah, but there *is* an Elephant Hotel. It is in Weimar, back home. I passed the night there once, Esther, and *guess* who else was sleeping there the same night?"

"Charlie Chaplin?"

"No, no, somebody *very* ugly. I'll give you a hint."

Hermann Feinstein put a black comb across his upper lip and coaxed a tuft of hair across his brow.

Esther chortled with recognition: "Der Hitler! Der Hitler!"

1944

SHANGHAI

Far away, the New Year began with the news that the Russians were cracking the two-year siege of Leningrad and bearing down on the Polish and Rumanian borders. But the liberation of Western Europe was an ever-receding mirage, though the towers of the Fatherland were toppling. The vaulting achievements of a millennium were being bombed to rubble. The Americans bombed by day, the British bombed by night. Every day, every night. The terrorization of the cities was relentless, unceasing. Berlin. Bremerhaven. Munich. Nuremberg. Hamburg. Essen. Duisburg. Wuppertal. Cologne. Münster. Rostock. Lübeck over and over. Why Lübeck?, Rebecca asked herself. Beautiful, peaceable, defenseless, unthreatening Lübeck. Berlin, Samuel . . .

"A necessary evil," Moritz Felcher said. "The sooner the Allies destroy civilian morale, the sooner the German people will demand a stop to the whole bloody mess."

"Just the opposite," David argued. "The more the Allies bomb, the more the Nazis will get their back up, the more the German people will feel that they are in the same boat with the Nazis and that the enemy is indeed the barbarian the Nazis say he is."

"They're not that pigheaded. Anyway, at least nobody's bombing Breslau."

"Yet," David added, to have the last word. Breslau, Mama . . .

Bombing was a reality for others, under different skies. Here, the pervasive reality was the cold. The air was damp nearly to saturation and cut like a scalpel. There were those who kept to their beds around the clock. Others went about swathed in everything that would adhere to their bodies— summer clothing under winter clothing, extra sheathings of blanket and bits of carpet and hanks of drapery and layers of newspaper pages—shameless as hobos.

"How did you sleep last night?"

"Cold."

"What's in the pot?"

"Cold."

"What's new?"

"Cold."

How was it that a subtropical city, which only yesterday had them begging for relief from the merciless heat, could so quickly transform itself into an arctic nightmare?

"Miriam," he would call softly from the foot of the stairs, and She took it as her cue to leave the house. It would have been unthinkable for her to stay there during Miriam's Tuesday and Friday un-à-trois, overhearing the sounds of love-making. She strolled and browsed, and found faint amusement that Miriam was in the house with her lover and *she* was the streetwalker.

Miriam could be said to be in good hands, if that was the phrase. Mr. Shabolov was a distinguished-looking man in his forties with silver hair and, peculiarly for the dead of winter, skin that looked sun-tanned. He came like royalty in his fashionably cut midnight-blue overcoat, pearl-gray derby, calfskin gloves, and sharply shined oxfords. He always came carrying some little lagniappe for Miriam.

Rebecca practiced and practiced at her typewriter. A complimentary announcement in *The Hongkew Reporter*—"Professional typewriter offers services at lowest rates in strictest confidence"—brought her her first paying customer. He was a Chinese law student, with a characteristically quaint command of English, who presented her with his brief.

"The Chinese studying law? Needing briefs?" Moritz Felcher hooted. "Let me tell you how the law works here. Back at the old Café Moritz a woman had her fur jacket stolen. We had the usual sign up about management not being responsible for personal property, but she filed a claim anyway. My solicitor was sure that I had an open-and-shut case. He kept telling me I couldn't lose, but to be on the safe side, just the same, we should slip the judge a little something. We did—and I was still

ordered to pay the woman for her coat. Was my solicitor embarrassed or ashamed? Not for one second. He just laughed
and said, 'I guess she slipped him more than just a little something.' "

"This young man sounds very high-minded, Mr. Felcher."

"Kohn-bahn-wah, Mrs. Wolf," he said, dismissing her defense of the law student. Good evening.

Mornings, it was "Oh-hah-yoh." Good morning.

"It just makes sense," Moritz Felcher said, explaining his
groping for a grasp of conversational Japanese. "We may be
here a long time."

His annoyance with Professor Spiller worsened, became
climactic.

Seconds after Kohn-bahn-wah-ing to Rebecca one night,
he stood at the historian-bookseller's door. "Where the hell
were you today, Spiller?"

Dead silence from within.

"Spiller, I am talking to you. Where the hell were you today?"

"Today?"

"Yes, goddamn it, today. I sent some fellow over to your
place. He was in my café, and I overheard he was trying to
obtain some damn book. I sent him over to you, and he was
back in half an hour setting me straight. Your shade was down,
he said, and you had a sign in the window—'Closed Today.'
Closed today? Where the hell were you?"

Silence.

"Spiller, I am speaking to you. Where the hell were you?"

"I—I was there. I was busy—with other things."

"Christ Almighty!"

David disliked the man. Joseph Schiff was a spook, a surly
misanthrope who deserved no better than he was getting. But
David's curiosity was piqued; where did the man go while his
wife was having her illicit tryst? One bitterly cold February
afternoon, when the sky was low and charcoal-gray, David's
curiosity got the better of him. He fell in step behind his neighbor.

Joseph Schiff was not taking his usual shuffling gait. He was walking purposefully, quite briskly, looking neither to the left nor to the right. At the end of Chusan Road he turned into Wayside Road. Joseph Schiff going to the police station? Some mysterious business with Minobe? The trail led on. He stopped in front of a crumbling brown frame building with a pagoda roof, looked around furtively, and slipped through a tin-plated door.

The building was an abandoned Chinese movie house that now served as a synagogue for overflow worshipers on the High Holy days. Who but Joseph Schiff would find refuge in such a forlorn building? David tried to visualize him standing—sitting?—in the Stygian gloom within, alone, a solitary communing with a lopsided makeshift ark and a sagging bimah encased in shadows.

"It would be an interesting experiment," Rebecca commented to David, "to stand at the intersection of Wayside and Chusan and ask every third European Jew how his new play was coming. I daresay you would never hear, 'What play?' "

Her typewriting business was quite active. A flow of aspiring dramatists wanted to see their plays in typescript. She smiled and sighed as she typewrote, and suffered qualms of guilt for accepting money for such amateurish efforts. The plays were about duped maidens or families gone awry or spies crawling out of the woodwork, and they had titles like *Proud Bertha of Alt Wittstein* and *Augsburg Agony* and *Betrayal in the Sudetenland* and *One Perfect Rose for Henrietta*.

On the heels of the playwrights came the players, who asked her to type out parts from the very plays that she had been typing. They would hand her the playwright's copy and say, "I'm playing Otto, please type only Otto's lines." The woman playing Frieda wanted only Frieda's lines. And so on. Such thrift was easily understandable, necessary, but what were rehearsals like when Otto and Frieda and Wolfgang and Henrietta and Bertha all came together with their memorized lines but with no comprehension of when they should be spoken? Could they, like Othello, say, "Were it my cue to fight, I should have known it without a prompter"?

At night, David still cried, remembering his mother, anguishing over her vulnerability and his terrible guilt in leaving Breslau without her. But the biting days were warmer in the knowledge there were two women in Shanghai, one under the same roof, the other in an internment camp, who were lifting his spirits. He loved one for sure, but was there another word that could more accurately pinpoint what he felt for Mrs. Wolf? Probably not. There was love, and love . . .

David read to Rebecca the portions of Rosalie's letter that might cheer *her* up, or at least give her a moment of amusement. He caught the measured merriment and was secretly thrilled with sensations of forbidden power. Why, Mrs. Wolf was a mite jealous. But what of himself and his own chilling sensations when she spoke of Doctor Pincus as the inspiration for her "first career" in the ghetto?

"The American Red Cross came through at last," he read from Rosalie's letter. "It took them only two years to find us. But there, at long last, were the coolies on the Common, unloading wagon after wagon of food cartons and stacking the cartons in piles almost as high as the walls. Enough for everybody here and then some, you would think. Not so.

"Some American bullies (excluding Aaron, thank God!) proclaimed that the food parcels were only for the Americans. The other nationals would have to wait for their own Red Cross to come through. One of the Americans and a Brit got into fisticuffs, and a carton accidentally split open. Eureka! Tins of butter and processed meat and salmon and liver pâté. Hard cheeses and cheese spreads. Chocolate. Bags of sugar. Mixed dried fruits. Powdered milk. Coffee, tea, preserves. Cigarettes. And more, much more.

"The Commandant tried to arbitrate. Each American should receive one carton, and that would leave one parcel for every two persons among the other nationals. Nothing doing, the loudmouth, greedy Yanks said. Okay, the Commandant said, the cartons stay right where they are until directions come from Tokyo. The drooling! Tongues were hanging to toenails.

Finally, after ten salivating days, Tokyo spoke: each person (no Americans excepted) would receive one-half of a carton. (The wisdom of Solomon!) The remaining cartons would go to the internees in Pootong. I give you one guess who 'the internees in Pootong' are."

David refrained from reading to Mrs. Wolf the end of Rosalie's letter: "Ah, well, as the English keep saying, 'Keep your pecker up.' "

They were going to the doctor—Rebecca was certain that Esther's sniffles required a check-up.

"On our way we can see what's going on at the Koos," Rebecca coaxed.

"A funeral's going on at the Koos. I don't like funerals."

It wasn't a funeral. Chang Kwon Koo, who owned the most formidable house in the neighborhood—a solid symmetrical cement block with a splendid red slate roof—had died a year ago. The funeral festivities went on for eight days while Mr. Koo lay in an open wooden coffin on wooden horses in the backyard and mourners sat in the winter cold at large circular tables feting his memory with copious intakes of food and drink. On the eighth day, Mr. Koo was cremated.

The first anniversary of Mr. Koo's death was now being celebrated. As Rebecca and Esther stood in the lane looking on, the oldest Koo son touched a long wooden match to an elaborate artistic creation. Chang Kwon Koo was being remembered and revered according to tradition. The owner of a gas station in this life, he had inspired a papier-mâché replica of a Packard touring automobile parked beside a gas pump. The detail was astonishing. The Packard had a body and tires black as coal, oyster-colored running boards, white front and back bumpers, and hubcaps sporting scarlet dragons. The gas pump was orange with a white gauge and a kelly-green hose. While the craftsmanship was going up in flames, the "mourners" laughed, cried, screeched, munched on platters of cakes and steamed meat dumplings, sipped hot rice wine, and passed around snapshots of the dead man.

Life and death in China. Again and again and again, the

paradoxes. Disregard for life but reverence for death. It was all right to consign an unwanted baby to the gutter or a creek. But there was the unimaginable fate of dying *alone*—the deceased was doomed to "come back" as a single atom in a universe devoid of any human element. Nonetheless, the Chinese were wary about extending a helping hand to the sick or the maimed; by some fiat of moral responsibility, that helping hand could never be withdrawn. The Chinese could gingerly step over bodies that had frozen in the street without so much as looking down. Life and death in China.

How happy she was to see Doctor Pincus again, to be swept up in his warm greeting and instant recognition after all these months. ("Ah, there're my sartorial arbiter and Little Miss Bright Eyes.") Secretly, Rebecca had nourished the hope that they would meet by chance again, without asking herself what could come of a chance meeting or a dozen chance meetings. She told herself that the pleasure of his company, fleetingly, could not be a forbidden one. But it was a pleasure that kept eluding her—he might have been living in Hong Kong!— while the company of others, less congenial, was too much with her.

"You must be so busy, Doctor Pincus, with all the sniffling and coughing and wheezing going around."

"*Busy*, Mrs. Wolf? Don't get me started. But you already have." His warm green eyes were twinkling again with merriment. "A doctor serving a Jewish community, in good times and bad, is always busy. Some of my patients refuse to take 'well' for a diagnosis. Some—not the Sephardics so much, but the Ashkenazics—as much as tell you that you don't know what you're doing. They all but say you wouldn't recognize a case of scarlet fever if the rash were staring you in the face. They scrutinize the certifications and commendations over the fireplace and imply they are forgeries. The first warm days of spring, I'll have a dozen people in here swearing that they have salmonella poisoning. If I can't talk them out of it, I'll say I'm only the doctor and they're probably right. That makes them feel better, and Doctor Placebo sends them off with an aspirin for their poisoning. If the symptoms and complaining start to grate on my nerves, I'll say something like, 'Let's talk of something cheerful. What do you hear about the beriberi plague in Pago Pago?' "

Rebecca and Doctor Pincus laughed together. The word came to her that described one facet of his humor: Nimbleness. It was a quality that she much esteemed. Nimbleness, as someone had observed, was the safest armor of a civilized mind in a barbarian world.

"Well, now, about that little cold." From a bottle sitting on a glass shelf Doctor Pincus poured a tablespoon of bright red liquid and asked Esther to open wide. "This tastes so good I keep hoping I'll get a cold."

Esther swallowed and licked her lips. "It is good. May I have some more?"

"Esther!"

"No, no, that's all right, Mrs. Wolf. Maybe an extra dosage will keep our pretty patient from having to miss another day of school."

"Then I don't want it."

"Very well. Then I'll give it to Mommy. Maybe it'll keep Mommy from getting your cold. That's what we call preventive medicine."

Rebecca thrilled to the spoon-feeding. His eyes looked straight into hers as she swallowed the sweet cough syrup. It was a moment that she wished could be held, stretched. She felt warm—maybe for the first time in this bone-numbing winter—and it was a warmth coming from more than the medicine and the chips of wood and briquettes burning in the small brick hearth.

David's obituaries were a popular feature in *The Hongkew Reporter*. It was always a surprise to discover that someone who had died so meanly and desolately had once been a person of consequence. He wrote of honors and achievements of the deceased, but also of the human qualities recalled by survivors and friends.

This time it was more than an obituary. It was a remembrance and a personal debt of conscience. In death, David must honor her more than he had in life.

" . . . She was forty-seven years of age but would have liked to have been on the sunny side of thirty. Until the Proclamation, she had done quite well as a saleswoman in a milliner's shop. She idolized Mae West and would mimic her mannerisms, style of dressing, and expressions. She, too, had a fancy for handsome young men, and would ask them to come up and see her sometime. In the Chaoufoong heim, she faded away. She sat on her bunk and stared. People who had known her in the other Shanghai would say to her, 'Why don't you do your Mae West imitations?' But she vowed, 'Never again. I have been such a foolish woman. By acting silly I have insulted the memory of my dear husband, and God is punishing me.' She forgot to remember important things, like eating and getting out of bed. Last week, this once vivacious lady died from what medical men delicately call 'loss of heart.' "

Would it have made any difference if he had been kinder, more gallant to Florenz Keyser when they both lived in his uncle's house? David shed tears of remorse for not having made the effort.

Spring came ambiguously to Hongkew.

There was no flash of yellows or greens. No robins hopped through grasses made lush by melting snows. There were no bursting buds that would turn into leaf on stately horse chestnuts, poplars, and lindens. There were no peonies, or hydrangeas, or tulips, or lilacs to gladden the eye.

Only the warming air and brightening sun defined the season of renewal and reawakened hope.

Another spring. But it was a mixed blessing. With the warmer weather came the odors of crematoria, excreta, and the multitudes of the unwashed. More people, destitute now, were moving into the heims. The cries of overcrowding and thinning rations intensified.

Most of the Central European Jewish refugees had now been in Shanghai for five years or more: a drop of water in the sea of world history. But in the time of a human life, five years was an age. Five years comprised the formative development of a child. Five years was the span of a university education. In an interlude of five years, people fell in love, married, and bore children.

Justin Spiller's bookshop was shut down for lack of rent money. David came home early one morning with a smudge of lipstick on his mouth. Moritz Felcher bubbled with plans for a roof garden at his café and discouraged his wife's new passion for crossword puzzles ("You don't have the vocabulary, Sophie"). Rebecca typed love letters for an aging Romeo and her thoughts drifted to Doctor Pincus. Esther clamored for a gorilla suit to celebrate the Year of the Monkey with Li Yang. Hermann Feinstein drank to excess and had crying jags and muttered foul stories in the night. Ada Hurwitz predicted that her dear old Mr. Spitzenberg was not long for this world. Miriam Schiff blossomed in her romance and was avidly reading the science books that Mr. Shabolov had brought to her. And Joseph Schiff killed himself.

They found him hanging in the Wayside Synagogue. He had strangled himself with the drawstrings of the curtain shielding the ark. In the pose of crucifixion, his long lifeless body—clad in a freshly pressed gray worsted suit—dangled from a noose tied to the railing of the women's gallery. He was draped loosely in the light blue silk curtain with its tableaux of grape arbors and lions of Judah. His small head was jerked upward, contorting his face and drawing his eyeballs so deep into his skull that only the bloodshot whites showed.

David understood much that had been mysterious, and was again remorseful. So that was why Joseph Schiff was so fascinated with Steppenwolf, another suicide. So that was what drew him to that spooky synagogue—the contemplation of suicide in the perfect place for suicide. The day that he had followed Joseph Schiff, if he had taken a few extra steps and followed him inside and offered friendliness (friendship was out of the question), would it have made a difference?

"Damnedest lunatic thing I ever heard of," Moritz Felcher charged.

"Crazy, crazy," Sophie Felcher concurred.

"Revenge," Ada Hurwitz said unequivocally. "Behind every suicide is the element of revenge. Vengeance was Joseph Schiff's. She'll have that to live with."

"Schiff had it so much worse than anyone else?" Hermann Feinstein asked. With gallows humor, he answered himself: "The poor fellow just got to the end of his rope."

"Will Mrs. Schiff go to heaven?" Esther asked her mother.

"I am sure that God will have mercy," Rebecca replied.

Joseph Schiff was taken to a Chinese mortician. The Wayside Sacred Burial Society washed his body and dressed him. In the immediate aftermath of the tragedy, he was just another fallen brother, another deceased of the Jewish faith to be wrapped in a white cotton shroud and his head covered with a yarmulke. A tallith was placed around his shoulders.

In extremis, Miriam Schiff was altogether remarkable, poised, apologetic to others, a paragon of equanimity. "I know we are taught that we are only lent our lives," she said, "but that is wrong. We own our lives and must be free to do with them as we please."

Rebecca agreed tenuously.

"Joseph must have a proper burial. He must be buried in a Jewish cemetery."

"Miriam, under the circumstances, there may be problems and . . ."

"There must be no problems. I am going to ask a favor of you, Rebecca. You are more persuasive and articulate than I. I want you to take this matter up with the rabbi."

Rebecca dreaded the metaphysical discourse with Rabbi Bernstein. With all respect to Sister Marina in the Lübeck school, she might have the aptitude but she had increasingly less appetite for philosophy or theory. Germany had produced the greatest philosophers in the world, but had their cumulative wisdom been able to prevail against the evil in their very own country? Rational inquiry was as impotent as music in its powers to soothe the savage breast.

"I needn't remind you of the Judaic abhorrence of suicide," Rabbi Bernstein cautioned Rebecca. "God says we insult Him if we forsake His gift of life. We are saying we do not feel one with God, and in so saying we deny the very existence of God. By this denial the deceased forfeits any right to immortal fellowship with God. That is the strictest interpretation of the law."

"Strictest, rabbi? That presumes lesser degrees of strictness."

"Arguably, there are always extenuating circumstances. One must not, in the first instance, accept circumstantial evidence. What appears to be suicide may, in fact, have been accidental or inadvertent. If it is conclusively suicide, it is pertinent to inquire if the deceased was in full possession of his faculties and aware of the action that he was taking. If he acts when he is not of sound mind, if his confusion or depression or derangement is so severe as to obscure his judgment, we can ponder whether he should be held accountable in the strictest interpretation of the law."

"I can certainly testify to Mr. Schiff's prolonged despondency," Rebecca said.

"Despondency?" the rabbi gainsaid. "Who of us does not know despondency? But what would happen to the future of mankind if we all threw a noose around our neck when we became despondent? I shall have to cogitate on Mr. Schiff . . ."

Cogitate on Mr. Schiff? Was there any other faith so riddled with complexities and contradictions? Puzzles lay buried inside enigmas residing within conundrums. Every question could have a thousand answers. Decisions were handed down in ambidextrous terms . . . on the one hand . . . but on the other hand . . .

In the end, the rabbi decreed that Joseph Schiff could be buried in the Jewish cemetery on Point Road. The yellow earth was now his bride.

Mr. Shabolov stopped calling at 22/158. Out of delicacy? Or were the lovers meeting elsewhere? Miriam became fuzzy, uncommunicative—the predictable let-down of someone who had sailed too stalwartly through a deep personal crisis? Perhaps. Or was there something more?

"He's gone," Ada Hurwitz sobbed into a drenched handkerchief, a prediction come true. "The dearest man I know. Mr. Spitzenberg always said that he wanted to live to his seventy-fifth birthday and not one day more. That's just how he went—

he never woke from his afternoon nap. Can anyone doubt that it's mind over matter? Look at that! Did you ever?"

She and Rebecca were sitting on canvas chairs on the pebbly patch that Moritz Felcher grandly called "the front lawn." Across the lane, in the rubble of an empty lot, four Chinese men squatted side by side. Their trousers were pulled down and sloshing around their clogs. They talked and laughed sociably like old friends meeting in a coffeehouse or a pub. It was a common-enough scene in mild weather, but it was as if Ada Hurwitz were seeing it for the first time. Entranced, she stared in their direction until they had finished, pulled up their trousers, and were gone.

"Imagine not using anything afterwards," Ada Hurwitz moaned.

"No wonder every other Chinaman is in the laundry business," Rebecca said.

After a long contemplative silence, Ada Hurwitz observed, "For centuries, Chinese women have not existed as human beings. They have been nothing more than vassals and perpetuators of the race. They have . . . "

"Giving them," Rebecca interrupted, "much in common with Jewish women."

"Yes, well, at least we're not like Chinese women. Chinese women have been as shadowy as the women of ancient Greece. That little sideshow across the road, that huddling together to do their number two, speaks volumes. What we were seeing was the next thing to an orgy. Whenever you have wholesale subjugation of women . . . "

The Second Front began.

"They've crossed the Channel and landed in Normandy," David yelped. "The Americans and the British and the Free French and the Canadians. Rommel was waiting in Brittany and Eisenhower landed far to the south."

D-Day. By nightfall, the B.B.C. in Delhi was reporting that the Allies were thirty-five miles into France.

"They'll be in Paris by Bastille Day," David averred.

"And MacArthur will still be hibernating in Hollandia!" his uncle retorted.

Summer was in fullest fury. The yellow oven in the sky was stuck on broiling.

"If I owned just Hongkew and hell," groused Hermann Feinstein, "I'd live in hell and rent out Hongkew."

"One of these days," Rebecca smilingly told Esther, "you'll come home from school and find Mommy has melted into a thimbleful of perspiration."

Again Rebecca was in a dying business. Gone, vanished (too improvident) were all the fledgling playwrights and actors. Thank heavens for the letter writers. Abraham Hofmeister, the corsetmaker with the green thumb from Leipzig—her chatty neighbor in the queue waiting to see Chief Examiner Minobe—wrote himself a letter once a week, signing it "Clara Lipschitz." He posted it, and it was duly delivered to him in the Ward Road heim by a blue-suited Chinese mailman. Old Mr. Schneider was expressing his love for a Miss Rothberg in immortal poetry. "Shall I compare thee to a summer's day?" "Had we but world enough, and time, this coyness were no crime." "Ah, love, let us be true to one another! for the world, which seems to lie before us like a land of dreams . . . "

"Please remove the quotation marks, Mrs. Wolf," Mr. Schneider instructed her.

"But surely Miss Rothberg will recognize that these lines are from . . . "

"Ach. She won't recognize a thing. She's just a poor seamstress from Dresden. I am her Werther."

Mr. Hofmeister. Old Mr. Schneider. What was left after dignity had fled? So many of the refugees, it seemed, were no longer themselves. The old hatmaker with his cock-a-doodle-dos. Hugo Raschenbaum in the street again, peddling the tawdriest junk. That Mr. Mitofsky who went up and down the lanes barking the most vile obscenities. ("Gilles de la Tourette's syndrome," Ada Hurwitz explained. "It's a compulsion. It's said to be peculiar to Ashkenazics.") Professor Spiller, now Schlepper Spiller without his bookshop, carrying meals from the Polish kitchen to the prideful widow Kirschner down the lane and being rewarded with a cufflink or a green visor or a stocking or a smile.

Was it the heat and hunger that was turning people inside out?

The heat expedited the reality of Moritz Felcher's roof garden. Carpenters measured, sawed, and laid planking, and over it went green carpeting to simulate grass. By the rubber tree in one corner there would be a dance band. People would "throng" in for a breath of air. (A breath of *this* air?)

Maestro Felcher conducted auditions for his band. Aspiring members arrived in the courtyard on the quarter hour. Such an array of virtuosos! A second oboist in the Berlin Philharmonia. A violinist who had been a protégé of Wilhelm Furtwängler. A tympanist in the Warsaw Symphony. The first clarinetist in the Amsterdam Concertgebow. Auditioning for the opportunity to play schmaltz in an open-air café in a ghetto in a Chinese slum.

"Any time you're ready, I'm listening," Moritz Felcher said to each of them in turn and handed out the same two pieces of sheet music.

Through a long afternoon the instrumentalists tried out.

Resting in bed with menstrual cramps, Rebecca thought, Hell is not a blazing inferno. Hell is having to hear ever again the *Beer Barrel Polka* or *Bei Mir Bist Du Schön*.

"That character couldn't play for sour apples," Moritz Felcher called to Rebecca between auditions. (Impresario Moritz Felcher, the connoisseur! The ex-fiddler from Stuttgart!) "The fellow you just heard needs a year with a metronome." "As the Chinese would say, that flutist has just disgraced the Court of Heavenly Harmonies."

A cellist rolling out the barrel was drowned out by a shriek of sirens. Their first air raid.

"Proceed to shelter," they had been told, "when you hear the sirens."

What shelter? There were no trenches, no basements, no dugouts. How could anything be dug out of a turf hardly thicker than a crust of bread? And their houses were no safer than the streets.

Flags of red triangles were raised here and there and sirens bawled. From across the Soochow came the blasting of big-gun fire. Overhead, a flock of long-winged silvery birds swooped inland in V formation, circled, traversed the city again, left their calling cards, and vanished over the East China Sea. The white star embedded in the circle of blue under the wings advertised the visitors as Americans.

"What is there to bomb in Shanghai?" Rebecca asked.

"Lots. The piers and the godowns," David said. "The ships in the Whangpoo. The oil tanks in Pootong. The aircraft-repair factories in the Great Western District. The Japanese headquarters and airdrome in Hongkew Park."

The bombers invoked the nuisance of a curfew. Shanghai was to be blacked out from twilight until dawn. Everybody must be off the streets by nine P.M.

Moritz Felcher grumbled over his earlier closing hour. Hermann Feinstein lost his "late show" at the Blaue Donau but said, "Who cares? They sit on their hands anyway." Only Miriam Schiff defied the order, persisting in the baffling new regimen that she had taken up only weeks after her husband's suicide. She had quit her job at the thrift shop and read in her room during the day. In the evening, she left the house gowned, perfumed, and coiffed, not to return until dawn. She revealed nothing—neither the whereabouts of Mr. Shabolov nor her diversions.

Rebecca was apprehensive for Miriam. She must say something to her, and say it in a flat-out way, without prying. And so she said, "Miriam, your business is your own, but I must tell you that I think you are inviting trouble."

"The curfew? Bless you for worrying. But the curfew doesn't apply to me. I have a permit."

"Permit?"

"Yes, if you are doing something vital or you are an entertainer, you may secure a permit. I have a new job. I am working at the Café Pacific, on Dent Road. Oh, I don't play the zither or sing coloratura ballads or dance in a chorus line. Still, I classify as an entertainer."

"You are an entertainer?"

"Well, yes, in a manner of speaking."

"You could have knocked me over with a butterfly," Moritz Felcher exulted. "I had not one second of notice, believe me. People remember things, you see. They remember the old

Café Moritz. I gave these two the best table in the roof garden and handled everything myself. There are certain things you cannot leave to Mrs. Felcher, though she tries. I am telling you that they could not have been politer. They know how things are over here and they didn't turn their noses up at anything. I put out Tyrolean ragout, boiled potatoes, and apple tart, and coffee."

The Pierce Arrow open touring car, a magnificent chariot of rich maroon, had rolled in ravishing spectacle throughout the designated area. Its route was spearheaded by nine dusty motorcycles with machine guns mounted in sidecars. To the rear were four more motorcycle escorts, also armed with machine guns.

Two pennants fluttered from staffs on the hood of the vehicle, one a red sun on a white field and the other a jet-black swastika set in a circle of white surrounded by blood red (a fat, ugly poisonous spider lurking in its nest, trying to eat the world). Both passengers sat bolt upright at opposite ends of the ivory leather rear seat. They were in full-dress regalia, their chests crowded with medals. Twenty-thousand Jewish eyes followed the ominous procession inching its way along Chusan and rolling into Wayside. At the Ward Road jail the visitors paid a call. There was another, briefer stop at the heim on Alcock Road. The caravan came to a final halt, as if by prearrangement, at the Café Moritz.

"How should I know what they were doing over here," Moritz Felcher snapped. "It wasn't my business to try to snoop or eavesdrop."

"Nogoodnogoodnogoodnogoodnogood," Hermann Feinstein chanted dourly.

"Nonsense," David jeered. "What use would the Nazis or Japs have for some starving Jews?"

Moritz Felcher threw Justin Spiller out of the house.

If it had been forty degrees cooler, would he have been a little less explosive, a little more compassionate?

"Out, Spiller! Get out of my house! I don't want to come back tonight and find you here."

"I beg of you, Mr. Felcher. If I could have one more week . . . "

"No more weeks! I've carried you for three weeks already. That's long enough to play the fool. Get out."

"I have some valuables . . . "

"You have nothing of value. Move. I'm not running a charity home."

Moritz Felcher was not the least bit interested to learn that the professor had moved into the Ward Road heim. But he was surprisingly forbearing when a drunken Hermann Feinstein struggled up the stairs, flung himself onto his bed, and broke into a lachrymose jeremiad:

" . . . 'Not funny, Jew . . . Make us laugh, kike.' . . . Funny? What's to laugh about? From the first nip at the nipple to the last breath—pain, pain, pain . . . Everything for baby brother. Everything for the Second Coming, 'you're Hermann the Good for Nothinn' . . . the little Jesus dies—diphtheria—and their eyes say, Too bad it couldn't have been Hermann the Good for Nothinn' . . . 'Hermann should be a pianist. Hermann should go far away to conservatory.' Kaput goes the smelting business—no piano, no conservatory . . . Gisella the shiksa: 'I love you, Hermann. You make me laugh, Hermann. You make me wet my pants, Hermann. You're King of the Kabarets, Kermann. Bye-bye, Jewmann. Keep 'em laughing at Buchenwald.' 'Make us laugh, kike . . . ' "

Conspiratorial German generals planted a bomb in a briefcase laid at Hitler's feet; instead of being blown apart, the Führer was only slightly injured. Pilotless missile bombers—Hitler's secret weapon of terror!—were buzzing into anxious British cities. In the Pacific, the Allies recaptured Saipan—in as bloody a fight as yet reported in this world-wide fight; tens of thousands of Japanese turned into suicidal human bombs and torpedoes—and the Allies landed on Guam and Tinian in the Marianas. After his navy suffered a crushing setback in the Philippine Sea, Prime Minister Hideki Tojo and his cabinet resigned in the extremity of self-castigation.

Here, an oppressive heat wave—what else was new!—the stoning of some Jewish schoolchildren by idle Chinese youths, and an epidemic of ringworm passed for events.

Rebecca remarked to Miriam Schiff that she had passed the place where Miriam worked, but tactfully omitted her unsavory impressions. "The Café Pacific isn't the Ritz," Miriam said defensively. "I wish they would do something about that sign that's ready to fall off. And they shouldn't let the soldiers who play dice at the sidewalk tables get so drunk and obstreperous."

For weeks, Miriam had not spoken of anything more personal than what she was reading. But Rebecca's mention of the café apparently struck a confessional chord and Miriam was eager to talk, to let Rebecca know something.

"I'm not telling you anything you haven't already suspected," Miriam said, "when I tell you it's all over with Mr. Shabolov. It never resumed after Joseph's death. I think Leonid had an attack of conscience and felt that he was partly to blame for what happened. I don't agree, but that's not the point. He said that he wasn't being fair to me and that as long as he was in the picture he would be standing in the way of my finding someone I could call my own."

"And I am sure he told you that you had so much to offer someone," Rebecca said.

"Oh, Rebecca, have you been through this, too?"

"Not exactly. But I used to see a lot of movies."

"So one thing led almost directly to the Café Pacific."

"Where you entertain?"

"Yes, well, that might be gilding the lily a bit. There are six or seven of us European women who work there every night. We each have our own table. If a gentleman would like to join us, we make him welcome. We always hope that he will be someone presentable, intelligent, considerate. Most of the men who come there are. A majority of them are from commerce or the military. A majority also happen to be Oriental. We do draw White Russians, though, and even some of our men. I would never have guessed there were so many lonely men who would buy a stranger a meal just for listening to him."

Neither would Rebecca have guessed it. Her skepticism must have been showing.

"Well, yes, that's not all some of them want," Miriam admitted with her frilly laugh. "There are those who want to go to the private rooms upstairs. The first time I was asked to go upstairs was the hardest; I thought I would die of embarrassment. To get to the rooms, you see, we have to pass through a smoky parlor where there always are lots of men playing bezique and chess. And can you believe this—not one of them ever looks up."

From Leonid Shabolov to nameless men who paid as they were pleasured. It would be easy for the moralist or the critic to say, "So it's come to this," or to ask, "Isn't there any other way?" Rebecca would only have risked ridicule by expressing such thoughts to Miriam. "Are the other women without husbands, too?" she asked, thinking the question fatuous.

"Quite the contrary. All the women except me have husbands. They make no bones of what they are doing, and their husbands go along with it. Necessity is the mother of ingenuity, too. We all need the money, so we look at it pragmatically. Some of the husbands even escort their wives to the café and call for them later."

Miriam was facile with self-serving rationalizations. Had she the gift of irony, she would note that the same woman who had refused to sell her cedar chest and linen to gain a visa to freedom was now willingly selling her body to pay the rent.

In a season when time hung so heavy, the arrival of the new tenant constituted a real event.

"He came into the café with another fellow," Moritz Felcher briefed the household. "He's about your age, David. His friend is a big, fair-haired, good-looking chap who works in the Reichsbank on the Bund. Mr. Fogelmann has no pass, so his friend comes over here to see him. I got into a little walla-walla at their table, and Mr. Fogelmann told me that he had had a run-in with his landlady. I said that it so happened that I had a vacant room. I asked by the bye where he worked. Now get this. He doesn't have work, but his friend, this Mr. Boehm, said not to worry about the rent, he'd be responsible until Mr. Fogelmann finds employment. See, they're not all no-good."

David recoiled. Something sounded familiar, unpleasantly familiar, but the impression was so fleeting that he could not nail it down.

"You'll have a new friend, David," his uncle said.

David didn't want a new friend. He wanted his lover. He resumed the churlish letter that he was writing to her. "Your father's misery is unearned. He is hungry. Who isn't? Innocent people who are thrown into concentration camps can complain that God put a mark on them . . . " He reviewed what he had written and tore it up.

Max Fogelmann was short and plumpish. He had thick, tousled auburn hair, pale freckles, large milky blue eyes, and long lashes that swept down and away. He was quiet and immaculate. He made a ceremony of his morning ablutions, carrying a basin of water to his room, sponging himself from head to toe, stropping his razor. He was nicely pressed and dressed—always a bow tie smartly in place—and he was redolent of cologne when he left the house in the morning. He was gone most of the day, presumably looking for work. In the late afternoon he would return and retire to his room. He smiled and bowed, meaning to ingratiate himself, but was too shy—secretive?—to be more communicative.

When David got around to asking him, Max Fogelmann said that he was from Schweim, in the Neanderthal.

"Your family?"

"They're in America. San Francisco, when I last heard. That was almost three years ago."

"They're in America and you're here?"

"Yes."

David caught the evasive tone. He did not press. He was not that curious. He could tell that he and Max Fogelmann were not going to become friends.

"Max."

David saw—and recognized—the handsome head calling over the bamboo fence of the courtyard. Of course. Boehm, yes, yes. Christian Boehm. The fellow who had been so friendly in Jessfield Park and had invited him to his flat for dinner that Saturday afternoon two years ago. ("And I always have a nice Moselle chilling.") Had Max Fogelmann also been admiring the swans in Jessfield Park?

Their eyes met.

Christian Boehm smiled familiarly. David betrayed not a flicker of recognition.

To Rebecca, who in little ways extended herself to make him feel at home, Max Fogelmann gradually revealed something of himself. The Fogelmanns had been furriers in Schweim "forever." Earlier than most Jews, Max's father had perceived the danger in Germany. After the Nuremberg Laws were passed, he applied for visas to the United States. The waiting period was fearsomely long, so Mr. Fogelmann brought his family to Shanghai as a way station. A clever and industrious man, Max's father started business all over again with one coat for sale—his wife's Persian lamb. Soon, he had a large showroom on the Avenue Foch, selling marten, sable, seal, mink, and leopard coats. In the summer of 1940, by which time the Fogelmanns were well off, word came from the U.S. consulate that their visas were ready. Max's father did not hesitate to book passage for California and practically gave away the business to his employees. Max was studying French history at St. John's and informed his family that he would be staying in Shanghai to finish his education.

"There must be many excellent universities in the United States," Rebecca commented.

"I just didn't want to leave."

"It must have been a wrench for your family."

"Wrench? A typhoon all the way to the Whangpoo. Their only son. Their beloved boy breaking the hearts of his mommy and daddy and little sister. And for what? For foolishness and spite. A boy so stupid he would throw away a future in America to stay here."

It did sound strange, and not altogether convincing. Max was not stupid. He was not one, seemingly, to cut off his nose to spite his face. There must be more to the story, but that was all he was saying. His long lashes fluttered and he smiled vacuously.

"I can't make this one out for tart apples," Ada Hurwitz confessed.

"Like that silly game of musical chairs that children play," Hugo Raschenbaum mused.

"Yes?"

With the sun pressing down like a hot iron, Rebecca had paused on the Chusan Road to chat briefly with him under his umbrella. She glanced at the dismal display of safety pins, buttons, the half tube of flea ointment, the hand mirror, the earmuffs, the lady's hairbrush, and a belt buckle from the First World War etched with the motto "Gott mit uns" (God's with us).

"Every time the music stops, there is one less chair to sit on," he said. "We scramble for vanishing bits and pieces of this and that. The bits and pieces get scarcer and shoddier every day. One day, they will all vanish or fall apart completely, and that will be the end of the game."

"And the players," Rebecca added.

Decay and privation. That was their story. *All* their stories. After a surfeit of decay and privation, could "the end" be very far behind?

In this morbid state of mind Rebecca returned to her room to typewrite another abject letter from Solomon Abramowitz to one Gustav Hahn. The correspondent was protesting again that the Proclamation did not apply to Polish Jews. He begged the influential Shanghailander on the Rue Flaubert to secure their release from this terrible place. ("We appeal to your magnanimous Jewish heart, Mr. Hahn, to convey to the authorities our profound respect for the honor of the Japanese nation and the extreme munificence of the Japanese people . . . ") Mr. Abramowitz implored Mr. Hahn to remember that Polish Jews were not stateless persons; their Polish citizenship papers were valid. There still was a Poland, if only a government-in-exile in London. Poland was not at war with Japan. Polish people here should be free to live where they chose and go about their affairs.

Conceding the rightness of Mr. Abramowitz' claim, Rebecca could feel little sympathy for its futility. If an injustice was being done to Polish Jews, the Polish Jews themselves could be capable of their own blind disregard for the welfare of others.

The Crysk Yeshiva offered a perfect case in point—those

bearded seekers of truth who trod solemnly amongst them in their black woolen suits and black broad-brimmed hats. For centuries, the yeshiva had pursued study of the Talmud in the Polish town of Crysk. At the approach of the Nazis, the scholars took up their Torahs, scrolls, and arks and found refuge in Lithuania. But not for long. As the Nazis closed in on the Baltic States, they fled across Russia and sailed from Vladivostock to Japan. They were received warmly in Kobe and lived there for a year. A couple of months before Pearl Harbor, the Japanese decided that these foreigners should move on to Shanghai—everybody was potentially a spy, an espionage agent. In the designated area, the yeshiva had passes permitting the men to take their book bags and phylacteries to the colossal Beth Aharon Synagogue, on Museum Road, where they were free to interpret the Torah from twelve to fourteen hours every day.

A committee from the heims had approached the leadership of the Crysk Yeshiva. In the name of compassion, would not the scholars help to buy food for children, pregnant women, and the elderly from the special dispensations that they had been given and were hoarding? The yeshiva said that it would have to weigh the request.

Weigh? What was there to weigh?

When the answer came, it was no. The yeshiva would not share funds with the needy. "Do not bother us with secular matters," it said in so many words. "We are not to be asked for sacrifices. If it is a matter of life and death, as you claim, some Jews are more important than others. We are the most important. We are guardians of Judaism. To keep Judaism alive, we must put our survival over the survival of others."

Nay-sayers wrapping themselves in pieties, again. Philosophy, the study of ethics, scholarship—what was the worth of any intellectual discipline if its first casualty was the humanity of its luminaries?

"Paris is liberated," David rejoiced, but his face fell on seeing how little joy the news evoked generally. Who had ever seen Paris for the first time—let alone had a "last" time to recall—and could remember when their hearts were young and gay? So Paris was freed. So nu?

David was becoming increasingly restive. "I really have to get out of here," he lashed out at no one in particular. "I am coming out of my skin."

Esther had an adventure on the outside. With her school class she went on a field trip to Kimpachai, "the pantry of Shanghai." She was reminded of *The Gleaners*, one of the paperweight classics. "Wrinkly people bending over the fields and working with their hands," she reported. "We counted twenty-six different kinds of vegetables, but no potatoes, Mommy. And you know what Rachel did? When Miss Greenbaum wasn't looking, she ate a tomato. A little Chinese girl gave her one and Rachel gulped it right down."

Rebecca's fingers typed out an adventure of her own, totally fantastic: "With the cessation of hostilities in the Greater East Asia Co-Prosperity Sphere, Mrs. Rebecca Langer-Wolf, of Lübeck—the jewel of Schleswig-Holstein—and Shanghai, is sailing for America. She was advised by her great and good friend Ambassador Seymour M. Whitfield IV that immigration papers for her and her enchanting daughter, Fräulein Esther Wolf, had been approved. Mère et fille have booked first-class accommodations on the *Grover Cleveland*, queen of the American President Lines. They will leave Shanghai on Monday next, calling at Hong Kong and Honolulu, en route to San Francisco. There, the vivacious and witty widow will be caught up quickly in the frenetic social whirl of that cosmopolitan city. Mrs. Langer-Wolf declined to identify the handsome, distinguished graying gentleman who has been keeping company with her these past evenings in the International Settlement's smartest spots . . . "

Max Fogelmann's friend had not visited him in more than a week and he was deeply despondent. He gave up the effort of leaving the house, and confined himself to his room. He was even lax about his personal hygiene, neglecting his daily sponge bath and shave.

"Lovesick," Ada Hurwitz diagnosed. "One of those unnatural affections, poor boy."

"Just the other day," Rebecca reminded her testily, "you were saying you couldn't make him out."

It was a conclusion that they were all drawing. David mumbled about it finally "making sense" why Christian Boehm had been so friendly to him that day in Jessfield Park. It was not something either of the Felchers could comment upon, but Hermann Feinstein waxed vulgarly witty: "Boy meets boy and they live unhappily ever after." Miriam Schiff observed appropriately that "on the human chessboard, all moves are possible."

"We saw so much of that sort of thing in Vienna," Ada Hurwitz expostulated. "Self-righteous people call it decadent? I don't agree. Did anyone ever call Michelangelo decadent? Or Leonardo? Or Socrates? Or Plato? Or Frederick the Great? What is there to fuss about? Some people are made that way and that is all there is to it. To my mind, Herr Doktor had the last word on the subject. A woman in America had written to him about her son who was 'that way.' Doctor Freud advised her that there was little hope for a change. She must accept the situation and let the boy live his own life."

Beware of pity, Rebecca cautioned herself. But her heart went out to this young man who was so alone and so wretched. One afternoon, when they were the only two in the house, she called to him in his room, "I do wish you would join me for a cup of tea, Mr. Fogelmann."

"I won't be good company," he apologized, but was quick to accept.

"We all have our ups and downs," she said gently.

His eyes were rimmed from crying and he laughed shakily, "May I borrow a cup of up?"

Christian Boehm might be dashing and devastating to gaze upon, but did he have any of the sweetness and charm of this forlorn youth? There was nothing like a cup of tea and a little sympathy to uncork confidences. Like it or not, she was hearing another tale of misbegotten love.

Christian Boehm, she learned, came from a noble family of Silesian industrialists and landowners. The Boehms were alte

Alemannen, conservative, rich, tradition-bound. Christian had been the student prince at Heidelberg for two years before becoming bored with his studies and the provincial city. He went to Berlin, the artistic center of the continent and the most uninhibited capital in Europe, to pursue the Muses and a hedonistic style of living. By day, Christian toiled listlessly at a banking job that had been arranged by his family. After dark he glowed.

Christian Boehm habituated a club on the Rumpelplatz called Herr Edna's—a flamboyant place of abandonment that attracted some of the freakiest denizens of the night. Herr Edna himself was a female impersonator who performed twice a night as the star of the floorshow. Christian would meet strangers at the club, each one more outré than the last, and invite them back to his flat. One night, he made the unfortunate selection of a youth who happened to be the special amour of nobody less than Ernst Roehm, the commander of the SA and the SS. Later that night, Roehm went to the club looking for the boy, and Herr Edna told him where he could be found. "How could you pull such a two-timing thing on someone who's been such a good customer?" Christian charged Herr Edna the next day. "Easily," Herr Edna said, fishing a fistful of Deutschmarks out of his brassiere.

Roehm had his revenge. Black boots kicked in Christian's door with an order for his arrest, and he was hustled off to a concentration camp near Bonn. It was a bad time in Germany for anyone found guilty of le vice anglais. The chicken farmer Himmler and his henchmen were propagandizing that "that degeneracy" would poison the Aryan race and it must be eliminated at all costs—by castration or extermination, if necessary. The detention site was a colony of tents, and Christian was made to wear a pink triangle, the badge of shame of all known homosexuals. "The pink triangles" were put to the hardest labor and fed the thinnest rations. They were ostracized. They suffered the abuse and derision of guards and fellow internees alike.

Christian's family was mortified and outraged by his deviation, but they were not about to forsake him completely. They had the means to bribe his passage out of Germany, and they found another banking post for him in Shanghai. It was their way of saying, "We've spared your hide. In exchange, we want you to get as far away from us as the globe will permit. And don't come back."

Max Fogelmann indeed met Christian in Jessfield Park. What an innocent Max had been! He had had no experience of this kind. He had never even thought of himself as *different*. When Christian invited him to go back to his flat for a Schnaps or some wine, Max refused, confessing abashedly that he did not drink. But, Max had to admit, he was strongly attracted to the charming Christian. There were more meetings in the park, a few dinners out. After seeing a sentimental movie together one evening, Max said, "I think I would like to have that Schnaps, if the offer is still open." Christian had not pressed him; he was no Svengali. This was Max's nature, too. If it had not been Christian, it would have been someone else, sooner or later.

"I love you and want to possess you," Christian had declared. "I want to settle down with someone. I am so weary of the chase and the one-night affairs."

After his family had sailed for America, Max moved into Christian's opulent flat in the Avenue Haig. Christian had said that Max was all he wanted. But, inevitably, he added, "Of course, now and again, I shall want to pluck a fresh daisy. Not to worry. I'll sip the nectar and be done with the flower." From time to time Christian had brazenly brought home a daisy and sipped the nectar in Max's presence, but as good as his word had discarded the drained flower.

"Now it's been nine days," Max anguished to Rebecca. "He must be plucking a whole field of daisies."

"Nine days isn't forever," she pointed out. But how limp and inadequate her response must sound to him. However, she could only think as a parent. From what little she had observed, such attractions contained the seeds of their own doom. She had no awareness of any homosexual relationship going down the years like a good marriage. "Did your mother and father suspect anything, Max?"

"No. But with all the rows that went on about my not going with them to America, I was tempted to tell them. Then I'd look at them and I couldn't—it would have killed them."

Axiomatically, bad news comes in multiples of three.

Esther's classmate who had clandestinely eaten the tomato on the field trip died. A wild fever, excruciating stomach pains, vomiting, and passing of blood and mucous were diagnosed as amoebic dysentery. Paregoric and prayers failed to save Rachel.

Esther bawled with the pain of grief and guilt. She and Rachel had shared the secret of the forbidden fruit. Shouldn't she tell Rachel's mother and father?

"You absolutely must not," Rebecca said firmly. "If there is one thing that could make them feel worse than they already do, it is the knowledge that Rachel disobeyed all the warnings that they must have drummed into her about eating raw food that hadn't been properly cleaned."

Several days later, Rebecca had a visitor. At first glance, she thought it was Teng. She prided herself on being one of those Occidentals who did not think that all Orientals were indistinguishable one from another. But Teng would not be wearing a western business suit. The young man introduced himself as the brother of Teng—ah yes, the medical student—and handed her an envelope. Inside were twelve Shanghai dollars—her share in the liquidation of the typewriter shop on the Boulevard St. Honoré—and a note from Teng: "I think about you many times, Mrs. Wolf. It is also bad for me and my comrades now. Soon the dark clouds will lift and everything will be better . . . "

"Where is Teng?" Rebecca asked.

"My brother behaved foolishly," Ho Wun Gon said. "His head ached with dangerous ideas. He could not keep them to himself. Some people who do not like those ideas found the place where Teng and his 'study group' were meeting, and they set fire to the building. Teng and his comrades ran out and were shot down. There were eleven of them."

Teng dead! Murdered! Sweet, thoughtful, caring, idealistic Teng. Here was Teng's own brother now giving this matter-of-fact account of Teng's assassination and as much as saying that Teng had invited his own death and deserved what he got. Her blood ran cold. She would never understand this country. She did not have to ask who found Teng's ideas "dangerous." If only the Generalissimo and his clique would direct their energies to fighting the Japanese instead of slaughtering their own people!

And David was missing!

"Aren't we a little too old for kids' games?" Natzie asked, but he let himself be persuaded.

David had been ruminating on the grimness of the Brothers Grimm and found his inspiration in *Hänsel und Gretel*. Natzie would be the perfect companion in this caprice. He saw too little of his friend; Natzie being Natzie, he was always on the runrunrun. In two rooms on Ward Road Natzie was making his peach, lard, and mustard concoctions. And he had inveigled two permanent passes—one for himself and one for "delivery assistant."

"I would like to write something about those delivery assistants," David teased his friend. "I wouldn't use real names, of course. I would merely report that there is a certain enterprising titan of industry in our community who manufactures delicacies and delivers them outside the ghetto. He needs someone to help him make these deliveries, and by an interesting coincidence that someone is always an attractive woman. Our entrepreneur has no bias—the woman may be married or not married, as long as she is not a tapir. After they make their rounds, the employer and his employee of the day spend an hour or so getting the lay of Fanwangtu Park. He claims that then—and only then—does he get to know how well his assistant delivers."

"I dare you to print a story like that," Natzie said, getting a hammer lock on the Hongkew reporter.

They set off on a languid Sunday afternoon in September. David, taking the lead, would be the Fox. Substituting kernels of rice for Hänsel's and Gretel's bread crumbs, he sprinkled a trail of single kernels for Natzie the Hound to follow. The Fox took a serpentine course through the lanes. Every five paces, he dropped another kernel of rice in the center of the street. His winding and looping route led north across Point Road, outside of the ghetto, and into the forbidden precincts of Hongkew Park.

It was foreordained that the Fox should be caught, and presently he was.

"I never saw a single kernel that you threw down," the Hound panted. "Some sharp-eyed Chinese boy kept picking them up and I just followed him."

"Life imitates literature again," David said, "the black crows of the forest become one starving lad of the lanes."

Freedom! Even Natzie should not be there—his pass did not apply for this Northern area. But there they both were, bold trespassers who had crossed the unguarded pass point.

The park was mangy and had large patches of dirt. But to the Fox it could have been the luscious gingerbread house itself. It was deserted except for a few Chinese family groups with their cooking braziers and Thermoses of tea. Across a roadway at the far end of the park sprawled the Japanese Naval Depot and Landing Party Barracks. Sentries stood like squat Prussians in front of the low sandstone buildings. A pair of overheated Voisins coughed along a central lane in the asphalt areaway and deposited three high-ranking Japanese officers into the somnolent depot.

The Fox and the Hound played tag, wrestled, kicked around a clump of dirt serving as a soccer ball, and "as twinn'd lambs that did frisk i' the sun, and bleat the one at the other," exchanging innocence for innocence. Tiring of their exertion, they stretched out on a blanket of trampled weeds. They picked out globs of whipped cream and scoops of vanilla ice cream in the cumulus clouds floating toward the sea, and dozed off.

David dreamed. It was another Sunday long ago. He was five years old, and he and Papa were hiking in Igls, up the mountainside from Innsbruck. They walked on a brambled ascending path through evergreens and Norway spruce so high they could hardly see the sky. David became cranky and asked his father to be picked up and carried. Papa said no, if David was that tired he would be too tired for the hot chocolate and Linzertorte that Mama would have waiting for them back at the inn. David didn't see it that way. If Papa would carry him, he would be rested and wide awake for the treats. Papa smiled and said, "You are a clever little fox . . . "

The Fox was kicked awake.

As was the Hound.

Japanese soldiers were staring down at them through telescopic sights on their rifles.

"Nein," Natzie pleaded. "Wir sind Ihre Freunde. Deutsche. *Germans.*"

The two "Freunde," arms high above their heads, were marched at bayonet point across the park and into a dark reception area in one of the crumbling barracks. A colonel barked at them through a triangular hole in a glass partition.

"Why are you in the park?"

"Relaxing," Natzie said. "Taking a snooze. A rest. Sleep."

"Your papers!"

"Wir sind Deutsche," Natzie protested. "Allies. Friends. No restrictions."

"You are not Germans."

Natzie's blandishments and fabrications were fruitless. The trespassers were manacled, gagged, and shoved into the back seat of a battered Buick, whose right-hand rear door was missing. The car bumped southward, across Point Road, and through the streets of Hongkew. At Soochow Creek, it swung into a crescent of roadway.

Seeing where they had stopped, David began to shake epileptically.

"Here we are into Tuesday," Moritz Felcher remonstrated, "and still no sign of him. Now tell me again exactly what he said when he left."

Rebecca, as distraught as the Felchers, said, "I wish there was something more I could tell you. All David said was, 'I've got to run. I'm a Fox and there's a Hound on my tail.' But I repeat, Mr. Felcher, he was in the best of spirits."

"It doesn't make sense."

In the windowless dungeon of the Bridge House there were no bunks, no cots, no stools, no mats. Sixteen white, yellow, black, and brown bodies meshed and melded in an obligatory embrace. In the center of the stone floor a shallow hole overflowed with waste. The air reeked of urine, feces, rancid breath, and gangrenous flesh.

David threw up. He voided in his clothes. He lost consciousness. He came to, hearing a blood-roiling cacophony, and blacked out. He awoke again to screams, yelps, shouted obscenities and profanities, maniacal laughter. A communal moan flowed through the vaulting tomb. Around him, bodies swayed in a dance of death . . . leaning, scratching, crouching, twisting up, down, down, up, a cruel charade of waking and sleeping. A siren shrieked. And shrieked and shrieked, like an aural drip torture designed to pierce the skull. Bowls of pus-colored gruel were pushed through the bars of the cell; sometimes the guards spat or pissed into the gruel. The scratching. Armpits, head, chest cavities, pubic hairs. Scratching, pinching, squeezing at the lush breeding grounds of the invincible crustaceans. Crazed nails ripped open flesh already violated with welts, gashes, burns, fractures, and depilations.

The crimes of the jailed were encyclopedic. Rumor-mongering. Thievery. Mendacity. Insolence. Licentiousness. Arrogance. Subterfuge. Treachery. Vandalism. Duplicity. Trespassing. The punishment for these crimes? A manual of sadism. Electric jolts to the genitals. Limbs severed. Truncheon blows to the buttocks, the kidneys, and the groin. Rackings. Mock crucifixions. Torching of flesh. Gouging of eyes. Naked bodies rolled down flights of sharp-edged stone stairways.

Dante's Ninth Circle . . . Devil's Island . . . Dachau . . . Paine, Dostoevsky, Dreyfus, Wilde. Other infernos of detention, other worthy men cast into inhuman degradation. It was no comfort for David to recall them.

The hours—the days?—froze in nightmarish limbo. The siren shrieked and shrieked. David stood and he squatted, he cried and he retched. And he couldn't stop scratching. He inhaled from his palms to mute the stench. Did he sleep?

"Booch-ben-der!"

The cell door clanked open, throwing back three corpses. David was hauled out. The muzzle of a rifle jammed against his tail bone prodded him along a pitch-black corridor. He halted at the bottom of a steep staircase and looked uncertainly into the darkness above. The muzzle rammed him in the testicles. David doubled up, cursed, and started to climb the stone steps. He climbed up and up, four flights, and was jabbed into a vast chamber. Two men were waiting for him. One of them was a jailer. Into the arms of the other, David collapsed.

And then Natzie the Hound was being thrown into the room.

"I would like to give the two of you a piece of my mind," Moritz Felcher fumed when they were clear of the Bridge House. "You're supposed to be grown-up men, not idiot kids. You should know what I went through to get you out of there. The bribes, the ass-kissing, and all the rest."

It was not just that David was filthy, tattered, and evil-smelling. Four days had altered him. He was bonily gaunt, his color was pale as wax, and there were black circles under his eyes. He could not stop shaking.

"David, oh my David!" Rebecca cried. "You must see a doctor."

"Yes," his uncle exhorted. "You look like a gargoyle. See a doctor, I'm ordering you."

"Doctor Pincus," Rebecca suggested.

Doctor Pincus was thorough and reassuring. "You young fellows can throw these things off pretty easily," he marveled. "The older men who come out of that place look like white-haired carcasses even the vultures wouldn't want." David was to bathe and shampoo thoroughly, apply the blue ointment to his armpits, scalp, and pubic area, and try to get some extra food into him.

Having the occasion to speak his name in a plausible context gladdened Rebecca. Months had passed since her last visit to his office. She could not put him out of mind. In daydreams and in the dark of night she had fantasized about him. The fantasies embarrassed her with their intimacy, their explicitness, their erotic abandonment. In one persisting image she was alone with him on a deserted beach on the Côte d'Azur. After he had caressed every pore of her body with his finger-tips and lips, she was raising her legs like a drawbridge to receive him. These were impossible dreams. Sometimes, she would abort them in the budding. Other times, she would indulge them, letting the fantasies build into an ethereal dream-world where all things were possible.

David could not write Rosalie about the Bridge House. In no way could he capture his terror and disgust, and he did not want to worry her. "I am bluer than Gainsborough's Blue Boy," he did write, and tried to be amusing about the blue ointment that he was applying to his pudenda. "I must have picked up the crabs from the crab bag I sleep in," he lied. "But I have considerable respect for crabs, and for cockroaches, too, for that matter. Both have this much in common with Jews—in five thousand years the world hasn't found a way of eradicating them."

"I wouldn't mind being the girl friend of the whirling dervish," Rosalie replied merrily. "But being the girl friend of the boy with the blue balls does give me pause."

Jealousy was too corrosive an emotion to harbor, Rebecca had been at the point of suggesting to Max, when Christian Boehm reappeared and Max Fogelmann was restored instantly to bliss.

Max, who had allowed Esther to climb all over him and pull his ears, let himself be drawn into her flirtatious web of interrogation. In amusement, Rebecca overheard:

Esther: Uncle David has a girl friend. Do you?
Max: Young girls shouldn't ask such personal questions.
Esther: Who should?
Max: Maybe the rabbi—if he's nosy, too.
Esther: If I were grown up and rich and beautiful, would you want me to be your girl friend?
Max: Let's wait to see if you are rich when you grow up.

The sexual comedy. From birth to the grave.

"Motherliness is the primary feeling of a woman," Bertha Pappenheim had said so long ago. It struck Rebecca, reflecting on both the anguish that she had felt when David was missing and her concern over Miriam, how true this was. And she thought it odd. She had begun life with no overwhelming passion to marry and bear children. But motherliness was indeed hers, inborn or acquired by growth and circumstance. In some form, her motherliness had reached out to every life that had touched hers, even to her own mother. To her sibling, she had been maternally self-sacrificing, saying, "Go pursue your life, Samuel, and don't worry about me." She had argued and gone against Meyer but had never withdrawn the bedrock of comfort that protected him from so many disagreeable realities. She had nursed him faithfully until he had closed his eyes forever. Teng had blossomed under her persistent interest and sympathy and conceded that not all foreigners in China were devils. She found herself reaching out to Max Fogelmann, who was trapped inside a nature that he could not shed, to steady him in his sloughs of despondency. David, apparently well and himself again, had started to have nightmares, crying out, "I wasn't spying, I wasn't spying." And Miriam. Miriam haunted her thoughts. She could babble on intelligently about Eve Curie's biography of her famous mother, and Rebecca would half-listen and think, "It's awful, awful, awful what you are doing. And here I sit, helpless to change a thing." Paradoxically, it was her own daughter who seemed least in need of mothering.

The news that David took off his radio might give him better dreams. The Allies had landed in the Philippines. MacArthur had returned, as promised. "So they're in Leyte," Moritz Felcher said. "I could say they have only six thousand nine hundred and ninety-nine Philippine islands to go. I could say that," giving David a love tap on the head, "but I won't."

It was autumn again. Another year was winding down. A golden moon had filled the sky and waned. The sun had deepened to apricot. Mists so fragile they could be brushed away with a hand had thickened into gentle rains.

"China is endurable only in these soft rains," Rebecca was thinking, when the light clicked off in the midafternoon sky.

The rain stopped and black clouds enveloped the ghetto in

darkness. Sounds trailed off into a chilling silence. Rebecca needed the flame of a candle to see the playing cards on the table before her. The wind stirred and began to rise. It swelled, overwhelming the candle. It ballooned to a sweep that was like a sucking vacuum or the rooting of swine. Vroom! Vrooom! VROOOOM!! The thunder exploded like bombs. Javelins of gold-orange lightning split the sky and set the air on fire. The house trembled, heaved, pitched, and rocked like an insane roller coaster. The two canvas-backed chairs in the courtyard flew like kites into the steel-black unknown. The fence buckled. Windowpanes burst, showering her arms with shards of glass. She clutched her typewriter as her anchor.

"Miriam!" she yelled upstairs. "Max! Mr. Feinstein!" Her voice was swallowed up in the raging blasts. Thunder pounded the earth like a giant's fist. Esther, thank God, was safe in that big school building. Rebecca kept her eyes and mouth shut tight. A single splinter from the Shanghai flotsam crashing through the broken panes could blind her. The wind could blow up her lungs. The rain started again, this time as belligerently as the wind. A sprinkle, a few tentative drops, became tumultuous. The water poured through the gaping window, slashing her across the face and body. She was drenched and frozen to the marrow. And she was crying.

The wind died as suddenly as it had come up. The sky lightened, there were long banners of red and yellow in the western sky, and the rain moderated.

At last, Rebecca dared to open her eyes. The waters had washed away the blood that the shards had pricked. She surveyed the detritus and almost swooned. The wardrobe and the cots were flooded. The floor was a sloshing lake. The mess, unspeakable mess from the outside world. A roof shingle. A brick. Drowned newspaper pages. A conical hat. A hearing trumpet. Clumps of mud. *Garbage.*

Soochow Creek was running through Hongkew. Rivers of ochre, scummy green, bowel-brown, brackish gray. The gushing waters rushed under wooden fencings, across yards, into houses, along hallways, beneath doors and scrims.

"Gott im Himmel! A Goddamn sewer. My home is a Goddamn sewer."

Coatless, vestless, his trouser legs rolled up to the knees and his purple silk shirt pasted to his skin, Moritz Felcher waded through the courtyard and into the house. He stood arms akimbo in a mounting sea of broken crockery, rinds and crusts, strips of clothing, clapboards split into kindling, sandals, and clots of dung. The Augean stables.

Rebecca stretched out her arms and he came into her embrace. They clung together, saying nothing. He was shaking, weeping silently. Be it ever so humble, there was indeed no place like home—and his had been ravaged. His hurt was eloquent, he touched her heart. She had never felt this close to him.

"It could have been worse," he said, pulling himself together.

"Oh, Mr. Felcher, do you really think so?"

"The typhoon of 1938 was worse, believe me."

"The typhoon of 1944 is enough for me," Rebecca said, and they were buoyed and laughing together.

Sophie Felcher became Queen of the Aftermath.

She alone was not immobilized by the carnage and the stench. She alone did not clamp her nostrils to shut out the smell of polluting waters, rotting fish, festering garbage, and floating feces. She rose to the moment with a cheerfulness and an energy that were almost perverse. In the wake of catastrophe her personality positively bloomed.

"You all must wear a bag of camphor balls around your neck," she instructed them. "The Chinese know from experience how to ward off disease."

Sophie Felcher commandeered the three other women in the house and two coolies. With brooms, mops, and wash buckets, the clean-up squad swept, swabbed, scoured, and pushed the sewage, silt, and slime out of the house. ("More Campho-Clinique, Mrs. Hurwitz. Keep dumping the Campho-Clinique.") But there was no pushing the muck out of view. Hongkew had no drainage or disposal system. It was choking in the miasma of typhoon afterbirth.

"I feel like Jean Valjean in the sewers of Paris," Rebecca said wryly.

"Who is he?" Sophie Felcher asked politely.

"Oh, just someone I used to know," Rebecca smiled.

It was more than the filth and the stink. The humidity and some indestructible rot in the air itself covered everything with a sickly green film, and they awoke in the morning to find even their faces coated with it.

"I like being a Martian," Esther declared.

Only the coming of winter's winds completely rid 22/158 of its odors.

The beginning of the second winter in the designated area also brought with it the warming news of the Allies' victory in the "Battle of the Bulge"—Rundstedt's last-gasp counteroffensive in the Ardennes. The Nazis had held out on three fronts for a long time, but now they were doomed. The miracle buzz bombs had fizzled. (Would the American plan to turn the Fatherland into an agricultural state drive the Chancellor into a death-to-the-last-German defense?)

Bundled up in ragged coats and mufflers, they sat around the damped clay pot toasting the coming year. Christian Boehm had given the household two kilos of brisket of beef, a treat so rare as to induce general conviviality. Sophie Felcher apologized for her borscht ("The beets were so weak"), but was drowned out. Esther jumped around her mother singing "Who's afraid of the big bad Wolf?" Ada Hurwitz recalled that fifty-seven trains passed through Kitzbühel every day, and someone charitably said, "How fascinating." And Hermann Feinstein finally had a joke that was neither off-color nor insulting:

Der Führer was having his fortune told. The fortuneteller hemmed and hawed and gnashed her teeth over the tarot cards, tea leaves, and crystal ball. Der Führer demanded to know what she saw. "The crystal ball is a little murky, my leader, and the tea leaves are in disarray. But everything is telling me that you will die on a Jewish holiday." "Jewish holiday?" der Führer bellowed. "What Jewish holiday?" "My Führer, any day you die will be a Jewish holiday."

Even Moritz Felcher laughed. Refilling everyone's glass of sweet red wine, he announced, "I bought some of us a ticket in the Solomon brothers' lottery. We guess when the war will end. Whoever comes closest wins the lottery. I'll go first and then I'll write down your guesses on these other tickets. I am guessing April 20."

"Hitler's birthday," David noted. "A good present."

"I'll go next," Ada Hurwitz cut in. "August 13. *My* birthday."

"You're still having birthdays?" Hermann Feinstein needled her.

"Mrs. Wolf?" Moritz Felcher prompted.

"If I said my birthday, I would have to mean the one after the one that's coming up next month—that would make my guess January 16, 1946."

"All right, Mrs. Wolf. January 16, 1946, it is. David?"

"July 4. America's birthday."

1945

SHANGHAI

This new year began inauspiciously.

Down the lane, two children died from rat bites. Seven refugees died of the cold, and nine more perished from causes "relating to malnutrition." The heims were appealing frantically for more food. Two Ashkenazic couples announced that for reasons that were nobody else's business they were exchanging spouses. The Shanghai School for Pickpockets opened a branch in the second story of a shop on Chusan Road. The ultimate in wedding-gift luxury was a tubful of hot bath water for the prospective bride. Many of the refugees warmed their hands on the outside walls of the crematoria. Irascible blackbirds hovered over Hongkew like harbingers of more bad news.

Rebecca was sleeping poorly. She drowsed throughout most of the long, frigid winter nights. (Esther beside her slept the sleep of the dead.) Perhaps she was paying the forfeit for some puritanical ethic that legislated "By the sweat of thy brow shalt thou earn sleep." She had less and less work, and this fed her anxiety and apprehensiveness. She was entering her forty-fifth year and her mind was flooded with baleful images.

Miriam lent her a volume of Chinese verse. The first line that her eyes fell upon was "So dim, so dark, so dense, so dull, so damp, so dark, so dead." So perfect.

But a melancholic Chinese poet of the sixteenth century could not solve her problems of employment and income. Fewer people could afford anything that was not crucial to their very survival. What else could she do if not typewrite? The spectre of ending up in a heim weighed on her like a millstone.

It was almost noon of a soot-gray January day before Miriam Schiff returned from the Café Pacific. Rebecca had been worrying and wondering about her. Gasping at the sight of her now, Rebecca saw that her worst fears concerning Miriam had been well-justified.

Miriam was trying to slink up the stairs, but her whimpering gave her away. The fur coat was draped over her shoulders and her hands were clasping her stomach. Despite the cold, she was barelegged. Her hair looked like a violated bird's nest.

"Miriam, what in the world?"

"Nothing."

"Nothing?" Rebecca remonstrated, following Miriam up the stairs and ignoring the unwritten rule of the house that no one ever stepped into anyone else's room without an invitation.

Miriam sat on her bed, shivering, keening, clutching her stomach.

"What is it, Miriam? What happened?"

Miriam shook her head.

"Miriam, look at me and tell me what it is."

Miriam looked up. Her eyes were dazed.

"Let me help you into bed," Rebecca said, "then we'll see about your stomach ache."

Miriam was helpless. Rebecca spoke soothingly as she hung up Miriam's coat and removed her shoes. Gently, Rebecca got her to her feet and coaxed her to raise her arms so that the dress could come off. She put the dress on a hanger and said, "Now, Miriam, we'll get your slip off and tuck you in."

Rebecca put her hand to her mouth to stifle a scream.

"Miriam, I'll go for a doctor right away."

"No, no," Miriam pleaded. "No doctor. Please."

Miriam fainted, revived briefly, then fell into a deep sleep.

Rebecca tiptoed in and out of the room while Miriam slept. She debated whether she should override Miriam and fetch a doctor. She could not believe what she had seen. What type of mind could have perpetrated anything so fiendish?

When Miriam awoke, she was surprisingly composed and let Rebecca swab her burns with gelatin. But she still wanted no attention from a doctor.

Rebecca's indignation was diffuse, indicting Miriam as well as her violator. "I'm not asking any questions," she said, "but I certainly have some thoughts as to the company you keep."

"He was a freak," Miriam conceded, with an echo of her frilly laugh.

Her "true confession"—Miriam all but insisted upon it, as if it were some kind of catharsis, her way of banishing a bad dream—was bizarre beyond the bounds of Rebecca's imagination.

How could Miriam have had her suspicions? Colonel Nagashubi, a courtly gentleman and often a guest in the Café Pacific, introduced Miriam to his friend Colonel Hakawana and importuned her to be nice to him. Miriam did not find this difficult. Colonel Hakawana was well-educated, a good conversationalist, and gentlemanly, too. He had spent a year in Germany training with the Heer. He was tall for a Japanese, attractive, and about thirty-five years of age. Miriam and Colonel Hakawana sat at her table so long that she began to think that conversation was all he wanted. Finally, though, he suggested that it would be pleasant if they would go to one of the rooms upstairs.

Miriam undressed there and lay down on the bed. Colonel Hakawana did not so much as remove his sword. He stood erect, gazing down peculiarly at her. She thought it was shyness and smiled at him reassuringly. But he just stood there. She reached out to unbuckle his belt. He drew away, shaking his head, meaning no, no, he wanted none of that. Why was he there then? What did he want?

"I began to feel queasy," Miriam told Rebecca.

Colonel Hakawana took something out of the breast pocket of his tunic and held it to the flame of the candle on the table beside the brass bed. Miriam smelled incense. He stared down at her again with that odd expression. He held the incense in one hand and began to rub her bare stomach with the palm of his other hand. Round and round the palm rubbed, the gentle motion of a caress. He did it for the longest while. It was so relaxing that Miriam was on the edge of falling asleep.

"I came to with a scream. I was being stabbed. I was on fire. It was the incense. He was jabbing the lighted end of the stick into my flesh. I pushed his hand away and he became furious. 'No,' he barked. He pointed to his sword and then to my throat. If I tried to foil him, he would hand me my head. I lay back and clenched my teeth."

Colonel Hakawana was both a sadist and an artist manqué. Which gave him the greater pleasure: inflicting pain or giving pain a framework? He bent his head close to Miriam's stomach and studied her skin. After much deliberation, he twisted the incense into a certain spot. Then into another. And another. He ignored her sobs. Stab and grind, stab and grind. He would step back for perspective. "Good, good," he complimented himself, and studied where next to dig his smoldering torch. Stab and grind, stab and grind.

Colonel Hakawana created two clusterings of ashen globules. One was to the left of Miriam's navel, the other was to the right. At last, she thought, he was finished and her deliverance was at hand. She was sadly mistaken. He began something even more excruciating and disgusting. He was singeing her pubic hair. He was making a design in her curly mound of Venus.

The torture lasted an eternity. When his incense stick burned its last stroke, Colonel Hakawana was in a state of palpable excitement. Perspiration streamed down his face and dribbles of saliva oozed out of the corners of his mouth. He was panting and chortling. "Perfection!" he cried. "Perfection! The Three Chrysanthemums. The Ceremony of the Three Chrysanthemums."

In near delirium, Colonel Hakawana ripped the buttons off the front of his trousers. He was fully tumescent. With both hands he shook his organ furiously. In a moment it was over. He took the semen in his fingers and traced the designs on Miriam's body like an artist affixing his signature to a painting. "Exquisite," he whispered, and was gone.

The Three Chrysanthemums. A barbarian adding insult to injury by branding a woman's flesh into floral designs. Recoiling from the tale of perversion, Rebecca said, "If you won't see a doctor, you must go to the police."

"The police? What for?"

"To report this abuse and desecration."

"Don't be naive, Rebecca. You can't think for a second that the police here are going to prosecute a Japanese colonel for what he did to an unlicensed whore."

"Miriam, please."

Miriam laughed hollowly. "Must I say prostitute? Why use three syllables when one will do?"

"Did he hurt you in any other way, Miriam?"

"Wasn't that enough?"

"I was just wondering about your swollen stomach."

"Oh, that's another story."

Black, gelid January made way for black, gelid February. The air was rife with complaints, raspings, and squabbles. The thin veneer of civilization grew thinner. Newspaper editorials noted the decline in good manners and courtesy and urged an end to the pettiness and bickering that was adding to the general discomfort.

Sophie Felcher began to have fits of weeping. Her ears were ringing and she feared the onslaught of madness. A specialist said that her hearing was very sensitive. The ringing could be coming from the American bombs blowing up the harbor or from the Chinese New Year's celebration. "That's your opinion," she snapped. Timorous, self-effacing Sophie Felcher talking impudently to a doctor!

"Two twerpy goons are monitoring my act," Hermann Feinstein grumbled. "They're out front every night."

"Nobody's there every night monitoring *that* act," Moritz Felcher jeered.

Screaming "Emergency, emergency," Ada Hurwitz beat on the door of the Throne Room when Moritz Felcher was inside and he yelled out, "Take your emergency and roll it up in one of your palanchinkas."

Christian Boehm told Max Fogelmann that he became depressed every time he came to Hongkew—Addis Ababa was lovelier by far—and Max wrung his hands over the thought of life without Christian.

David exulted that in New York his friend Erika Zuckerman had found a way of getting around America's Trading with the Enemy Act. Co-op funds would start coming back into the heims. American dollars would be sent to Saint Gallen, in Switzerland, and converted there into Swiss francs, which would be sent on to Shanghai. The Japs would skim off the cream, of course, certifying it as "postage and handling charges," but enough of that money would get through to keep the soup pot cooking. "Ten thousand miles away," David marveled, "and she's still worrying about people in the heims."

"Worrying, no doubt," Rebecca said tartly, "while sipping cocktails at the Stork Club."

Rebecca was equally testy with David on another day, and she wondered what was taking possession of her. He had said, "You will never guess whom I saw today."

"If I'll never guess, I won't guess at all."

"Elsa and Inge! The two girls from the *Hannover.* I hardly recognized them. They looked awful. So hard and washed out. And guess what they were up to?"

"It's not my day for guessing, David."

"They came into Mr. Frankenberg's with some wall calendars they said they would sell him cheap. The only trouble was that the calendars were three years old. The girls had pasted a '5' over the '2' in '1942.' Mr. Frankenberg soon showed them to the street."

"Where I dare say they fared better."

Nor was Rebecca properly amused or apprehensive over the latest tidings from David's girl friend via Ah Chang.

"Tonight, we are putting on our crude version of *Pride and Prejudice,*" Rosalie wrote. "See if you can guess who's playing Elizabeth Bennet. Hint: she has a face rendered uncommonly intelligent by the beautiful expression of her eyes, a light and pleasing figure, and a lively, playful disposition, which delights in anything ridiculous . . .

"*Two days later:* I am in Shanghai General Hospital. (Was that your jaw I just heard hit the ground?) Not to worry. I had been taking Marilyn's barbiturates and feeling draggy, so I dragged myself over to the camp quack. He agreed with my diagnosis that I have a thyroid condition and should go into hospital. I am in very good hands. They belong to a nice young White Russian doctor here—Doctor Zamarov, Doctor Andrei

Zamarov—who says I need lots of rest and attention and should not look to be released very soon . . . "

"Can you figure it out?" David asked Rebecca.

"If you're asking me for an honest opinion," she said, "I'd say that she's a clever girl who tricked her way out of the internment camp and has found an obliging doctor who will keep her from having to go back in a trice."

Rebecca saw that David was annoyed with her. He must have hoped for some other answer. But what? Should she be telling him that he had reason to be jealous of the doctor? Absurd.

Scarcely two weeks after her defilement, Miriam Schiff was back at the Café Pacific. "Miriam," Rebecca said, "there seems to be no fool like an old fool, if you will excuse me."

"So they say. Still, a woman has to live—I guess."

"Hilda's bleeding and her mother says she's a woman now," Esther confided to her mother. "When do I get to be a woman, Mommy?"

"Soon enough," Rebecca snapped, and was instantly remorseful. It had not been a badgering query. Soon, too soon, this child would be flowering into young womanhood, and Rebecca ached with conflict. Part of her wanted to hold on to the child forever and part of her rejoiced that her precious one could grow and blossom in this desert.

"I've said my last oh-hah-yoh and kohn-bahn-wah," Moritz Felcher announced. "Now look, everybody, I want you to be witnesses."

He took the Japanese phrase book in hand and strode to the Throne Room. With the flourish of a baseball pitcher he flung it—plop—into the honey pot.

"A propos," Hermann Feinstein smirked. "Japanese is a crappy language."

"I've done this," Moritz Felcher explained, "to indicate my confidence in the Allies. With MacArthur back in Manila and convoys coming into China over the Burma Road for the first time in three years, I'm now betting the war is kaput very soon." He turned to Rebecca and said, "A little rachmones for an old man. Please typewrite some new menus for me. There are things on the old ones I can't get any more, even with squeeze."

Ada Hurwitz gurgled on and on about a "perfectly enchanting" new friend. Once a week, Mrs. Sarnoff left her "luxurious home" on the Rue Thibault to carry parcels of food and clothing to one or the other of the heims. She stopped always at the Mozart Pâtisserie to chat and bemoan the hardships of the refugees. "Our people should be doing so much more for the people over here," she lamented.

And Natzie took it upon himself to deliver some peach nectar to Shanghai General and report back to David.

Rosalie was lallygagging in a semiprivate room on the top floor. She "went out of her skull" at the sight of Natzie. There were squeals, hugs, and kisses. She was blooming, the picture of perfect health.

"What the hell's wrong with you?" Natzie asked her.

"There are things, Ignatz, that nice girls don't like to talk about."

"Aw, come on, Rosie, you can tell *me*."

"Well, you're not hearing this. It's classified information, if you must know."

Doctor Zamarov had moved her into this nice setup, which she shared with another girl. "You should see Rosie's roommate, Davie. You know a girl has to be a goddess if she looks great even with her legs in traction. Veronica's supposed to have phlebitis. Personally, I think they're both faking. Veronica calls herself an interpretative dancer. Interpretative dancer, my foot; we all know what that means."

Natzie was in his teasing, infuriating prime—throwing up his freedom at David, taking him by surprise, and salting everything with sly innuendoes. David would not give the imp the satisfaction of prompting him or appearing anxious.

"This Veronica, would you believe it, has a boyfriend who is number three in the German embassy. Herr Klaus Mainbocher! Listen to this, Davie. While I'm there, Mainbocher comes in carrying a big box all done up in ribbons. I naturally thought that it was a gift for his sweetheart. Not so at all. He hands it to Rosie and says, 'You'll never know what I went through getting some of these things. They took me for a transvestite.' I was dying of curiosity but Rosie wouldn't open the box while I was there. Then in breezes Doctor Andrei Zamarov himself, a handsomer devil you've never seen, Davie, and I decided it was time to twenty-three skidoodle. A girl and her doctor, you know, deserve to be left alone together. Hey, Davie, what's a gynecologist doing examining a thyroid condition?"

David wanted to punch that grinning face. He wasn't going to hear a thing that he wanted to hear. What he had heard only made him more miserable and bewildered.

"Oh, before I forget, Rosie asked me to give you this."

Natzie startled David with a long, full, wet kiss on the lips.

Edith Sarnoff, Mrs. Hurwitz's new friend from the White Russian community, paid a surprise call on 22/158 en route to an appointment with Rabbi Bernstein. She was a tall, willowy woman in her sixties with bluish hair and a face congealed behind a thick coating of make-up. She was wearing a matching mink coat and hat, sealskin gloves, and calf-length boots. She could scarcely mask her dismay over the premises. The Chinese, yes. But white people living like this?

"There is a way that we can help," she said. "It may not be the happiest of solutions, but there comes a time for being realistic and facing facts." She spoke slowly, selecting her words carefully—a dress rehearsal for her meeting with the rabbi? "Hard as I find it to believe, babies are still being born over here, in these conditions. The outlook for them, you must admit, is bleak at best. You, Mrs. Hurwitz, and you, Mrs. Wolf, know as well as I that these babies are at a disadvantage from the second breath they take. The hygiene, the nutrition, everything. In our community there are childless couples and others who would be overjoyed to adopt these babies. They would pay for them, and pay a pretty penny. I know this may sound horrible, crass, and calculating, but surely what is best for the baby should be the overriding consideration."

"Oh, Mrs. Sarnoff," Ada Hurwitz gushed, "it sounds most generous and thoughtful."

"Yes," Rebecca said, "but I don't think you'll find much—

if any—precedent for Jewish parents giving up their babies, even in the worst of times."

"Babies?" Miriam Schiff interjected. She had paused on her way across the courtyard to overhear the discussion. "Is it babies you want? I know of one you can have in a few months."

Edith Sarnoff regarded her with intense interest, appraising her shrewdly. "There is just this about it," she said, speaking directly to Miriam. "Any mother should think carefully before making such a commitment. She should not be acting out of the desperation of the moment. There would be no chance for second thoughts. These adoptions would be permanent. Nobody in our community is interested in temporary or foster parenthood."

The Chief Examiner was accessible, but almost nobody was seeking a pass anymore. What was the use? What was there to find on the outside? A change of scene at best, but neither help nor hope. The talk rose and stayed aloft that the Allies would invade China. Who wanted to be caught in the cross fire when infantrymen stormed off landing barges in the Whangpoo?

David was befuddled. Did he wake or dream? Was there really such a person as Rosalie Balaban—who loved him? Or was she but some chimera of the mind shaped from the depths of his loneliness and longing? Their meeting, their time together—so achingly long ago—was receding into the murkiness of myth. He must see her.

There was no way of telling if the Chief Examiner remembered him. Minobe was busy pasting snapshots of children—his?—into a black photograph album. He wasn't to be bothered. Why should he look up from his table and listen to some whining stateless person at the railing when he had more amusing things to distract him?

David had almost forgotten how very ugly this swarthy dwarf was. Studying the warty face and simian features and the tufts of wild hair sprouting from his ears and nostrils and the stiff black spikes rising from his head, he saw him as an anthropological phenomenon. Dabbing glue on the back of the snapshots, he looked like a baboon that had been trained to imitate humans.

"Pass for what?" Minobe asked, still focusing on the album.

"To visit a friend in hospital."

"*Visit?*"

"Visit, sir."

"Is that what you call it?"

"Yes, that is what I call it."

Minobe was silent. He dipped a knobby index finger into the paste pot and brushed the back of another snapshot. He centered the photograph on a fresh page in the album and tamped it down, then slammed the album shut. The stumpy little legs that had been gliding like swings leapt to the top of the table. He danced up and down, gleefully shaking his fists over his head.

"No pass, no pass, no pass. I remember you, pretty-boy. You diddle women here? For pay? Like I told you? You must be rich. No pass for *visit* in hospital. Visit head off here."

Why hadn't someone strangled this obnoxious toad? As soon as the war did end, Minobe had better run a sword across that belly before someone else did the honors for him. And people were still saluting him as King of the Jews!

"Come to the meeting, journalist," Minobe was calling after him.

The timing for the meeting with the leaders of the ghetto—whatever its purpose—was not propitious. Minobe would be in a ferocious temper. The night before, American raiders had all but fire-bombed Tokyo off the map. Reports of the human devastation were numbing—more than one hundred thousand men, women, and children had been burned alive.

What now? Rabbi Bernstein asked himself. What new challenges would be put to his rabbinical ratiocination? Just last week, there had been that business with the Sarnoff woman.

"We have no orphans here, Mrs. Sarnoff," he had told her. "Poor we are, yes, but when we are blessed with issue, we forget we are poor. And the last thing we would think of would be to put a price tab on God's ultimate gift to man."

Minobe, paradoxically, was wreathed in smiles and unctuous with pleasantries. Spring would soon be back, hee-hee,
excuse this musky community house, ah, but it was the only
place available. All things considered, their life here had not
been too bad, true? Had not the Japanese been most fair and
correct in their treatment of stateless people?

Minobe grinned in the direction of Rabbi Bernstein and
paused, waiting for some confirmation of Japanese rectitude.

"You do not hear us complain," the rabbi equivocated.

You do not hear us complain? David sniffed to himself. Anyone would have to be stone-deaf not to hear the bitching.

"Japanese have highest honor for Jewish people," the
Chief Examiner resumed. "Jewish people very good to us.
They give us money to beat Russians. They give us money to
help after earthquake. Jewish people run from Bolshies and
come to us in Manchukuo. They do very fine in Harbin, Da-
rien, Mukden. In Manchukuo, new Jerusalem in new Japan.
Jewish people have power everywhere. Most power in America. The President Jewish—President Rosenfeld. Banks Jewish.
Morgan—Morgensteins, Rockefellerheimers. Newspapers, radio, movies—all Jewish. Government Jewish. Jewish people
here have power, too. Power to make war end soonest."

Minobe paused, nodding to Rabbi Bernstein and awaiting
gratitude for his complimentary remarks and for some sign of
encouragement to continue.

"You must not overestimate us," the rabbi said at length.
Correct? Or was there any correct response to such demented
oratory as Minobe's? "We have our strengths, spiritual
strengths I should emphasize, but no political power."

"Too humble, rabbi," Minobe said, sweetness evaporat-
ing, the eyes hardening into two black coals.

"Accurate, not humble, but so be it if this is the way you
see us. What, then, are you asking of us?"

"We want you make broadcast. Wireless broadcast. You
tell brothers in America we treat you nice. You tell them Japanese people not like Nazis. Japanese people show courtesy and
respect. You tell Americans they can end war. Then everybody
go home. We all go home. Minobe goes home to babies. Nice?"

All go home? Was he mad? Or just abysmally ignorant? Where was "home" for the banished, forsaken, no-return refugees of Hongkew?

"Yes, rabbi. You make talk on wireless?"

"I beg your patience, Mr. Chief Examiner," Rabbi Bernstein said, still doubting the evidence of his ears. "Neither I nor anyone else here is empowered to give you an answer. Surely you have observed that we are a people who speak with many voices. We shall need a little time. We must present this idea to the whole community and attempt to arrive at a consensus."

"Take little time," Minobe said, crimson blotches flushing his cheeks. "Tell your people this important for them."

"We shall report to you after our Sabbath," Rabbi Bernstein promised.

To David, this stratagem was as transparent as it was deranged. It had to come straight from the Chief Examiner's warped brain. "Their cities are being bombed to kingdom come," David declaimed. "Tokyo and Osaka, Yokohama and Nagoya and Kobe. American Marines have captured Iwo Jima. The Nips are so scared they're forcing children into factories to make bombs. The Jews of Hongkew speaking to the American Jews? Insanity! In the first place, the broadcast would never reach America. In the second place, the American Jews don't know that we even exist! The Japanese are licked, and Minobe wants us to try to save their ugly brown asses."

The synagogue that Sabbath was a babel of tongues:

"Suicide to consider it. The Americans would call us undesirable aliens. Nobody would have a prayer of getting into the States."

"Lift a finger to oblige these barbarians?"

"We must think about Japanese face."

"Sit on Japanese face!"

"We should think of some compromise and try . . . "

"Compromise, you collaborator!"

The walls vibrated in the passion of rhetoric and epithets. In the end, there was unanimous agreement on one thing: The broadcast must not be made.

"It is settled then," Rabbi Bernstein said. "Nevertheless, I am going to inform Chief Examiner Minobe that we will be cooperative, but before we go ahead . . . "

"No!"

"Never!"

"We won't, we won't."

"For shame, rabbi!"

"Patience, patience," the rabbi resonated above the din. "Please, hear me out. Before we go ahead, I shall tell Mr. Minobe that the authorities might wish to reconsider some of the consequences. When the American Jews hear our voices speaking to them at this great distance, will they not wonder if we are acting spontaneously? Might they not suspect that there has been coercion? If they did suspect such a thing, would they not interpret the broadcast as an act of desperation on the part of those doing the coercing? Would the Japanese military in Shanghai, I shall ask Mr. Minobe, want to assume the responsibility for risking that interpretation of a signal sent to America?"

An appreciative murmur swept the synagogue.

The Festival of Jewish Deliverance was celebrated for the second time in the ghetto. But again without hamentaschen or groggers. Embroidering, taking scriptural license, Esther retold the story of her Old Testament namesake, "the most beautiful girl in all of Persia":

"Her mother and father died when she was a little girl, and she went to live with her cousin Mordecai, a fine and important man. One day, the great King Xerxes was looking for a new queen, and many girls went to the palace hoping to be chosen. The king took one look at Esther and—naturally—picked her right away. Queen Esther had a secret, though. She didn't tell King Xerxes, her husband, that she was Jewish. She didn't . . . "

"Smart girl," Hermann Feinstein interrupted.

"Now, Mordecai overheard some bad men tell how they were going to kill the king. Mordecai ran to tell his cousin Queen Esther about it and she told the king. King Xerxes was so pleased that there was such a loyal subject as Mordecai that he gave Mordecai many nice presents.

"There now came to the palace a wicked prince. His name

was Haman, and he wore a three-cornered hat. He expected all the officials to bow to him, and all of them did, except Mordecai. Mordecai said to Haman, 'I am a Jew. I bow only to God.' This made Haman hate Mordecai so much that he asked King Xerxes to punish all those of 'a certain people' in his kingdom, and the king told Haman to go ahead and punish them. Haman ordered that all the Jews—those 'certain people'—were to be *killed*, and he put the king's seal on the order. Mordecai heard about the order, and he begged Queen Esther to ask her husband the king to save their people, the Jews. Queen Esther, being very clever, of course, knew that because the king was busy with his wars, she would have to talk with him at just the right time. She planned a big banquet to honor him. Being a marvelous hostess, Esther invited all the people the king liked best and made sure that the tables would be full of the foods and wines that were most pleasing to him. The king was overcome with delight and his love for Queen Esther. He told her that anything in the world would be hers if she would just name it. 'Your majesty,' the beautiful Esther said, 'the order has gone out for all Jews to be killed. I myself am Jewish, and all I ask of you is to spare me and my people our lives.'

"So that was Queen Esther's way of telling her husband her big secret—that she was Jewish.

" 'My darling,' King Xerxes said, 'why have you kept that from me? What were you afraid of? I love you more than anything in the world. It doesn't matter what you are. And who, may I ask, dares to hand down such an order?'

" 'That man over there,' Esther said, pointing to Haman. 'He is the enemy of the Jews. He has built gallows to hang my cousin Mordecai—Mordecai, who saved your life.'

"The king became very angry. He ordered that Haman himself should be hanged on the gallows, and he sent out orders for the Jews to defend themselves if they were attacked. And that is what the Jewish people did. Instead of being killed, the Jews killed their enemies. And on this day of Purim every year, Jews all over the world hail good, brave, clever Queen Esther for saving her people."

"And dumping them here," Hermann Feinstein muttered into the applause greeting Esther's version of the biblical story.

The cold rains stopped. The mud and macadam dried. The sun came nearer. The shrubbery brightened and the scrawny ginkos leafed again. Hummingbirds flinted northward in flashes of yellow. Another spring.

As winter layers of clothing were shed, deterioration stared everyone in the face. Bodies were shrinking, decaying. Teeth were furry. Winter's pallor did not yield to the warming sun. This was the Valley of the Bones. But where was their Ezekiel, who, at the Lord's command, would breathe life into these withering souls and put flesh on cadavers?

People complained to the police of feathery fingers that snatched from handbags the bit of salami or the cabbage that was to be their supper, and the police said, "This is not my lane." In the heims they wailed, "Only pig slop and wormy bread." David told Mr. Frankenberg to run off just a few copies of *The Hongkew Reporter*—"It's only a penny, but it's a penny that more and more people don't have."

"I informed Mr. Minobe of our willingness to make the broadcast," Rabbi Bernstein told his congregation. "And I pointed out those things that he should bear in mind, what a broadcast from us in behalf of the Japanese might really convey to the Americans. I was dismissed with a wave of a hand. Minobe mumbled something about being much too busy with important matters to discuss radio broadcasts with stateless persons."

Esther had bruised her shins learning to ride a classmate's bicycle, and Rebecca went to Solomon's Apothecary Shop for iodine.

"Not arsenic, I hope."

Rebecca wheeled around to confront Doctor Pincus. He grasped both her arms and held her for the longest moment. His smile was warm and eager.

"Lovely as ever," he said.

"Please, I looked in my glass this morning and screamed."

"Lovely is in the eye of the beholder," he reminded her.

"How are you? And Esther? I have thought of you a hundred times."

"And I have thought of you," Rebecca admitted, but didn't confess that it had been more than a hundred times. Nor did she say that he looked pale, drawn, and fatigued.

"You can see how you've changed my life, Mrs. Wolf."

The early April day was warm and he was wearing the beige knee-length shorts, short-sleeved cotton shirt, and light cotton stockings that she had bought him in the Forbidden City. Time was so tricky here. That must have been going on two years ago.

"You have your iodine, and I have my mustard plasters," he said, drawing her with him out of the shop. "Tell me truly how things are going."

"Oh, magnificently," she laughed, "just don't ask for any of the particulars."

"That's something I don't hear very often. You may be the last person around with any sense of gaiety. I look at you superficially and you indeed appear well, though much too thin. But what can a doctor prescribe for underweight? Except a very obvious palliative—dinner with me one evening soon. Is that possible?"

She hid her happiness behind frivolous self-deprecation. "Have you read *Beware of Pity*, Doctor Pincus?"

"I have, and it doesn't apply."

But why, then, was he inviting her now, after this accidental encounter? Something else baffled her, too. As she hesitated, he must have seen a shadow on her face.

"Mrs. Pincus? It's all right. We have our understanding."

Before Rebecca had her evening with Doctor Pincus, a calamitous event intervened, stunning the ghetto and throwing everyone into mourning. The President of the United States was dead.

None of the refugees had seen in the flesh the man they had romanticized into heroic dimensions. Some had heard recordings of his "fireside chats." Most of them had strong visual memories of him from newspapers and magazines and newsreels. His charm, his self-assurance, and his aristocratic mien had haunted their imaginations and inspired hope. "President Roosevelt and Adolf Hitler came to power within weeks of each other," Rabbi Bernstein sermonized. "But God in His perplexing ways takes the virtuous man first."

"What did Roosevelt ever do for the Jews?" Hermann Feinstein asked deprecatingly.

"You could just as well ask what the American Jews do for the Jews," David rejoined. "My Marine friend, Joe Gordon, told me there were influential Jews that Roosevelt would have listened to, but they were too afraid of rocking their own boat. The most respected political commentator in America is a man named Walter Lippmann, and he keeps his Jewishness a secret. Not once during the 1930s, Joe said, did Lippmann write a word about what the Nazis were doing to the Jews."

"Roosevelt's policies endeared him to the Jews already in the United States," Rebecca temporized. "But like most leaders, he didn't like to hear bad news. Nor did the Congress of the United States. And the whole subject of Jewish immigration *was* bad news."

"Hitler must be walking on air," Moritz Felcher said. "He'll see Roosevelt's death as a miracle, a sign that the Almighty is looking out for him. He'll start thinking that he can survive Churchill and Stalin, too."

"Then he's as nuts as Minobe," David snorted. "The Allies have Berlin by the short ones."

The Japanese came for Hermann Feinstein.

Feinstein had gone too far.

"Can we talk?" he asked audiences at the Café Blaue Donau. "Listen, I've been keeping score. By my count, just reading what they put out in their own newspapers, the Nips have sunk the whole American Navy four times over. They have shot down the entire American Air Force three and a half times over. They've killed every Allied soldier five times over." For a closing ditty, Feinstein sang, "Hitler's gone, tee-hee-hee / Now we'll hang Hirohito from a sour apple tree."

The men who took him away were the "two twerpy goons" who had been monitoring his act night after night.

"And I didn't believe anybody could be listening to him night after night," Moritz Felcher said. "He should have stuck to his lousy jokes instead of making with the needles."

"The Bridge House," David shuddered. "They'll charge him with blasphemy, slander, and inciting to demoralize."

"If that's where they've got him," Moritz Felcher said, "he'll have to joke his way out. I'm not going through all that again. I can't afford it."

But David could not leave it at that. He had been there. He could not think of anyone except Adolf Hitler whom he would not try to rescue from that colossus of miseries. He presented himself at the Bridge House as a journalist, not the concerned housemate, but the jailers were adamant. He could not see prisoner Feinstein.

Nobody at 22/158 except Esther honestly liked Hermann Feinstein, but they had adjusted to him, and he did bring them an occasional smile. His absence, his incarceration appalled the household. As the days passed, it became apparent that Feinstein's flip lip was not going to secure his freedom. His empty room gaped at them like a silent rebuke. "I should look for another tenant," Moritz Felcher said. But he didn't.

"You must borrow one of my dresses," Miriam Schiff said, "and look your best."

Rebecca was relieved to be on good terms with Miriam again. After calling Miriam a fool for going back to the Café Pacific, a coolness had developed between them. Rebecca still could not expunge the word "fool" from her mind—and it was foolishness compounded for a pregnant woman to be selling herself to men with quirky yearnings—but she *had* to burble out the news of her invitation to someone.

She was too old, she told herself giddily, to be playing Cinderella. But that's exactly how she felt in Miriam's long pink organdy gown with the ruffled sleeves. "I'd forgotten there were places like this," she gushed to Romeo.

The Café St. Petersburg was an oasis of charm and substance in a forlorn quarter. Its pastel green walls held a small fortune in contemporary European art, and there was Aubusson carpeting. Under steel-bladed ceiling fans stirring the air, patrons sat on mahogany chairs at mahogany tables covered with starched napery and centered with vases of fresh-cut flowers. In a far corner a harpist in a décolleté lime silk evening dress unobtrusively played melodies from Tchaikovsky and Rachmaninov.

The Café exuded a bewildering prosperity, a patronage of prosperous Japanese, White Russian, and Chinese businessmen. But no one was nearly as handsome or as elegant as the man across from Rebecca in his midnight-blue suit with the gold chain looping across the vest. His navy polka-dotted bowtie contrasted smartly with a light blue Shantung silk shirt.

"I think beautiful restaurants are created with women like you in mind," Doctor Pincus said gallantly.

"You mean women who can't afford to go to them?" she smiled.

Her eyes swam at the temptations listed inside the long suede-covered carte. "How can I ever choose? If only I were one of those hibernating animals, I could eat my way through the whole menu and go to sleep and not have to worry about eating again for six months. You order, Doctor Pincus. Anything . . . "

"Werner, please."

"Anything will be absolutely what I was craving, Werner."

"A lady could get into trouble by deferring too much," he twinkled, and addressed himself to commanding chilled schav, herring salads, chicken Pojarski, and a bottle of Liebfraumilch.

Again, the innuendo that teetered on the naughty. The intimacy of it, the soft lighting, the glissandoes now of a Victor Herbert medley ("Slumber on, my little gypsy sweetheart . . . "), and the impending miracles from the kitchen filled her with the wildest expectation.

"I see you glancing around with just the faint edge of—je ne sais quoi," her companion said. "Surely I am not to feel guilty if after months and months of unremitting toil I invite a lovely lady to a fancy restaurant."

"Please, you may invite whomever you please wherever you please."

"You are very nimble in sidestepping compliments."

"That's easy enough. I don't have to get out of the way of too many of them."

"Now who is going to believe that?"

"I am going through a stage with Esther where I get the impression that I don't have one redeeming human quality. I asked her the other night if she could think of anything that she liked and admired about me. She spent at least half an hour in pensive thought. And you know what she said? 'You have marvelous handwriting, Mommy.' "

He laughed and said, "The next time she gets a cold, no more of that sweet cherry syrup. I'll give her some medicine that tastes like Fernet Branca."

"All these people, I can't help thinking, stuffing themselves," Rebecca sighed, "with the starving so near by." And thinking, where is Mrs. Pincus? And with whom is *she* having dinner?

"Yes, yes, but for a minute let me play one of those disputatious rabbinical scholars who can always find the contraindication to the most palpable truths. Will you believe me if I tell you, cross my heart, that there are refugee men who owe their lives to being put into the ghetto? Otherwise, they would have been dead by now from gout or diabetes or gallstones or heart disease or high blood pressure. But here, with no chance for most of them to indulge their gluttony, they are leaner and in better health than they've been for a long time."

The food arrived and Rebecca cautioned herself to eat slowly. Her shrunken stomach could not absorb too much. May God give her the discipline to leave something on her plate! And to sip the wine sparingly, or her head would spin off.

"I look at someone like you," she said, " and I wonder for the thousandth time about a country so masochistic that it cuts itself off from so much of its richest natural resource—its brain power—from Einstein on down, through thousands upon thousands of brilliant scientists and mathematicians, doctors, scholars, and artists."

"Did you have to rank me lower than Einstein?" His smile deepened the weary creases around his eyes, and Rebecca noticed, with a pang of sadness, how much grayer that steely close-cropped hair had become since she first met him.

"I was being serious," she said. "And I was about to ask what your career might have been but for Shanghai."

"You're really asking for the story of my life. Surely you would not find that interesting."

"Yes, I think I should," she blushed.

"Well, I'll tell you mine if you tell me yours," he said, and Rebecca thrilled with the anticipatory pleasure of setting out on an expedition. "Please stop me when it gets boring, or if you've heard it before. I was a poor boy—bored already?"

"No, heard it before," she laughed.

"Not truly poor. My father was in civil service—a postal inspector—but he had four sons with voracious appetites to feed. That was in Kassel. We were quite ordinary—the usual family with a frustrated father, a martyred mother, and squabbling sons. The dog's name was Nebuchadnezzar, and I had a wonderful kite made from the flags of Germany and her colonies—the Cameroons, Togo, East Africa, Southwest Africa, Fiji, the Bismarck Archipelago, the Marshalls. My first memory—could I have been two? two and a half?—was being at Lake Constance. It was a very hot day, and my father had taken me for a ride on a ferry boat. A summer storm came up while we were still on the lake, and he pressed me to him saying, 'Don't be afraid, don't be afraid.' Afraid? The more it thundered and lightninged and the more it rained and the higher the waves came, the more I liked it. I always remembered the excitement of being on the water in that storm, and I guess it directed my future course. I became a merchant seaman. For three years I drifted and pitched on the high seas on the freighter *Kiel*. I swabbed decks and cleaned latrines and stoked coal and worked the officers' mess. Around the world in a thousand days. One day, the radio operator stumbled into the hold and I just happened to be going by when the ship's doctor called out for me to give him a hand. One of Sparks' arms was broken and I stayed with the doctor through all the setting and taping. Like many a ship's doctor, ours was there because of a weakness for Schnaps. Doctor Krueger took a liking to me and during his occasional spells of sobriety I learned a great deal from him. I became his assistant and did routine things like give inoculations and swab throats and treat fevers. I felt the murmur of a real calling. But along came the Great War and I joined the Kaiser's navy. I served under Admiral Hipper at Jutland—well, you know about that, we won but we lost. After the war, I drifted and looked for work. There was no money for a medical education. When things are very bad, some people find the escape of illness. That may be what kept me in Davos for three years, as a spiritual brother of Hans Castorp. Tuberculosis hardened my resolve to go into medicine. After leaving the sanatorium, I spent two and a half years tutoring a count's blockhead son in mathematics and Latin. I hoarded every Pfennig to enter the University of Jena, where I toiled and troubled for seven years. On the doorstep of middle age I received my medical degree and entered into general practice with an older doctor in Bad Nauheim. In September of 1937, I came to Shanghai to live happily ever after. There you have it—all anyone could ever want to know about the life and hard times of Werner Pincus, doctor of medicine."

She smiled tenuously. Was that all he was going to tell her? The sommelier refilled their glasses as she framed a response. Again, something was amusing him.

"Did I leave out something?" he asked.

"A good deal, I should say."

"Mrs. Pincus?"

"Well, yes," she said, her cheeks flaming.

"Pardon me while I take a deep breath." He inhaled deeply, sonorously. "Did you ever notice how many stories have a way of beginning, 'You won't believe this, but . . . ' Doctor Blumenthal, who had taken me into his practice, in Bad Nauheim, had some good friends who were vintners in Rüdesheim. These people had a daughter who had always been high-strung and nervous. As she became a young woman, her problems began to multiply. She would be in and out of asylums that treated the emotionally disturbed, but she also had long spells when she was well, active, and cheerful. Then the darkness would descend and she would become catatonic. Manic-depressive, they diagnosed her. The Third Reich, as you know, looks very harshly upon people with mental weaknesses. These friends of Doctor Blumenthal were very worried that during one of their daughter's periods of hospitalization she would be seized, put into a van, and carried off for extermination. The Nazis were beginning to do this quite freely and openly—and with the physically unfit as well. Doctor Blumenthal came to me one day with an extraordinary proposition. Mind you, I had never met the Bruders, much less laid eyes on their daughter. You have to put this in the framework of its time. 'I have had my life,' Doctor Blumenthal said to me, 'but for you, Werner, things will only get worse here. One day, they won't let you attend anybody.' The proposition was that I marry Rita Bruder and help her get away from there. Her parents would pay for our passage to the only place that would immediately take us. The Bruders would tend their vineyards through the coming season and then join Rita here in Shanghai. They would become her custodians again and the marriage would be annulled. They even insisted on giving me a modest sum to set up a practice here. 'You'll be doing them a very big mitzvah,' Doctor Blumenthal told me, 'and it's for just a little while.' Rita's parents, of course, never made it here."

He stopped with a whimsical smile. As if that were truly the end of the story. "Oh, Werner."

"What does 'Oh, Werner' mean?"

"Well, I wasn't bored and I really hadn't heard it before."

"Meaning you can bear to hear more?"

"Yes, yes, anything."

"When we first came here, I rented a bungalow on King George Road and set up my office there. I put a notice in the newspapers announcing my services. By then, there had been such a flood of doctors from Europe that the International Settlement wasn't waiting for one more. But soon, the tide of refugees began to swell, and many of them went right into the heims here in Hongkew and needed the services of a doctor. I decided that I had better move over here, too. Rita was very upset: 'You expect me to live in a slum like this. Wait until my parents get here and see how you are treating me.' In her less lucid moments she accused me of having kidnaped her. She still had the monthly allowance that her family was sending through a bank in Amsterdam and its branch on the Bubbling Well Road. During her good spells Rita is an energetic and gregarious woman. Many people must find her immensely attractive, and do not suspect that there is anything wrong with her. But if she had to live in Hongkew, damned if she'd stay here night *and* day. She never told me where she was going in the morning or where she had been, and I never asked. But when people asked me where my wife was, I would be tempted to answer, 'She disappeared across the Soochow Creek a year ago and that's the last I've seen of her.' Many a time I had only to pick up a newspaper to find out where she had been. Her face would be gazing out of the brown pages of the rotogravure section. It was a polo match here or a pool party there or some fashion benefit for Chinese orphan children. She had a terrible spell after the Führer invaded western Europe and the allowances stopped and she realized that her parents would not be able to get here. But then she was up and off being the social butterfly again. And that's the way it's been. She's either on the move or inert in black humors. She is not restricted to the area, of course, because our arrival predated 1938, but what she finds to do these days in the Concessions is beyond me. She has a right to her amusements, of course; I am buried in my work. Life goes on."

He put the tips of his fingers together, as much a gesture of finality as if he had placed them across his lips. End of story. Now she knew so much, but her deepest curiosities were unsatisfied. For the moment it must suffice. The moment must be complete unto itself, the excitement of his nearness and this glow of supreme well-being.

"What can I say? There are so many things I should like to say."

"Save them until I've heard the story of your life. It's your turn and I'm all ears."

"I warn you, you'll be bored and you'll certainly have heard it before. Once upon a time in Lübeck, there was . . . "

She stopped. Something dreadful was about to happen. The lights in the lamps flickered nervously. Overhead, the blades of the ceiling fans stuttered, stammered, and died. Waiters and captains scurried about frantically. The walls trembled with slight paroxysms. A long blast rent the hushed air and was followed by a short blast. In the next instant came a sustained blast signaling danger.

"Under the table, Rebecca. Get down."

Rebecca obeyed Werner unquestioningly. It was like a

game of hide and seek, crouching under the tablecloth that dropped to the floor and shielded them from the world. Their knees touched and their heads came close together. Her fear fled in the deliciousness of contact and the absurdity of their position. Within seconds, bombers were thundering straight above them. She began to shake.

"Don't be afraid," he soothed her, and cupped his hands over her ears.

She shivered and said, "It's only Lake Constance."

"An air raid to remember," he smiled, dropping his hands to caress her arms.

"Yes, but it's interrupting the story of my life."

"What does the St. Petersburg have that the Café Moritz doesn't have?" Moritz Felcher teased Rebecca the next morning. "Except swell food, a wine cellar, atmosphere, nice people, and good service."

"Self-deprecation becomes you, my dear Mr. Felcher," Rebecca said. Thanking Miriam for the loan of the pink organdy dress, she asserted, "It brought me good luck."

"Keep it then. That's more than it ever did for me."

"I can't keep it, Miriam."

"Yes, you can, and you must. And I have a couple more you may have. The truth is, Rebecca, I am leaving. I have someone who will be looking after me very well."

"Miriam!"

"Yes, I am going. I am leaving the ghetto, as a matter of fact."

"You can't be serious."

"It is true. There is someone who wants to take me away from all this, as they are always saying in the movies—and under about the same circumstances. He is a major in the Third Marines Regiment and holds to the samurai code of honor. He is concerned about my welfare and has arranged for me to live in my own flat in the Rue Lafayette."

Boxes within boxes. One high-ranking Japanese officer coming forward to protect Miriam after her body has been mutilated by another and impregnated by still another.

Miriam leaving—the word itself had the sharp edge of a reproach. Rebecca's feelings for Miriam were complicated and confusing. The one constant was affection. But at one time or another she had felt pity, admiration, and anger for this desperate woman who stumbled from one mess to the next. Still, Miriam was the one woman in the house with whom she shared a friendship. In common, they had an intelligence, a sensibility, and a curiosity transcending gossip. She could talk to Sophie Felcher, so wispy and uxorious, only in the pedestrian language of Hausfraulichkeit. Ada Hurwitz was amusing and generous but too flighty and layered with affectations for a dependable line of communication. It was not just the accident of geography, of propinquity; "in the real world," in the familiar parlance, Rebecca and Miriam could easily have been friends.

"For myself, I couldn't be sorrier," Rebecca said to Miriam. "How I shall miss you! But it will be better for you, and it will certainly be better for the baby."

"Oh, the baby. The baby will be going straightaway to Mrs. Sarnoff."

Others were not so fortunate as Miriam. Some of them could not face up to the options closing in on them. Landlords were being called heartless and avaricious because they were evicting tenants who could no longer pay their tiny rent. The landlords defended themselves by asking where it was written that deadbeats should pull the rest of the world into the gutter with them. On the eve of her forcible removal to the Alcock heim, the widow Kirschner down the lane swallowed strychnine and died agonizingly, and somebody took red paint to the fence of her landlord and wrote "Murderer."

"I have no heart for it," Moritz Felcher said, "but I should open the roof garden again. Help me with these menus, Mrs. Wolf, and we'll just forget about any more rent."

More ominous rumblings raced across the community. Those most nauseating of rumors were revived. This time they were passed from person to person in whispers, which took on a hysterical edge. The bedrock of truth seemed to be that something horrible was happening in Europe. Somebody knew of somebody who had talked to people who had seen "death camps" with their own eyes and smuggled word out about unimaginable crimes. It was almost beyond belief that such terrors could be transpiring.

"I close my ears to all those tales," Moritz Felcher declared. "They remind me of the last war—remember what they said the German army was doing with its bayonets to Belgian babies. It's only propaganda."

Better by far to be hoisted over the moon by one fact than cast to the ground by a hundred rumors. "The Golem" was dead!

Their nemesis, the perpetrator of their agony and dislocation, was gone. But there was no overt rejoicing, no celebration of a curse lifted from their heads—only a ravenous hunger for information. Only detail laid upon convincing detail could assure them that the greatest scourge on the planet had met his demise.

Even the matter of death was riveting, transfixing. The man who had threatened to bury his enemies had taken his own life. The Führer of the Master Race a suicide! In the bowels of the earth he had blown out his brains.

Four months earlier, Hitler had moved into the eighteen tiny rooms of the submarinelike bunker under the Reich Chancellery and may never have seen the light of day again. He despised Berlin, but nevertheless he would stay there until the end. He wished to share his fate "with the millions of others who have chosen to remain inside the heartbeat of our beloved Reich." He said he chose death willfully, joyously, knowing of the immeasurable deeds and achievements carried out in his name by the peasants, the workers, and the youth.

A few minutes before his suicide, Hitler married his secret companion of many years, the blonde Eva Braun, and she chose to die with him. Each of them swallowed a pellet of cyanide and, simultaneously, the Great Dictator put a revolver to his head. Their corpses, in accordance with a final order, were carried out of the underground lair and burned to ashes in a bomb crater. It was his dying wish that no Jew should ever be able to see in his remains anything recognizable as Adolf Hitler.

Adolf Hitler was dead. It had to be all over in Europe—and it was.

Götterdämmerung came like collapsing jackstraws. German armies in northern Italy surrendered. Mussolini and his mistress were captured and executed by Italian partisans. Soviet armies seized Berlin. The German armies in Holland, Denmark, and northwest Germany surrendered. The German army in Austria raised the white flag. The Americans were at the Brandenburg Gate. Generals Jodl and Friedeburg and Admiral Dönitz surrendered the Fatherland unconditionally to the Allies. Propaganda Minister Goebbels killed himself and Reichsmarshall Göring (The Gas Bag, The Iron Hermann) was captured. The Third Reich that was to have been the glory of the world for a thousand years was kaput after only twelve.

Bloody, beaten, brought to its knees, Germany was free of its tyranny. Murderous evil had been annihilated by something mightier—the invincibility of goodness and justice. But Germany was not a country that any of the refugees yearned to return to. The memories were so bitter, so painful. Some talked vaguely of "fresh starts." But where? Maybe in America . . . the Holy Land . . . Australia. How could any of them know where? Someone else was still dealing. They would have to wait to see what cards turned up.

"Let joy be confined," Rabbi Bernstein revised a familiar maxim. "It is not wise to spread your wings when others near you may soon have theirs fatally clipped. We still have another victory to wait upon. Patiens et fortis."

Hope for loved ones left behind, which had long languished, revived afresh. The cities of Germany were ruins. But human beings could be less vulnerable than architecture—they had mobility, a sentient yearning for survival. Those vile, vomitous rumors aside, there was even reawakened hope for the pitiful creatures who had ended up in the camps of eastern Europe. How could prison inmates have gone on with their labors for the Fatherland's war effort unless they had been at least minimally fed and sheltered? (How often Rebecca had wished that Samuel might have turned himself into some furry little animal of the night, a mole in a warm hole, who would crawl out into the sunlight when the nightmare was over.)

"Six close relatives," a suddenly voluble Sophie Felcher recalled. "My brother, Dieter, in Augsburg. My sister—married 'out' to the hops warehouseman—in Duisberg. Uncle Frank and Uncle Otto, my bachelor uncles in Baiersdorf. Cousin Katya, the kindergarten teacher in Bonn. Aunt Karoline—'Crazy Karoline,' they called her—she went light in the head and begged the Ursaline sisters to convert her."

"I hope God has shown a little mercy to my sister," Moritz Felcher said.

"Please, God, give me back Mama," David prayed silently. "I promise that I shall stop saying You do not exist."

"I shan't be going back to Vienna," Ada Hurwitz divulged. "I will never forget the day I saw a rabbi being beaten up there by Jews pretending they were not Jews. If there was ever a more anti-Semitic city on Earth, I confess I don't know where it is."

"Will the New Germany be safe for all genders?" Max Fogelmann wondered wryly.

Rabbi Bernstein need not have cautioned them about an excess of high spirits. Euphoria faded quickly and they were unable to follow his stricture on patience. It is in the nature of man to clamor for total gratification as soon as total gratification becomes a possibility. Victory in Europe yesterday—why not victory in the Pacific today? But grim reality foreclosed on optimism. The days were an inferno. The air reeked of burnt rubber and burnt corpses. At night, the mosquitoes buzzed like dive bombers. Tighter curfews were imposed, and black curtains went back up. More trenches had to be dug—unsightly gashes magnifying the irreducible squalor of Hongkew. Cholera, dysentery, rabies, salmonella poisoning, and exhausted hearts took a higher toll. One breathless middle of the night, a patent-medicine maker from Cracow put his hands around the neck of his sleeping wife and strangled her.

David colored the world shit-brown. His mouth tasted of ashes. He moved the colored pins on his war map but it was an exercise in frustration. The Allies would never finish mopping up the Philippines. It would take forever to finish off the Japanese "bullet brigades" on Okinawa. He was putting out his newssheet only once a week—just as well, nothing much new was happening. Or was it that he had stopped seeing things? Were his brains frying or atrophying?

"Shake the grates," Natzie urged him. "Take some little honeysuckle rose into the bushes and get to the bottom of things."

"You think that screwing is the cure for everything," David countered peevishly.

"Do you know of a better cure? I think it was that Doctor Johnson you admire so much who said whoever is tired of screwing is tired of life."

"He said it about London, you ass, and you know it."

Everything crept under David's skin. Aunt Sophie was nodding but not listening to a thing anyone said to her. Ada Hurwitz's voluminous drawers hogged the clothesline like a row of soaked parachutes put out to dry. "Seen anyone, David," his uncle pestered him, "who'd like a nice room cheap?" Max Fogelmann kept fluffing his locks and tweaking his eyebrows. Even Mrs. Wolf was primping and fussing with her appearance. Everybody must be going daft, himself included.

Rosalie, too. "I'll give you a little hint" was the latest word from Shanghai General. "I'm getting weller and weller . . . "

Clue to what?

"Soon," he had said, touching Rebecca's cheeks.

Soon. "Soon, maybe not tomorrow . . . " A maddeningly elastic word. Soon is a thousandth of a second to the infant crying for the breast. Soon is the few million years it takes for one primate form to evolve into a higher adaptation. "I will pay you soon" the debtor assures his creditor, meaning possibly never. Soon, sooner, soonest. Was there anything in the world that wasn't relative?

Evening in steamy Hongkew, and Rebecca was alone in the yard trying not to think about Werner Pincus. In her loft Ada Hurwitz snored lightly. Esther was sleeping the sleep of content, having outjumped her friend Helena in four games of Parcheesi. The Felchers were still at the café. David was off somewhere. Max Fogelmann was watching a refugee group—the Saucey Savoyards—put on *The Mikado*.

"I tried out for Yum Yum," Max said in passing, "but they said the part would have to be played by a girl."

"How little imagination some people have," Rebecca commiserated.

Max was displaying a new independence that was heartening. Christian Boehm's visits had become sporadic, but Max seemed more resilient, less injured by the neglect. "Christian says that intellectually he praises monogamy," Max had said quite calmly, "but that his heart is hopelessly polygamous."

Across the lane several people were bent toward a flickering candle, losing themselves in canasta. Farther along Kimpei the Kwon children were lighting strings of firecrackers that popped like machine-gun fire. From a shack came the monotonous twang-twang of a samisen. Lin Su-san shuffled past, the orange macaw on his left shoulder screeching "Piss on you, piss on you"—the three-word vocabulary owed to its previous master, a British sailor.

Soon. A ridiculous hope, a longing that should be dismissed from mind. It was a relationship that could have no future—not even a present. There was already one Mrs. Pincus, however tenuous the marriage, and she shared his bed and board, however marginally. It was foolish to daydream about other possibilities, about altered positions in a triangle. And yet. And yet . . .

"Excuse me, madam, please."

Startled from her reverie, Rebecca looked up to see an extraordinary presence at the gate to the courtyard.

"I do not wish to disturb," the visitor said.

"May I help you?"

"Is this—is this—the place of Mr. David Buchbinder?"

"Yes, Mr. Buchbinder lives here."

"Permit me to inquire if Mr. Buchbinder is in residence?"

The English was clipped British, and excessively formal. The girl was probably Eurasian.

"He is not present at present," Rebecca told her.

"It is quite necessary that I see him. Would you give me permission, please, madam, to wait here until he returns."

"It isn't a matter of permission. It's simply that I have no way of knowing how long that might be."

"For Mr. Buchbinder, I should wait forever."

Mockery? Some quaint exaggeration of courtesy? Rebecca unlatched the gate to let in the stunning young woman. It was like welcoming a fashion model from the glossies. The girl's slender figure was exquisitely encased in a high-collared gown of green antique brocade, rich and heavy, slashed to the thighs. Her shining raven-black hair was like a helmet, covering her brow in a dense row of bangs. Her eyes were almost the identical jade green of her dress, and they were ringed in kohl. Her face was as white as chalk and her mouth was lacquered with thick scarlet lipstick. She was smiling sweetly and batting her long sweeping eyelashes.

"Is Mr. Buchbinder expecting you?"

This simplest of questions threw the girl into a quandary. She pondered at length before replying, "It is my humble opinion—and I hesitate to speak slightingly of him—that he is not quite deductive enough to be expecting me."

Deductive? Would not a simple "yes" or "no" have sufficed? The girl's feet, Rebecca noticed, now that they both were seated on the camp chairs, were not as dainty as her speech. They were not Oriental feet, and they were too large for the green satin pumps into which they were squeezed.

"Then am I to deduce that at least you know Mr. Buchbinder?" Rebecca said to the stranger.

There was another long pause while this remark was put through the grinding mills of deliberation. "Know? *Know?*" the eyelashes batting furiously. "Are you asking me if I have biblical knowledge of Mr. Buchbinder?"

The lovely face was all innocence and inscrutability, but there could be no mistaking her meaning. Who was this—this piece of goods anyway? Some remnant from David's free-ranging days across the Soochow? She was certainly not a streetwalking tart. Could she be someone who had trained her-self in the arts of coquetry and badinage?

"What I thought I was asking is," Rebecca said precisely, "is Mr. Buchbinder an acquaintance of yours?"

"*Acquaintance?* Raw-ther—to say the very least!"

Ignoring the innuendo, and glancing at the heavy brocade dress, Rebecca remarked, "You must be very warm."

"Warmer than warm, thank you very much. To put a point upon it, I am quite as hot as the proverbial firecracker."

The smile was still sweet as sugar, and those bristles of lashes went on flicking like camera shutters over eyes wide with innocence, despite the heavily weighted sexual insinua-tion.

"I am afraid, Miss—Miss . . . "

"Blossoms. Peony Blossoms. But please, madam, call me Peony."

"I am afraid it is my bedtime. I shall have to say good night to you."

Peony Blossoms, my eye! Whoever she was, this caller was impertinent and exasperating, and was deserving of no further hospitality—at least from her. Let her sit out there and enter-tain herself with her snide whimsies and double entendres. Ah, but would David, when he did return, be any match for her?

First, the girl had Moritz Felcher to contend with. Now in bed, Rebecca could smile in bitter humor at the overheard ex-change.

"Mr. Felcher . . . "

"What? Who are you?"

"Look at me closely, kind sir, and tell me that you do not know me."

"Get away from me. I don't know you. What are you do-ing here?"

There was the sound of purring. "I have business with your nephew."

"What kind of business?"

"What am I to say? But if you must know, it is business of the most intimate kind."

"You had better get off my property right now or you will be sorry."

"Yes, I should be sorry. But your nephew would be just as sorry. And he would be extremely vexed with you."

"Miss, I don't know who you are, but . . . "

"They call me Peony Blossoms. *You* may call me Miss Blossoms, sir,"

Moritz Felcher snorted and bolted off to his bedroom. It *was* funny. A cunning Oriental, half their ages, getting the better of two educated middle-aged people. A glamorous siren who hinted euphemistically of erotic abandonment and neither one of them had managed to get out of her the most elementary of facts—who she was!

It was well after curfew when Rebecca heard the familiar step along the lane and the latch lifting on the gate. David's visitor was still waiting.

"Mr. Buchbinder?"

Rebecca heard a gasp. David must be levitating.

"Mr. David Buchbinder?"

There was dead silence.

"So again we meet, David Buchbinder."

"Again? I have never laid eyes . . . "

"Oh, Mr. Buchbinder. After all we have been to each other?"

Oh ho, David, dear David. The vixen would make mincemeat out of him and feed him to the tigers. Where in the world could their paths have crossed? Some night, many a moon ago, when David, befuddled with rice wine, wound up in her arms and made undying promises to her?

"Look at me closely, mon cher, and tell me that you really don't remember."

"Who—who are you?"

"You can ask, after all we have been to each other?"

"I have never seen you before. Please believe me, I would remember."

"Peony Blossoms did not please you as much as you said she did?"

"Is this some joke? Did Natzie Stern . . . "

"Do not be stern with me, sir."

What must be going through his mind? Was she a wily impostor? A blackmailer? Someone trying to nail him for breach of promise—or a charge of paternity? And a girl like *that . . . ?*

"It has to be one of Natzie's jokes. I know, you've been delivering pig fat and he put you up to this."

"You have laid a good deal more than eyes on me, my impetuous Lothario."

Lothario?

"And I shall prove it to you," Peony Blossoms said, "quick as the shake of a lamb's tail. Lend me your handkerchief and turn your back to me."

A zipper unzipped and there was the rustling of a garment being removed and thrown to the courtyard. "And now to take off my face and my head." There was a long mute minute for the handkerchief to work its magic. "Okay, Mr. David Buchbinder, turn around."

The voice had changed, too. The accent was plain, unstilted—American?

"It's me!" she shrieked.

David was dumbfounded.

"It's me! David, it's me!"

David let out a Tarzanic roar. "Rosalieeeeeeeeeeeeeeee!"

"Daviiiiid!"

The screams of ecstasy and the whoopings and the leapings and the bouncings and the huggings and the smoochings and the squeals of joy and wonder. David and his Rosalie—*united!* But how . . . ?

"Is it really you?" David asked for the tenth time.

"It's me."

"Pinch me, I can't believe it." Then he screamed, "Not down *there!*"

The story tumbled out of Rosalie Balaban, in the backyard, in the middle of the night, for all of Hongkew to hear. "As I wrote you, I took those pills of Marilyn's to make myself so groggy the camp doc would agree with me that I was having a thyroid crisis and that I had better be put in Shanghai General. Doctor Zamarov, the one I teased you about, was a perfect doll and would have gone along with anything to keep me from having to go back to camp. He moved me into a semiprivate with a White Russian beauty named Veronica, and it was Veronica who was struck by genius. She said there was a way of getting out of the hospital without having to go back to Chapei. If I were to walk out of there looking like an Oriental, no one would give me even a first glance and try to stop me. So we made up a shopping list, and Veronica got her boyfriend to buy the stuff—that gown, the wig, the gunk for my face. As luck would have it, Veronica's boyfriend came back with the whole megillah at the very time Natzie was visiting. I was so afraid Natzie, that yenta, would guess what was up and spill the beans—I so wanted to knock you off your feet."

"I don't believe it. I must be dreaming."

"Should I pinch you again?"

"Yes—any place but *there*."

Soon, David was taking Rosalie to his room. He was quickly out of his own clothes. It could not have been more natural or unabashed. The fragile house throbbed the rest of the night to the cries and the beat of love-making.

Rebecca lay awake with an ungratified sexual hunger that all but made her ill. She wanted "a blue miracle," too—the surprise of all surprises.

David was too happy for shame, too starved for inhibition. If he held back, the dream would disappear. If he slept, he would wake to find that it had been a mirage after all. She was here. She was real. She was really here to stay.

Only yesterday, a hundred years ago, they had met in that snow-white movie-set flat in Broadway Mansions. Everything had changed, nothing had changed. In their rhapsody of reunion, the days and months and years fell away like the leaves of a calendar denoting the passage of time in a film.

"You're so skinny," Rosalie said, stroking his cheekbones and the concavities of his cheeks.

"You're so delicious, Miss Blossoms," David said, and again feasted on succulent fruit.

"You're so horny," she gasped.

In three years, David had not seen anyone so lovely. She looked older, more woman than girl. Her copper hair was in a bun on the top of her head now, and her eyes, green as emeralds, still danced with merriment. The winged eyebrows floated delicately. Her nose and lips and long smooth neck had their same elegant lines. She was pale, but the June sun would soon dispel the hospital pallor. (In the broad light of day, Rosalie inspected 22/158 and, giggling, whispered to David, "What . . . a . . . dump!")

Rosalie was a princessly new presence in an exhausted household. She brought the refreshment of novelty. She was young, very pretty, an American girl who loved one of them very much. She was a clever and daring heroine who had taken risks and outwitted authority to come and live with them. Moritz Felcher welcomed her with the offer of the Schiffs' room. (Propriety must be observed, if only in the breach.) Sophie Felcher flitted like a mother hen, collecting a wardrobe out of the second-hand shops. Rebecca found Rosalie artless, charming, and good company, and envied her her sexual abandon. Ada Hurwitz clucked with satisfaction (oo-la-la, all that business in the hay). Esther was mesmerized; here was a big sister home from exotic lands and full of fascinating tales ("Shirley Temple had straight brown hair until they got to work with a bottle of dye and the curlers . . . They taped Judy's breasts so she would look girlish enough to play Dorothy").

Love brought a first, fine, careless release of tightly coiled springs. But in the satiety of early rapture, all was not sunlight in paradise. It was an inelegant time and place for intimacy. The mirror that David and Rosalie held up to each other began to crack with imperfections. She was not as infectiously gay and garrulous as he had remembered her. She often went inside herself. She could be abrupt and sarcastic. She complained that he was short-fused and monomaniacal about developments in the war.

"Tell me why you are morose," David said to her. "Is it your parents?"

"They are always on my mind," she admitted. "I know one thing now—Marilyn's the stronger of the two. And I used to think that she was only a doormat."

"Do you feel you should be back there with them?"

"I don't feel guilty, if that's what you mean. They were actually happy I was in hospital and out of the camp. But I doubt that if they could see me now, they'd say it was a far, far better world I've gone to—present company excepted, of course."

Esther started and Rebecca stopped.

"I did just what you told me to do, Mommy. I went to the w.c. and used the terry-cloth napkin. I wasn't afraid at all."

And so it had come to pass. Esther had become a woman. And she had done so naturally and unfearfully—spared the Dark Ages voodooism that had surrounded this rite of passage in Rebecca's own life. But how swift and few were the days of childhood.

"Now will you please call me Miss Wolf, Mrs. Wolf?"

"No, but maybe your classmates will."

The same subtropical climate that could hasten a child into womanhood, the doctors advised, could also hasten menopause. But a pause in the menstrual cycle should not be mistaken for the onset of menopause. Blame the severity of the heat. Blame progressive malnutrition. Blame the worrisome conditions of their lives. Try to relax and dispel anxiety, the medical men counseled. The worst threat to health was excessive concern over minor symptoms.

Temporary or permanent, Rebecca anguished over the drying up of her wellsprings. Middle age weighed heavily enough. Any vestige of oncoming old age was intolerable. She had thought about it. She had tried to prepare herself for it. But the stopping of the flow was like the stopping of hope for any new life. Just now, for reasons too irrational to articulate, it was especially agonizing.

In another moment, she was laughing and flying.

A lame coolie delivered a note from Doctor Pincus. "I enclose a dance program for your approval. But between us and the ball stands an incipient epidemic of cholera. It is highly infectious, and I want you to show a healthy respect for it. Please double-boil the water and don't eat any melon—merchants are injecting melons with water to increase their weight, and that water may be contaminated. I do have some cheerful news, but it must wait. Bis später."

On the homemade dance program—for that mythical Ball of the Century—there were dance numbers from one to twenty and her name had been written on every line.

Fuses were getting even shorter and voices raspier.

In the Pingliang Road heim a cook took a meat cleaver to a man who had predicted that the war in the Pacific would go on for another three years.

A Pao Chia guard ratted on another guard for being ten minutes late in relieving him.

One Felix Grossmann forced his wife to wear a scarlet A on her blouse for cuckolding him.

God must have loved the yellow men to make so many of them, a letter to the *Chronicle* complained, but did He have to make them so thieving and evil-smelling?

Moritz Felcher asked Ada Hurwitz for overdue rent and she asked him if he remembered that Jesus had driven the moneychangers out of the Temple of God.

"A man from Berlin is to a man from Warsaw," a Mr. Dresler said to a Mr. Kadinsky, "as an imperial wagon-lit is to a boxcar."

Again it was some physiological yearning—hunger this time—that was inspiring Rebecca with images of poetry. She saw the sun as an egg yolk frying in the pale blue skillet of the summer sky.

"You had better be careful," she warned Rosalie and Max Fogelmann, who were sitting on the canvas chairs in the court-yard. "That sun is out to murder."

Rosalie had gone out of her way to be kind to Max, without patronizing him. "Yes, I have been there, and it is the most beautiful city in America," she was saying. "American cities don't win beauty contests, but something happened and they got San Francisco just right. I was there only once, when I was about six years old, and I still remember the cable cars clanking up and down hills as steep as mountains. One night, we were in a hotel roof garden and I remember feeling as though I was an angel in the sky looking down thousands of feet at all the twinkling lights. I can also remember going to a wharf and eating clams and oysters that had just been pulled out of the nice clean waters."

"I want so much to go there," Max said. "It's nearly five years since I have seen my family. I am so homesick for them."

Time hung suspended in the seething air.

The denouement had passed. The outcome was irreversible. The war everywhere would soon be over. But how soon? Would the brown zealots let their floating island be invaded? Would they persist until every last soldier and civilian alike had perished—until there were no Japan Japanese left? And what would the Japanese in Shanghai, in bitterness and humiliation of defeat, have in store for the ghetto?

Sometime in the night, David would leave Rosalie's room to waken in his own bed or on the mattress he had moved into the lane to catch a whisp of air. By day, the two of them wandered. They watched a soccer game behind the Ward Road heim. ("How can they kick the ball, David? Those boys are skin and bones.") They sipped grenadine seltzers and played cribbage on the roof garden of the Café Moritz. They audited a course in calligraphy at the ORT workshop. They read aloud to each other from *Sonnets from the Portuguese*. They repaired mosquito netting in the house. Rosalie helped Esther with her mathematics. ("If someone gave each person in this house—all eight of us—fourteen Pekingese puppies, how many dogs would there be in this house?") One evening Natzie treated the lovers to supper and *The Countess of Gerolstein*. And they talked about the China they had only read about and probably would never, never see: mists asleep in long-forgotten valleys . . . houses built in water with roof beams of cassia and rafters of orchids . . . the Gobi dust that fell like snowflakes . . . deep porcelain-blue heavens and mountain peaks above the clouds . . . the men who drowned hugging the moon in their courtyard pond . . . cities carved out with fingernails . . .

"Are you and Aunt Rosalie going to get married?" Esther asked them.

"Don't be so curious," David admonished her. "Remember what happened to the cat."

"Cats have nine lives, so I still have eight left. Are you and Aunt Rosalie going to get married?"

"Seven!"

David *felt* married enough. If this was not love, what *was* love? How could he be more intimate, lose himself more completely, be *so* involved. He was coming to know her heart and mind as well as he knew her body. There were things he could never tell her, but she must have things she could never tell him, also. Most of their lives had been so completely different. But for the horrifying events of recent years, a shared Jewishness would not have been strongly bonding. If at times he was too serious for her and she was too light for him, if each drifted away and looked at the other through glazed eyes, what did that matter? They were lovers and good companions under the worst of circumstances. Still, he hesitated to speak of this last token of commitment. There was always the possibility that he would be refused. She had said nothing. He well knew that American and English girls who thought progressively could give themselves to passionate love affairs that they had no intention of cementing with matrimony. And how, for that matter, could he pledge himself to another when he did not belong to himself yet? His fate was still in other hands.

Yet, saying nothing, intimating nothing, nagged at him. He felt presumptive, cavalier. Should not there be at least some kind of understanding—well, if such and such happened and this came to pass and both individuals were agreeable, then a certain situation would be neatly resolved, yes?

David broached the subject gingerly. "Customs are so different. If this were Germany, when I was growing up, people would think ill of me living conjugally out of wedlock with a well-born marriageable young woman. An honorable man always . . . "

"Did the right thing by his intended? Married her before opening the pleasure chest?"

"Yes," he blushed. "Our code was very strict. Everyone knew what was . . . "

"Expected of him? Oh, David, you are not proposing marriage, are you? Trying to make an honest woman out of me?"

"In my own way I guess I am."

"Why—why buy the cow when the milk is so cheap?"

Her crudity befuddled him.

"David, you prude," she went on. "Let's talk of cabbages and kings, not of weddings and marriages."

"People do get married—even here."

"Well, it is my idea of nothing at all. I always wanted my first wedding to be absolute perfection. A million-dollar reception, the best caterer, the most . . . "

"*First* wedding?"

"You goose, David." She kissed him impulsively. "Don't ever change. Promise to keep falling into my Venus's-flytrap."

The cholera epidemic moved from threat to reality.

Rebecca's impressions of cholera, though the disease was no stranger to Shanghai, had been formed mainly through her reading. In fiction of the Far East, cholera was something that struck down Orientals or was used as convenient plot device to kill off some corrupt or adulterous colonial. But the intestinal microorganism Vibrio comma was no respecter of race or virtue. In seventeenth-century England, a cholera epidemic claimed twenty-five thousand lives. It was happening in Shanghai again. How bitterly ironic to be this near to the end of the war, only to be done in by a tropical virus!

The Washing Road hospital and the heim clinics were filling with the stricken. Every day, more and more of the infected arrived with their soaring fevers, watery diarrhea, vomiting, and retching. The fatal danger was dehydration. A person would perish unless his bodily fluids were restored. Rebecca had visions of Werner Pincus on an endless round of duty, swabbing brows as hot as sunbaked bricks, tunneling water through tubes, affixing syringes to emaciated arms. She tried to project herself as Florence Nightingale. There must be something she could do to help.

Another note, this one agitating, was delivered to Rebecca.

"You must see me," it read. "Your appointment is at nine o'clock tomorrow morning. Don't be alarmed."

Don't be alarmed? What should she think? Was there something he knew that she didn't—and should, *must* know?

Did he have some divining rod that could test her susceptibility to the malady at a distance? Was he going to inoculate her, give her medication, subject her to examination? What about Esther?

Rebecca slept wretchedly, and rose to see the drenched silhouette of her body on the sheet. She sponged herself carefully and splashed all over herself the Joie de Paris cologne that Miriam had given her. She put on one of Miriam's hand-me-down dresses, a light lemon chiffon with a ruffled hemline.

The half-dozen wooden folding chairs in the hallway-waiting room of Doctor Pincus were already occupied. A door opened to let out an elderly woman in a thin housedress, her bare legs revealing a bad case of varicose veins. Werner Pincus nodded to Rebecca, and she swept in past the others who had been waiting before her. He held both her arms in a half-embrace.

"You are very obedient," he smiled.

"When a doctor summons . . . "

"I am so happy to see you again."

"And I you. And I'll be even happier after you've told me what's wrong with me."

"Wrong with you? That will be the day when I see anything wrong with *you*."

"Then what do you see?" she asked, almost flirtatiously.

She saw a fatigued man who looked as if he had not slept in days. He was in his summer gear without the covering of his smock or the stethoscope around his neck. She saw amusement shining through the weariness, and felt his warmth.

"What do I see? I see a magnificently fair woman in her prime. I see her fine features and lovely skin and honey hair and wish I were a Titian or a Bronzino or a Rossetti."

Rebecca smiled to herself. Could that silly architect back in Lübeck, who had praised her beauty so fulsomely, be whispering into Werner's ear?

"It's very warm for July," she tittered, "don't you think?"

"Yes, a person really expects July to be on the cool side," he laughed. "My, you look as cool as a cucumber."

"Or possibly a melon. A waterlogged melon."

They laughed together and she rejoiced in the benediction of laughter.

"Are you aware," Werner Pincus was teasing her, "that you are in the presence of a significant statistic?"

"I'm not even aware of what a significant statistic is," she confessed.

"You will be. You will be."

He bantered about "significant statistics" and she longed to ask bluntly, "What *am* I doing here?" Particularly just now, when every claim on his time must be better than hers. Could the strain he had been under be throwing him off balance a little? "You look so tired, Werner," she said. "Are you getting any rest?"

"You have just led me into my news. I don't think that I have ever in my life been so bone-tired as I was the night before last. On top of all my office calls, I visited my patients twice that day. It was way beyond ten o'clock before I gave my last intravenous infusion of potassium chloride. I had a bit of food before coming home. By this time it was almost midnight, and who should be waiting up for me but Rita. I could hardly keep my eyes open, but she said, 'I think you had better stay awake until you've heard what I want to say to you.'"

He stopped, rather dramatically. Some prompting was expected of Rebecca, and she murmured, "How interesting."

"Rita made it short and sweet. Four little words: 'I want a divorce.'"

Rebecca stared at him.

"You're speechless, Rebecca. So was I."

Rebecca struggled for something, anything, to say in the floodtide of her emotions. "Werner, I—I—I— can't believe it."

"That's what she said, and I have never heard her sound so clear-headed and determined."

"Werner, Werner."

"Let me go on a bit, Rebecca. Houses built of cards are meant to collapse. I am only surprised by the extremity of her demand. It never pretended to be more than it was—a marriage of convenience. But the best-laid schemes of man indeed gang aft a-gley. We had developed a modus vivendi. She went where she went, and I went to my office. In the last year,

Rita seemed to be feeling well for longer and longer periods—the depressions, when they came, were shorter and shorter. One night last February, she came home with her left hand in a cast. She had slipped in an icy lane and had broken it. I asked why she had not come to me, her own husband, who was a doctor, and she said that the idea had not occurred to her. The accident also marked the beginning of a change in her. She stopped running so much and was content to stay home several evenings a week just reading, which was something she had never done. There was no sign whatsoever of a depression coming on. She began taking elaborate care of her personal appearance. I remarked that her hair was getting lighter, and she confessed that it was due to something called Celestial Rinse. She became almost chatty and quite solicitous of me. Something was going on, but I was too tired to lie awake wondering about it. A week or so ago, Rita came to me with a little speech she must have rehearsed and rehearsed. She thought it only fair to let me know that she had become deeply attached to someone. In fact, she was wildly in love with him. It did not seem suitable that she should go on living under my roof. She said that I had always been kind to her and that she wanted to ask for one more kindness. Would I be good enough to lend her enough money so that she could rent a room of her own and to provide her with a modest allowance? I was to keep careful records, and somehow, some day, she would repay me with interest. As I was prepared to go along with her arrangement, but without the interest part of it, I didn't think it was presumptuous to ask with whom she was in love. I see that you have guessed, Rebecca. Yes, nobody else than the other doctor, the one who fixed her broken wrist. I told her to make her arrangements and let me know what she would need, I was sure things could be worked out amicably. Then came the bombshell. The way that she planned to handle things was fine with her, she explained, but not with Herbert. He said he had no interest in any backstreet romance. Herbert was insisting that she marry him, and it was now her wish to do so."

Rebecca's head was reeling. "Extraordinary, extraordinary."

"And then some. That's the meaning of significant statistic. Have you any idea of how uncommon divorce is here?"

"It's the sort of thing that David Buchbinder—the young man in my house—keeps track of. I think he said there were eleven in 1943 and eighteen last year."

"But I dare say few of those were women divorcing their husbands, and I may have the distinction of being the only doctor in the ghetto to be divorced by his wife."

Striving for just the right tone of neutrality, Rebecca said, "This is totally irrelevant, but I heard one of the rabbis commenting on divorce. He said that in adversity the most cherished bonds were sometimes strained to the breaking point."

"That rabbi, I would say, has been well trained in banality."

"What will you do, Werner?"

"Do? I shall comply with her wishes." He laughed mirthlessly. "I was prepared to give her money, and all she wants is a divorce."

So this was the purpose of the "appointment." He wanted to give her the news, and give it to her at the earliest possible moment. The implication was clear, and her heart was racing. She noticed for the tenth time how handsome his legs were. One did not usually think of men's legs cosmetically. She looked nervously in the direction of the foyer.

"Don't worry about them," he said. "They're here every morning. One of them ran out of symptoms yesterday and said, 'It's my hair, Doctor Pincus. It hurts so.' "

"Remind me never to become your patient," Rebecca smiled.

He took both of her hands and held them. "I have denied myself so much," he said. "I don't want to go on doing that. I want you to be much more than my patient."

Rebecca slept not at all that Bible-black night. She was feverish with longing and anticipation. Not since that Lübeck springtime when Meyer was courting her had she been so consumed with desire. All those ancient yearnings that she had thought were dead forever had revived. It couldn't be the same, she was no longer young, or virginal, but it *felt* the same. Once to every woman—twice to the anointed.

As she lay awake, recalling the forthrightness of that earlier courtship, she composed what she would say to Werner when she saw him the next night. "I am yours on any terms at all," she would tell him. "And I am ready right now. You do not have to promise me a thing. I do not care about the proprieties. I, too, am weary of being deprived. It would make me happy trying to make you happy."

Her images of another's ardor responding to hers were intruded upon by cries from the lanes.

"Peace! Peace!"

It could not be. Not in one day could she be hearing the two things that she most wanted to hear. "I want you to be much more than my patient" and "Peace!"

The cries were real. The whole household was astir. Rebecca threw on a robe and straw sandals and pressed herself into the bacchanalian ballet choking the lanes. All the refugees had heard the cry. They were hooting and weeping and yodeling and cheering and laughing. And singing *The Star-Spangled Banner.* Under a sky dimly lit by starlight and plaited yellow bamboo flares, delirious strangers embraced and kissed and passed hoarded bottles of wines and bits of cake to one another. Such release, such hysterics. Let joy now be unrefined.

The voice of Abraham rose to end their revels. "Jewish people, stop this," it commanded them from an unseen platform. "Be quiet. Go home. There is no peace. There is no peace."

Morning brought another day of deadly terror to the dead center of summer. The sun rose angrily from the East China Sea and the heat rained down. The sky was a molten blue drained through a filter of calcified dust. The air, breathless as a corpse, hung in shrouds. The leaves on the exhausted ginkos drooped like the ears of a basset hound. The macadam roads were gum.

Rebecca saw Esther off to school and a heaviness weighed on her heart. What would she tell Esther? How much would Esther be able to understand, accept? Rebecca suspected that

Esther, being in love with the idea of people being in love, would be pleased. But if she asked, "Are you going to marry Doctor Pincus?" and got a vague answer, she could be displeased. In that case, Esther would have to ride out her mood. There was a limit to what even Esther could demand.

In the yard, Rosalie was trying to make a pencil portrait, and David was balking.

"It's too hot to sit still," he complained.

"It's hotter fidgeting around the way you are."

"You already have one portrait of me."

"That was ages ago. How exotic and beautiful I thought you were then. Franz Kafka without the flapping ears, remember?"

"But you don't think so anymore?"

"We all change. You're a little lean and hungry-looking now."

"Such men are dangerous."

"You're only dangerous in bed. Grrrrr."

"Grrrrr yourself."

She sketched and commented, "Now that you are thinner and your face is asthenic, you look even more saintly. Like maybe a Saint Francis of Assisi. Or one of El Greco's religious subjects—St. Jerome. Your eyes are still violetish, but your hair is lighter, kind of a cocoa auburn. That dear dimple in your chin is deeper. The swoop at the end of your eyebrows is so sexy. A face to remember, I feel."

In her room, Rebecca pondered the weighty problem of what she would wear that evening. Not the lemon chiffon dress, which he had seen the day before. Not the pink organdy she had worn to the Café St. Petersburg. It came down to the burgundy silk dress with the loose lines, another of Miriam's bequests, or the white linen with the pleated skirt. Why must she be asked to shoulder such decisions? And should she treat herself to a visit to the bathhouse?

("I haven't a thing to wear tonight," Max Fogelmann said, amused at Rebecca's confusion. "May I borrow something you're not going to wear?" They were all becoming so silly.)

The banter in the courtyard was infectious. Peace, if it should break out, she reflected ludicrously, would be an interference. "Peace, peace, go away, come again another day." Peace, you cannot come between me and my big moment. On second thought, peace was a phantom consideration. Peace, if it broke out today, would change nothing. They would all still be here, waiting, waiting for some word from the captains of their destiny. They would be here until they heard America or the United Kingdom or Australia calling—and someone sent them the fare.

Rosalie tried another tack to distract her fidgety subject. "On a day like this, if it was before we went to the mountains," she recalled, "I'd be at the Race Course with a bunch of friends. We'd sit around the pool ordering liveried slaves to bring us watercress sandwiches and tall iced teas. The boys were always trying to impress us with their swan dives and jackknives and somersaults off the highboard. And the girls would say real snotty things in loud voices. Like, 'Personally, I thought it was only circus animals that did stunts.' Or, 'Don't you just hate it when a boy doesn't have *any* hair on his chest?' We'd play a few hands of gin rummy or auction bridge and go to somebody's house for dinner. The same boys we had insulted at the pool would come over and we'd dance around the Victrola. One summer, the Lambeth Walk was all the rage. Another summer, we were all snaking around in conga lines and the antsy boys were always bumping their weenies against our tuches. It was very pleasant. Not their weenies—the Race Course life, I mean."

"Do you know what you sound like? A bunch of spoiled brats."

"Poof, David. Why don't you sharpen my pencil and stick yourself with it you-know-where."

"You have a vulgar mouth."

"The better to bite pompous pricks."

Rebecca smiled. Different times, different cultures. No German girl, much less a German *Jewish* girl, would express herself so earthily. It was jarring to the ear, as were the voices edged in irritability, but of no primal importance. Young lovers, trapped in idleness, indignities, and the suspension of waiting, working their way under each other's skin. Soon, with luck, they would all be returning to some kind of civilized manners. Tonight, she would wear the white linen for that pristine look that augured fresh beginnings. Outside, the strained silence that had followed the last testy exchange between the young lovers was broken.

"David, you're right," Rosalie said. "I do have a vulgar mouth. I never used to talk like this. Do you think I'm tetched from the sun?"

"It may have been Chapei."

"This has to stop. And you have to help me. I want you to wash my mouth out with boric acid the next time you hear me say fuck or cunt or cock or prick or any of the other disgustees. Promise me you will?"

"I'll start right now."

"Wait till I've finished the sketch. Then I'm yours to do with as you will."

"How about a lecture?"

"From you?"

"No, no," he chuckled. "Hannah Bratowski."

"Again? What is she talking about this time?"

"Jewish Women: The Timeless Matriarchy—chapter forty-two."

"Jesus Christ!"

"Where's the boric acid?"

Rosalie hooted, and David laughed with her. He basked in her approval of his laughter. For her approval, the miracle of her love and being *here*, he would move the mountains only faith supposedly could accomplish. He closed his eyes and slumped blissfully in the low-slung canvas chair. He tamped the moisture from his face, but immediately there was a fresh stream flowing downward. When it reached his lips, he tasted the salt of tears. He opened his eyes and through a mist saw the beloved face contemplating his. Her pencil was firming the line of his lower lip on the yellow legal pad. He smiled and closed his eyes again.

"Are you sleeping?" she wondered.

"Mmmmm."

"A penny for your thoughts. Well, a ha'penny."

"Do you want to know that bad?"

"That's more than I've bloody got to my name, David! What were you thinking? You had the smile of an angel."

"What was I thinking? I was thinking that I am happy. Here I am in a suffocating sewer and I am happy."

It was a word that sounded strange falling from David's lips. It was a word that Rebecca had doubted she would ever use to describe herself. She decided against the white linen. So what if he had seen the lemon chiffon with the ruffles only yesterday? As she looked then, hadn't he wished he were a Titian or a Bronzino or a Rossetti?

"Damn and botheration," Rosalie cursed. "*Them* again."

"They're your planes," David said. "*Our* friends."

The familiar and infernal bzz-bzz-bzzing. They were like a nest of hornets charging across a sky bleached by the noonday sun. The streaking flashes of silver left entrails of thin white plumes that scriggled like ganglia. Directly overhead, the twin-tailed Liberators went into spread-eagled formation and bzz-bzz-bzzed toward the interior. "Go indoors," a voice on the community's public address system barked. "Take cover."

"Take cover, my ass," Rosalie scoffed.

"Boric acid."

"Where are we going to take cover, David?" Shielding her eyes from the sun, she wondered, "Why do they go way out there and then come back?"

"They get two chances at their target. One on the way in, one on the way out."

"I wish they'd bomb whatever it is they are trying to bomb and get it over with. This bzz-bzz-bzz day after day is driving me batty."

The raids *were* nervous-making, Rebecca agreed. Was there really such a thing as becoming inured to them? People in London and the German cities and Tokyo, the reports went, had learned to take bombings in stride—there seemed to be no limit to the possibilities of human adaptation. But it would take an awful lot of adapting to accommodate oneself to that infernal noise in the sky.

By some sudden change of wind or bewitchment of air currents, the droning stopped. There was a moment of stunned stillness. Into the eerie silence, Rosalie shouted, "I am afraid."

"Afraid? You afraid?"

"Yes."

"There's no need to be."

"But I am. Very."

Another surge of warmth welled through David, making his eyes glisten again. This frightened cry was so endearing and childlike of her. After all those months in the internment camp and the intricacies of that hospital maneuver, she was suddenly afraid. "Come," David said, "come sit in my lap and I'll tell you a little story."

Obedient as a child, Rosalie came to him. Like a child, she snuggled into the protection of his lap and arms. David smiled at the prospect of two adults curled up together on a frail canvas chair and falling through the bottom. A tide of ineffable sweetness swept over him. Let the chair collapse, their bodies would still be glued to each other. Forget those noisy planes that were heading back on their way to the harbor. Forget the sweat and the heat and the dirt and the din. This . . . was happiness.

"Once upon a time," he began his story, "there was a little princess with beautiful green eyes and copper-colored tresses and she lived in a big snow-white . . . "

Hongkew heaved, rocked, and became supernaturally still.

The tables in the Café Moritz swayed, bounced, and slid. Cutlery jitterbugged. Crockery fell to the floor. The walls shuddered. A swatch of ersatz grass from the roof garden dropped through the ceiling and into the rinsing cauldron in the kitchen. Six dazed diners were knocked off their chairs.

An earthquake? Lightning literally out of the blue? A cyclone? The gasworks exploding? The munitions dump? Moritz Felcher waited the longest minute of his life. Ascertaining that Sophie was steady though stunned, he wrapped a soaked handkerchief around his face and ran from the restaurant.

The light had gone out of the day. Smoke dark as graphite drifted in whorls like fog off the Baltic. Brigades of frantic people were pressing through curtains of gray gauze. Shops and houses, or the remains of shops and houses, were like ghosts on photographic negatives. Reptilian tongues of flames were licking in all corners. The stink of burning assaulted the nostrils; the air itself smelled scorched.

"What happened?" Moritz Felcher yelled into the milling mob. "WHAT HAPPENED?"

"We've been bombed."

His house! He must get to his house. What if that, too, had been set aflame and was burning down?

"Out of my way, get out of my way," he shouted, plunging into the seething, braying maw of white, yellow, and brown faces. He made pistons of his elbows, forging a path for himself. Through the mask of handkerchief, he breathed in gasps. He steeled himself against the assault to his ears of the anguished screams of pain and helplessness.

"Frieda! Frieda! Where are you? Where are you?"

"Help me! Help!"

"My arm! I can't find my arm."

"Water! Please, water."

Moritz Felcher was panicking. He was not in control. With all the shoving and pushing at cross currents, he was only moving at a snail's pace. Everything was mayhem.

A penny-whistle shrieked.

"Coming through! Make way! Lorry coming through!"

Two coolies, grinning insanely, were pulling their burden by long wooden shafts. They trotted almost in place, moving only by inches as the unmalleable hordes gave way reluctantly. The truck inching through the gummy macadam had no sides and was piled to overflowing with its cargo.

"Jesus Christ!" Moritz Felcher swore. "Jesus Christ Almighty!"

The truck carried a junk heap of dismembered human flesh. A pyramid of dead, burnt, ripped, mutilated flesh. Arms. Legs. Hands. Feet. Chests. Heads. Ears. Breasts. Penises and testicles. Human beings reduced to bones and scraps from a butcher's block. From near the top of the mangled mound, a single eye, Cyclops, black as agate, stared at him and he turned his head in fright and shame. His heart was thumping wildly with some unspoken terror.

At Dent Road, the truck turned into the lane leading to the crematorium. As the coolies hauled their burden into the lane, the vaporish cloud of dust lifted and the afternoon light seeped back into the sky. An apricot sun shone wanly on the ravaged quarter and its deranged citizens.

A house could burn to the ground by the time it took a man to get around a corner—but another minute or two of pushing and jabbing would bring Moritz Felcher into Kimpei Lane. He must get a grip on himself. He must quiet his heart. He must think coherently. He would have to get out of his sticky, stinking clothes and wash himself from head to foot. David would know what had happened; he would ask David for all the details. On certain matters, his nephew was the only one worth listening to. David. This would be over soon and their paths would part. He and Sophie must not try to hang on to him. David had his girl friend and he had his life before him. The way all of them had been forced to live, who would ever want to see a single day of it back? But in time to come, memory, as it always did, would blot out the worst, and there would be a yearning for something that had been lost forever. If they had not been thrown together, trapped together, how could he ever have developed this feeling for Gertrud's wonderful son? With the stars in his eyes—love, the future—did David have any notion of how much pain it would give his Uncle Moritz to be losing him? Did he know how much his Uncle Moritz—in his clumsy way—had come to love him?

Moritz Felcher wiped his sweaty brow on a sleeve of his jacket and laughed uneasily. To have held high standards through thick and thin and then act like a coolie when it was nearly over. At least Mrs. Wolf wasn't watching him. How he would miss her, too. (And darling Esther.) In the Old World their lives would not have touched. Being in a position to help such a fine person had bolstered his self-esteem more than he could admit. Something was afoot with her, she was acting skittishly—it probably had to do with that doctor—and he felt another stab of pain (and jealousy). He would be losing her, too, not only to circumstance but quite probably to another man's protection.

Turning into Kimpei Lane, Moritz Felcher adjusted his spectacles. He smoothed his rumpled suit and tugged at his necktie, as if he must pass inspection. The lane was a patchwork quilt of blasted masonry, splintered wood, charred bits and pieces of frames, roofing, and fencing, and hunks of uprooted earth. But there were no fires, and the first few houses on either side were intact. The rubble underfoot could be cleared away with a broom and a little brawn.

But as he picked his way along the curiously deserted lane—a minute ago the Maelstrom, now nobody—Moritz Felcher was engulfed with waves of foreboding. Something was terribly wrong. The silence was spooky. A baby was wailing, but that was far off, in some other lane. The houses, stark and still, looked like petrified artifacts.

There it was, that grotesquerie of the freestanding staircase, Esther's play castle. Out of the corner of his eyes, he saw, as he had seen a thousand other times, the concrete base and the sweep of two-floor hard teakwood steps that rose steeply and trailed off into thin air. As he came nearer, he looked at it directly. But beyond? The staircase was standing against a backdrop of—of *nothing*.

Where was his house?

Where an hour ago he would have seen his house and two neighboring houses, Moritz Felcher now looked into an oblong crater. Three homes and their contents had been blasted out of existence. Transfixed, he stared and stared into the yawning red hole. Nothing remained. Not a thing. Not a remnant. From a slash in the bottom of the pit a sluggish pool was oozing out of the bowels of Hongkew.

Something yellow, a scrap of yellow paper, teetered on the far rim of the cavity. Moritz Felcher looked over at it numbly for the longest while, as the subject regards the raised finger of the hypnotist. Rousing from his paralysis, he edged around the gaping canyon and picked up the scrap of paper. It was a fragment of page from a lined yellow tablet. He held it close to his eyes and saw the pencil sketching of the upper half of a handsome young man's head.

He fell to his knees and drove his fists into the steaming earth.

Moritz Felcher screamed.

EPILOGUE

It was a tragic miscalculation.

The intended targets of the American Liberators on that July 19th were Japanese fuel storage tanks in Hongkew Park and airplane repair shops in the Western District, miles and miles away.

The erring bombs killed two hundred and eighty people and wounded almost one thousand others. Among the thirty-one Jewish fatalities were Rebecca Langer-Wolf, David Buchbinder, Rosalie Balaban, and Max Fogelmann. Their bodies were never found.

Three weeks after this bombing of Hongkew, the United States Air Force—in an act of unprecedented devastation—unleashed on Hiroshima and Nagasaki "the force from which the sun draws its powers." On August 8, the Soviet Union opportunistically joined the war in the Pacific and attacked Japanese forces in Manchukuo. On August 14, 1945, the Japanese surrendered unconditionally and the Second World War, which had cost sixty million lives, was over.

Peace brought few immediate changes to the lives of the Jewish refugees in Shanghai. Classified now as displaced persons, they were deghettoized and no longer confined to the designated area in Hongkew. A few of the younger people found temporary work with the United States Armed Forces occupying Shanghai, Nanking, and Peking. Most of them, however, were not so fortunate—they had no employment, nowhere to go. They were hungry, weak, and destitute. Their frustration became almost intolerable. They waited as pawns to be moved, for their lives to begin anew elsewhere—still another time. Any lingering fantasy of returning to Europe was put to rest by the reports drifting in of the Nazi death camps.

Eventually, Jewish philanthropies throughout the world,

the United Nations Relief and Rehabilitation Agency (UNRRA), and the new Communist government of China helped the refugees to leave Shanghai and find new homes in Australia, Hong Kong, Canada, South Africa, Great Britain, Latin America, and the United States. Thousands of them migrated to "the promised land" of Israel after its creation in 1948.

Only the young looked to the future with optimism. Their elders felt that nothing could ever compensate them for the hell they had been put through. Many ripened into seasoned skeptics, cynical about the very existence of civilization. Had not a nominally Christian nation, in the middle of the twentieth century, perpetrated horrors beyond comprehension? Had not another nominally Christian nation inflicted instant genocide on two Japanese cities? How could Christianity, with so much blood on its hands, look to any kind of future? Purged of its "impurities," could a new Germany ever again give birth to the glories of creativity and discovery that had been so suicidally snuffed out?

Moritz and Sophie Felcher emigrated to Australia. With the financial aid of cousins in Melbourne, they opened still another Café Moritz. It became one of the temples of gastronomy in that restaurant-bleak city. Today, Moritz Felcher is a widower residing in a prosperous retirement colony in Geelong. Sophie Felcher died in 1974. (Gertrud Felcher Buchbinder, David's mother, Moritz' sister, died in Auschwitz, in 1944.)

Ada Hurwitz used the money that she had won in the Solomon brothers' lottery—she was only a day off on her guess of the date that the War would end—to move to a kibbutz near Elath, in Israel. She later opened a Viennese-style coffeehouse in Haifa. In 1963, she married a much-decorated officer who had been blinded in Israel's War of Independence; he died two months after the wedding. Ada Hurwitz-Katzenellenbogen lives today in suburban Tel Aviv.

Miriam Schiff, during the brief resurgence of British power in postwar Shanghai, married a senior vice president of Jardine Matheson and Company. Today, the Eadweard Farnsworths live quietly in England, on a farm near Faversham, in Kent.

Professor Justin Spiller also emigrated to the "land of milk and honey" and taught the history of the Diaspora at Hebrew University, in Jerusalem. He died in 1957 during a visit to his native city of Trier, in the Palatinate. His history of Jews in China was never completed.

Hermann Feinstein presumably perished in the Bridge House.

Esther Wolf, who had been at school during the bombing, and was orphaned by the death of her mother, came briefly under the guardianship of Ada Hurwitz in the Ward Road heim. With the help of the Hebrew Immigrant Aid Society, she returned to Germany to live with her Uncle Samuel. She earned honors at the University of Grenoble and married a French biologist. Esther Wolf-Benoit died in childbirth, in Clermont-Ferrand, in the spring of 1967, in her thirty-fourth year.

Doctor Werner Pincus was one of the few Shanghai refugees to be repatriated. He established a private practice in Munich and lectured on tropical diseases at Kaiser Wilhelm Institute. He never remarried, and died of a heart attack in 1971.

Hugo Raschenbaum was also a victim of the bombing of Hongkew. He was one of twelve men killed by a direct hit on the kitchen of the Chaoufoong heim.

Ignatz (Natzie) Stern became an American citizen and settled in New York City. He owns a company that imports precious gems from Sri Lanka. He lives with his wife, a former Miss Kentucky, and their three sons in a triplex on Central Park South.

Aaron and Marilyn Balaban returned to the United States. He became a vice president in charge of exploitation at Paramount Pictures. The Balabans are deceased.

Christian Boehm was stabbed to death by an American sailor in the Terminal Bar in Shanghai's Blood Alley on Christmas Eve 1945.

U.S. Marine Lieutenant Joseph Stone Gordon, who was Rosalie Balaban's cousin, and briefly David Buchbinder's newfound friend in Shanghai, survived the Bataan death march and was a prisoner of war for three and a half years in northern China. He became a Rhodes Scholar and joined the State Department as a specialist in Far Eastern Affairs. He accompanied

President Nixon on his historic state visit to China in 1971. Mr. Gordon is retired and lives with his wife in Falls Church, Virginia. They adopted two Chinese children.

Samuel Langer, Rebecca's brother, survived two years in the concentration camp Theresienstadt. In failing health, he chose to remain in Germany after V-E day. He made no effort to revive his prewar paperweights business, and he (and Esther for a time) subsisted modestly on reparations from the West German government. In 1968, Samuel committed suicide in his West Berlin apartment by swallowing Veronal; he was seventy-one years old.

In August 1980, nearly a thousand of the surviving "Shanghai Jews" convened for the first time in thirty-five years. It had taken this long for some wounds to heal, for any general desire to meet and look back to that shared chapter in their lives. In Oakland, California, they gathered with their families from as far as Sydney and Geneva and Toronto and San Juan. Among the illustrious was W. Michael Blumenthal, a U.S. Secretary of the Treasury in the Jimmy Carter administration, who recalled that during his teen-age years in the designated area he had peddled sausage by the quarter-slice.

The same tide that had swept the Jewish refugees out of Shanghai took with it all the other Caucasians as well. The end of the Second World War reactivated the Chinese civil war, whose origins went back to 1927. Mao's Communists pushed Chiang Kai-shek into the sea, ended all extraterritorial treaties, and by 1949 were in possession of all of mainland China. (Before escaping Shanghai, Chiang's son was paid $5,000,000 by every Chinese war profiteer in return for a "pardon.") A new China was in the making—at the sacrifice of fifty million lives. It was a China that had no place for the white man.

Today, there is scarcely a remaining vestige of the Jewish presence that began in China a thousand years ago. The Sephardic Jewish families that founded dynasties in Shanghai at the end of the last century were obliged to transfer their operations to Hong Kong, Bombay, Paris, and London. Jewish graveyards in Shanghai were razed by the Communists to make way for factories and apartment blocks.

A handful of the Jewish refugees were, however, allowed to stay on in Shanghai for compassionate reasons. A seventy-five-year-old man from Lodz in Poland, Max Leibowitch, died there in January 1982. For many years he had been disabled by Parkinson's disease and was beyond speech. After the death of his mother, he was cared for by two elderly Chinese male nurses who were paid by American Jewish philanthropies. His obituary called him "the last Jew in Shanghai."